About the

Brenda Harlen is a multi-award winning author for Mills & Boon True Love who has written over 25 books for the company.

Since her first venture into novel writing in the mid-nineties, **Kristi Gold** has greatly enjoyed weaving stories of love and commitment. She's an avid fan of baseball, beaches and bridal reality shows. During her career, Kristi has been a National Readers Choice winner, *Romantic Times* award winner, and a three-time Romance Writers of America *RITA* finalist. She resides in Central Texas and can be reached through her website at kristigold.com

Susanne Hampton is the mother of two adult daughters, Orianthi and Tina. Her varied career titles have included dental nurse, personal assistant, contract manager and now Medical Romance author. The family also extends to a Maltese shih-tzu, a poodle, three ducks and four hens. Susanne has always read romance novels and says, 'I love a happy ever after so writing for Mills & Boon is a dream come true.'

Princess Brides

Princess Brides: Second Chance

BRENDA HARLEN

KRISTI GOLD

SUSANNE HAMPTON

MILLS & BOON

First Published in Great Britain 2024
by Mills & Boon, an imprint of HarperCollins*Publishers* Ltd
1 London Bridge Street, London, SE1 9GF

www.harpercollins.co.uk

HarperCollins*Publishers*
Macken House, 39/40 Mayor Street Upper,
Dublin 1, D01 C9W8, Ireland

ISBN: 978-0-263-39775-8

MIX
Paper | Supporting
responsible forestry
FSC
www.fsc.org
FSC™ C007454

This book contains FSC™ certified paper and other controlled sources to ensure responsible forest management.

For more information visit: www.harpercollins.co.uk/green

Printed and Bound in the UK using 100% Renewable Electricity at CPI Group (UK) Ltd, Croydon, CR0 4YY

THE PRINCE'S
SECOND CHANCE

BRENDA HARLEN

In memory of Catherine Elizabeth Witmer

~writer, reader, reviewer & friend~

Chapter One

"Do you have a minute?"

It wasn't every day that Cameron Leandres looked up from his desk to find Rowan Santiago, his cousin and the prince regent of Tesoro del Mar, standing in the doorway of his office.

"Of course," Cameron said, because he couldn't imagine responding in any other way to the ruler of the country. "But not much more than that—I'm meeting with the Ardenan Trade Minister at nine-thirty."

"Actually, that meeting has been…postponed," Rowan told him.

Cameron frowned. "No one told me."

"I just got off the phone with Benedicto Romero."

He immediately recognized the name of Ardena's king and waited silently, apprehensively, for his cousin to continue.

"He's furious about this morning's paper and threatening not to renew our trade agreement."

"I skimmed the front section," Cameron said. "I didn't see anything that would impact our negotiations."

"Did you check the society pages?" The prince regent tossed the paper onto his desk.

The photo and the headline battled for his attention, but it was the bold words that won out: *Prince Cameron Adds New Notch to His Bedpost?*

It was a mockery of the headline that had run on the front page only a few days earlier, *Prince Cameron Adds New Title to His Portfolio*, announcing that he'd been named the country's new Minister of Trade. He didn't want to know what *this* article claimed, but his eyes automatically began to skim the brief paragraph.

Apparently his new responsibilities on the political scene haven't curbed the prince's extracurricular activities. In fact, just last night the prince was spotted at Club Sapphire making some serious moves on the dance floor—and on the King of Ardena's youngest daughter.

Cameron clenched his jaw, holding back the vehement curse that instinctively sprang to his lips. He glanced at the photo again, recognizing the woman who had plastered herself against him on the dance floor.

"I didn't know that she was the king's daughter," he said, ruefully acknowledging that truth wasn't much of a defense.

"The king's seventeen-year-old daughter."

Cameron dropped his head into his hands, and this time he didn't manage to hold back the curse.

"Did you sleep with her?" Rowan asked bluntly.

"No!" Maybe he shouldn't have been shocked by the question, but he was. And while he might have told anyone else that it wasn't their business, he couldn't say that to the prince regent. They both knew his actions reflected on his office.

He was relieved to be able to assert his innocence in this situation, because even if he hadn't guessed that the woman in the photo was underage, he had known that she was far too young for even a serious flirtation. While he hadn't always been discriminating in his choice of female companions, he was thirty-six years old now and long past the age where he was easily seduced by a warm body and willing smile.

"I was there with Allegra de Havilland," he explained, naming his frequent if not exclusive companion of the past six months, "and this girl—she only said her name was Leticia— came up to me on the dance floor while my date was in the ladies' room. We didn't even dance for two minutes. When Allegra came back, she and I left."

His cousin nodded. "Then there's no reason to believe that this can't be salvaged."

Cameron didn't know how to respond. His cousin had taken a chance on him six years earlier when he'd first appointed him to his cabinet, after Cameron had done everything in his power to undermine Rowan's position. At the time, he'd suspected that Rowan was subscribing to the old adage "keep your friends close and your enemies closer" and he couldn't blame him for that. But over time, as they'd worked together on various projects, they'd developed a mutual respect for one another. And Cameron would forever be grateful to his cousin for giving him the chance to be something more than a worthless title in the history books.

When he finally spoke, it was only to say, "I regret that this has caused a problem with the king."

Rowan nodded. "You need to be extra cautious and remember that, as a royal and a member of public office, everything you say and do is subject to media scrutiny."

"Do you want my resignation?" He held his breath, waiting for his cousin's response.

"No, I don't want your resignation. You've been an asset to this administration."

Cameron exhaled. "Do you want me to talk to the king?"

"No," Rowan said again. "I've invited him to join me for lunch. Hopefully I can smooth things over with him then."

Cameron refused to consider what the repercussions might be if his cousin failed. Rowan hadn't been born for the position he was in, but he'd stepped in without missing a beat when Julian and Catherine, his brother and sister-in-law, were killed in a fluke explosion on their yacht.

Maybe Cameron had resented Rowan's appointment back then, because he'd felt that he was just as qualified and capable of doing the prince regent's job. But over the past half-dozen years, he'd realized that he didn't want those duties and responsibilities, even on an interim basis. And he regretted that his own actions—however inadvertent—were making his cousin's job more difficult.

"I also contacted *La Noticia*," Rowan continued. "Because I was annoyed that Alex would run such a headline without at least giving us a heads-up."

Alex Girard was the society columnist for the local paper whose fair and objective reporting had earned him several invitations to the palace and the opportunity to write exclusive stories about the royal family. Now that Cameron thought about it, it wasn't only out-of-character for the reporter to launch an attack on a member of the prince regent's cabinet but potentially detrimental to his own career.

"As it turns out, Alex didn't have anything to do with the story. He's out of the country for a couple of weeks so the society pages are being covered by another staff writer—Gabriella Vasquez."

Cameron should have guessed that. Not that she'd always hated him. In fact, there was a time when they'd been extremely close. But that was long before she'd become "Dear Gabby" and started using her column to vilify both his character and his activities. And while her references to him had always been unmistakable, she was usually more subtle in her condemnation. Now she'd apparently taken the gloves off.

And he was prepared to do the same.

* * *

Gabriella wasn't surprised when she received the summons to her editor's office, but she did feel the tiniest twinge of guilt when she saw Allison Jenkins—one of her oldest and dearest friends—rubbing her forehead, as she often did when a major headache was brewing.

"You wanted to see me?" Gabriella said.

The editor looked up. "I'm sure you know why."

"Since there wasn't anything particularly controversial in my 'Dear Gabby' column this week, I'm guessing this is about the 'Around Town' segment."

"Would you also like to take a guess as to how many phone calls I've received this morning? Or how many emails have flooded my inbox?"

Gabriella's own office computer had actually been so overloaded with incoming messages that it had crashed, but she was unconcerned. Everyone knew that the newspaper business was suffering and anything that increased circulation—as her contribution to the society pages had done exponentially— couldn't be a bad thing.

"So put your big girl panties on and deal with it," Gabriella said. "That's why they pay you the big bucks."

Alli shook her head. "You're not even sorry."

"Why should I be? I didn't write anything that wasn't true."

"You may have created an international scandal," her editor warned.

"*I* wasn't dirty dancing with the King of Ardena's underage daughter," she pointed out.

"They were dancing," Alli repeated. "There is absolutely no evidence of anything more than that."

"I never said that there was."

"No," her boss agreed. "But your text implies that the prince is a seducer of virgins."

Gabriella knew that he was, but she didn't intend to admit

that to her boss. "Royal headlines sell papers," she reminded Allison.

"And we get a lot of inside news because we've worked hard to establish a good relationship with the palace."

"Do you really think anyone at the palace even noticed an article buried in the middle of page twelve?"

"I don't think it, I know it," Alli told her. "Because one of the multitude of phone calls that I received was from Prince Rowan."

Gabriella swallowed. "The prince regent called you?"

"And he wasn't very happy."

"Then I'll apologize for putting you in an awkward position," she said. "But I can't apologize for what I wrote. Prince Cameron uses his title and his charm to lure women into his bed and innocent girls should be forewarned."

"Then take out a public service announcement with your name on it but don't use this newspaper to pursue what is obviously a personal vendetta."

Gabriella felt the sting of that reprimand because she knew there was some truth in her boss's words. When Alex Girard had asked her to cover the celebrity watch while he was on vacation, she'd had mixed feelings about the request. For the better part of sixteen years, she'd been careful to steer clear of anyone connected with the royal family. Of course, that hadn't been too difficult for a commoner who didn't move in the same circles they did.

But this new assignment would require Gabriella to seek them out, to go to the places they were known to frequent, to rub elbows with their friends and acquaintances. Of course, the assignment was broader than the royal family, but everyone knew that the Santiagos and the Leandreses were the real celebrities in Tesoro del Mar.

"For Monday's paper, I wrote about the prince regent's picnic at the beach with his family. Tuesday, I covered Princess Molly's book launch and her reading at the library. Yesterday,

I was out of town interviewing the Hollywood elite who are filming a romantic comedy in San Pedro. In fact, I didn't even want to go to Club Sapphire last night, but I got a tip that 'several people of note' were going to be there, so I went."

"Who else was there?" Alli wanted to know.

"Most of the Hollywood contingent," Gabriella admitted.

"Why didn't you get any pictures of them?"

"Because I already have a ton of photos that were taken during the interview sessions."

Alli dropped her head into her hands. "Are you trying to give me an ulcer?"

"I did my job," Gabriella said.

"Which you could have done just as effectively by concentrating on the visiting actors—what they were wearing, what they were drinking, who was hooked up with whom."

"And ignoring the prince's presence?" Gabriella challenged.

"It would have been enough to reference the fact that Prince Cameron was there," her editor insisted.

"With the king's daughter," Gabriella reminded her.

"I'm going to end up with an ulcer and a pink slip," Alli muttered. "But at least I'll have you to keep me company when I'm unemployed."

"I didn't cross any lines."

"Tell that to the legal department when we get slapped with a libel suit."

"It's not libelous if it's true," Gabriella insisted.

"But the truth is often a matter of opinion, isn't that correct, Ms. Vasquez?"

Gabriella recognized that voice. Even after more than sixteen years, the smooth, sexy tone hadn't faded from her memory, and her breath caught in her throat as she spun around to face the door.

Cameron.

"This day just keeps getting better and better," Alli grumbled, but not so loudly that the prince could hear.

Gabriella didn't see her friend move—she couldn't seem to tear her eyes from the man lounging indolently against the doorjamb—but she heard the chair slide and knew that Alli was rising to her feet in deference to the man at her door. She would probably even curtsy.

Gabriella refused to do the same. She wouldn't bow and scrape to this man. Not now, not ever again.

But she couldn't deny that seeing him made her heart slam against her ribs, and while she was determined to play the scene out coolly and casually, her knees had gone just a little weak.

He hadn't changed much in sixteen years. His hair was still thick and dark and slightly tousled, as if he couldn't be bothered to tame it. His golden-brown eyes were further enhanced by thick, black lashes and bold, arched brows. His perfectly-shaped and seductively-soft lips were now compressed in a firm line, the only outward sign of his displeasure.

He was dressed in a charcoal-colored suit with a snowy white shirt that enhanced his olive skin and a black-and-silver patterned tie. But in his case, it was the man who made the clothes rather than vice versa, and not just because he was a royal but because of the supreme confidence he wore even more comfortably than the designer threads on his back.

On closer inspection, she realized that there were some subtle signs of the passing of time: a few strands of gray near his temples, laugh lines fanning out from his eyes, but certainly nothing that detracted from his overall appearance.

His shoulders seemed just as broad as she remembered; his body appeared as hard and lean. He'd always known who he was, what he wanted, and he'd never let anything—or anyone—stand in his way. He was as outrageously sexy and devilishly handsome as ever, and she'd never stood a chance.

"Do you think we could speak privately in your office?"

Cameron asked her, his tone as casual as his posture—and in complete contradiction to the anger that she saw glinting in the depths of those hazel eyes.

Gabriella lifted her chin. "I don't have an office, I have a cubicle. Not all of us are handed cushy jobs with—"

"You can use mine," Alli interrupted hastily, shooting daggers at Gabriella as she moved past her on the way to the door. "I have to get to a meeting with the marketing director, anyway."

"Thank you," Cameron said, inclining his head toward her.

Gabriella had no intention of thanking her boss. She was feeling anything but grateful at the prospect of being stuck in Allison's tiny little office with a man who had always made her feel overwhelmed in his presence. But she squared her shoulders, reminded herself that she wasn't seventeen years old anymore, and faced him defiantly.

In the more than sixteen years that had passed since he'd dated Gabriella Vasquez, Cameron hadn't forgotten about her, but many of the details had faded from his mind. Facing her now, those details came flooding back, washing over him in a powerful wave that left his head struggling to stay above water.

When they'd first met, her hair was a tumbling mass of curls that fell to the middle of her back. Now, the sexy sun-streaked dark tresses grazed her shoulders and the shorter style drew attention to her face, to the dusky gold skin, cocoa-colored eyes, long, inky lashes, and soft, full lips that promised a taste of heaven.

His gaze drifted lower. From her full, round breasts to a narrow waist and the subtle flare of slim hips and down long, lean legs. His hands ached to trace the familiar contours as they'd done so many years before, and he had to curl his fingers into his palms to resist the urge to reach for her.

But even more than her physical attributes, what had attracted him was that she had spirit and spunk—even when she knew she was outgunned, she didn't surrender. From the first time they met, she'd been a challenge—and an incredible pleasure. He pushed aside the memory, firmly slammed the door on the past.

"Sixteen years is a long time to hold a grudge, wouldn't you agree?" he asked her.

"I would," she said easily. "And while I realize you may find this difficult to believe, the page twelve article wasn't about you."

He snorted, confirming his disbelief.

"The 'Around Town' section of the newspaper covers celebrity sightings and rumors. I saw you at the club with Princess Leticia and it seemed obvious to me that royalty hooking up with royalty would make some pretty good headlines."

"So it was just about selling papers?"

"That's my job," she said pleasantly.

"Why don't I believe you?"

She shrugged. "I've been writing an advice column for *La Noticia* for twelve years—my editor could confirm that fact, but you scared her away."

He felt a smile tug at the corners of his mouth, but refused to give into it. "Maybe because your editor has more sense than you do."

"Maybe," she agreed.

"You don't think I could have you fired?" he challenged softly.

Her eyes flashed, but her tone remained even when she responded. "I'm sure you could, but then I would have to sue for unlawful termination and all the gory details would be revealed, putting far too much importance on one little article."

His gaze narrowed. "That 'one little article' may result in

the King of Ardena walking away from a trade agreement that has been in place for more than fifty years."

"That would be unfortunate," she said, "but hardly my fault."

"You implied that I seduced his daughter."

"Did you?" She held up her hands. "Sorry. Forget I asked. I don't want to know and it's none of my business."

He gritted his teeth, but before he could respond, the ring of a cell phone intruded.

"Excuse me," she said, turning away from him to check the display on the slim instrument he hadn't realized was in her hand. Frowning, she connected the call. "Sierra?"

He couldn't hear what the caller was saying, but judging by the way Gabriella's face paled, the news was not good.

He was more than a little annoyed with her, irritated by her easy dismissal of him, and furious about the headlines she'd manufactured. So why did seeing the obvious distress on her face bother him? Why did he wish she would turn *to* him rather than turn away?

Gabriella's hands were unsteady as she closed the phone. The call had obviously shaken her, but when she turned back to him again, her face was carefully composed.

"As fascinating as this conversation has been," she said lightly, "I have to go."

"We're not done here, Gabriella."

She lifted her chin in a gesture that intrigued him as much as it irked him. "If you have any other concerns about the job I'm doing, take them up with my editor."

He let her brush past him and head out the door, and he tried to ignore the regret that gnawed at his belly.

There was no point in wishing that he'd handled things differently sixteen years earlier, no point in wondering where they might be now if he had. He'd been given more than enough second chances in his life; he couldn't expect another one from Gabriella.

And even if he wasn't still royally ticked about her creative reporting, she'd made it more than clear that she had no interest in him whatsoever. Not that he was entirely sure he believed her claim. Because if she truly didn't have any feelings for him, why did she continue to target him in her column? Why had she written a headline that she had to know would get his attention?

I did my job.

Her words echoed in his mind and he wondered if it really was as simple as that. Maybe he only wanted to believe that she'd never forgotten about him because he'd never forgotten about her.

They'd dated for only a few months, and although he'd dated a lot of other women both before and after his brief affair with Gabriella, no one else had ever lingered in his mind the way she had done.

She'd been both naive and inexperienced—and not at all his type. But there was something about her innocence that tugged at him, something about her purity and sweetness that had thoroughly captivated him.

She hadn't been similarly entranced. While a lot of women had wanted to be with him because he was a prince, Gabriella had seemed more intimidated than impressed by his title—and determined to keep him at a distance. But he'd never been the type to take a detour just because someone had set up a roadblock, and that was an aspect of his personality that hadn't changed in the past sixteen years.

No, Gabriella, he thought as he followed her path out the door. *We're not even close to being done.*

Chapter Two

Gabriella was still shaking as she exited through the automatic doors and stepped into the bright sunshine, but she knew it wasn't Sierra's phone call alone that was responsible for her distress. Learning that a child was in the hospital would be enough to send any parent into a panic, but hearing her daughter's voice had reassured Gabriella somewhat. Of course, she wouldn't be completely reassured until she'd held Sierra in her arms, so she unlocked the door and sank into the driver's seat, anxious to get to the hospital to do just that.

She tried to put Cameron Leandres out of her mind as she drove, but her thoughts were torn between worry for her daughter and worry for herself—and the secret she'd been holding on to for sixteen years.

It was her own fault. She should have realized that there would be repercussions if she continued to taunt him in print. But she'd been so angry with him for so long, and when she'd seen him at the club, up close and personal for the first time in so many years, she'd been overwhelmed by memories and emotions. And then she'd seen him dancing with the young Ardenan princess, and she'd recognized the look on the teenager's face when she'd gazed up at the prince because she'd once looked at him exactly the same way.

And for just a little while, Cameron had looked back at Gabriella as if she was the center of his world, and she'd let herself believe that she could be. She'd deluded herself into trusting that he truly cared about her, that she actually mattered to him. She wasn't the first woman to make that mistake, and she certainly hadn't been the last, though that knowledge didn't lessen her heartache in the slightest.

But that was a long time ago, and she was over him, wholly and completely. And if her heart had done a funny little skip when she'd seen him standing in the doorway of Allison's office, well, that wasn't really surprising. He was still an incredibly attractive man and any woman would have responded the same way. In fact, she'd be willing to bet that even Alli's cynical heart had gone pitter-patter. Not that she was going to question her editor about it. In fact, if she never again heard his name from her friend's lips, it would be too soon.

But just as she pulled into the hospital parking lot, her phone beeped to indicate an incoming text message. She drove into a vacant spot and checked the display.

where r u? r u with the prince? i came back to my office and u both were gone and i picked up some pretty heavy vibes btwn the 2 of u.

So much for thinking she might be able to avoid the topic, but it was easier to lie to her friend when she didn't have to look her in the eye. So she texted back:

I got a call from Sierra. She was in a fender bender with a friend. I'm at the hospital now, will check in with you later.

Then she tucked the phone in her purse, put both Allison Jenkins and Cameron Leandres out of her mind, and went into the hospital.

"Sierra Vasquez?" she said to the nurse behind the desk.

"First room on the right, third curtain on the left."

"Thank you."

She found her daughter exactly where the nurse had indicated. She looked so small and pale on the narrow hospital cot, the fluorescent yellow cast on her arm a bright contrast to the pale green sheets on the bed. Her heels clicked on the tile floor as she crossed the room, and Sierra's eyes flicked open.

"Hi, Mom."

"Hi." She brushed a dark curl off of her daughter's forehead and touched her lips to the pale skin there. "You told me you weren't hurt."

"I'm not," Sierra said. "Not really. And I didn't want you to freak out."

"Do I look like I'm freaking out?"

Sierra's lips tilted up at the corners. "I know when you're freaking out, even when no one else does."

"Well, it's a mother's prerogative to worry about her child." She pulled a chair up beside the bed. "How's Jenna?"

"Not a scratch. Her mom came and got her already. Mrs. Azzaro wanted to wait to see you, but she had a deposition or something that she had to get back to court for."

"I'll call Luisa tonight," Gabriella said, and took Sierra's hand in hers. "So what happened?"

"A cat ran across the road. Jenna swerved to avoid it and ended up hitting a lamppost."

"I didn't even know Jenna had her license," she noted.

"She got it three weeks ago," Sierra admitted.

"And her parents let her drive to school?"

"Probably the first and last time."

"Probably," Gabriella said. "Although I'm sure Don and

Luisa arc just as relieved as I am that no one was seriously injured."

"I wish I could say the same about the car."

"Cars can be fixed," Gabriella said.

"Speaking of fixed," Sierra said. "Why are you all fixed up today?"

Gabriella glanced down at her matching skirt and jacket. She'd always told Sierra that one of the greatest advantages of working from home was being able to work in her pj's. Not that she usually did so, but she also didn't dig "the good clothes" out of the back of her closet or torture her feet in three-inch heels except for rare visits to the newspaper offices.

"I had a meeting with my editor this morning."

Her daughter's brows rose.

"Don't ask," Gabriella told her.

"I'm sorry if I dragged you away from something important," Sierra said.

"Nothing is more important than you." She put her arm across her daughter's shoulder, hugged her carefully. "And I don't think I need to point out that this accident wouldn't have happened if you'd been at school, where you were supposed to be."

"I had a free period, Mom."

"During which you're supposed to do your homework or study."

"Jenna wanted to get a new pair of shoes for her date with Kevin tonight and there was a sale…" her explanation trailed off when she caught the look on her mother's face. "Okay, I won't leave school property again without getting your permission first."

"And to make sure you remember that, you're grounded for a week."

"A week?" Sierra squawked indignantly.

"Are you angling for two?" Gabriella asked.

Her daughter sighed. "Okay—a week."

Gabriella stood up again. "Now I'm going to find the doctor to get you out of here, then we'll go rent some movies and spend the night—"

"You're not staying home with me tonight, Mom."

She frowned. "Why not?"

"Because Rafe's flying in for the weekend, and he said he was going to make reservations at L'Atelier." Sierra frowned at her. "You forgot, didn't you?"

"No," she denied, although not very convincingly. But she hadn't forgotten so much as she'd pushed the information to the back of her mind, not nearly as excited about Rafe's plans as her daughter seemed to be.

"This could be the night," Sierra continued, "and I'm not going to be the one to screw things up for you."

She didn't need to when Gabriella was perfectly capable of screwing things up entirely on her own, and probably would. But she wasn't going to think about that now. She wasn't going to worry about what might or might not happen with the American businessman who had started dropping hints about the future he wanted for them together.

"Honey, Rafe and I can have dinner another time. I don't want you to be alone tonight."

"Paolo could come over to watch movies with me."

Gabriella raised her eyebrows. "And I certainly don't want you alone with your boyfriend."

Sierra rolled her eyes. "I didn't expect we would be alone— Grandma will be home, won't she?"

Still, she hesitated.

"I only broke my wrist," Sierra said. "That's no reason for you to break your plans with Rafe."

"Rafe will understand."

Sierra sighed. "Mom, he's going to ask you to marry him tonight."

"He didn't tell you that, did he?"

"No, but I'm not an idiot. An impromptu visit, dinner at L'Atelier, something important to discuss…"

No, her daughter definitely wasn't an idiot. And Gabriella knew she should be pleased that Sierra obviously liked and approved of the man her mother had been dating for the past year and a half. Of course, everyone liked Rafe. He was a wonderful man—handsome and successful and generous and giving, and Gabriella cared for him a great deal. But marriage?

She was almost thirty-four years old and she'd lost her innocence a long time ago, but she was still relatively naive and inexperienced. She'd fallen head over heels in love only once, when she was barely seventeen years old, and her life experiences after that had been very different from most other girls her age. She'd survived first love and first heartbreak, but it had taken her a long time to put the pieces of her shattered heart back together.

While she'd long ago abandoned her girlish dreams of walking down the aisle, she'd believed that her heart was sufficiently mended that she could fall in love again. But as wonderful as Rafe was—and he truly was—something still held her back.

She refused to let herself think about what that something— or who that someone—might be.

Cameron didn't feel like going out. After being ambushed by the underage princess at Club Sapphire the night before, he wanted only to stay home, far away from the prying eyes of the paparazzi.

Maybe he was getting old. Since his thirtieth birthday, more than six years ago, he'd started to think that he wanted more than an endless parade of interchangeable women through his life. Spending time with friends and family members who were happily married had further convinced him that he wanted that same kind of close connection with someone—someday. But it seemed that he could never stay with any one woman long enough to allow that kind of closeness to develop. Or maybe he'd just never met the right woman.

When Michael's daughter was born, Cameron had become even more aware of the emptiness of his own life. The realization that he wanted a family wasn't just unexpected but shocking, considering how screwed up his own family had been.

His father—Gaetan Leandres—had been a farmer by birth and by trade and he'd been content with his lot in life, at least until he'd had the misfortune of falling in love with a princess. They'd married against, and possibly to spite, her father's wishes, and they'd had three children together. Cameron believed that Elena had loved her husband, but when Gaetan had died and left her alone, she'd suddenly resented everything that she'd given up to be with him.

So she'd tried to pass her dreams and ambitions on to her children. Michael, her firstborn, had always known what he wanted and had refused to let her manipulate him. Marissa, her youngest child and only daughter, had mostly escaped Elena's attention by virtue of her gender. So it was almost by default that she'd focused her efforts on her second son.

And Cameron, still looking for his own place and purpose in life, had been much more susceptible to his mother's manipulations. As a result, he'd done some things he wasn't proud of, hurt a lot of people who never should have been hurt, and walked away from the only woman he'd ever loved.

Walked away? His lips twisted wryly. No, what he'd done was push her away—so forcefully and finally that she'd never wanted to look back. And Cameron had never let himself look back, either. He'd never let himself admit that he might have made a mistake, that every woman he'd been with since had been little more than a pale substitute for her.

Until today when, for the first time in more than sixteen years, he'd found himself face-to-face with her again.

Gabriella Vasquez—the only woman who had ever taken hold of his heart.

He closed his eyes, as if that might banish her image from his mind. He didn't want to think of her now, to remember what they'd once shared, to imagine what might have been. There was no point. Gabriella was his past and he had to look to the future.

Not that a status-conscious socialite like Allegra was a woman he could imagine being with for the rest of his life. But hopefully a casual meal with his frequent companion would generate some positive publicity to counteract all the negative headlines of last night's fiasco at Club Sapphire.

And there would be publicity—of that he had no doubt. Gone were the days when he only had to worry about card-carrying members of the media shoving cameras in his face—now they hid in the shadows and used telephoto lenses. And even if no paparazzi were around, there would be someone with a camera in a cell phone eager to snap a shot.

He arrived at Allegra's condo at seven-fifteen, knowing she would keep him waiting at least fifteen minutes. He didn't usually mind, but for some reason, he found the delay to-night more than a little irritating. When Allegra swept into the room, however, he couldn't deny that she was worth the wait.

She was wearing a sheath-style dress of emerald green that molded to her slender frame and enhanced the color of her eyes. Her long, blond hair was styled in a fancy twist that was both sexy and sophisticated. Round emeralds surrounded by diamonds glittered at her ears and a matching pendant dangled between her breasts.

"I'm sorry I kept you waiting," she said.

"You look lovely," he said, his response as automatic as her apology, though probably more sincere.

"Would you like a drink before we go?" she asked, gesturing toward the well-stocked bar in the corner.

He shook his head. "We have reservations at L'Atelier and if we don't leave now, we'll be late."

"L'Atelier?" Her eyes lit up and her lips curved as she tucked her hand in his arms. "Aren't you full of surprises tonight?"

When they were seated at one of only a half-dozen tables in the exclusive upper-level dining room, Cameron ordered a bottle of Cristal because he knew it was Allegra's favorite.

During the course of the meal, they sipped the champagne and talked about nothing of importance. When the waiter cleared away his empty plate and the remnants of Allegra's coq au vin—because she never did more than sample her dinner—a flash of color near the doorway caught his eye.

A swirling red dress wrapped around luscious feminine curves. A tumble of dark curls that grazed sexy shoulders. A low, throaty laugh that shot through his blood like an exquisite cognac.

His breath caught; his throat went dry.

No, it couldn't be.

Then she turned, and his heart actually skipped a beat.

It *was* Gabriella.

He didn't recognize the man she was with, but he didn't really take a good look. He couldn't tear his eyes off of the woman who had preoccupied far too many of his thoughts since their encounter earlier that morning—the same woman who had haunted his dreams for far too many years.

She looked absolutely stunning. Sensual. Sexy. Seductive.

The return of the waiter with their dessert dragged his attention back to his own table. He noticed that Allegra was frowning slightly, obviously displeased by the wavering of his attention but reluctant to say anything about it.

He reached across the table for her hand, and she smiled at him. She was always quick to forgive and forget—and willing to disregard troublesome newspaper headlines. It was unfortunate, he thought, that he wasn't even close to falling in love with her.

"Allegra—"

She leaned forward, her eyes bright and filled with anticipation. "Yes?"

He drew in a breath. "I think we should take a break."

She blinked. Once. Twice. "*Excuse* me?"

He couldn't blame her for appearing shell-shocked. He had no idea where those words had come from. And yet, now that he'd spoken them, he felt an immense sense of relief—and more than a little bit of guilt.

"You brought me here tonight…to dump me?"

"No," he said. "I didn't plan— I mean, I'm not dumping you."

Her eyes filled with tears, but she valiantly held them in check. He breathed a silent sigh of relief, grateful that she wasn't the type of woman to make a nasty scene.

"It sure sounds that way to me." Her voice was cool and carefully controlled as she pushed her chair away from the table. Then she picked up her champagne glass and tossed the contents in his face. "You son of a bitch."

So much for thinking she wouldn't cause a scene, Cameron thought, as he wiped up the Cristal with his linen napkin.

Gabriella had escaped to the ladies' room for a moment of quiet to catch her breath and settle her nerves. As she'd readied herself for her date with Rafe, she'd worried about Sierra's prediction. When they'd arrived at the restaurant and been led to the upper level, her apprehension had increased.

She knew there were about half a dozen tables in the exclusive dining room, but the arrangement and décor were such that the diners at each table had the illusion of complete privacy. There were tall columns and lush greenery, soft lights and romantic music, and just walking into the scene had her stomach twisting into knots. Because in that moment, she knew that Sierra was right—Rafe had brought her here tonight because he was going to ask her to marry him, and she didn't know how she would respond to that question.

She considered calling her daughter and begging Sierra to call *her* with some trumped-up emergency that required Gabriella to immediately return home. The only reason she didn't make the call was that she knew she couldn't count on Sierra's complicity. Her daughter clearly thought it was a good idea for Gabriella to marry Rafe and wouldn't understand her hesitation. A hesitation that had led her to hiding out in the ladies' room rather than facing a perfectly wonderful man who wanted to spend his life with her.

As she was reapplying her lip gloss, the door to the ladies' room flew open. When a weeping woman flung herself onto the chaise lounge and buried her face in her hands, Gabriella realized that some people had bigger problems than she did.

She dropped the lip gloss back into her purse and glanced around, but the spacious room was otherwise empty. So she plucked a handful of tissues from the box on the counter and went to the sitting area, lowering herself to the edge of a chair facing the distraught woman.

Wordlessly, she offered the tissues.

The blonde lifted her head, looked at her through beautiful, tear-drenched eyes.

Gabriella barely managed to hold back a shocked gasp.

It had been awkward enough to imagine that she'd been trapped in the washroom with a broken-hearted but anonymous stranger. But she knew who this woman was—she was Allegra de Havilland, Prince Cameron's consort.

As quickly as Gabriella identified the woman, she also recognized that the juiciest headline of her career was in the palm of her hand.

Chapter Three

She immediately pushed the thought aside, ashamed that she would consider—even for a second—capitalizing on someone else's pain for the purpose of advancing her career. It wasn't as if she aspired to take over Alex Girard's "Around Town" column, after all, she was just having some fun with it while her colleague was on vacation. But it would be cruel to exploit Allegra's obvious heartache for a headline. So Gabriella didn't ask what the callous prince had done, she only asked, "Do you want me to call you a cab?"

The gorgeous heiress dabbed carefully at the mascara streaks under her eyes. But instead of answering Gabriella's question, she said, "I thought things were moving along nicely, that we were moving toward being exclusive."

"Men are usually a few steps behind women when it comes to relationships," Gabriella said lightly.

"I could have handled it if he said he needed more time, but he said we should take a break, spend some time apart."

Gabriella winced, understanding how harshly those insensitive words would slice through a heart that was filled with love. On the other hand, they weren't nearly as cold as the words—and the fistful of cash—he'd once thrown at her.

"Everyone warned me that he was a snake," Allegra continued, "but I didn't believe them. I didn't want to believe them, because he was always so considerate and charming."

Calling Cameron Leandres a snake was an insult to snakes, but Gabriella kept that assessment to herself, knowing that it would do nothing to ease Allegra's pain.

"After almost six months, he's suddenly changed his mind about what he wants?" Her eyes filled with tears again. "I want to hate him. There's a part of me that does hate him. But a bigger part really does love him." She dabbed at the streaks of mascara again, then her eyes suddenly went wide. "I'm so sorry—you must have a husband or a boyfriend or someone waiting for you—"

"It's okay," Gabriella assured her. "He won't mind."

"He must be a real prince of a guy," Allegra said softly.

She smiled at the irony. "He really is."

"Then you're a lucky woman."

Gabriella nodded. "So what are your plans for the rest of the night? Are you going back to your date—" she deliberately didn't use Cameron's name or title because she didn't want Allegra to know that she'd guessed his identity "—or do you want the maitre d' to call a cab for you?"

"I can't go back out there. I threw my champagne in his face."

Gabriella nearly choked trying to hold back a laugh. "Then you don't have to," she assured the other woman. "You wait here, and I'll come back to get you when your cab has arrived."

"You're being very kind," Allegra said gratefully.

"I've been where you are," she said, then, taking in the luxurious surroundings, she smiled wryly. "Well, not exactly.

But I've had my heart broken before, so I can relate—at least a little—to what you're feeling right now."

She took a quick detour to where Rafe was seated, to let him know what she was doing before she tracked down the maitre d'. She tried to apologize for the interruption of the romantic evening he'd planned but, Rafe being Rafe, he understood.

After she watched Allegra's cab pull away, she turned—and came face-to-face with Prince Cameron Leandres for the second time that day.

"I can just imagine the headlines that are scrolling through your mind," he said, a definite edge to his voice.

She smiled, unable to resist taunting him. "I doubt that you can."

"Why don't you give me a chance to tell my side of the story?"

"Because I'm not interested in anything you have to say." She started to move past him, but he caught her arm.

The jolt of heat that shot through her veins in response to the contact was as unwelcome as it was unexpected. As low as her opinion was of him, she had to wonder what it said about *her* that the briefest touch could send her pulse racing. Except that her heart had been pounding even before he'd touched her—even before she'd seen him standing there. It was as if she was hardwired to respond to this man as she'd never responded to anyone else before or since their long-ago affair.

But while she couldn't deny her instinctive reaction to him, she had no intention of letting him know the effect he had on her. Instead of yanking her arm from his grasp, as she wanted to do, she simply looked at his hand and lifted her brows, deliberately cool and unaffected.

His fingers uncurled, his hand dropped away. "Of course not," he said sardonically. "It's just about selling papers, right?"

"That's my job," she reminded him, then moved past him to return to her date.

But she was obviously more flustered than she wanted to admit, because as soon as she got back to the table, Rafe was on his feet, his brow furrowed with concern. "Are you okay?"

She forced a smile. "Yeah. It's just been a really long day."

"I ordered pizza," he told her.

She glanced up, startled. "Pizza?"

"From Pinelli's," he explained. "We can pick it up on the way back to your place."

"But—"

He touched a finger to her lips, silencing her protest. "We'll do this again some other time," he promised her.

"I'm sorry."

And she *was* sorry that she'd ruined the mood he'd so carefully set—but she was also relieved that he wouldn't be getting down on one knee tonight.

"Don't be," he said, and brushed his lips against hers.

The gentle kiss was as steady and reliable as the man who kissed her. There was no startling jolt of awareness, no unexpected surge of heat, nothing she couldn't handle. And Gabriella was glad for that. She didn't ever want to feel out of control again.

Rafe tossed more than enough cash on the table to pay for the bottle of champagne they'd barely touched and compensate the waiter for the tip on the hefty dinner tab he was missing out on as a result of their premature exit. Then they picked up two extra-large cheese and pepperoni pizzas on the way home, to share with Sierra and Paolo and Katarina, Gabriella's mother who had canceled her own plans in order to stay home and chaperone the young couple.

In the comfort of her home, surrounded by family, Gabriella found herself relaxing again. And when Rafe said that he was going to call it a night, she exhaled a silent sigh of relief as she walked him to the door. Obviously her suspicions about his intentions tonight had been off-base. As she'd told Allegra, women usually started thinking about commitment before men and Rafe was obviously happy with the status quo.

Or so she thought until he pulled a small, square box out of his jacket pocket.

Her eyes went wide, her breath caught, and she felt a fine sheen of perspiration bead on her brow.

Rafe chuckled, but the sound was strained. "Honestly, Gabriella, I've never known another woman who would blanch at the sight of a jeweler's box."

She swallowed, forced a smile. "I don't like to be predictable."

"No worries there." He flipped open the lid, and her eyes dropped back to the box with the same combination of fascination and trepidation that compelled passersby to gawk at the scene of an accident.

"Wow," she said, and swallowed again.

"I've had this ring for a couple of months now. I brought it with me tonight because I thought—I'd *hoped*—you might finally be ready to wear it." He closed the lid again and pressed the box into her hand. "But I know you're not, so I'm only going to ask you to hold on to it until you are."

She looked up at him, hoping he knew how truly sorry she was that she couldn't take the ring out of the box and put it on her finger. And hoping, just as desperately, that someday she would be ready.

It was with more than a little apprehension that Cameron unfolded his newspaper the next morning. Seeing nothing on the front page that was cause for concern, he turned the page. By the time he got to the "Around Town" section, he was mentally drafting his resignation, certain that nothing he could say or do would save his political career after Gabriella

Vasquez had pried all the intimate details of his latest failed relationship from his obviously unhappy ex-girlfriend. But the headline at the top of the page—*American Actress Storms Off Set*—gave him pause.

Although he didn't usually read the gossip columns, he forced himself to do so now, to ensure that he wasn't somehow to blame for the actress's behavior.

He skimmed several paragraphs about the drama that had taken place during filming of a romantic comedy in San Pedro, and then he found his name at the bottom of the page.

In other news: a rep for native supermodel Arianna Raquel has confirmed that the twenty-four-year-old is expecting her first child with Russian composer, Pavel Belyakova; and Prince Cameron and long-time girlfriend Allegra de Havilland were spotted dining at L'Atelier Friday evening.

He turned the page, looking for more. But that was it— barely a footnote at the very bottom of the page.

He exhaled a sigh, as surprised as he was relieved, and even more curious.

It was the curiosity that led him to track her down at her home and ask, "Why?"

Gabriella stared at him, appearing as surprised by his presence at her door at this early hour as by the inquiry.

"What are you doing here?" she demanded, completely disregarding his question to ask her own.

There was something in his tone that warned him she wasn't just surprised that he was there but…scared?

No, he was obviously misreading the situation. As she'd already proven that her pen was mightier than his sword, she had nothing to fear from him.

He shrugged. "I wanted to talk to you, but I didn't want

to have another conversation where we'd be surrounded by reporters."

"How did you know where I lived?"

"I called your editor." He'd expected a downtown address and had been surprised to find himself driving toward the outskirts of the city. He'd been even more surprised to pull up in front of a modest but well-kept two-story home on a quiet cul-de-sac.

It was a house made for a family, and it made him wonder if Gabriella had one. It wasn't unreasonable to expect that she'd married and had children at some point over the past sixteen years, even if she still looked more like a centerfold fantasy than a suburban mom.

He cut off his wandering thoughts before they could detour too far down that dangerous path, but cast a quick glance at her left hand and found that it was bare.

As bare as the long, slender legs that seemed to stretch for miles beneath the ragged hem of cutoff shorts she wore low on her hips. As bare as the sexy, curve of her shoulders peeking above the neckline of her peasant-style blouse. As bare as—

Gabriella's soft groan drew his attention back to their conversation. "You called Alli? Thanks. As if I didn't get enough of an interrogation after your appearance at the office yesterday, now you contacted her for my home address."

He cleared his throat, suddenly uncomfortably aware of her nearness, of the soft feminine scent that had always clouded his senses when he was near her. "I didn't realize that would be a problem."

"As if that would matter to you," she muttered.

"Can I come in?"

"No."

Her response—immediate and definitive—had him lifting his brows. "Do you really want to take the chance of someone spotting me standing on your doorstep?"

"If you didn't want to announce your presence to everyone on the street, you should have driven something a little more inconspicuous than an Aston Martin." But she did, reluctantly, step away from the door so that he could enter.

Of course, she didn't move any farther into the house than the foyer, and she faced him squarely, arms folded across her chest. The open-concept design allowed light to spill into the entranceway from the east-facing windows, and it surrounded Gabriella now, giving her an almost ethereal appearance. Although the dark scowl on her face spoiled the illusion somewhat.

He glanced around, appreciating how the sunny yellow walls complemented the terracotta floor. Her furniture was simple in design and neutral in color, with bold splashes of turquoise, lime and purple used as strategic accents.

"Nice place," he told her.

"Thank you," she responded stiffly. "But since I don't think you stopped by to compliment my décor, why don't you tell me why you're really here?"

"Because I can't figure you out."

"I don't know why you'd bother to try," she told him.

Her tone was dismissive, and yet, he couldn't forget the flare of awareness he'd seen in her eyes when he'd touched her arm the night before, confirming that she'd felt the same jolt that had shaken him to the core.

It had been like that between them since the first time they'd met. But he wouldn't have expected that there would be anything left of that long-ago connection, not after so many years, and especially not considering the way their relationship had ended.

He'd been young and scared of the feelings he had for her, and he'd treated her badly. He had no excuse for his behavior—and no reason to expect that she'd forgiven him, which made the absence of any mention in the gossip column of his argument with Allegra all the more puzzling.

"You could have completely skewered me in today's paper," he noted.

Her brows rose. "Because you stomped all over some poor woman's heart? That's hardly news."

"I didn't realize how badly I'd stomped on yours," he said.

She waved a hand dismissively. "Ancient history."

"Is it?" He took a step closer, watched her eyes narrow, darken.

"Yes," she said firmly.

But he could see the pulse point at the base of her jaw, and it was racing.

"I never forgot about you, Gabriella. And I don't think you forgot about me, either."

"How could I when your face is plastered on the tabloids on an almost daily basis?"

"You're not going to give me an inch, are you?"

"I've already given you a lot more than I should have." She slipped past him and reached for the handle of the door. "Now I have things to do and I'd really like you to go."

But he wasn't ready to leave. Not yet. "Who was the guy you were with last night?"

"Newsflash," she said. "I'm the reporter, you're the object of the public's curiosity. Therefore, I get to ask the questions and you get to smile and look pretty."

"Who is he?" he asked again.

She sighed. "Rafe Fulton."

The name didn't mean anything to him, but he wanted to know more than the man's identity—he wanted to know what the man meant to her. "Boyfriend?"

"Yes."

He frowned at that, but before he could say anything else, footsteps sounded overhead.

Gabriella's gaze shifted to the stairs. "You really have to go now."

He didn't particularly want to hang around to meet the boy-friend, but he was baffled by Gabriella's sudden and obvious desperation to get him out the door. Was her boyfriend the possessive type? Would he disapprove of her having a conversation with another man? Would he—Cameron's blood boiled at the thought—take out his displeasure on Gabriella?

"Gabriella—" He reached for her hand, found it icy cold.

She tugged her hand from his grasp, wrenched open the door. "Please, Cameron. Just go."

The footsteps were coming down the stairs now. Not the heavy tread he'd anticipated, but light, quick steps.

"What's for breakfast, Mom? I'm starving."

Cameron froze, his mind spinning.

Mom?

"I'm making French toast as soon as Gram gets back from the market with the eggs," Gabriella called, then hissed at him, "Please go. I don't want to explain your presence here to my daughter."

Daughter.

She wasn't trying to get rid of him for the benefit of an angry husband or possessive lover, but because she didn't want him to meet her child.

Except that the voice he'd heard didn't sound like that of a pre-schooler or even a pre-teen, but more like that of an adult.

"Mmm, I love French toast," the voice replied.

And then she stepped into view and he saw that his assessment had been right. Gabriella's daughter wasn't a little girl, but a young and stunningly beautiful woman with her mother's dark tumbling curls and distinctly feminine curves. She was dressed similarly to her mother, too, in shorts and a T-shirt, with the addition of a sling around her neck to help support the arm that was encased in a neon-yellow cast.

Except for the cast, looking at her was like looking at Gabriella sixteen years ago, and the realization nearly knocked him off of his feet.

"Whoops." The girl stopped in mid-stride when she spotted Cameron standing in the foyer beside her mother. "Sorry—I didn't realize you had company."

"It's okay," Gabriella said pointedly. "Cameron was just on his way out."

He ignored her, focusing instead on her daughter, who was eyeing him with unbridled curiosity.

As she drew nearer, he saw that the child's eyes were lighter than her mother's—more hazel than brown.

More like the color of his own eyes.

His gaze flew back to Gabriella.

She tilted her chin, as if daring him to ask. But he didn't need to ask.

In that moment, all of the pieces fell into place.

A long-ago conversation. Tear-filled eyes looking to him for answers. Desperate panic. Fierce denials. Reassurance. Relief.

He'd worked hard to forget her, to forget what they had been to one another, but she hadn't been able to forget. She'd lived with the reminder of their long-ago affair every day for the past sixteen years.

The girl standing in front of him was that reminder.

Gabriella's daughter was his daughter, too.

Mi Dios. He was a father.

As his gaze lingered on the beautiful young woman, he couldn't help but think: *Lord, help us both.*

Chapter Four

"Hey, aren't you—" Sierra's sleepy brain woke up in time to halt the impulsive flow of words. She had almost asked her mother's visitor if he was one of the royals, but thankfully she realized how ridiculous the question was before she embarrassed herself by asking it.

She shook her head but still couldn't shake the feeling that she recognized him from somewhere. "Sorry, for a minute I thought you looked…familiar."

"I am Cameron Leandres," he said, and bowed.

Sierra held back a snicker.

Was this guy for real?

Then the name clicked, and her head suddenly felt so light, she thought that she might faint.

"Then you are—ohmygod—you're *Prince* Cameron?"

"I am," he agreed, in the same casual tone.

Sierra's gaze flew to her mother, who seemed neither surprised nor impressed by this revelation.

Of course, her mother worked in the newspaper business

and she'd been covering the "Around Town" section while Alex was on vacation. She knew everyone in the country who was newsworthy. Obviously she would have recognized him immediately. But that still didn't explain what the heck the guy—the *prince*—was doing in her house. And wouldn't Jenna just die when she heard about this?

"And you are obviously Gabriella's daughter," Prince Cameron noted.

"Sierra Vasquez," she responded automatically, wondering if she was supposed to bow or curtsy.

She glanced at her mother again, as if for guidance, and noticed the stiffness of her posture, the deepening of the faint lines that bracketed her mouth. Whatever had brought this member of the royal family to their door, it was apparent to Sierra that Gabriella wasn't pleased by his presence.

"It's a pleasure to finally meet you, Sierra." The prince's comment drew her attention back to him and further piqued her curiosity.

Before she could say anything else, her mother interrupted.

"Thanks for the information, Your Highness," Gabriella said. "I'll be sure to pass it along to Alex when he returns from his vacation."

"There's no need for such formalities between old friends, Gabriella," the prince chided.

Old friends?

Sierra felt her jaw drop.

She turned to her mother, noted the spots of color that rode high on her cheeks, a telltale sign that she was either embarrassed or angry. Because she used to rub elbows with royalty? Or because she didn't want Sierra to know that she used to rub elbows with royalty? It made her wonder how long her mother had known the prince—and just how close they used to be.

Curiosity was eating away at her, but she didn't dare ask her mother those questions. At least not right now.

"What happened to your arm?"

It was the prince who spoke again, his tone was casual and friendly, as if he was unaware of the tension in the room. Or maybe he was just unconcerned about it.

She glanced cautiously at her mother, because she knew Gabriella was still angry about the events of the previous day. "Car accident."

He frowned. "You can't be old enough to drive."

"Your Highness—" Gabriella began to interject again, with obvious impatience.

"Not yet," Sierra responded to his statement. "My best friend was driving."

"I hope no one was badly injured."

She shook her head, lifted her arm slightly. "This was the worst of it."

The crunch of tires on gravel was unmistakable through the open window, evidence that her grandmother had returned from the market.

"Go help with the bags, Sierra," her mother said.

It was obvious that she was being sent out of the room so that her mother could finish her conversation with the royal visitor in private, and Sierra was itching to know why. What business had brought the prince to their home? And why was her usually composed and level-headed mother so obviously flustered by his presence?

"I think you're forgetting which one of us has the broken arm," she responded, hoping for a brief reprieve.

"Now," Gabriella snapped.

Sierra's brows lifted in response to the unexpectedly sharp tone. Her mother was definitely unnerved, and as much as she wanted to hang around and hear the rest of the conversation between them, the sound of the back door opening prompted her to do as she was told.

* * *

Gabriella breathed a silent sigh of relief when Sierra finally exited the room. She knew she'd only been granted a brief reprieve, that her daughter would have plenty of questions for her later. And she would face them later. But right now, she had to face the prince, who wasn't likely to be nearly as patient nor understanding as Sierra.

"So how old is she?" Cameron asked.

Gabriella crossed her arms over her chest. "My daughter is none of your business."

"Unless she's my daughter, too."

He'd kept his voice low, his tone even, but she couldn't resist glancing toward the doorway through which Sierra had disappeared to confirm her daughter was not within earshot. "She's not."

"How old is she?" he asked again.

She lifted her chin. "Fifteen."

"When's her birthday?"

"What gives you the right to barge in here and ask me all these questions?"

"Her birthday," he said again.

Her reply wasn't a date but a directive, and he responded to her crude words with a casual lift of his brows. His unruffled demeanor only irritated her further. Of course, he could afford to be cool—he didn't have anything to lose.

"Look, Your Highness—"

"I don't remember you ever being as hung up on my title then as you seem to be now," he mused.

She hadn't even known he had a title when they first met. If she had, she probably would never have got up the courage to even speak to him. But to her, he'd just been one of a group of college kids who regularly came into the restaurant on Friday nights. Maybe he was a little more handsome than the others, a little more charming. And he was the only one whose smile made her heart beat faster.

Even not knowing that he was royalty, she'd known that he was out of her league. Not just because he was older and more sophisticated, but because it was obvious that his family had money while her family worked for those with money. If Gabriella wanted to go to college someday, as she'd intended to do, she would have to earn the money to pay for her education. Which was how she ended up serving wood-oven pizzas and pitchers of beer to spoiled frat boys like Cameron and his buddies.

"Obviously I wasn't as discerning then as I am now," she said coolly.

"Ouch," he said, but smiled after he said it.

It was the same smile that had always made her knees a little bit weak. So easy and natural, so completely charming and utterly irresistible—at least to a seventeen-year-old girl. But she wasn't seventeen anymore and there was too much at stake to let herself to succumb once again to his considerable charms.

"Cameron." She used his name this time, and was rewarded with another smile.

"Isn't that much better, *Gabriella?*"

His pronunciation of her name was as sensual as a caress, and she felt something unwelcome and unwanted stir inside of her. "What would be much better," she told him, "would be for you to leave so that I can enjoy the rest of the day with my family."

"But we have so much to catch up on," he insisted.

Despite the casual tone, she knew the words weren't an invitation but a threat.

"Another time," she offered.

"You're only delaying the inevitable," he warned her.

She knew that might be true. But she also knew that "the partying prince" had a notoriously short attention span, and she was confident that he would soon forget about her and Sierra and this impromptu visit entirely.

"I'll be happy to meet with you at a mutually convenient date and time," she lied.

"All right," he finally said. He pulled a BlackBerry from his jacket pocket and scrolled through some data, no doubt checking his calendar. "Next Saturday afternoon. Two o'clock in front of the Naval History Museum."

"I'll have to check my schedule," she told him.

His gaze narrowed. "Next Saturday at two o'clock," he said again. "If you're not there, I'll come back here. And I won't leave until all of my questions have been answered."

"I'll be there," she agreed, because she knew that she had no choice. And because she was hoping that, at some point in the coming week, something more important would come up and he would forget.

Gabriella knew *she* wouldn't forget. Because nothing was more important to her than her daughter—and keeping the secret of Sierra's paternity.

Cameron didn't want to wait a whole week to get the answers he sought. But he wasn't entirely sure he trusted Gabriella to tell him the truth, and he knew that if he had some time, he could uncover some of the answers himself.

By Thursday afternoon, he had the most important one. As he stared at the copy of the birth certificate in his hand, his gaze focused on the date that confirmed his suspicions. Sierra Katarina Vasquez was born on June fifteenth—nine months after the weekend he and Gabriella had spent together on the northern coast. Which proved that Gabriella's beautiful fifteen-going-on-sixteen-year-old daughter was also his daughter, even if the father was listed as "unknown" on the registration of her birth.

The sight of that single word had filled him with burning fury. He was as stunned as he was incensed that she would deny the role he'd played in the creation of their child. But his anger faded almost as quickly as it had built, as snippets of a long-ago conversation filtered through his memory.

They'd had the occasional stolen moment together over the period of a few months, and then one glorious extended weekend at Cielo del Norte. When he'd dropped her off after their brief holiday was over, he'd promised that he would call her—but he never did. In fact, several weeks passed before he saw her again, before she tracked him down.

He remembered the exact moment he'd spotted her standing beside the stone archway that guarded the entrance to his campus residence. His initial surprise had been replaced by pleasure, then guilt and regret.

He wanted to go to her, to take her in his arms, to tell her how much he'd missed her. Because he had, and every time he'd thought of her, he'd felt an aching emptiness deep inside. But he'd made up his mind—he was too young to get seriously involved with any one woman—and he'd been sure that, in time, he'd get over her. So instead of going to her, he walked right past, as if he didn't even see her.

He'd thought she would take the hint, that she would turn away. But she'd raced across the field, chasing after him.

"Cameron, wait."

He couldn't pretend he hadn't heard her, so he halted, and tried to look vaguely puzzled. "Hi, uh, Gabriella, right?"

Her eyes—those beautiful, fathomless dark eyes that haunted his dreams—went wide, her face drained of all color. But then she firmed her quivering lip and lifted her chin. "Yes, it's Gabriella," she told him. "We spent a weekend together at the beach last month."

"Yeah," he nodded, as if only now remembering. As if the memories hadn't preoccupied his every waking thought and haunted his every dream since he'd said goodbye to her. "It was a good time."

She hesitated, as if she wasn't sure what else to say to him.

Then she tilted her chin another fraction and met his gaze dead-on. "I think I might be pregnant."

He couldn't see his own face, but he would have guessed that it was even whiter than hers now. He took an automatic step in retreat. "No. No way."

"I don't know for sure," she admitted, her gaze sliding away from his now. "But I thought you should know."

He shook his head. He didn't want to know. He didn't want to believe it was possible. They'd been careful. He was always careful. Except for that last morning. He'd realized that he'd run out of condoms, but he'd thought that it would be okay—he'd convinced her that it would be okay—just one time.

"When—" he managed to clear his throat, but his mind remained fuzzy "—when will you know...for sure?"

"I can pick up a test...on my way home."

He nodded and reached into his back pocket for his wallet. He didn't even count out the bills—he just pulled out all the money that he had and thrust it toward her.

She stared at the money in his hand, her eyes filling with tears.

"Just take it," he said. "In case you need anything."

She knocked the money out of his hand and turned.

"Gabriella."

"Don't worry," she said, her usually warm voice colder than he'd ever heard it before. "I don't need anything from you."

Then she'd walked away, but the tight, panicky feeling that had taken hold inside his chest didn't go away, not for a long time. But as the days turned into weeks and the weeks into months and he didn't see her or hear from her again, he'd been relieved. He'd assumed that she'd made a mistake, that she hadn't been pregnant. Now he knew otherwise.

In retrospect, he could hardly blame her for refusing to name him on her child's birth certificate. If anything, he should thank her. Because at twenty years of age, he hadn't been ready to be a parent. He didn't imagine that Gabriella had been any more ready than he, but she'd taken on the responsibility, anyway. She could have terminated her pregnancy or given the baby up for adoption, but she'd done neither. She'd given birth and raised their child on her own.

Maybe not completely alone, since it seemed that her mother had stood by her. But as far as he knew, she'd never even attempted to contact him again. Not once in the past sixteen years had she tried to get in touch with him to let him know that he was a father.

He knew he couldn't blame her for that. And yet, when he looked at the young woman who reminded him so much of Gabriella when he'd first met her so many years before, he couldn't help but resent having been excluded. Not just excluded but explicitly disavowed by that one little word: *unknown*.

And what would have been different if she'd named him on the child's birth certificate?

He instinctively winced in response to the question that echoed in the back of his head. Even now, more than sixteen years later, he couldn't pretend that everything wouldn't have spun out of control. There would have been a media circus, at the very least. As soon as anyone had seen his name on the birth certificate, the existence of his illegitimate child would have been in the headlines. And he would have responded the same way he'd responded to every scandal that he'd faced: with bald-faced, blatant denials.

He would have been instructed by his royal advisors to deny even the possibility that he was the father of Gabriella's baby. If there had been any proof that she'd spent the weekend at Cielo del Norte with him, then he'd produce a dozen more witnesses to testify to the fact that they weren't alone. She would have been portrayed as a girl of loose morals who'd gotten herself into trouble and was looking for a quick payoff by claiming he'd been with her. And if she'd tried to force the issue by demanding a paternity test, well, the Leandres name and money were more compelling than science.

Yeah, he was still mad at Gabriella Vasquez, but he figured his residual anger couldn't begin to compare to hers.

She'd had sixteen years to resent who he was and what he'd done—how was he ever going to make up for that?

Chapter Five

Gabriella never considered not showing up at the museum. She didn't dare disregard Cameron's threat about returning to her home, and if they were going to have it out about Sierra she wanted to do it somewhere else. But a full week had passed since he'd knocked on her door, and she did let herself hope that he had forgotten about this meeting, that he'd forgotten about her daughter.

Her daughter.

She repeated the words to herself, a soft whisper that couldn't be heard by anyone else, and found solace in them.

Sierra was *her* daughter. From the very beginning, Gabriella had known it would only be the two of them, that they would have to make their own way together. Cameron had made his feelings very clear and if Gabriella had let herself imagine that he might change his mind once he'd had a chance to think about the possibility of their baby, the princess royal had disabused her of that ridiculous notion.

Her own mother had been stunned when Gabriella told her

that she was pregnant. Worse, she'd been disappointed. Gabriella had seen it in her eyes, and it had shamed her. Her father had passed away when Gabriella was only ten years old, and her mother had taken on a second job after his death in order to ensure they didn't lose the house they'd always lived in. It hadn't been easy for Katarina, working two jobs and trying to be both a mother and father to her only daughter, but she'd always been there for Gabriella.

When Gabriella started showing an interest in boys, Katarina had sat down with her and talked to her about love and lust, impressing upon her the importance of respecting her body so that others would, too. Gabriella had assured her mother that she had no intentions of falling in love or falling into bed with anyone. She had plans for her life. She wanted to go to college and build a career before she even considered getting seriously involved.

And then she'd met Cameron. Prior to the first time he walked into Marconi's Restaurant, Gabriella hadn't realized that lust could race through a woman's body with such intensity, making her want with such desperation that there was no thought or reason. She'd tried to resist, but she'd been so completely inexperienced and totally unprepared to withstand his easy charm.

Or maybe she hadn't tried as hard as she should have, because even then she'd thought it was more than lust. She'd convinced herself that she was in love with him, and she'd believed him when he'd said that he was in love with her. And though her mother's warnings had echoed in the back of her mind, she didn't think there was anything wrong with two people in love making love.

It hadn't taken her long to realize she'd been duped, by her own hormones as much as his words.

But that was a lot of years ago—and she was a different woman now.

A woman who glanced at her watch for the tenth time in half as many minutes. It was almost two o'clock.

She shifted her gaze to the crowd of people who were milling around the entrance, but she didn't see Cameron anywhere. Maybe he wasn't going to show up. Maybe—

"You look like you're ready to bolt."

His voice, deep and warm and tinged with amusement, came from behind.

Gabriella whirled around, her heart pounding furiously against her ribs. "Not before two-oh-five," she assured him.

He smiled, his teeth flashing white in contrast to his tanned skin, and her knees went weak. Silently she cursed him, then cursed herself louder and harder.

"Where's your entourage of bodyguards?"

"I'm flying beneath the radar today," he told her.

She didn't see how that was possible. Even as casually dressed as he was, in well-worn jeans and a faded Cambridge University T-shirt with a battered Baltimore Orioles baseball cap on his head, there was something about him that made him stand out from the crowd. Although he dwarfed her five-feet-four-inch frame, he was probably just about six feet tall, and he was more slender than muscular. But his shoulders were broad, and he carried himself with a confidence that edged into arrogance. He was the type of man who would never go anywhere unnoticed, and the realization made Gabriella wary.

"The museum closes at three," she told him, anxious to commence and conclude this unwanted meeting.

"I didn't actually plan on going inside," he replied.

She frowned. "Then why are we here?"

"I thought we could take a walk." He offered his arm to her.

Gabriella only stared at him. "In the middle of downtown on a Saturday afternoon?"

His lips curved again, and her heart pounded.

"Are you worried about what the gossip columnists might say if we're seen together?" he teased.

"I'd think you should be the one to worry," she said, unable to deny that being seen with the prince made her uneasy. Because his baseball cap really wasn't much of a disguise.

He just shrugged. "I stopped letting rumors and innuendo bother me years ago."

She wished she could say the same thing, but the truth was, she'd always hated the idea of anyone talking behind her back, spreading gossip and lies. She only had herself to blame for the worst of it. By refusing to name the father of her baby, she'd given people reason to talk, to speculate, to sneer.

"Gabriella?"

She pushed the painful memories aside. "Where are we walking to?"

"The harbor front."

It would be even busier down by the water, but maybe that was his plan—to hide in plain sight. So she fell into step beside him, grateful that she was wearing low-heeled sandals. She'd changed her clothes four times before she'd left the house—not because she wanted to impress him but because she wanted to ensure that she didn't give that impression.

"Have you had lunch?" he asked her.

"I had a late breakfast." Truthfully, she'd barely nibbled on the omelet her mother had made for her, because her stomach was tied up in knots in anticipation of this meeting.

"We could pick up some sandwiches at The Angel and take them to the park for a picnic."

"I wouldn't have taken you for the picnicking type," she said.

"A lot changes in seventeen years."

"True enough," she agreed.

"Although you look the same," he noted. "Aside from some subtle changes. Your hair's a little shorter, your curves are a little fuller, but you still knock the breath out of me every time I see you."

"And you still have all the best lines," she retorted.

"You don't believe it's true?"

"I learned a long time ago not to believe any words that come out of your mouth."

A muscle in his jaw flexed. "I guess I can't blame you for that," he finally said.

Gabriella didn't respond. She'd promised herself that she wouldn't let him get to her, that no matter what he said or did, she would remain cool and unruffled. But after less than ten minutes in his company, she was feeling decidedly uncool and extremely ruffled.

He paused on the sidewalk outside of the café. "Proscuitto and provolone with mustard?"

She was surprised that he remembered. She'd thought it was only a coincidence that he'd chosen to stop at The Angel. She wouldn't have expected him to remember that they'd been there together once before—stopping in for provisions on the Friday afternoon before they'd stolen away for the weekend. Not only had he remembered that they'd stopped at this café, but he'd remembered what she'd ordered.

But as he'd pointed out, they weren't the same people now that they were then, and she'd changed a lot more than he could imagine. "Turkey and Swiss with mayo."

"Iced tea?"

She nodded. While he ducked inside the café, she waited outside, watching the crowd.

When Sierra was little, Gabriella would often bring her down here on weekends. They would browse through the little shops that lined the waterfront and eat sandwiches in the park, throwing their crusts to the ducks that paddled in circles around the pond. Then they'd walk a little farther, and she'd hold tightly to Sierra's hand as she said a silent thank-you to the playboy prince who lived in the fancy house that was just barely visible at the top of the hill, because he'd given her the greatest gift in the world. Then they'd go back to Lorenzo's for some lemon ice before they headed home.

She smiled at the memory, the smile slipping as she remembered that Sierra still loved to spend Saturday afternoons at the harbor front, though she usually preferred to do her shopping with Jenna and Rachel now. Gabriella had a moment of panic then, when it occurred to her that she might run into her daughter here in town. She wasn't sure what Sierra's plans were for the day, but she figured it would be just her luck to meet Cameron downtown in order to avoid him seeing Sierra again—and then running into her anyway.

"Gabriella?"

Her breath caught in her throat, but she chided herself for the instinctive reaction. The deeply, masculine voice obviously didn't belong to her daughter. As she turned to respond, the initial sense of relief was replaced by guilt and remorse when she found herself face-to-face with Rafe.

Cameron walked out of the café with a paper bag in hand and a smile on his face. He wasn't sure he could explain his good mood. He'd been furious beyond reason when he'd realized that Gabriella had given birth to his child and never bothered to tell him about his daughter, and even if he thought he understood why she'd kept that information to herself, he knew it was going to take them both some time to get past all of that history.

But he also knew that he wanted to get past it. He wanted to get to know his daughter, he wanted Sierra to know that he was her father, and he wanted a second chance with Gabriella—a first chance for the three of them to be a family.

Family. The word made his chest feel tight. At first, he'd thought his reaction was panic at the idea of being tied down to one woman and her child, but the more he thought about it, the more he'd realized what he was really feeling was a yearning. A yearning that had been stirring inside of him since he'd seen her standing in her boss's office.

Or maybe the yearning had been there for the past seventeen years. Maybe that was why he'd never had a long-term relationship with any one woman—because he'd never gotten over Gabriella. Because he couldn't help but compare every other woman he'd been with to her, and no one had ever measured up.

He shook his head, banishing the ridiculously romantic notion from his mind. He'd barely been twenty years old when they'd had their brief affair so many years ago and he hadn't been pining for her since. Truthfully, he'd hardly even let himself think about her during the intervening years. But when he'd realized she was the author of the offending "Around Town" column, he'd grasped the excuse to track her down. Yes, he'd been frustrated and angry—but he'd also been curious. He'd wanted to see her again, to find out what she'd been up to over the past seventeen years, and he was curious to know if there was anything left of the chemistry that had always sizzled between them.

There was still sizzle—and a whole lot of baggage that he never could have anticipated. But he wasn't going to worry about that today. Right now, he just wanted to spend a pleasant day with Gabriella, to learn about his daughter and convince her mother that he wanted to be part of her life again.

And maybe, if he was lucky, he might have a chance to test the potency of that chemistry. He pushed open the door, his smile fading as soon as he saw that Gabriella wasn't alone.

She was with a man, holding his hand, and the man was smiling at her in a way that left Cameron in no doubt about the fact that they'd been lovers. Maybe they still were. His fingers automatically curled into fists, and it was only when he heard the crinkle of the paper bag that he remembered it was in his hand.

"Ready, Gabriella?" His tone was deliberately casual.

She started and turned, her cheeks flushing with color. He thought she tried to tug her hand from the other man's grasp, but he held on, his smile looking a little strained now.

"Oh. That was quick," she said.

He lifted a brow, silently questioning.

"Cameron, this is Rafe Fulton. Rafe, this is Cameron."

He offered his hand, not because he felt compelled by social custom but in order to force the other man to release his hold on Gabriella, as he finally did.

"It's a pleasure," Rafe said, although the look in his eyes warned that it was anything but.

"You're American," Cameron noted, immediately picking up on the accent.

"That's right," Rafe agreed.

"New York?" he guessed.

The other man nodded. "Although I seem to spend more time traveling than I do at home these days."

"Rafe's in international banking," Gabriella explained.

"Is that why you're in Tesoro del Mar?" Cameron asked him.

"That's the reason I first visited Tesoro del Mar almost two years ago," Rafe told him, then shifted his gaze to Gabriella. "But not the reason I keep coming back."

The flush in Gabriella's cheeks deepened. "Cameron and I have some things—business—to discuss."

"Then I'll leave you to your...business," Rafe said, taking a step back. "And I'll look forward to seeing you at seven."

She nodded.

"Busy day for you today," Cameron mused, as the other man walked away.

"You picked the date and time for this meeting," she reminded him.

"I guess I did," he agreed. "I didn't realize your boyfriend would still be in town."

"Would it have made a difference if you did?" she challenged.

"No," he admitted, and began heading toward the park.

Gabriella fell into step beside him. When they found a vacant picnic table in the shade, he spread a couple of paper napkins on top before setting out their food. She opened her iced tea, took a long swallow.

Cameron took a bite of his sandwich, although his appetite had diminished. "How serious is it?"

She frowned. "What?"

"You and Rafe," he clarified. "How serious is it?"

"Is that why you wanted to see me today—to talk about my relationship with Rafe?"

Actually, that was the absolute last thing he wanted to talk about. "No—I wanted to talk about what you're planning for Sierra's birthday."

Every muscle in Gabriella's body went completely still. "What are you talking about?"

"It's June fifteenth next week," he pointed out to her. "I just assumed you'd be having a party for the big occasion."

Her cheeks paled, but her gaze never wavered. "As a matter of fact, I am."

He nodded. "A girl's sixteenth birthday is a special occasion." Then, when Gabriella remained silent, he pressed on. "It is her sixteenth birthday, isn't it?"

"Obviously you already know the answer to that question."

"Birth registrations are a matter of public record," he reminded her.

"Her age doesn't prove anything," she said.

"No," he agreed. "But I imagine a DNA test would prove plenty."

She wrapped up her untouched sandwich, her appetite obviously gone. "Do you really want to subject yourself to the sort of scandal that would entail?"

"Maybe the better question is: do you want to subject Sierra to that sort of scandal?" he challenged. "Because I'm not the one denying that she's my daughter."

She rose to her feet, facing him across the table. "You have no right—"

"I think the courts would agree that I have plenty of rights," he assured her.

Her eyes filled with tears. "You bastard."

"Actually, *my* parents were legally married when I was conceived."

"Which just goes to prove that having both a father and a mother isn't a guarantee of anything," she snapped.

"You never did pull your punches," he mused.

She stormed away. He abandoned the remnants of their lunch to follow her into a stand of trees.

"What do you want from me?"

He wasn't sure there was a simple answer to that question, so he only said, "I want a chance to know my child."

"Why?"

"Because she's my child."

Gabriella didn't waste any more breath trying to deny it. When she spoke again, it was only to say, "She doesn't know you're her father."

"Maybe it's time that she did," he told her.

Her gaze flew to his—her dark eyes filled with anger and frustration. "What gives you the right, after sixteen years, to make that decision?"

"How about the fact that, for sixteen years, I didn't know I had a child?"

"You didn't want to know," she reminded him.

He couldn't deny that was true, at least in the beginning. But the situation was different now, and he had no intention of continuing to deny his relationship to Sierra. "When is her party?"

"You're not invited."

"That wasn't what I asked," he said mildly.

She huffed out a breath. "Saturday night. Eight o'clock. And you're not invited."

"Where?"

"Cameron—"

"At your house," he guessed.

"Yes," she admitted. "It's a surprise and you're not invited."

"Do you really think you can keep me away?"

"I think you should be able to see the potential for disaster if you show up. It only took Sierra a few minutes to figure out who you are and once her friends realize you're royalty, well, there will be pictures of you all over the internet before the birthday candles are even lit."

"I might be more inclined to appreciate your concern if you weren't responsible for so much of my bad press of late."

"Honestly, I don't care what kind of photos or videos the kids snap of you. I *do* care how your presence at the party might impact Sierra. What possible explanation could you give for being there?"

"Other than the truth, you mean?"

She glared at him. "Other than that."

"I'll be your date," he suddenly decided.

"I don't think so."

"I'm sure you could accept that more easily than explaining to all of the guests that I'm the birthday girl's father."

She folded her arms across her chest. "And how am I supposed to explain to my daughter that I'm dating someone other than my fiancé?"

He frowned at that. "You and Rafe are engaged?"

"Yes," she told him, but her defiant gaze flickered away.

"Then why aren't you wearing his ring?" he demanded.

She blinked, as if startled by the question. "It's, uh, it's a little big, so I've decided not to wear it until I've had a chance to get it adjusted."

"Really?" He considered her explanation for a moment, then shook his head. "If he was serious enough to buy a ring, he'd make sure it was the right size so he could slide it on your finger as soon as you said 'yes.'"

She didn't respond.

"Or maybe that's the real reason you're not wearing it," he continued. "Because you haven't said 'yes.'"

"My relationship with Rafe isn't any of your business."

"It is when you keep using it as a roadblock between us."

"There is no 'us,'" she said again.

He hadn't seen her in more than sixteen years, so her statement was hardly unreasonable. And yet, something about her adamant tone irked him, made him want to prove differently. Unable to think of any words that might convince her, he kissed her instead.

Chapter Six

Gabriella had all kinds of reasons for not ever wanting to see Cameron Leandres again, and only one for acceding to his request: Sierra. She'd thought—desperately hoped—that she might convince the prince that he had no reason to believe her daughter was also his. She hadn't let herself think of her own feelings. Or maybe she hadn't believed that she could have any feelings for the man who had broken her heart so many years before. But the moment his lips touched hers, she knew that she'd made a very dangerous miscalculation.

Because in that first whisper-soft brush of his mouth against hers, she was catapulted back in time. It was as if everything she was feeling was new and unfamiliar and all-encompassing. She hadn't just been a virgin when she'd met Cameron, but an innocent in far more ways than she'd realized—completely unprepared for the depth and breadth of the emotions and desires that he brought to life within her. But she'd been an avid pupil of his experienced seduction, an eager participant in their lovemaking.

This was only a kiss—and should have been simple enough for Gabriella to resist. But she had never been able to resist Cameron. She'd known from the beginning that a relationship between them could never work out—his family was blue-blood, hers was blue-collar—but she'd somehow got caught up in the romantic fantasy, anyway. She'd let herself hope and dream, and she'd had her heart shattered.

Afterward, she'd convinced herself that what she'd felt with him hadn't been all that she'd remembered. That it was only an unfortunate combination of teenage hormones and inexperience that had made her behave so recklessly and impulsively. She'd found some solace in that, and a certain amount of relief that she'd never felt so out-of-control with any other man. Not even the man who'd asked her to marry him.

But suddenly, hidden in the shadows of the trees, she was feeling it all again. The same desperate, burning need; the same fiery, raging desire. And she was no more prepared for the feelings now than she'd been when she was seventeen. As his lips moved over hers, demanding rather than coaxing now, she responded, giving him all that he wanted, showing him all that she wanted. His fingers tangled in her hair and he tipped her head farther back, deepening the kiss. Her lips parted, their tongues met, desires tangled.

He nibbled on her bottom lip, murmured some words that her swirling mind couldn't begin to decipher. Then his hand slid up to her breast, his thumb brushing over the crest, and she whimpered low in her throat.

She knew this was wrong—being here with him, kissing him, wanting him. But she couldn't seem to help herself. She couldn't stop her heart from pounding, her blood from pulsing, or her body from yearning. But she could hate him for it. And she did.

She pulled away, her eyes burning with tears that she refused to shed. Not for this man. Not ever again.

He cupped her chin, forced her to meet his gaze. "You're not going to marry that American."

"Whether or not I marry Rafe has nothing to do with you."

"If you were really in love with him, you wouldn't have kissed me back."

"Kissing you only proved to me how lucky I am to have Rafe," she retorted.

He stepped closer, his gaze dark and foreboding. "You should be careful about throwing his name in my face," he warned. "Especially when your lips are still warm from mine."

She tilted her chin, met his stare evenly. "Don't worry. It won't happen again."

"Don't make promises you can't keep," he warned her. "But putting that aside for now, it is you who has a decision to make."

"What decision is that?" she asked warily.

"Whether to uninvite your American friend to Sierra's birthday party so that I can be your date—or to introduce me to our daughter as her father."

Of course, they both knew what her decision would be. She'd spent the better part of sixteen years protecting Sierra from the publicity that would be generated by the truth of her paternity, and she had no intention of subjecting her daughter to the headlines now. "I guess I'll see you next Saturday at eight."

Cameron understood why Gabriella was concerned about the media discovering the truth about Sierra's paternity. While being a royal entitled one to many perks, the status also came with restrictions—one of which was the inability to talk about personal issues without worry that confessions would end up on the front page of the morning newspaper. Experience had taught Cameron that the only people he could trust to keep his secrets were his family, so when he and Gabriella parted ways after their lunch in the park, he drove toward his brother's house in the exclusive gated community of Verde Colinas.

Michael and his wife had lived there happily for thirteen years, and when Samantha died almost two years earlier, Cameron had expected that his brother would want to move out of the home they'd shared together. But Michael had no intention of going anywhere, and only those family and close friends who had known him when Samantha was alive knew how much of a toll her death had taken on him. Their sister, Marissa, had contacted Cameron several times over the past few months, hoping that he would have some advice or insights on how to reach Michael, to make him see that he still had family who cared about him and—most importantly—a daughter who needed him.

Their efforts had been unsuccessful, but Marissa remained optimistic. "I'm sure he just needs time," she'd said to Cameron during a recent conversation. "Samantha was such a huge part of his life for so many years—it can't be easy to get over that kind of loss."

Cameron wouldn't know. He didn't think he'd ever been all the way in love. In fact, the closest he'd ever come had probably been with Gabriella, and that was too many years ago to even count. Since then, he'd mostly avoided personal entanglements, and—Allegra's dashed hopes aside—most of the women he dated knew he wasn't looking for anything serious or long-term.

He'd had more than a few women claim to be in love with him over the years, but he knew that what they really loved was being with a prince. Too often the words had been followed by a request—"I love you and I miss you so much when you're gone. Maybe this time I could go to Australia/Bermuda/China with you." Or a demand—"If you loved me, you would get me tickets to the concert/talk to someone about that parking infraction/buy me that condo at the waterfront."

That was a favorite of his mother's tricks—playing the affection/demand card to get what she wanted, and it had taught Cameron that everyone wanted something from him.

Everyone except his sister, he realized, when Marissa answered the door. She was the one person who always gave so much more than she ever asked for. She led him into the kitchen now and immediately began to make a pot of coffee.

"Michael's not here?" he guessed.

She shook her head. "He's at the office."

He heard music coming from the other room, and he peeked around the corner to see his twenty-one-month-old niece spinning in circles to the music.

"On a Saturday?" he responded to Marissa's statement about his brother's whereabouts.

"He said something about a big project outline he had to finish," she explained.

"And you're here watching Riley again," he guessed.

"The nanny only works until six and not at all on weekends, so I've been helping out when I can," she admitted.

As if on cue, the little girl raced into the room. She halted when she saw Cameron, then smiled shyly before she lifted her arms to her aunt.

Marissa scooped her up with one arm and an ease that revealed she'd done the same thing countless times before.

"How often is that?" he asked.

His sister shifted the child to her other hip, and shifted her gaze away from his.

"Marissa?" he prompted.

"I've moved into the spare room downstairs," she admitted.

"You've moved in?"

She shrugged. "It got me out of Mother's house."

"I'm sure she had something to say about this arrangement," he noted dryly. The princess royal always had an opinion, especially when it came to her children.

"I don't even know if she's realized I'm gone," Marissa told him.

He frowned but didn't argue her claim. It was a well-known fact that Elena paid scant attention to her only daughter, choosing to focus her energies and ambitions on her two sons. Both he and Michael had disappointed her in that regard, making Cameron wonder if their mother might have made a mistake in disregarding her daughter's potential. Except that his sister was too pure of mind and soft of heart to fall in with their mother's machinations, which was one of the reasons that he'd come to her now. Because she was also too loyal and sweet to judge the brother who had made more mistakes than he cared to admit.

"She hasn't come around here in a while," Marissa continued, rubbing the baby's back. "I think she's finally realized that Michael may never forgive her."

"For what now?" Cameron asked.

"For convincing Samantha to get pregnant—in order to ensure the continuation of the Leandres line."

And it was as a result of complications that arose during childbirth that Samantha had lost her life.

"Then, when the baby was born, Mother didn't want to have anything to do with her."

"Because she was a girl," he guessed, pouring himself a cup of the freshly brewed coffee.

She nodded.

"Then I guess there's no reason that I should feel compelled to share my news."

"What's your news?"

"That she has another granddaughter."

Marissa gaped at him. "You're a daddy?"

He smiled as he nodded. "I can't imagine her calling me

'daddy,' though, considering that she's almost sixteen years old."

His sister sank into a chair. "A teenager."

He nodded again.

"I can't believe it."

"I'm still getting used to the idea myself," he admitted.

"You didn't know?"

"Not until a few days ago."

"Are you...sure?" she asked hesitantly.

"That she's mine, you mean?"

Now it was Marissa's turn to nod.

"Yeah, I'm sure. If for no other reason than that Gabriella tried so hard to deny it."

"I'm assuming Gabriella is the mother."

"She is," he confirmed. "Gabriella Vasquez."

"Oh, this just keeps getting better and better," Marissa said, amusement evident in her tone. "And it certainly explains why the columnist always seemed to have a chip on her shoulder where you were concerned."

"Don't tell me you read that drivel."

His sister's chin went up. "It's not drivel, it's interesting. And while she strikes me as a very savvy lady, I do have to wonder how and where the two of you ever hooked up."

"She was a waitress at Marconi's," he admitted. "And from the first moment I laid eyes on her, I was seriously smitten."

Marissa's brows rose. "How did I not know any of this?"

"You were away at school at the time, and we weren't together for very long," Cameron explained.

"Long enough, obviously," she remarked dryly.

He couldn't disagree with that.

"So what went wrong? What did you do that prevented Gabriella from telling you that she was pregnant? Because I know that you have your faults, but I also know that you wouldn't walk away from your responsibilities."

He stared into the mug of coffee cradled between his hands

and wondered what he'd ever done to deserve her loyalty. "I think she tried to tell me, but I didn't want to hear it. I was young and scared and I'd just been subjected to another of our mother's endless lectures about the duties and responsibilities of being royal and—"

"And you let her come between you and the only woman you'd ever loved," Marissa told him.

He frowned. "I was twenty years old. What did I know about love?"

"You probably knew more then than you do now—because you've spent the past sixteen years trying to forget about her."

"You're such a hopeless romantic, Mar."

"Because I can believe in love even though I've never experienced it myself?" she challenged.

"Because you believe that the chemistry that draws a man and a woman together is based on elusive emotion when the reality is that the male-female attraction is founded on lust rather than love."

"Lust flares hot and bright and burns out quickly," she told him. "Love endures."

"And you know this how?"

"It's obvious—at least to me—that you still have feelings for Gabriella Vasquez, even after all this time. The only question now, big brother, is what do you intend to do about those feelings?"

It was a question that Cameron couldn't begin to answer.

When Gabriella returned home, it was to an empty house. Not wanting to think about Cameron or Rafe or the million things she had to do before Sierra's birthday party the following weekend, she decided to spend some time working on her column instead.

Unfortunately, the first letter she opened proved that escape from her own problems was impossible.

Dear Gabby,

My boyfriend of two years recently asked me to marry him and although I'm now wearing his ring, I'm not sure that I'm ready to make that kind of lifelong commitment. I said "yes" when he proposed because I do love him and because I figured a long engagement would give us both the time we needed to be sure that we want to be together forever.

But he insists that he doesn't want to wait, that he wants to start our life together right now. He says that if I really love him, I'll marry him.

I do love him, but I'm only twenty-one. He insists that he's ready to settle down and has warned that if I'm not ready to start a life with him, he'll find someone else who is.

Should I set a date or bide my time?

Signed,

Muddled about Marriage

The email address from which the letter had been sent clearly identified "Muddled" as the VP of a local telecommunications company, a title that carried more prestige than power and was granted to her upon graduation from college by the president—her father—only a few months before his death. Now, less than a year later, her twenty-first birthday celebration had been big news because it meant unrestricted access to her trust fund.

Gabriella considered for a moment, wondering if this additional information would impact the advice she intended to give "Muddled," and decided that it would not. Even if the letter writer wasn't an heiress and her fiancé wasn't so obviously a fortune-hunter, her response would be the same: ditch the jerk *now* before you're stuck with him forever.

Of course, she was a little more subtle in her formal response.

Dear Muddled,

If you're not sure that you're ready to make a lifelong commitment, then you're definitely not ready and your fiancé shouldn't be pressuring you and he definitely shouldn't be issuing ultimatums.

If he loves you, he will wait, and if he finds someone else while he's waiting, then he obviously isn't as committed to you as he claims to be—and if that's the case, it's much better to find out before you speak the vows that will tie you together.

If he continues to pressure you, then you should set a date—to move on with your life without him. Because if you let him propel you down the aisle before you're sure that it's what you want, you'll find yourself standing at the altar and kissing a frog!

Good luck,

Gabby

Gabriella re-read the letter and her response, then clicked to save it on her computer. She felt comfortable with the advice she was giving to the young woman, but as she lifted her gaze to glance at the clock above her desk, the light blue box on the shelf caught her eye and she sighed.

"Muddled" was right to be concerned—she was young, she'd barely had a chance to experience life and shouldn't be rushing to tie herself down—especially when she had reason to suspect her boyfriend's motivations. Gabriella had no similar excuse.

She was almost thirty-four years old and she'd known Rafe for two years. He was handsome, charming, intelligent, successful and wealthy, and she'd been attracted to him from the beginning. So why was she hesitating?

She lifted the box down from the shelf and opened the lid, blinking at the flash of white fire that seemed to erupt from within. The ring was truly dazzling—a three-carat heart-shaped diamond in a platinum bezel setting—and she was sure it had cost Rafe a small fortune.

He hadn't pressured her, but she knew that her almost-fiancé had believed it was only a matter of time until she took the ring out of the box and put it on her finger. Gabriella wasn't so certain.

What if I'm never ready?

But, of course, she hadn't actually spoken those words aloud. She hadn't dared ask the question that might have alerted him to the reality of her emotional scars. She'd been too afraid that he would walk away from her forever. And though she wouldn't blame him if he did, she wasn't ready to lose him. She couldn't commit to spending the rest of her life with him, but she didn't want to live her life without him, either. She didn't want to be alone.

She carefully—almost cautiously—took the ring out of the box and slipped it onto the third finger of her left hand. It fit perfectly, as Cameron had correctly assumed it would, but it felt heavy. Part of the sensation was a direct result of the size of the rock, but she knew that it felt a lot heavier than it really was, that it was the weight of expectations that felt so cumbersome when she put the diamond on her finger. With a sigh of sincere regret, she put the ring back in the box.

She'd hoped that she could wear it someday, but she knew now that it would never happen. She'd thought her heart was sufficiently mended that she could fall in love again, but as wonderful as Rafe was, something had always held her back. After the kiss she'd shared with Cameron in the park, she knew that it wasn't something but some*one*. And she knew that she would have to tell Rafe the truth about her feelings.

She was still at her computer, staring unseeingly at another reader letter, when the doorbell rang. She automatically rose to respond to the summons, surprised to find Rafe on the step.

"It can't be seven o'clock already," she said, wondering how she could have lost track of so much time.

"It's not," he admitted. "But I decided I couldn't wait until then to see you."

She moved away from the door so that he could enter. He stepped into the entranceway, but didn't go any farther.

"Something's wrong," she guessed.

"I've decided to go back to New York. Tonight."

Her throat was suddenly tight and dry, so that she had to swallow before she could ask, "Why?"

"Because as long as you're still hung up on Sierra's father, you're never going to be able to make a commitment to me."

She dropped her gaze, felt her cheeks flush, but she had to ask, "How did you know he's Sierra's father?"

"It wasn't anything obvious," he assured her. "It certainly isn't as if she looks like him—it was more the way he was looking at you. And the way he looked at me when he saw me with you, like he wanted to tear me apart for daring to touch his woman."

She shook her head. "It isn't like that. We're not…involved."

His smile was wry. "I can't tell if you're really that naive or if you think I am."

"We're not," she insisted. "Until last week, I hadn't even seen him in more than sixteen years."

Rafe looked unconvinced. "I always figured you were still harboring feelings for the man who'd fathered your daughter, but I also figured, with time, you'd get over him. Of course, I never expected that he would turn out to be a prince."

"What difference does that make?"

"Maybe none," he allowed. "Maybe your feelings have nothing to do with his title and everything to do with the fact that he was the first man you ever loved—the man you still love."

She shook her head again, refusing to acknowledge that it might be true, refusing to even consider that she might be so foolish as to harbor any feelings for a man who had proven years ago that he'd never really cared about her.

But Rafe only lifted a hand and laid his palm against her cheek. She closed her eyes, savoring the warmth of his touch, and wishing she could feel more.

"I can't make you love me," he said, as if reading her thoughts. "And I can't accept any less." Then he dipped his head and kissed her softly. "Goodbye, Gabriella."

She watched him drive away, as she had so many times before, but this time, she knew that it truly was goodbye.

Chapter Seven

The morning of Sierra's sixteenth birthday was sunny and bright, and the only thing that put a damper on her spirits was the cast that still weighed heavily on her broken arm.

Her grandmother brought a tray to her bedroom, preserving the "breakfast in bed" tradition that had been a birthday ritual in the Vasquez household for as long as Sierra could remember.

She sniffed the air, hummed her approval. "Fresh chocolate chip waffles?"

"They are your favorite," Katarina said, settling the tray across her granddaughter's lap.

Sierra took in the glass of orange juice, the bowl of fresh fruit with a dollop of yogurt, the small pitcher of warm syrup, the plate of waffles—already cut up, in deference to her injury—and the vase with a single white rose, and smiled. "You spoil me."

"That's what *abuelas* are supposed to do."

"If I eat all of this, I won't fit into the dress I was planning to wear tonight," Sierra warned, spearing a piece of waffle with her fork.

"Then you should have bought a bigger size," Katarina said, with only the slightest hint of disapproval in her tone. Though they didn't often battle over Sierra's wardrobe, the teen knew that her grandmother didn't favor the figure-hugging fashions that were currently in style.

"What if I share my waffles with you instead?"

"You're just like your mother at your age—with an answer for everything," Katarina said, shaking her head in what Sierra took to be a combination of exasperation and affection.

"Where is Mom?" Sierra asked, popping another piece of waffle into her mouth.

"Right here," Gabriella said, carrying an enormous vase overflowing with tropical blooms. She set the flowers on the table beside the bed and leaned over to kiss Sierra's cheek. "Happy Sweet Sixteen."

"Where did those come from?" Sierra asked.

"Rafe sent them," Gabriella told her.

"Is he coming for dinner with us tonight?" she asked.

Her mother and grandmother exchanged a look, and then Gabriella shook her head. "Rafe went back to New York."

"Oh." Although Sierra couldn't deny her disappointment, she was more concerned about her mother's apparent reluctance to share the information. "Is everything okay with you two?"

"Yes. No." Gabriella sighed, then lowered herself onto the edge of the mattress as Katarina hustled away on the pretext of cleaning up the kitchen. "Rafe and I… We're not seeing each other anymore."

Sierra felt her jaw drop open. "But…why?"

"He wanted more of a commitment from me than I was ready to make."

Though her tone was casual, Sierra knew that her mother's

feelings for the American were not, and that knowledge only baffled her more. "You're not going to marry him?"

Gabriella shook her head.

Sierra narrowed her gaze. "Is it because of Prince Cameron?"

Her mother's head shot up, her eyes went wide. "Why would you ask something like that?"

"Because you've been acting kind of weird ever since that day he showed up here."

Her mother hesitated, just long enough to convince Sierra that her suspicions weren't unfounded.

"I was just surprised to see him after such a very long time," Gabriella said. "But even before Cameron showed up, I knew I couldn't marry Rafe."

"So I guess that means we won't be going to New York City, either," Sierra said, aware that she sounded like a spoiled child.

"There's no reason we can't go for a visit on our own sometime," Gabriella promised her. "If we save our pennies."

Sierra sipped her juice and tried not to resent the fact that they wouldn't have had to worry about pennies if her mother had decided to marry Rafe. He could have flown them all to New York City—and anywhere else they wanted to go—on his company's private jet.

"So it's just you and me and Grandma tonight," Sierra clarified. She knew her mother had planned a party and that all of her friends would be at the house later, but she played along, not wanting to ruin the surprise.

Gabriella fussed with the flower arrangement, repositioning an enormous pink lily. "And Prince Cameron might stop by later."

Sierra nearly choked on a piece of pineapple. "Why?"

"To wish you a happy birthday," Gabriella said.

But Sierra suspected that the real answer wasn't nearly as simple as her mother wanted her to believe.

* * *

Gabriella hated being less than completely honest with Sierra, but she wasn't nearly ready for the life she'd built with her daughter to come crashing down around them, and she hated knowing that that was exactly what would happen when the truth about Sierra's paternity came to light.

And she knew that it would eventually come to light. Now that Cameron had figured it out, there would be no stopping it. And as concerned as Gabriella was about her daughter's potential response to the news, she had more reasons than that to worry. Because when Sierra was only a baby, she'd struck a deal, and she knew now that it was only a matter of time before the promise she'd made would be broken. And though the bargain might be destroyed through no fault of her own, she knew there would be repercussions.

A knock at the door startled her from her reverie.

She set down the knife she'd been using to chop veggies and made her way to the door, expecting Beth or Rachel, who had volunteered to come by to help set up for the party while Jenna kept Sierra occupied and away from the house. She wasn't expecting Cameron, and her heart gave a traitorous thump against her ribs when she opened the door and found him standing there.

"You're about five hours early," she told him.

"I know," he admitted, unfazed by her lack of welcome. "But I wanted to show you what I picked out for Sierra before I gave it to her tonight."

"You didn't have to get her a gift," Gabriella protested.

"I could hardly come empty-handed to a sweet sixteen birthday party."

"And yet, your hands are empty," she noted.

"It's an expression," he chided. "The gift is parked across the street."

Parked?

Gabriella's stomach twisted into painful knots as she looked up and spotted the shiny yellow sports car with an enormous pink bow on its roof.

"You've got to be kidding."

He frowned. "What's wrong?"

"What's wrong?" she echoed, incredulous. "Do you really think that's an appropriate gift?"

"I can exchange it for another color, if she doesn't like it. Of course, I don't know what she likes and doesn't like, but I noticed that her cast was yellow and thought she might be fond of the color."

"It's not the color—it's that it's a car," she said, incensed. "You can't give her a car."

"Why not?"

She stared at him, stunned by his obvious lack of comprehension. "Firstly, because she just turned sixteen and doesn't even have her driver's license yet. Secondly, because it's far too extravagant a gift from someone who is supposedly only here as my date."

He frowned. "Considering that I've missed sixteen years of birthdays, I don't think it's extravagant at all."

"Of course you wouldn't," she muttered.

"Every teenager wants a car," he pointed out reasonably.

"That doesn't mean they should have one."

"Why are you being obstinate about this?"

"Maybe because I'm her mother and I know that Sierra isn't old enough or responsible enough for a car of her own, and even if she was, I wouldn't let her drive around in a brand-new lemon-yellow sports car."

"So it's the specific kind of vehicle and not the car itself that you have a problem with?"

She shook her head. "Take it back."

He frowned. "And get her what instead?"

"A gift certificate for the movies. A basket of bath products. A teddy bear." She ticked the suggestions off on her fingertips.

He lifted his brows. "A teddy bear?"

"Something casual and inexpensive," she explained.

"I think she'd rather have the car."

"She'd love the car," Gabriella admitted. "Just as she'd love an unlimited shopping allowance or a trip to New York City, but she doesn't expect to have either of those things handed to her, either."

Cameron frowned. "Why would she want to go to New York City? Did your American friend offer to take her there?"

She sighed. "This isn't about Rafe—it's about you getting that car away from here before Sierra gets home."

"All right," he finally agreed, but when he looked over at the car again, regret was clearly etched in his features. "It's too bad, though. She's a beautiful vehicle and drives like a dream."

"What is a dream to you would be a nightmare to me, because I'd worry every time she drove away from the house," she told him.

"I'm sure you've had enough worries, raising Sierra on your own for sixteen years, and it certainly wasn't my intention to add to that."

She was surprised by the sincerity in his tone, touched by his understanding. "I haven't been entirely on my own," she reminded him. "I've had my mother to help out along the way."

"And now you have me."

"Cameron—"

He touched his fingers to her lips, silencing her protest. "I realize that we have a lot of details still to work out, but I want you to know that I'm not going to walk away this time. Not from Sierra, and not from you."

Somehow his words left her feeling more apprehensive than reassured.

* * *

Cameron decided to go with the teddy bear. Of the options Gabriella had enumerated, it seemed the best choice. Or so he thought, until he began to search and realized there were many different sizes, colors and styles of bears. In the end, he found what he was looking for in a specialty children's shop down at the waterfront.

When he returned to the house, just before nine o'clock, the party was in full swing. Gabriella had suggested that it would be simpler if he came after the "surprise" part so he didn't have to explain to anyone who he was or answer too many questions about why he was there. As it turned out, most of Sierra's friends either didn't recognize him or didn't care, because they barely paid any attention to him when he arrived. Music was pumping out of speakers and many of the party guests were crowded together on the small patio and moving to the music while others danced happily on the lawn. To be relatively unobtrusive in a crowd was a new experience, but he didn't mind. It allowed him to hover in the background and observe Sierra.

His daughter.

He watched her move through the crowd, stopping now and again to talk and laugh with her friends, or swaying her hips and tossing her head in tune with the music. For some reason, he found himself thinking of Riley—his brother's daughter, and the way she'd spun in circles watching the skirt of her dress twirl around her legs. And suddenly he was thinking about how much time he'd missed with his own child—who was already a woman.

He wondered what she'd looked like as a baby, whether he would have recognized any parts of himself in her features. Had she been a shy toddler who hid behind her mother's legs whenever a stranger spoke to her, or one of those precocious children who was happy to make friends with everyone who crossed her path? And the more he thought about all these things that he didn't know, the angrier he got.

He heard a soft, familiar laugh and glanced over as Gabriella stepped onto the porch, a glass of wine in each hand. It was her fault. As far as he was concerned, she was the one who had deprived him of the opportunity to share in all of Sierra's milestones and moments—and not just the big events, like her first day of school and special occasions, but all of the ordinary days in between.

He wanted to hate her. He *should* hate her. She was the reason he didn't know the beautiful girl on the dance floor who was his daughter. But just looking at Gabriella—in a halter-style top that left her tanned shoulders bare and a long swirling skirt with painted toes peeking out beneath—he felt a complicated mix of emotions, none of which was hate.

She was somehow even sexier now than she'd been when they first met, and despite their history and secrets, he was just as attracted to her now as he'd been back then.

Lust flares hot and bright and burns out quickly. Love endures.

He pushed the echo of his sister's words from his mind. He was *not* in love with Gabriella. Maybe he didn't hate her, but he didn't forgive her, either. Which only made it all the more difficult to figure out how the hell he was supposed to deal with her.

He watched her approach. Her bare feet made no sound on the deck, but there was a rope of gold chain slung low on her hips that jangled with every step she took. She'd always had an innate sensuality that stirred his blood, and his response was immediate and intense.

She was smiling, as if she was truly happy to see him. He knew she was only playing her part, giving him an excuse for being there. And while part of him wanted to curse her for the fact that he needed an excuse, a bigger part was content to simply enjoy looking at her.

As his gaze zeroed in on her mouth, he couldn't help but remember the day of their picnic in the park. Kissing her in the shadows of the trees. The taste of her sweet lips, the press of her soft body against his, the passion of her response. As he pushed the memories to the back of his mind, he couldn't help but wonder if his feelings for Gabriella had always been more complicated than he'd wanted to acknowledge.

She offered him one of the glasses she carried. "It's a cabernet. Not up to your usual standards, I'm sure, but decent."

He took the glass, sipped, and nodded in agreement with her assessment. "Was she surprised?"

Gabriella's lips curved. "She pretended to be. But more importantly, she's with her family and friends and having fun."

"Not all of her family," he noted.

She sighed. "Tell me again why I let you come."

"Because you knew you couldn't keep me away."

"I guess that would explain it." She nudged him toward a long table that was laden down with enormous platters of food. There were hot and cold hors d'oeuvres, crudités and dips, little sandwiches and quiches, mini-pastries and assorted sweets, and an enormous bowl of punch. "But since you're here, you might as well have something to eat."

He picked up a plate. "It's quite a spread you've put out."

"Teenagers—even teenage girls—like to eat, and my mother likes to fuss."

"She did all of this?"

"Most of it," Gabriella admitted. "I was assigned a few simple tasks—chopping vegetables, cutting sandwiches— basically, things that I couldn't screw up too badly."

"You're not much of a cook?"

She shook her head. "That domestic talent seems to have skipped my generation. Sierra, on the other hand, is a natural in the kitchen."

Just one more thing that he hadn't known. But before he

could comment on it, someone lowered the volume on the music to announce that it was time for Sierra to open her gifts. Gabriella tugged on his arm, drawing him closer to the crowd that had gathered around the birthday girl.

The presents had been set on another table, and he'd added his to the pile when he'd arrived. Sierra took her time opening each one, exclaiming over every item and sincerely thanking the individual giver. There were CDs and DVDs and books and clothes, and she seemed genuinely delighted with each item. And yet, when she picked up the glossy pink bag that contained his gift, Cameron felt his palms go damp and his breath catch in his throat.

She read the card, then her eyes searched for him in the crowd. He'd signed it simply "Cameron" and she took the cue, introducing him to the gathering as a friend of her mother's without mention of his title. Then she pulled the tissue out of the bag and reached inside, making a soft sound of surprised pleasure when she found the bear. She held it to her breast, her eyes sparkling and her lips curving wide, and Cameron's heart started to beat again.

Gabriella watched her daughter cuddle the teddy bear that Cameron had given to her, Sierra's first gift from her father, and her heart simply melted.

It wasn't the casual, inexpensive gift that Gabriella had suggested. Even from a distance, she could see the tag on the left ear that identified the bear as a Steiff. But Sierra's appreciation of the gift had nothing to do with its price tag and everything to do with her pleasure at being able to add the gorgeous blond mohair bear to her collection.

"Good call," she murmured to Cameron.

"It was your idea," he reminded her.

"And thank you—for backing down on the car."

He shrugged. "You know her better than I do, obviously,

and if you say she isn't ready, then I'll respect your judgment on that."

"It's not the only thing she isn't ready for," she warned.

"You're worried about her learning the truth about who I am," he guessed.

She nodded.

"When do you think she will be ready?" He was trying to be patient, but he'd already lost sixteen years with his daughter and he didn't intend to lose any more.

"I don't know," she admitted. "I'm just asking you to give her a chance to get to know you first, before you turn her whole world upside down."

"Is it really Sierra's world that you're worried about—or your own?"

She heard the challenge in his voice, and thought she understood. Finding out that he'd fathered a child so many years ago had obviously affected him, but he still didn't—couldn't—know what it meant to truly be a parent. He couldn't know that Sierra's world and her world were one and the same, that when Sierra hurt, Gabriella hurt right along with her.

"In a lot of ways, Sierra is very mature for her age. So much so that I sometimes forget that she's only sixteen, that her heart is still vulnerable. And while I have no doubt there's a part of her that still yearns for a father as much as she did when she was ten, she's not going to be as unquestioning or accepting of your sudden appearance in her life as she would have been back then."

"Then maybe you should have found me six years ago," he retorted. "Better yet, sixteen years ago."

"Because you would have been thrilled to learn that you were a father," she said, not even trying to mask her sarcasm.

"No," he admitted. "But at least I would have known."

"I tried to tell you," she reminded him. She didn't want to talk about what was still a painful memory for her, but she couldn't let him continue to play the injured party without bearing any responsibility for the choices they'd both made. "You didn't even know who I was."

He winced. "That's not true—"

"Don't," she said, her voice sharp. "I'd heard the rumors. I knew that you were just looking for a good time. But I let myself believe that we had something special, that you really cared about me. Of course, you made sure I believed it— because you knew it was the only way you would get me into bed."

"I *did* care about you, dammit."

She turned away, refusing to listen to his lies, refusing to acknowledge that there was still a tiny part of her heart that wanted to believe him. "I'm going to get the cake."

Chapter Eight

Cameron followed her into the house.

He wasn't ready to let their conversation drop, but he realized that their daughter's birthday party might not be the best time or place to continue it. He wanted answers. There was so much he wanted to know, but he also knew that he had to be prepared to face Gabriella's questions—and Sierra's, too—to explain the things he'd said and done so many years ago, to accept responsibility for his own actions.

For now, he only watched as Gabriella carefully arranged sixteen pink candles around the elaborately scrolled letters that spelled out "Happy Sweet Sixteen, Sierra."

"More of your mother's work?" he asked.

Gabriella nodded.

"It's beautiful."

"Wait until you taste it," she told him. "Dominic Donatella has been trying to wrangle her buttercream icing recipe out of her for more than twenty years."

"Donatella—as in Donatella's Bakery?"

She nodded again, but her eyes—still focused on the cake—filled with tears.

"Gabriella?"

"Sorry, birthdays always make me a little nostalgic, and I can't believe it's her sixteenth already." She blew out a soft breath. "When she was little, she used to think really hard about her wish, then she'd squeeze her eyes shut and blow with all of her might. She was so serious about her wishes, so certain she could make them come true."

"Do you know what kinds of things she wished for?"

"A lot of the usual things—dolls and puppies and ponies. And then, the year she turned ten, she told me that what she really wanted, more than anything in the world, was to be a princess."

She made a show of counting the candles again, while Cameron considered this revelation. He was sure it wasn't an unusual wish for a little girl, and he couldn't help but wonder how Gabriella had responded to her daughter's statement.

"You could have made that wish come true for her," he felt compelled to point out. "All you had to do was acknowledge the truth about her paternity."

"I thought about it," Gabriella admitted. "Not because it was Sierra's wish, but because I wanted her to know her father, and for her to know you."

"Then why didn't you?" he demanded. "If you really wanted me to know, why didn't you ever make any effort to contact me? Why is it that the only reason I found out about my daughter is that I tracked you down and came face-to-face with her?"

She glanced away. "I couldn't get in touch with you."

He scowled. "Are you claiming you didn't know how to reach me?"

"No, I'm saying that I couldn't. Because I'd made a promise."

"What kind of promise?" he demanded. "To whom?"

"Gabriella—"

They both started at the interruption.

"—are you bringing the cake?" Katarina's question preceded her entry into the kitchen. "Oh." She glanced from Gabriella to Cameron and back again. "I didn't realize I was interrupting."

"You're not," Gabriella responded quickly. "I was just looking for the matches."

"In the cupboard over the fridge, where we've always kept them," her mother pointed out.

"Right." Gabriella moved away from him, rising onto her tiptoes to retrieve the long box.

Cameron hovered in the background, feeling uneasy under the older woman's scrutiny. He'd never had occasion to meet Gabriella's mother before. When he and Gabriella had first started seeing each other, they'd each had their own reasons for wanting to keep the relationship a secret. He wondered if Gabriella had ever told her mother that he was Sierra's father, and guessed not. Katarina looked like the kind of woman who would have tracked him down and kicked his ass to hell and back if she'd known. But he also guessed, based on the narrow-eyed stare that pinned him now, that she'd figured it out—or at least had some suspicions.

"You must be Gabriella's mother." He thought about offering his hand, but decided against it as she looked more inclined to swat it away than accept it. "I'm Cameron Leandres."

"I know who I am and who you are," she said. "I didn't come in to exchange pleasantries, only to check on the cake."

"*Madre!*" Gabriella chided, her cheeks coloring slightly.

"I will not apologize for speaking my mind," Katarina told her. "And while I appreciate that you are Sierra's mother and want what is best for her, I don't see how encouraging a relationship between your daughter and this man—a man who wasn't there for you, who did nothing to help when your baby almost died—could be best for her. It would be far better for her to never know the identity of her father than to know he is a man who could turn his back on the girl he got pregnant and the innocent child she bore."

He didn't respond to Katarina's outburst but turned to Gabriella for clarification. "What does she mean—your baby almost died?"

But she only shook her head, shooting an angry look at her mother. "I'm *not* going to do this now."

"Dammit, Gabriella. I deserve to know—"

"Today is a celebration," she interrupted, her voice deliberately calm as she tucked the matches under arm and picked up the cake. "And Sierra is waiting."

So he bided his time. He wasn't particularly happy about it, but he waited. He watched the birthday girl blow out her candles and eat her cake, saw her kiss her grandmother's cheek and wrap her arms—cast and all—around her mother. There was such easy affection between the three women, evidence of the solid bond between all of them.

Gabriella had given their daughter a good life—with help from her mother, of course—and Sierra was obviously happy. What right did he have to barge into their lives at this late date and upset the status quo?

Yes, he was Sierra's father, but that was an accident of biology rather than any particular planning on his part. As Katarina pointed out, he hadn't been there for Gabriella through her pregnancy or childbirth or any of the other stages of Sierra's life until now. And why was he here now?

He frowned over that question as he helped Gabriella tidy up the kitchen. She was right—he hadn't been ready to be a father sixteen years ago, and he wasn't entirely sure he was ready now. But he was thirty-six now—old enough and mature enough to own up to his responsibilities, to be a father to his daughter—even if she didn't seem to need him.

He looked through the window over the sink. Most of the guests had already gone, but a few of Sierra's closest friends had lingered, along with a guy who was—in his opinion—far too close to his daughter.

"Who's that with Sierra?" he asked Gabriella.

She squeezed out the dish cloth, wiped around the outside of the sink. "Paolo."

He didn't want to ask, but the question sprang from his lips anyway. "Boyfriend?"

She nodded. "They've been seeing each other for about six months now."

"Isn't she too young to have a boyfriend?"

"She's sixteen," she reminded him.

"Just turned sixteen," he shot back.

She only smiled. "Paolo's a good guy."

He frowned. "Are you really okay with this?"

"Let's just say that I've learned to pick my battles."

"You seem to have a really good relationship," he commented. "I can't imagine you having any battles."

"If you stick around long enough, you'll see plenty of them," she promised.

"But you don't think I will stick around, do you?"

She was silent as she carefully folded the dish cloth, then draped it over the faucet. "I don't have any expectations one way or the other."

"I guess I can't blame you for that," he said. "But I can promise you that I'm sticking around this time."

"Because you think it's the right thing to do?"

"Partly," he admitted.

"But what if it's not?" she challenged.

"What do you mean?"

Her gaze went to the window, and when she finally turned back to him, he saw the confusion and uncertainty clearly in the depths of dark eyes. "What if telling Sierra the truth about who you are isn't the right thing for her?"

"Would you be asking that question if I wasn't a prince?"

Her hesitation confirmed that his title was a concern to her. Most people wanted to exploit his royal status; Gabriella would prefer it didn't exist.

"The fact is, you are a prince," she said. "And when word gets out that you have an illegitimate child, there will be a media frenzy with Sierra at the center."

"She'll deal with it," he said confidently.

"But why should she have to?"

"Because whether you want to acknowledge it or not, she is a Leandres, a princess and a member of the royal family of Tesoro del Mar."

"I'm not the only one who might not want to acknowledge it," Gabriella warned him.

"What's the supposed to mean?"

She shook her head. "Nothing. Forget it."

"Obviously it was something," he said. "And I'm growing frustrated by the way you continually dodge my questions."

"I'm not dodging," she denied.

He lifted a brow. "Just picking your battles?"

She gave him a half-smile. "Something like that."

"If you're not dodging, then tell me what your mother meant about Sierra almost dying."

"It really wasn't as dramatic as that," Gabriella said.

"Sounds like a dodge to me."

"She was born with an atrial septal defect—more commonly called a hole in the heart," she finally admitted. "It wasn't anything that was immediately apparent. She came out crying and she had ten fingers and ten toes, but her skin had a slightly bluish tinge and she seemed to struggle a little with her breathing, something that became more apparent during nursing.

"When it was diagnosed, the doctors were optimistic that it would close on its own. But it didn't, and when she was six months old, she had open heart surgery."

"Why do I get the feeling you're glossing over a lot of details?"

"Because I am. Because I really don't want to go back to that time, even in my mind, and remember how terrified I was."

He couldn't blame her for that. And he could understand why her mother resented him. Katarina was right—he hadn't been there for Gabriella, he'd done nothing to help when her baby had almost died, and now he'd stormed back into the life she'd built for herself and her child and was threatening to turn it upside down.

"The worst thing," she said to him now, "was knowing that Sierra needed the surgery and not knowing if the doctors would do it."

"Because she was so young?"

She shook her head. "Because I couldn't pay for it. I had no medical coverage, no savings." She looked down at the hands that she'd linked her lap. "I had nothing but my baby, and I was so scared I was going to lose her."

He couldn't even begin to imagine. Even now, only knowing about his daughter for a few weeks, he would be devastated if anything happened to her. Gabriella had carried their child in her womb for nine months, she'd struggled through he-didn't-know-how-many hours of labor to bring her into the world, and then she'd been given a medical diagnosis that forced her to face the possibility that her baby might die.

"But they did the surgery," he said, trying to refocus her thoughts on the positive outcome rather than the obstacles she'd faced.

She nodded. "I would have done anything, given anything, to save my baby."

Something in her voice alerted him to the fact that there was more to the story, some other detail that she wasn't telling him, something that he wasn't sure he wanted to know. "But you didn't come to me," he noted.

"No," she admitted. "I couldn't."

He didn't understand. She had to know that money wasn't an issue for him. Not only could he have taken care of the bill for Sierra's surgery, he could have bought a hospital—and would have—if it was necessary.

Maybe, after the way things had ended, she'd decided that she couldn't count on him for anything. But by her own admission, she'd been alone and scared and desperate. It seemed to him that desperation would have trumped everything else, and yet she still hadn't come to him.

"Why not?" he demanded.

She met his gaze evenly. "Because I'd made a deal with your mother."

Gabriella's tone was matter-of-fact. She refused to feel any guilt for what she had done and the only regret she had was that it had been necessary. But she'd meant what she said— she would have done anything to save her baby. And when the princess royal had visited her in the hospital and offered the chance to do just that, there had been absolutely no doubt in her mind.

She'd wondered about the other woman's motives in offering to help. Elena Leandres had made it clear to Gabriella the first day she visited the hospital that she didn't for one minute believe that Cameron was Sierra's father, although she'd kept close tabs on her son and knew about the weekend he'd spent with Gabriella. And she'd warned Gabriella of the havoc she would wreak if she ever dared suggest otherwise.

Gabriella knew it wasn't an empty threat. She knew it didn't matter that she hadn't ever been with anyone but Cameron. The truth had no force compared to a royal decree and if the princess royal claimed that she'd slept with a dozen men, any of whom could be the father of her child, she'd no doubt find a parade of men who would support her claim.

Gabriella resented the implication, but she didn't argue.

What was the point, anyway? Why should she insist on putting Cameron's name on her baby's birth certificate when he'd made it clear that he had no interest in her or the baby she carried? So she'd claimed the father was "unknown" and the princess royal had ensured that Gabriella had the money she needed to pay for Sierra's surgery.

It was, she'd thought at the time, more than a fair trade. And if she'd had occasional twinges of doubt over the years, she'd only needed to look at her happy and healthy daughter to push those twinges aside.

With Gabriella's confession, all of the pieces fell into place in Cameron's mind, like a jigsaw puzzle finally taking shape. Since coming face-to-face with his daughter that first day, he'd struggled to understand how Gabriella could keep their child a secret from him for so many years, why she would lie to him about Sierra's paternity. But now he knew. And long after he'd left the party and begun to drive the familiar winding streets that led to his mother's home, frustration and fury continued to burn inside of him.

Elena had already settled into bed for the night, the butler advised him, and Cameron knew she would not be happy to be disturbed. He didn't care. Nor did he wait in the parlor for her, as the butler suggested. He'd waited too damn long already.

Elena was just shoving her arms into the sleeves of a robe when he pushed open the door of her suite. She glanced over, irritation evident in the furrow of her brow. "Honestly, Cameron, do you have any idea what hour it is?"

"Just after midnight on the day of my daughter's sixteenth birthday," he noted.

Her hands paused in the act of tying a knot at the front of her robe. "So you know."

He stared at her, incredulous. "That's all you can say?"

"If it were up to me, we wouldn't be having this conversation at all," she reminded him.

"How could you not tell me? How could you have known that Gabriella had given birth to my child—*your grandchild*—and not tell me?"

Elena sniffed disdainfully. "I only knew that you'd shown poor judgment in dating a commoner—a waitress, no less—who later had a baby. I had no way of knowing that the child was yours."

"And yet you went to visit Gabriella in the hospital, to see the baby."

"I was curious."

"Curious enough to have the baby's DNA typed?"

"I don't need to explain my actions to you."

He shook his head. He'd known his mother was manipulative and self-centered and yet, throughout the drive to her home, he'd dared to let himself hope that there was some reasonable explanation for what she'd done.

"You knew she was mine."

"All I knew was that you were careless and immature and irresponsible—no greater crimes than most young men are guilty of—and I didn't want you to be stuck paying for those crimes for the rest of your life."

"But it was okay for Gabriella to pay?"

"She wanted the child."

"How could you know I didn't?"

She laughed at that, though the sound was abrupt and without humor. "You were little more than a child yourself, neither ready nor willing to be responsible for anyone else."

"It wasn't your decision to make."

"You'd already made your decision, by finally ending your relationship with the little slut."

He felt his hands curl into fists. He'd never wanted to hit another human being and the fact that he had to fight against the urge now—and that the human being in question was his mother—made his stomach churn. Deliberately, he blew out a long breath and unfurled his fingers. "She wasn't a slut, she is the mother of my child, and you will speak of her with respect."

"I am your mother and you will speak to *me* with respect," Elena said sharply.

"I can't speak to you at all right now," Cameron told her. "Just thinking about what you did, your lies and manipulations, makes me ill."

"I did what was best for you and this family."

"My daughter is part of this family," he shot back.

Elena's eyes narrowed. "You've worked hard to get where you are now," she reminded him. "What do you think will happen to your image in the press and the future of your career if you try to claim that bastard child as your daughter?"

"Do you think I care?"

"If you don't, you're a bigger fool than I thought. And maybe that's partly my fault," she continued. "I let you be the spoiled prince for too long, trusting that you would find your purpose and direction when you were ready. And I thought you had found it when you joined Rowan's cabinet. But this renewed fascination with Gabriella and your sudden determination to be some kind of father to her daughter prove you're as unfocused as ever."

"Actually, I think I may have finally found my focus," he told her.

"Walk away from her," Elena said. "If you don't, you're going to lose everything."

Cameron walked away from his mother instead. Because he'd finally realized that Gabriella and Sierra were everything that mattered, and he wasn't going to give up on them and the future he hoped they could build together. Not again.

After Cameron had gone, Elena sat at the antique desk in her upstairs office waiting for the supervisor of her security detail. As she was considering the most appropriate course of action, her gaze fell on the silver tri-fold frame—a gift from her late husband that contained photos of each of their three children.

She'd been blessed with two sons, and she'd had dreams and ambitions for each of them. Unfortunately, her disappointment had been as great as her plans when first Michael and then Cameron had chosen to pursue his own path. Though she'd been frustrated, she couldn't pretend not to understand where the defiance came from. She herself had defied her father's wishes to make a good match for her when she'd run away to marry a farmer.

It had seemed so romantic at the time. And she truly had loved Gaetan, at least in the beginning. When he'd died, just a few months after his forty-seventh birthday, she'd grieved—and she'd felt released. The idealistic life she'd envisioned had been painted over by the reality of trying to build a life with a man who wanted different things than she did—and who made no secret of the fact that he disapproved of her plans for their sons.

But he'd been gone a lot of years before she'd approached Michael about making a play for the throne. Her eldest son had refused to even consider her proposition. She'd tried to make him see that he'd been meant for greater things than his little advertising company, but he'd been adamant that his career and his wife were all he wanted.

He didn't even plan to have children, a decision which Elena viewed not just as a disappointment but a betrayal. As the oldest son, he had a duty to provide an heir. He needed a son of his own to extend the royal line and carry the family name. But while Michael remained steadfast, Samantha was eventually persuaded. Unfortunately, when she finally did give birth it was to a girl, and then she'd died only a few hours later, leaving Michael alone with the burden of an infant daughter.

He'd taken his wife's sudden and unexpected death hard, and Elena allowed herself a moment to wonder if Michael had yet adjusted to the loss before she focused her thoughts on her second-born son. Cameron had always been more malleable, more eager to please. In his youth, he'd been occasionally irresponsible and frequently reckless, but for the most part, he'd fallen in line with her expectations. Aside from that brief rebellious period in college when he'd been sneaking around with Gabriella, of course, but she'd nipped that in the bud. She'd helped him see the error of his ways and convinced him that he was destined for bigger things.

She didn't regret keeping the existence of his child a secret sixteen years ago. She only regretted that he'd found out now. But far worse than his knowledge was his intention to publicly claim the child as his own—as if he couldn't see that such an announcement would be an unmitigated disaster. He'd skirted the edge of scandal too many times already, and it was quite possible that the revelation of his youthful indiscretion would be the final nail in the coffin of his political career.

It wasn't that Elena had a problem with Cameron being a father, although she'd naturally been disappointed by the child's gender. If she didn't know better, she might have thought that both of her sons had fathered daughters on purpose just to spite her. But at least Michael had been married to the mother of his child, and while Elena and Samantha had never been close, her son's wife had come from a good family, she'd been well-educated and she'd been both understanding and respectful of Michael's background.

Gabriella Vasquez was a completely different story. She'd been nothing more than a starry-eyed waitress who saw the young prince as her ticket to the easy life. The quickness with which she'd snatched at Elena's offer of money in exchange for her silence about the baby was proof enough of that fact.

And now, sixteen years later, she thought she could renege on that agreement without consequence?

No way in hell.

Chapter Nine

Gabriella was usually up with the sun, but the day after Sierra's birthday party, she slept late. So late, in fact, that she only awakened when there was a knock on her bedroom door. She lifted a groggy head from her pillow when her mother poked her head in the room.

"What time is it?" Gabriella asked, squinting to focus on her clock.

"Almost time for me to be leaving for mass," Katarina said, stepping into the room. "But I didn't want to go without checking on you first."

Gabriella pushed herself up in bed. "I'm okay. I guess I was just more tired out from yesterday than I realized."

"It was a busy day," her mother agreed. "And an emotional one."

She just nodded.

"I overstepped," Katarina said. "With your prince."

"He's not mine," Gabriella told her. "And I understand why you feel the way that you do."

"I was so angry with you, when you refused to tell me the name of your baby's father."

"I couldn't. I didn't dare. It was all too easy to imagine you storming the gates of his family's estate, demanding that he marry me and give his name to my baby."

"He should have married you," Katarina insisted.

"We were both too young to marry."

"But old enough to make a baby."

Gabriella sighed. "And don't you think I'm a little too old for this lecture now, *madre?*"

Katarina shrugged. "Perhaps. It's just that I look at Sierra sometimes and she reminds me so much of you that it's scary. She's so beautiful and willful and I worry that she will follow her heart as you did, and have it broken."

"A broken heart heals," she said.

"And yet, you have never loved anyone else," her mother noted.

Gabriella thought, fleetingly, of Rafe, and wanted to protest, but the words stuck in her throat. Her mother was right. As much as she'd wanted to love Rafe, to share her life and build a future with him, she'd never been able to give him her heart. Because she'd already—foolishly—given it away too many years before. "I have you and Sierra. I don't need anyone else."

"If I had known—" Katarina shook her head. "I should have known. I should have seen that you were in love and always making excuses to get out of the house."

"I was pretty industrious," Gabriella admitted.

Her mother nodded. "But he was older, more sophisticated and experienced."

"And I was blind and naive," Gabriella interjected. "I know, and I'd rather not go down that road again." She'd spent enough time, during the darkest hours of the night, remembering what she'd had, what she'd lost, and wondering how things might have turned out if both she and Cameron had handled the situation differently.

"He broke your heart." There was anger and accusation in Katarina's tone.

"He gave me my daughter," Gabriella said softly.

"You always did look on the bright side of things."

"And she is the brightest part of my life."

Katarina smiled and touched a hand to her daughter's cheek. "I know how you feel."

When her hand dropped away, Gabriella reached for it, held on. "I'm scared," she admitted.

"Of telling Sierra?" Katarina guessed.

"Of losing Sierra," she admitted softly. "He can offer her so much more than I can."

"Things, perhaps." Katarina waved a hand dismissively. "But he cannot love her more than you do, and nothing he can offer her now will undermine the solid foundation you have given her over the past sixteen years."

"I hope you're right."

"You believe, then, that he is planning to acknowledge that he is her father?"

"I think he would have done so already, if I hadn't convinced him to wait—to give Sierra some time."

"He doesn't strike me as the patient type," Katarina mused.

"Not at all," Gabriella agreed.

"Which makes me wonder if maybe I was wrong."

"About what?"

"About what he wants from you." Her mother's tone was quiet now, reflective, and made Gabriella squirm uneasily.

"He wants a relationship with his daughter," she pointed out.

"Maybe that's true," Katarina agreed, "but it might not be the whole truth."

"Care to explain that? Because it's too early for me to wrap my head around one of your riddles."

"It's not early at all," her mother denied. "In fact, if I don't hurry now, I will be late for church."

Then she dropped a kiss on her daughter's cheek and was gone.

After she'd taken a quick shower to clear the last of the cobwebs from her brain and tugged on some clothes, Gabriella made her way down to the kitchen, following the scent of the coffee her mother had already brewed. She knew that some of her friends and colleagues had wondered about her living arrangement—a thirty-four-year-old mother of a teenage daughter living with her own mother—but Katarina had truly been her rock, not just since that fateful day when the results of an over-the-counter pregnancy test had changed her world, but for as long as she could remember.

She'd been so scared to tell her mother that she was pregnant. Not because she worried that her mother would turn her out of her home, but because she knew she would be disappointed. She'd raised Gabriella with traditional values and morals, and learning that her unwed teenage daughter was pregnant was a slap in the face to everything she believed in. Still, she'd never wavered in her support of her daughter, and the only time they'd seriously argued was when Gabriella refused to reveal the name of her baby's father.

In fact, it was only a few weeks earlier, after Cameron's first visit to her home, that Gabriella had been shaken enough to confess the truth. Based on her mother's reaction to the news—and her uncensored comments to Cameron the night before—Gabriella had been wise to keep that information to herself for so long.

But now, the secret that she'd so closely guarded for so many years was about to be revealed. And she couldn't help but wonder how the princess royal would respond to that.

Gabriella had kept her end of the bargain—she'd never told

Cameron about his child. In fact, she'd gone one step further and denied that he was the father when he'd asked. She hadn't counted on Cameron making any further inquiries on his own, and she didn't think Elena would have anticipated such interest, either.

The doorbell rang as she was refilling her mug with coffee and she carried it with her when she went to answer the summons. Cameron was on the step, but unlike his first visit to her home two weeks earlier, this time she didn't hesitate to step back and let him inside.

"Coffee?" she asked.

"Please," he said, sounding desperately grateful.

She returned to the kitchen, pulled a second mug from the cupboard. "Cream? Sugar?"

"Just black."

She glanced over her shoulder as he dropped into a chair at the table. "You look like you had a rough night."

"I haven't slept," he admitted.

She pushed the mug across the table to him. "At all?"

He shook his head. "I haven't even been home. After I left here last night, I went to see my mother. And then I just drove."

"That's a lot of driving," she said lightly.

"I had a lot of thinking to do."

"Do you want something to eat? I could scramble some eggs."

He glanced up, the ghost of a smile hovering at the edges of his lips. "I must really look like hell if you're offering to cook for me."

"I don't cook," she reminded him. "Scrambling eggs doesn't count as cooking."

"In that case, I would love some."

Gabriella took a handful of eggs out of the fridge, cracked them into a bowl. She added some milk, a dash of salt and pepper, then whipped them until they were frothy.

"For someone who doesn't cook, you know your way around a kitchen."

"I can handle the basics," she assured him, setting a frying pan on top of the stove.

"Do you have a recipe that might make a serving of crow more palatable?"

She slid a couple of slices of bread into the toaster, then turned to him. "A recipe for what?"

"Crow," he said again.

"Are you planning to eat crow?" she asked him.

"At the very least."

Gabriella took the coffee pot to the table, refilled his mug. "Eat your breakfast first," she instructed. "Before it gets cold."

He picked up his fork and dug into the eggs. The meal was simple but delicious, and in minutes, he'd completely cleaned his plate.

"I owe you an apology."

"I appreciate the sentiment," she said. "But I'd rather focus on where we go from here than rehash the past."

"That's generous of you."

"Not really," she denied. "We've both made mistakes."

He nodded. "So where do we go from here?"

She folded her hands around her mug. "I know you're anxious for Sierra to know who you are."

"I am," he agreed. "But it might be better if we spent some time together first, getting to know one another without the father-daughter labels hanging over our heads."

"I think that's a good idea."

"Does she like boats?"

"She's never been on one," Gabriella admitted. "But she's usually game to try new things."

"Then why don't we plan an outing for Wednesday afternoon?"

"Wednesday?"

"School's out for summer break now, isn't it?"

Gabriella nodded. "Sierra wrote her last exam Friday morning."

"Good," he said. "My morning is booked solid with meetings, but I should be able to get away from the office by noon and there won't be nearly as much traffic on the water then as on the weekend."

Maybe it should have irritated her that he didn't ask about her work schedule, but the fact was that as long as she got her columns in to her editor on time, her hours were completely flexible. And the idea of spending an afternoon out on the water instead of in front of her computer was too tempting to resist. "Do you want me to pack a lunch?"

"No. I'll have my chef put something together for us."

"Well, then, I'm sure we'll eat better than tuna sandwiches."

He frowned at the obvious pique in her tone. "It bothers you that I have a chef?"

"No," she denied. "I guess it just reminded me that you aren't like the rest of us common folk." And she was glad for the reminder, because allowing herself to think otherwise could be very dangerous.

"I could fire him, if that would make you feel better," he teased.

"Yeah, because putting some guy out of a job would make me happy," she said dryly.

"I don't understand why my title and status are such an issue for you."

"Of course you don't, because you're the one with the blue blood."

"It's not quite as blue as Elena would like everyone to believe," he told her.

"Your father wasn't of noble birth?" she guessed, aware that his mother had a direct connection to the throne.

"My father was a farmer," he told her. "It was quite the scandal when they got married."

"She must have really loved him," Gabriella mused. But try as she might, she couldn't imagine the woman who had heartlessly bargained with Sierra's life caring that much about anyone.

"Or she really wanted to piss off her father," Cameron suggested.

That scenario was much easier for Gabriella to envision. It also made her wonder, "Is that why you were with me?"

"I was with you because you were beautiful and sexy and smart," he said patiently. "And because the moment I laid eyes on you, I didn't want to be with anyone else."

The words sounded good, and Gabriella wanted to believe them. She wanted to believe in *him*. But she couldn't help remembering how careful he'd been to ensure they weren't seen in public together.

At the time, she'd thought he was protecting her from the media spotlight. Later, she'd accepted that he'd been protecting himself. After all, it would have damaged his image to be seen in the company of a waitress.

Sixteen years later, not much had changed. Although "the partying prince" didn't grace the covers of the tabloids as frequently as he had ten years earlier, he was still accustomed to being photographed in the company of the world's most wealthy and beautiful women. Gabriella didn't fit into either category. She was a single mother who had obtained her journalism degree while her daughter was in diapers and the simple fact that her child was also the prince's child couldn't magically bridge the distance that separated their two worlds.

"How many staff do you have on your yacht?" she asked him now.

"Three."

"Do you trust them?"

"Implicitly," he assured her without hesitation.

"Then I guess we'll see you around noon on Wednesday."

On Tuesday, the long-standing trade agreement between Tesoro del Mar and Ardena was officially renewed. Afterward, Cameron tracked down the prince regent in his office.

"I'm going to play hooky tomorrow afternoon," Cameron said.

"It's not really hooky if you tell me," Rowan informed him.

"Okay then, I'm not really playing hooky tomorrow afternoon."

Rowan pushed aside the document he'd been reviewing. "Obviously there's a reason you thought I should be aware of your plans."

"I just wanted to give you a heads-up, in case some enterprising photographer catches a picture of me and/or my guests."

Rowan waited, patiently, for him to continue.

"I'm going to spend the afternoon on my yacht with Gabriella Vasquez and her daughter—my daughter—Sierra."

The prince regent's brows shot up. "Your daughter?"

He nodded.

Rowan frowned. "Your personal life isn't any of my business—except when it reflects on this office. And when I appointed you to the cabinet, you promised me that you were finished living the life of a carefree playboy."

"And I meant it," Cameron assured him.

"Then can you tell me how in hell this happened?"

Cameron couldn't blame his cousin for being pissed. Because what Rowan hadn't said, but Cameron knew was that when he'd named his cousin to the cabinet, it was against the recommendation of several key advisors—and probably both of his brothers, too.

"A youthful indiscretion?" he suggested.

The furrow in Rowan's brow deepened. "Dammit, Cameron, you're thirty-six years old—"

"And she's sixteen."

His cousin's face drained of all color. "The mother?"

"*Dios,* no! My daughter."

"Oh." Rowan exhaled. "Thank God."

"I can't believe you'd even think—" Cameron shook his head. "That's just sick."

"I'm sorry." The apology was automatic but sincere. "I guess the headlines about the king's daughter are still on my mind."

"I only recently learned about Sierra's existence," Cameron explained. "And Gabriella and I have agreed to keep the truth of her paternity under wraps until we've had a chance to tell her."

"How many people do know?"

"Other than myself and Gabriella, just her mother, my mother, Marissa and now you."

"How did your mother respond to the news?"

"Let's just say that it wasn't news to her." Cameron's gut still burned with fury whenever he thought about his mother's lies.

Rowan, being well-acquainted with Elena's manipulations and machinations, only nodded. "Then I'd suggest you don't wait too long to tell your daughter," he warned. "Secrets have a habit of blowing up when we least expect it."

It was a truth that Cameron understood only too well.

"This is so lame," Sierra grumbled. She'd been on the phone with Beth, making plans to go down to the waterfront. They were going to spend the afternoon doing some shopping and hanging out, and then she was going to meet Paolo when he finished work.

It was, in her opinion, the perfect way to spend a summer

afternoon. Except that her mother had kiboshed those plans because she wanted Sierra to spend the day with her. Which wouldn't have been such a hardship, really. Gabriella was pretty cool, as far as mothers went. She didn't harp on Sierra all the time about her clothes or her make-up, the way Rachel's mother did. And she was usually flexible about her curfew, as long as she knew where Sierra was and who she was with.

But when Sierra tried to wriggle out of spending the afternoon with her, this time she was completely *in*flexible. And it wasn't even because she wanted some private mother-daughter time, it was because she wanted Sierra to get to know Prince Cameron. And maybe Sierra had thought it was sweet when she'd first met him and realized the man standing in her living room was royalty, but now, it was kind of weird.

She'd Googled him, out of curiosity, and she'd been stunned by the amount of information that was on the internet about him. The basic facts were well-known. He was the second son and middle child of the princess royal, Elena Marissa Santiago Leandres, and her deceased husband, Gaetan Rainier Leandres, which meant that Prince Cameron was fourteenth in line to the throne—not likely to ever rule the country but not completely out of the running, either, which was sort of cool. He'd been educated at St. Mary's College in Port Augustine and at Cambridge University and had spent several years traveling abroad before returning home to accept a position in the royal cabinet. His Royal Highness Prince Rowan Santiago, the current prince regent, had made the original appointment and recently named him the country's new Minister of Trade.

Aside from all of that, most of the other stuff she found was gossip—photos of women he'd dated, rumors of engagements, reports of break-ups. He'd dated *a lot* of women, but not any one woman for any length of time, and even if only half the stories she read were true (because she was savvy enough to know she couldn't believe *everything* she read on the internet), she felt that she had reason to worry about his interest in her mother.

Gabriella was every bit as beautiful as any of the other women he'd dated, but she lacked their worldliness and sophistication. Sierra couldn't help but wonder how her mother had caught his eye and what his intentions were toward her. And she decided that, as much as she resented having to change her own plans, it was probably a good idea for her to keep any eye on things.

Gabriella finished wrapping the plate of brownies. "I thought you would enjoy an afternoon on the water."

"With my mother and her new boyfriend?" she asked, not even trying to hide her sarcasm.

"It's not like that," Gabriella said. "Cameron and I are just friends."

Sierra wondered whether she was trying to convince her daughter or herself.

"I may only be sixteen," she reminded Gabriella, "but I'm not a child and I'm not an idiot. You dated Rafe for six months before you brought him home to meet me, now this prince is suddenly in your life and you're pushing me to get to know him.

"So is that the real reason you're dragging me along?" she pressed. "Am I your chaperone—so he doesn't pressure you to go too far?"

Gabriella pushed her hair back off her forehead and sent her daughter a baleful glance. "Honestly, Sierra, you have the most vivid imagination."

"I wasn't imagining the way he was looking at you."

"I'm not worried about Cameron behaving inappropriately," her mother insisted.

"Because you're as hot for him as he is for you?"

Gabriella's cheeks flushed. "Sierra."

It was her don't-mess-with-me tone and usually succeeded in getting her daughter to back down. But the color in her face confirmed that Sierra wasn't far off the mark. Not that she could blame her mother for being attracted—Cameron was incredibly good-looking, for an old guy, and he was a real-life prince, too. In any event, she knew there was more going on here than her mother was telling her, and she wasn't going to let up until she got to the truth.

Except that before she could say anything else, Cameron was at the door.

Chapter Ten

Twenty minutes later, they were at the harbor. Sierra didn't want to be impressed, but it was impossible not to be. She didn't know anything about boats and couldn't even have guessed at the size of the yacht—except to say that it was huge, and gorgeous. It shone brilliantly in the afternoon sun—as stunningly white as a pearl in the sapphire blue waters, and when she stepped onto the glossy wood deck, she felt as if she'd stepped into another world.

Cameron gave them a quick tour. She had expected that the inside would be dim, but it wasn't, as natural light shone through wide windows on every side. There was an enormous saloon with more glossy wood cabinets and tables with leather stools, cushy leather sofas and an impressive home theatre system, a small office, a master cabin with ensuite, plus two more guest cabins, each with its own private bath, and separate crew quarters.

While he'd been showing them around, the yacht had been making its way away from the island. When they finished the tour and returned to the main saloon, she was surprised by how much distance they'd put between themselves and the shore in such a short time.

"Are you hungry?" Cameron asked.

Sierra shrugged, trying to act casual.

"Starved," Gabriella admitted, shooting her daughter a look that Sierra chose to ignore.

"Good." He smiled at both of them, his even white teeth flashing white against his tanned skin. "Emilio has set up lunch on the deck, if that's acceptable. Or we can eat inside, if you'd prefer."

"Outside," Sierra answered automatically, before she remembered that she wasn't supposed to care.

"Gabriella?" he prompted.

There was something about the way he said the name that made it sound like a caress, and the color that infused her mother's cheeks confirmed that she'd heard it, as well.

"Outside sounds wonderful," Gabriella agreed.

He gestured for them to precede him, and again, Sierra had to give him points for presentation. The table had been set for three, with linens and fancy crystal and silverware that was probably the real deal and not the stainless steel stuff in their own drawer at home.

Cameron and her mother chatted easily over the meal, almost as if they really were old friends, and Sierra found herself wondering if maybe she'd been wrong about their relationship. But when he reached over and casually touched the back of her mother's hand and Gabriella's fork slipped from her fingers, she knew that she hadn't been wrong at all.

"Do you like to swim?" he asked, turning his attention to Sierra.

She nodded, because the fact that she did was one of the reasons she'd thought the afternoon on his yacht might not be a total bust.

"Then you should take a dip after lunch," he suggested, lifting his glass of wine. "The water out here is heavenly."

Yeah, he'd probably love for her to take a swim—while he put the moves on her mother.

"I can't swim," she said, holding up her arm in case he'd forgotten about the cast on it. Which he probably had, because he was too preoccupied with thoughts of getting her mother naked to worry about something as insignificant as her broken wrist.

"Sierra." Her mother's sharp response warned that she hadn't missed the disdainful tone of her daughter's voice. "Dr. Granger gave me some waterproof sleeves, if you want to go in the water."

The prince, to his credit, responded smoothly. "Or you could try the jet ski if you don't want to swim."

"Jet ski?" she echoed, her interest piqued despite herself.

"As long as it's okay with your mother," he hastened to add.

Now she did look at Gabriella, trying to convey a mixture of apology and pleading in her gaze. Her mother's hesitation was a warning to Sierra that she expected her best behavior from this point on. She gave a brief nod to telegraph her understanding.

"It's okay with me," Gabriella finally said. "As long as you have your cast covered and wear a life jacket."

Sierra opened her mouth to protest, then closed it again without uttering a word.

"Impressive," Cameron said to Gabriella later.

Lunch had been cleared away and they had taken their wine where they could watch Sierra who, now properly attired, was making waves out on the water.

"She's always loved the water," she told him.

"It shows," he said. "Although I wasn't talking about that."

Gabriella looked over at him. "Then what were you talking about?"

"The wordless communication between the two of you."

"It's not always as effective as I'd like," she said. "Which leads into my turn to apologize to you. She was being deliberately difficult and I don't know why."

"Don't you?"

"She's a teenager, which is probably enough of an explanation for a lot of her behavior, but it was more than that today."

"The 'more than that' being her feelings about the relationship between you and I?"

"That's exactly it," she admitted. "She's somehow got it into her head that we're more than friends and—"

"We *are* more than friends," he said.

The hand she'd raised to reach for her glass dropped away. "We have a history," she acknowledged.

"I think I understand now why she's worried."

"You do?"

He nodded. "Because our daughter is obviously more insightful than you are."

"Cameron."

"Gabriella."

She frowned at the amusement evident in his tone.

"After the kiss we shared in the park, do you really doubt that I'm attracted to you?"

"Considering your reputation, the fact that I'm female should be enough to assuage my doubts," she told him.

He shifted closer. "If you're trying to distract me by making me mad, it's not going to work."

"Didn't I make it clear, after that kiss, that you were wasting your time?"

"That's what you said," he agreed. "But I don't think it's what you meant."

She swallowed, glanced away. "I'm not playing hard to

get—I promise you. I just can't risk getting involved with you again."

"Because of Sierra?" he guessed.

"I want her to get to know you and have a relationship with you. But I don't want her to hope that we'll end up together like one big happy family."

"Because that's not what you want?"

Because it *was* what she wanted, more than anything. But she could hardly admit as much to Cameron. He'd already broken her heart once before—she wasn't going to give him the power to do so again.

"I'm trying to be realistic here, Cameron."

"Reality's overrated."

"Said the prince from his ivory tower," she retorted.

"Being royal has given me a lot of advantages," he acknowledged. "It has also presented a unique set of challenges."

"I'll bet none of those challenges included siphoning money from the grocery fund to pay the electrical bill so that the little food you had in the fridge didn't spoil."

"You're right," he admitted. "I can't begin to imagine how difficult it was for you, struggling to hold down a job and raise a child. And while I can tell you now that I would have helped, the words don't change anything."

"No," she agreed, then reached over to take his hand. "But thank you, anyway."

"I hate knowing that you didn't come to me because you didn't trust me not to turn you away. Because I had already turned you away."

"It was a long time ago," she reminded him.

He reached out, wrapped a strand of her hair around his finger, and tugged gently. The unexpected gesture threw her off-balance, and she had to step forward or risk stumbling.

"Gone but not forgotten?"

She had to tilt her head to meet his gaze, but pride wouldn't let her step away again. "What does that mean?"

"You keep saying that there's no point in dwelling on the past, that it's the future that matters. But you refuse to consider that we could have a future together, and I can't help but think that you're reticent because you haven't let go of the past."

"Maybe I'm reticent because I've never known you to talk about anything further into the future than dinner."

"Ouch." He dropped his hand from his hair, wrapped it around her waist. "So what if I did want to make plans for dinner?"

She could feel the strength in his arm, the heat of his touch, and had to swallow before she could speak. "We just finished lunch."

"We didn't have dessert."

"Sierra made brownies," she reminded him. Not that the brownies had been made specifically for this occasion, it was just that Sierra had been playing around in the kitchen and Gabriella had pilfered half of the pan to bring on this outing. Despite knowing that Cameron had a chef, she didn't like to show up empty-handed.

"Then we should wait for Sierra to have those. In the meantime…" His head lowered toward her.

Gabriella put her hand on his chest. "Don't play games with me, Cameron."

"Is that what you think I'm doing?"

"I don't know," she said. "My brain is spinning in circles right now so that I can't seem to figure any of this out. You invited us here today so that you could spend some time with Sierra—"

"And with you," he told her.

And when he looked at her like that, his eyes burning so intently with heat and hunger, she believed him. More, she felt herself responding.

"This is a mistake," she warned him.

But even before the words were completely out of her

mouth, the hand that she'd laid on his chest curled into the fabric of his shirt.

His mouth came down on hers, hard and hungry; her lips parted for him, eager and willing. She could taste the wine they'd both drunk, and the darker and more potent flavor of the passion that flared between them. Her hands slid up his chest, over his shoulders, linking behind his head. Her fingers toyed with the strands of hair that brushed his collar, so soft and silky in contrast to the lean, hard body pressed against hers.

She felt weak and hot and dizzy, and though she wished she could blame the hot Mediterranean sun, she knew her response had nothing to do with the weather and everything to do with the man. She'd always responded to him like this, completely and instinctively. And while she'd once thrilled to the discovery of such intense and all-consuming desire, she was embarrassed and ashamed to realize that she could still feel such depth of emotion for a man who had broken her heart—and a lot of other hearts, too.

He was used to having whatever he wanted, whenever he wanted, women included. She had been one of those women once, willingly and happily, but she wouldn't let herself be cast in that same role again. Not just because she wanted to protect her heart, but because she wanted to provide a better example for her daughter.

The daughter who, even now, could be on her way back to the boat.

She pulled away from him. "I can't do this."

Cameron took a minute to draw in a breath before he responded. "I'd say we were doing just fine."

"We both know how to go through the motions," she agreed. "But it's never been just that for me. I can't separate the wants of my body from the needs of my heart."

"And you assume that I can?"

"I'd say that history speaks for itself."

"Gone but not forgotten," he said again.

She shook her head. "I'm not referring to our history but your reputation."

"Deserved or not?" he challenged.

"Cameron, I work in the newspaper industry. I know as well as anyone that information is sometimes slanted, the truth is often stretched, and headlines are frequently exaggerated. But I also know it's a fact that you've dated more women in the past year than a lot of men date in their entire lifetimes."

Cameron had never been particularly concerned about his reputation, nor about the fact that it had been greatly exaggerated through the media. He enjoyed spending time in a woman's company, and he'd been fortunate that a lot of women seemed to enjoy his company in turn.

"But not one of those women—not any one that I've ever dated, in fact—has ever made me forget about you," he told Gabriella.

"Cameron, we haven't had any contact in more than sixteen years." She spoke patiently, as if she was talking to a dim-witted child. "You probably didn't even remember I existed until the photos of you with Princess Leticia were published."

She was wrong, but he didn't know how to convince her of the truth. He could hardly blame her for being skeptical. After the weekend they'd spent at Cielo del Norte, he'd realized that he was more than halfway in love with her—and he'd panicked. He was only twenty years old, still in college and with no real direction for his future—what did he know about love? How could he know for certain that she was "the one" when there were so many women out there? So many women who wanted to be with him?

He'd decided to take some time to figure things out. He'd promised to call her, but he didn't. As anxious as he was to hear her voice, he refused to give in, refused to admit—even

to himself—how much he needed her. Because needing someone was a weakness, and weaknesses could be exploited, and
those of royal blood could not afford to be weak.

The day that she'd tracked him down on campus, he'd been
so happy to see her, but he'd pretended that he didn't even
remember her name. He'd been deliberately cruel, acting as
if the time they'd spent together had meant nothing to him.
And still, she'd had the courage to look him straight in the eye
and confide her suspicion that she might be pregnant. That
was when the real panic had set in.

Afterward, he'd thrown himself at other women, desperate
to forget about Gabriella. Eventually, over time, the memories
faded. But he'd never truly forgotten her. No one else's arms
had ever felt so right around him, no one else's kisses had ever
touched him so deep inside. No one else had ever loved him
as freely and unconditionally as she had done, if only for a
short while.

He'd been such a fool. He'd missed out on so much time
with Gabriella—and the entire first sixteen years of Sierra's
life—because he'd been a selfish and self-centered fool. That
was time that he could never get back and, because he'd so
completely and effectively isolated Gabriella so many years
before, it was entirely possible that he'd blown any hope for
the future, too.

"I guess it's going to take some time to convince you that
I'm not the man the press has portrayed me to be."

"You don't need to convince me of anything," she said.
"But if you say you want a relationship with Sierra, you better
mean it. She needs a father who will be there for her, even—
or maybe especially—when she's pretending that she doesn't
need you at all."

"I'll be there for her," he promised.

And I'll be there for you, he silently vowed. *Even when
you're pretending that you don't need me at all.*

The sound of the jet ski grew louder, signaling Sierra's

return. "Why don't you and I take that swim Sierra claimed she didn't want?" he suggested. "Then maybe she'll be enticed to join us."

"The water does look inviting," Gabriella admitted.

"Go put on your bathing suit," Cameron encouraged.

While she was changing, he did the same, and they were both ready by the time Sierra had returned. She declined the invitation to join them, opting instead to plug into her iPod and blast out her eardrums. Cameron decided that she needed some time, and turned his attention to the woman by his side.

"Maybe we should just head back," she suggested. "I know this day isn't turning out quite how you'd planned."

"I have no complaints," he assured her. "Unless you renege on your promise to go swimming with me."

With a shrug, she pulled off her cover-up. It dropped onto the deck—right beside Cameron's jaw.

Even at seventeen, Gabriella had the kind of beauty that stopped men in their tracks and the type of body that inspired them to fantasize about her. And he'd spent a lot of long, lonely nights doing just that before he'd finally known the pleasure of that sweet, lush body stretched out beneath him, wrapped around him, moving against him. She was somehow even more beautiful now, her body even more lush and breath-taking. And while the two-piece bathing suit she wore was modest by current standards, just one glance and his blood—already pumping hard and fast through his veins—quickly detoured south.

Oh man, he was in trouble here. Big trouble. And he suddenly found himself questioning the wisdom of getting half-naked with a woman who had always turned him on more than any other. Not that he would tell her as much, of course. Because even if he was foolish enough to make such a confession, she would never believe him. It was going to take time—time and a concerted effort—to break through Gabriella's resistance and convince her that the feelings he had for her were real.

In the meantime, he would have to take a lot of cold showers. But a cold shower not being immediately available, he decided a dip in the Mediterranean would have to suffice.

He dove deep, relishing the coolness of the water as his body sliced through it. Kicking hard, he pushed himself deeper. He swam downward until his lungs ached with the effort of holding his breath in, then he turned abruptly and pushed hard toward the surface. He broke through and drew in a deep, shuddering breath—and felt something smack into his shoulder.

Blinking water from his eyes, he saw Gabriella was in the water with him. Her hair was dripping wet, and her eyes were huge in her pale face.

"Goddamn you, Cameron."

The relief Gabriella had felt when he broke through the surface was overwhelming, but her heart was still pounding too hard and too fast. For almost a whole minute or maybe even longer—it certainly seemed like so much longer—he'd been gone. One minute he'd been standing beside her on the deck, the next he'd executed a clean dive into the water, and then he'd disappeared.

She should have called for the captain. That would have been the smart thing to do. But she hadn't been able to think— she'd just acted, and apparently that meant flinging herself over the edge and into the water after him.

She'd gone under three times, mindless of the salt that stung her eyes as she desperately scanned the crystal clear waters for any sign of where he'd gone. And then, finally, she'd seen him. Not injured or unconscious beneath the surface, but determinedly swimming toward it.

Cameron frowned at her. "What's got you all bent out of shape?"

She stared at him as she continued to tread water beside him. "You were underwater forever. I couldn't see where you'd gone, if you'd hit or head on something and—"

"And you jumped in to save me?" His lips curved, just a little, as if he was amused by her instinctive response.

She wanted to hit him again. "I don't know why I bothered."

"I think you do," he said. "I think maybe, just maybe, all of your claims to the contrary aside, you still care about me."

"I would try to save anyone I thought was drowning."

"Hey." He moved closer, lifting his hands out of the water to cradle her face in his palms. "I didn't mean to scare you."

"Well, you did." This time she did smack him again. The violent action splashed more water, hopefully masking the moisture that swam in her eyes. "You big idiot."

"I'm sorry." He dipped his head, brushed his lips lightly against hers.

She wanted to cling to him, to hold him and feel the solid warmth of his flesh beneath her hands. But she didn't, because to do so would only prove what he already suspected—that she still cared about him. And while she might be able to convince herself that it was perfectly normal and reasonable to care about the man who was the father of her child, she knew that her feelings for Cameron weren't that simple or straightforward.

"Stop that." She started to pull away, but he caught her, tangled his legs with hers. Their bodies bumped, once, twice, and the slick slide of wet skin against wet skin was incredibly and unbelievably arousing.

"I can't." His hands slid down her back to curl around her bottom and pull her closer. "I've tried, really I have, but I can't stop myself from wanting you."

The words, the tone, and the man were far too seductive—or maybe she was far too naive, because she wanted to believe he meant what he'd said. Because then it might be okay to admit that she wanted him, too.

"This is crazy," she said instead.

"You've always made me crazy." He nibbled his way along her jaw, down her throat, as they bobbed in the gentle waves.

"I thought we were going to swim."

"This is so much better than swimming."

"Right now, I'm having a hard time disagreeing with that," she admitted. "But this isn't the time or place."

Cameron suckled on her earlobe. "So tell me when and where."

His voice was warm with desire, silky with promise, and far too tempting. But somehow Gabriella resisted the impulse to let her head fall back, to let him lead where she was only too willing to follow. Because she'd been down that road before, and she'd found herself alone at the end.

"You make it sound so easy," she said.

"It could be," he told her.

She shook her head as she disentangled herself from him. When he was touching her, she couldn't think straight. When she was wanting him, she couldn't remember all the reasons that she shouldn't. "*I'm* not easy," she told him. "Not anymore."

"I never thought you were easy," he denied. "And I always believed you were worth the effort."

"I have to get back." She started swimming toward the ladder.

Cameron matched her, stroke for stroke. "You're running away."

"No. I have a column to finish and send in to my editor."

He was right behind her as she climbed out of the water.

"How about dinner?" he asked, as she started to towel off.

"I told you—I have work to do."

"Not tonight," he said. "Saturday."

She hesitated. "I think Sierra has plans with Paolo."

"I'm not asking Sierra, I'm asking you."

"I'd have to check my calendar."

"I'm trying to prove that I'm capable of thinking long-term," he told her. "Not just as far away as dinner, but dinner three days in the future."

"Should I be impressed?"

"You should say 'yes.'"

"Don't you need to check your calendar?" she challenged, knowing that his professional obligations—and his social life—were far more demanding than hers.

"No," he replied, without hesitation. "Because even if there's something else on my schedule, it couldn't possibly be as important as taking you to dinner."

He had the right answers to all of her questions, which only made her more cautious. He'd always been a player, and she couldn't take the chance that he was playing her—again.

"I think being here with you today is enough tempting of fate for one week."

"Would it really be so terrible to be seen in public with me?"

She'd always thought he was the one who didn't want to be seen with her. But now, she was wary. "It's not you, Cameron, it's the paparazzi that follows wherever you go. And I don't want my daughter reading headlines that label me as your latest conquest just because we were having dinner together."

"Our daughter."

She cast a glance toward Sierra, relieved to see that she was still listening to her iPod and apparently oblivious to their conversation. "Our daughter," she murmured in agreement.

"I promise you, no one will know where we're going and there will be no paparazzi hiding anywhere in the shadows waiting to snap pictures of us."

"How can you make that kind of promise?"

"Trust me," he said. "I've not only lived most of my life in the spotlight, I've learned how to court that attention when it serves my purpose—and how to circumvent it when necessary."

Still she hesitated.

"Seven o'clock," he suggested.

She sighed. "Okay. But I have to be home by midnight."

"Is that your curfew?" he teased.

"It's Sierra's, and I need to be home to know that she is."

"Then I will have you home by midnight," he promised.

Chapter Eleven

Dear Gabby,
The first time I fell in love, I was fifteen years old.
Maybe I was naive to believe that Carlos and I would
last forever, but he claimed to love me, too, and we spent
hours talking about the future. After high school graduation, we went to different colleges, but I continued to
believe that we would get back together again when we
both finished school. Except that when Carlos finally
came home, he was married to someone else.

I was devastated, but because I didn't want anyone to
know how heartbroken I was, I started dating someone
else. After a while, I convinced myself that I was in love
with him and, within a few months, we were married.
It took less time than that for me to realize that our
marriage had been a horrible mistake and that I'd never
stopped loving Carlos.

A couple of years ago, our paths crossed again. I
immediately realized that I still had strong feelings for

him. And since it turned out that he was divorced, too, it almost seemed natural to start dating again. We've been together now for almost a year and a half, and Carlos has been starting to drop hints about the two of us getting married.

I have never loved anyone else as much as I loved him, but no one else has ever hurt me as much as he did, either. I'm afraid to give him another chance, afraid that he'll break my heart all over again.

Should I play it safe—or risk it all for a chance to live happily-ever-after?
Signed,
Still Sorting Out the Pieces

Over the years that Gabriella had been writing her "Dear Gabby" column for the newspaper, she'd occasionally found that a reader's questions and concerns reflected current events in her own life. Those were always the most difficult letters to respond to because they required not just a dose of common sense but a fair bit of introspection and Gabriella wasn't always willing to look into herself. It was far easier, in her opinion, to respond to other people's problems than examine her own.

In this case, however, the issue was one at the forefront of her mind. Cameron had been more than hinting about wanting a second chance, and Gabriella was still reluctant to even consider the possibility.

Dear Sorting,
A man who can abuse your trust and break your heart once shouldn't be given a chance to do so again.

Gabriella sat back and studied the words on the screen. It was a valid point, she thought, but not quite the response that her readers expected. On a sigh, she held down the backspace key until the screen was blank again. Because as justified as she might have felt in writing those words, they were a personal response rather than a professional one.

Don't think about Cameron, she reminded herself. *Don't think about the fact that he claimed to love you and then dumped you. Don't think about the fact that he disappeared from your life for more than sixteen years and now expects to pick up right where things left off.*

She pushed him out of her mind—or at least tried to—and focused on her response again.

Dear Sorting,
There is nothing quite as intense as first love. And nothing quite as devastating as a first heartbreak.

It's not surprising that you would still be holding on to your hurt and using it as a shield to protect your heart this time around. But you and Carlos are different people now than you were in high school. You're not just older and more mature, you've lived separate lives and had distinct experiences, taken different paths that have merged to bring you together once again.

It's time to let go of the past and look to the future— and decide if you want him to be part of that future. It's not always easy to forgive and forget, and only you can decide if you're ready to take that next step.

The only thing I'll add to that is that second chances are rare. If you decide you want this one, grab hold of it with both hands.
Good luck,
Gabby

It was good advice—objectively, she knew that was true. But did she have the courage to listen to her own guidance? Did she want a second chance with Cameron? Or was she a fool to think he was even offering her one?

Had he really changed—or was he just playing her? He claimed that he wanted to be a father to his daughter, and Gabriella had no intention of standing in the way of that.

So what was his interest in her?

There was no shortage of women wanting to be with him, and no reason for Cameron to be with Gabriella unless that was truly what he wanted.

But what did *she* want?

She pondered that question as she rifled through the clothes in her wardrobe.

She wanted Sierra to have a relationship with Cameron, but she was also afraid to acknowledge that relationship. As soon as the truth came out, everything would change. Sierra wouldn't be her little girl anymore—she'd be the prince's daughter and a princess in her own right. Her life wouldn't be her own—she would be thrust into the spotlight, her every action and word scrutinized by the media. Gabriella wanted to protect her from that, for just a little while longer.

And yet, here she was—watching the clock and mentally calculating the time that she had left to get ready for her date with the prince.

Was she making a mistake?

She didn't want to think so, but the truth was, she'd never been able to think very clearly where Cameron Leandres was concerned. There was just something about the man that affected her on a basic level, stirring her blood and muddling her brain so that rational thought was all but impossible.

But she did know that playing it safe was no longer an option. She was playing with fire and she knew it. All she could do now was hope that no one got burned.

Cameron knew he was early, but he'd hoped that arriving ahead of schedule would give him a few minutes to talk to Sierra. The first time they'd met, she'd been obviously surprised and adorably flustered to realize who he was. Since then, however, her demeanor toward him had cooled noticeably. As he'd done nothing to justify this change in her attitude, he could only speculate that it was a reflection of her feelings about his relationship with Gabriella.

He thought he could understand her wariness. He knew that Gabriella had been dating Rafe for a long time, then suddenly Rafe was out of the picture and Cameron was in. And Sierra really had no idea who he was, aside from his title, and no reason to trust him or his motivations.

He heard footsteps approach in response to the ring of the bell, then Sierra was standing in front of him. The welcoming light in her eyes dimmed and her easy smile slipped when she recognized him. "Oh. I thought you were Paolo."

Gabriella had mentioned that Sierra probably had a date with the boyfriend tonight, and apparently she did. The teenager was dressed casually, in a simple knitted tank and a long flowing skirt that Cameron could easily picture Gabriella wearing. Obviously Sierra had inherited her mother's innate sense of style and—unfortunately, at least from a father's perspective—her ultra-feminine curves.

He wanted to suggest that she put on a sweater but knew she would look at him as if he was crazy. And maybe he was crazy to think that he had any business trying to parent a teenage girl that he'd only met a few weeks earlier. But it was more than a recently developed sense of responsibility that urged him to get to know his daughter, it was—from the moment he'd learned of her existence—an instinctive and irrefutable desire to claim her as his child. To be the type of father to her that he'd had been fortunate enough to have for the first dozen years of his life.

He forced himself to ignore what she was wearing and only said, "Can I come in anyway?"

Her cheeks flushed. "Yes, of course. You can have a seat in the living room. My mom should be down in a few minutes."

"Why don't you wait with me?" he suggested.

"Why would I?"

He wanted to call her on her rudeness, but he gritted his teeth to bite back the instinctive response and shrugged, deliberately casual. "It will give us a chance to get to know one another better."

Sierra paused in the arched entranceway of the living room and turned to face him. "Look, I know you're royalty and you're used to people bowing and curtsying. And I should probably be welcoming and gracious and oh-so-thrilled that you're dating my mother, but the truth is, I don't think you're good enough for her, even if you are a prince."

She spoke bluntly, unapologetically, and he was sure that Gabriella would be appalled if she heard the words coming out of her daughter's mouth. And while Cameron wasn't thrilled by her obvious lack of respect, he couldn't help but admire her strength of character and conviction. "You're probably right."

Her eyes narrowed suspiciously. "You're agreeing with me?"

"I've known your mom a long time," he told her, settling himself onto the sofa. "Although truthfully, in some ways, I hardly know her at all. But I do know that she's an incredible woman and I enjoy spending time with her."

"So that's all this is?" She folded her arms over her chest in a gesture that was so like her mother he had to fight back a smile. "Spending time with her?"

"We're taking things one step at a time," he said cautiously.

She inched a little farther into the room. "She was dating Rafe for almost two years. He asked her to marry him."

"Did you want her to marry him?" The idea sliced him to the quick. It was uncomfortable enough to think of Gabriella with the other man, but to imagine that her daughter—*his* daughter—had approved of that relationship and maybe even looked at the other man as a father figure, was unbearable.

But Sierra hesitated before answering, and he knew that she was considering her response. "I don't want her to be alone," she finally said.

"I don't imagine she thinks of herself as being alone."

"But I'm not going to be living here forever. I've only got two more years of high school and then I'll be going away to college. Hopefully."

Her frown warned that this was a subject of much debate between mother and daughter, and that no final decisions had been made. If it was a matter of finances, Cameron knew that he could alleviate their concerns, but that was hardly a discussion he intended to initiate now.

"And my grandmother's great," she continued. "But, come on, she shouldn't live with her mother forever, either."

He couldn't help but smile at that.

"And she doesn't have a lot of experience with men," Sierra confided. "I mean, I don't even remember her dating anyone, aside from Rafe. And you've dated a ton of women."

His brows rose. "Have you been reading the tabloids?"

"I did some internet research," she said, unapologetically. "And though I'm sure some of the stories are exaggerated, it's obvious that you've been around a lot more than she has."

"You're right," he acknowledged. "And there's probably nothing I can do or say to alleviate your concerns, but I can promise that my only intention tonight is to enjoy a quiet dinner with your mother."

"Okay." Then, almost reluctantly, she added, "She likes to dance. So you could maybe take her dancing, too, if you wanted."

"I'll keep that in mind," he promised.

"Okay," she said again.

The doorbell sounded, and her head turned automatically, her eyes lighting up.

"I need to get that," she said, just as her mother stepped into the room.

Cameron's attention shifted automatically, and his breath caught. Gabriella had put her hair up in some kind of twist and fastened simple gold hoops at her ears. Her make-up was mostly subtle—some shadow to highlight her eyes, a touch of blusher on her cheeks—aside from the mouth-watering red that slicked her lips. It matched the color of her dress, a sleeveless wrap-style of scarlet silk that dipped low between her breasts and clung to every delicious curve. And her feet were encased in shoes of that exact same shade that added almost three inches to her height and drew attention to her long, shapely legs.

Mi Dios, the woman knew how to tempt a man.

And he was more than tempted.

Thankfully, after a quick smile to acknowledge his presence, Gabriella had focused her attention on Sierra, giving him a moment to complete his perusal and recover his composure.

"Twelve o'clock," she reminded her daughter.

Sierra rolled her eyes. "As if I could ever forget."

Gabriella touched her lips gently to her cheek. "Have a good time."

"Yeah, uh, you, too." Sierra glanced past her mother to him, whether in acknowledgement or warning he couldn't be sure, but he knew that she was right to be worried. Because his promise to Sierra aside, one look at Gabriella, and suddenly he was wanting a lot more than dinner.

"You look…exquisite."

Gabriella felt her fingers tremble as the prince kissed her hand, and she hoped Cameron wouldn't notice. She was more nervous than she wanted to admit—like a seventeen-year-old girl on her first date.

"Thank you," she murmured.

He looked wonderful, too. But then again, he always did. The day they'd spent on his yacht, he'd been casually attired in shorts and a T-shirt. Tonight, he was wearing a suit—dark navy in color and conservative in cut. He moved easily, with a fluid grace and inherent dignity, whatever he was wearing and wherever he went.

It hadn't always been like that, she remembered. He'd once chafed at the restrictions that came with being a royal—except when he was outright ignoring them. He'd been the rebel prince, unconcerned with politics and protocol, determined to make his own mark in the world. And often, it had seemed to her as she'd followed his escapades through headlines over the years, desperately unhappy.

He had changed. She didn't doubt that any more. He was more comfortable in his own skin now, happier in his career and with his life. And she was happy for him—and hopeful that he could now be the kind of father her daughter deserved. But she was still unwilling to hope that he could be a part of her life.

He kept her hand in his as he led the way to the door. "Did you need to check in with your mother before we head out?"

She smiled, a little, in response to his gentle teasing. "Usually I would," she agreed. "But she's at her water aerobics class until nine."

"Water aerobics?"

"She loves to bake—and to eat what she bakes—so she does yoga or water aerobics almost every day, sometimes both, to balance it out."

"She sounds very…energetic," he decided.

"She only retired a couple of years ago," Gabriella told him, pausing to lock the door. "Until then, she'd worked two jobs. Having time on her hands was a huge adjustment for her."

"What kind of work did she used to do?"

Gabriella looked at him, surprised by the question. "I

thought you knew—she worked early mornings at the bakery and then cleaned houses the rest of the day."

He helped her into the limo, then settled himself beside her on the wide leather seat. "Why would I know that?"

"Because—" she broke off, shook her head. "It doesn't matter."

"My mother," he guessed flatly.

"I really don't want to talk about this tonight."

"Dammit, Gabriella. I need to know what she did."

"It won't change anything."

"No," he agreed. "But I'm tired of the lies and deceptions. I want the truth."

"When she first came to me, wanting to buy my silence with payment of Sierra's medical expenses, I refused. I believed, naively, that my mother and I would somehow find a way to pay the bills. The very next day, my mother lost her cleaning job at the Gianninis'."

"Elena and Roberta Giannini have been friends—or at least acquaintances—for years," he acknowledged.

She nodded. "And Roberta Giannini was good friends with Arianna Bertuzzi, so if my mother wanted to keep *that* job, I was told I'd better rethink my decision regarding Sierra."

He took both of her hands now. "*Dios,* Gabriella, I can't tell you how sorry I am."

"I hated her for a long time," she admitted. "And I was scared for even longer, afraid that the day might come when she wanted more than my silence."

"You were worried that she would try to take Sierra," he guessed.

"She'd already proven that she had the money and power and influence—all I had was my daughter, but she was everything to me."

He squeezed her hands gently as the limo rolled to a stop. "You were right. Let's try to put this aside for tonight and enjoy our dinner."

"Gladly," Gabriella said, and meant it.

The driver opened the door, and Cameron slid out first, offering his hand to her again.

She hadn't asked where they were going and, looking at the elegantly scripted letters on the huge plate glass window beneath the green-and-white-striped awning, realized now that had been a mistake.

But she never would have guessed—couldn't have guessed. Marconi's wasn't even in business anymore. After a falling-out with his son, Franco, who had moved to San Pedro to open his own restaurant six months earlier, Alonzo Marconi had closed down the business and put the building up for sale.

Cameron gestured for her to precede him up the walk, but Gabriella stood frozen in her tracks. "What are we doing here?"

"We're having dinner," he reminded her.

"But—" she faltered, as she caught a whiff of the tantalizing and familiar scent that drifted on the air.

"I promised to take you someplace where no one would guess we were going and where there would be no paparazzi hiding in the shadows."

"And you thought an abandoned restaurant would fit the bill."

"Not entirely abandoned," he assured her. "Alonzo Marconi himself is behind the stove tonight."

Still, she hesitated. It was obvious that Cameron had gone to quite a bit of trouble to set this up, but she wasn't entirely sure how she felt about this turn of events. She'd told him that the past was over and done, except that a lot of their shared past was now only a few steps away.

Already, just looking at the door, she could hear the familiar jangle of the bell that would sound when it was opened. And she knew that the sound of that bell would tear the lid off of the box of memories she'd worked hard to keep tightly closed.

Memories of the day she'd first met Cameron, the first time he'd kissed her. Memories of hanging out with him after the restaurant closed, talking for long hours or dancing to the music that blared out of the jukebox. Memories of hiding out in the bathroom, fighting against tears, after he'd dumped her, when she'd realized her period was late, and finally—when she'd been fired from her job after confiding to Mrs. Marconi that she was pregnant.

The memories were both plentiful and painful, and she knew that she could avoid them no longer.

Chapter Twelve

As Cameron followed Gabriella through the door, he began to wonder if he'd made a serious miscalculation. He'd thought she would be pleased with the arrangements he'd made, instead, she seemed apprehensive.

On the other hand, she'd seemed apprehensive since she'd agreed to have dinner with him, as if she'd been having second thoughts from the very beginning. But he was hopeful that he could get her to relax. They'd share a good meal together, an excellent bottle of wine, some pleasant conversation, and maybe, when the night was finally over, a good-night kiss.

He turned the key that had been left in the lock, so that no one could wander in off the street and disturb them.

She moved automatically toward the round table in the middle of the room, the only one that was set. The candle, stuffed into a squat wine bottle, had been lit, and the gentle flame illuminated the shine of flatware and the gleam of crystal.

"Something smells good," she said.

He agreed, although what he could smell was her scent, something light and citrusy, decidedly feminine and undeniably sexy.

"My sincere apologies, Your Highness." Alonzo Marconi rushed into the dining room, stopping in front of Cameron to execute a deep bow. "I did not realize you had arrived."

"It's not a problem," Cameron assured him. "And thank you again for your indulgence tonight."

"How could I refuse a personal request from a prince?"

A personal request—and the offer of a significant sum for the retired chef's time and trouble. But it was worth it to Cameron, to guarantee that he and Gabriella would have privacy tonight. He'd made her a promise, and he intended to prove to her that she could trust in his promises.

"You remember Gabriella?" he prompted.

"Of course." Alonzo took both of her hands before kissing her lavishly on each cheek in turn. "*Bella,* you are even more beautiful than I remembered."

"And you are just as charming as I remember," she told him.

"You are well? And your mother and your little girl?" he prompted, as he held out her chair for her.

"We are all very well, thanks. Although Sierra is not a little girl anymore. She had her sixteenth birthday last week."

"*Mi Dios*—where did the years go?"

As Cameron glanced around, he wondered the same thing. The restaurant hadn't changed at all in the six months that it had been closed. In fact, it looked to Cameron that not much had changed in the past sixteen years. Even the layout of the tables was the same, as familiar as the cane-back chairs set around them, the red-and-white-checked tablecloths draped over them and the candles in wine bottles that served as centerpieces for each one. The jukebox was still in the corner, silent now.

It had never been a high-end eating place but was undoubtedly an extremely popular one, having long ago established a reputation for serving quality food at reasonable prices. Primarily marketed as a family restaurant, it had also become a favorite of the college crowd, as it was located within walking distance of the dorms.

"I have the wine you requested," Alonzo told him, hustling over to the bar to retrieve it.

He hurried back, showed Cameron the label. He checked the date, nodded, and Alonzo quickly and efficiently uncorked the bottle. He poured a small amount in the prince's glass, allowing him to test and approve the burgundy before he filled Gabriella's glass. After topping up Cameron's, he set the bottle on the table.

"There is a set menu for this evening," Alonzo announced. "Crostini with basil pesto and tomatoes, followed by linguine with freshly made pomodoro sauce, then a main course of chicken piccata, finishing off with a simple green salad with an olive oil and red wine vinaigrette. And finally, for dessert, warm poached pears sprinkled with goat cheese."

"It sounds perfect," Cameron assured him.

Gradually, as they sipped their wine and nibbled their way through Alonzo's impressive menu, Gabriella began to relax. It helped, Cameron thought, that they talked mostly about Sierra. Although garnering more information about his daughter wasn't the primary purpose for the evening, he looked at the opportunity as a bonus. And Sierra was the one topic of conversation that seemed to break through Gabriella's reserve.

She happily recounted stories of Sierra's childhood, reported on every illness and injury, and detailed all of the important milestones of her first sixteen years until he finally formed a picture, not of the young woman she was now but of the little girl she'd been.

While he smiled at Gabriella's charming retelling of her antics, he was again painfully aware of how very much he'd missed. But he wasn't angry at Gabriella anymore. There was no reason to be. He knew now that he'd missed out on sixteen years of his daughter's life because he'd been too damned selfish and self-absorbed to worry about an ex-girlfriend's concern that she might be pregnant. Okay, so maybe he'd sweated over the possibility for a while. Maybe he'd waited to hear back from her, regarding the results of the pregnancy test. But when she'd failed to contact him again, he'd assumed that she'd been wrong—or that she'd taken care of it. And he'd been selfish and self-absorbed enough to be relieved by that thought.

Gabriella pushed away her salad bowl, the action drawing him away from the uncomfortable memories of his past and back to the much more enjoyable present.

"The whole meal was spectacular," she said. "But I can't possibly eat another bite."

"You have to have room for dessert."

She groaned. "I wish I did. Really. But—"

Her protest trailed off when Alonzo came out with the poached pears. Her eyes shifted to the square plate of neatly arranged pear halves drizzled with a Reisling reduction and sprinkled with goat cheese, and he could tell that she was tempted, at least a little.

"A few bites," he cajoled, after the chef had slipped away again. "So as not to hurt Alonzo's feelings."

"I'll have to start going to water aerobics with my mother," she muttered, but picked up her dessert fork.

He didn't think she needed to worry about indulging in a few desserts, but he refrained from saying so. He knew that kind of comment would catapult them out of neutral conversational territory into the decidedly personal zone and result in all of Gabriella's barriers locking firmly back into place.

She broke off a piece of pear, popped it into her mouth. Her lips closed around the tines of the fork, her eyelids lowered, and she hummed in blissful pleasure. "Mmm."

"That sounds like a positive endorsement," Cameron mused.

She nodded as she chewed, swallowed. "Oh. Wow. It's... fabulous. It's sweet and tart, and the cheese adds a little bit of creamy texture, and the flavors just explode on your tongue."

She sliced off another piece of fruit, held it out to Cameron. It was a spontaneous gesture, certainly not one that was intended to be deliberately seductive. But when his lips parted and she slid the fork between them, they were both suddenly aware of the intimacy of the moment.

She pulled the utensil away, her cheeks flushing. Cameron's eyes remained on hers as he chewed slowly, savoring the bite she'd shared with him. The air nearly crackled with the attraction between them, proving that the illusion of neutrality had been exactly that.

Alonzo bustled in again, offering coffee or tea.

Gabriella tore her gaze from his, and turned to smile at the chef. "Not for me, thanks."

"Nor me," Cameron agreed. "But I think we'll linger for a while, to finish up our dessert and the wine."

"Of course," Alonzo said. "If it's acceptable to you, I will come back tomorrow to finish cleaning up so that you will have some privacy."

Cameron nodded. "We'll lock up when we go. And thank you again."

"My pleasure, Your Highness." He bowed deeply to Cameron, then turned his attention—and a warm smile—to Gabriella. "And it's always a pleasure to see you, *bella*."

"*Grazie, Signor Marconi.*" She touched his hand. "*Grazie per tutto.*"

He captured her fingers and raised her hand to his lips. "*Buona notte.*"

With a last bow, Alonzo slipped away, leaving them alone.

"Do you want to tell me what that was about?" Cameron asked.

"What are you talking about?"

"I'm talking about Alonzo flirting with you—right in front of me."

"He wasn't flirting with me," Gabriella denied.

"It sure looked like that from where I'm sitting—and that you were flirting back."

She shook her head. "I've known Signor Marconi for a long time," she reminded him. "In a lot of ways, he was like a father to me. He gave me more than a job—he gave me advice and guidance and support."

Her gaze shifted away from his, her fingers slid down the stem of her wineglass, traced a slow circle around the perimeter of the base.

"Obviously there's more to the story," he guessed.

"Let's just say that *Signora* Marconi was a little less supportive."

"His wife?"

She nodded. "She fired me. When she found out... Well, she said that this was supposed to be a family restaurant and that it wouldn't do to have an unwed, pregnant teenager waiting on tables.

"Alonzo was furious with her. He didn't approve of my condition any more than she did, but he understood that I needed some way to support myself and my child. So he gave me a new job—washing dishes." Gabriella shrugged. "The money wasn't as good as working in the dining room, but at least it was something."

"I'm sorry," Cameron said. "I brought you here tonight because I'd hoped it would help you remember the good times. I didn't realize how much history you had here."

"Most of it was good times," she said, then her lips curved a little at the edges. "Aside from the occasional night when I had to wait on tables filled with obnoxious college boys."

"You can't be talking about my friends."

"You guys used to take turns paying the bill," she recalled. "And I always knew when it was your friend Andre's turn, because I would find my tip—in nickels and dimes—in the bottom of the beer pitcher."

Cameron winced. "Okay. He was obnoxious. But another one of those guys used to hang around after closing sometimes, staying late to help you clean up—and just to be with you."

She frowned, as if she wasn't sure she remembered what he was talking about, but the teasing sparkle in her eye assured him that she did.

He pushed his chair away from the table and went over to the ancient jukebox against the wall. He dropped some coins into the slot, punched in the numbers from memory. He watched Gabriella as the first unmistakable notes of "Why Can't This Be Love?" filled the air. The half-smile on her lips faded, and every muscle in her body went still.

She'd been a die-hard Van Halen fan and when she'd locked the doors after the last customers had gone, she'd crank up the music and dance around while she wiped down the tables and stacked the chairs. The very first time he'd kissed her, it was this song that had been playing. Thinking about that now, he couldn't help but wonder how it was that he struggled to remember the names of half the women he'd slept with in the past dozen years, but he'd never forgotten a single detail of the time he'd spent with Gabriella.

"Dance with me."

She hesitated.

"Come on," he cajoled. "You don't want to disappoint Sierra."

"How does this have anything to do with Sierra?"

"She suggested that I take you out dancing. I know the ambiance here isn't the same as a club, there's no flashing lights or pulsing bass or—"

"No," she agreed. "This is better." Then she finally put her hand in his.

He drew her gently to her feet. She came willingly, if not quite eagerly. She was still wary, he understood that, so he would content himself with little steps. Right now, all that mattered was that she was in his arms.

It wasn't exactly a slow song, but they'd always danced to it like this, close together. They fell into that same familiar rhythm now, and with each whisper of contact, even the most subtle brush of flesh against flesh, the sparks between them flared hotter.

Less than two and a half minutes into the song, he gave up any pretense of following the music and settled his hands on those seductively swaying hips, pulling her hard against him. Gabriella's eyes widened, but her lips curved, and she lifted her arms to his shoulders.

There was no hesitation when he kissed her this time, and nothing tentative in her response.

Her lips were soft and yielding, deliciously and intoxicatingly familiar. Of course he remembered her taste—he'd kissed her on his yacht only a few days earlier. But he'd remembered her taste even then; he'd been haunted by her scent and her warmth and her passion for years.

There had been a lot of women in and out of his life over the years. Probably too many women. But none of them had ever lingered in his mind or taken hold of his heart the way Gabriella had done.

It was more than the rush of blood through his veins, it was the rush of joy he felt when she smiled at him. It was the way his pulse leapt when she so much as glanced in his direction, the way his heart pounded when she touched a hand to his sleeve. It was the unexpected and undeniable bone-deep contentment and rightness that he'd only ever felt when she was in his arms.

Seventeen years ago, he'd told her that he'd loved her. But

even when he'd said those words to her, even when his heart had felt as if it would burst with happiness when she said them back, he hadn't fully understood what they meant. He hadn't fully appreciated the true depth of his feelings while he was with her—and he certainly hadn't anticipated the intensity of the emptiness he would feel when she was gone.

But she was here with him now, warm and willing, and he had no intention of ever letting her go again.

He combed his fingers through her hair. Pins scattered as the soft mass spilled down onto her shoulders. He'd always loved her hair, the way it looked spread out over his pillow, and the way she looked at him, sleepy-eyed and contented. The image was sharp and vivid in his mind, and he wanted her like that again. Now.

He tore his lips from hers to trail kisses down her throat. He lingered at the racing pulse point at her jaw, and she sighed with pleasure. He moved lower, tracing the deep V at the front of her dress, dipping his tongue into the warm hollow between her breasts. She shuddered but didn't pull away. He found the tie at her waist, released it. There was another tie inside, but he made quick work of that, too, and suddenly his hands were inside the dress, on her bare, quivering flesh.

A quick glimpse of the red lace bikini panties and matching bra had him groaning aloud. She was so lush and perfect and...his. He backed her up against the jukebox and curled his hands around her buttocks, lifting her off of the ground. She braced her back against the machine and wrapped her legs around him, pressing herself more intimately against him, and he groaned again as all the blood rushed from his head.

He unfastened the front clasp of her bra, letting her breasts spill free. He filled his hands with them, brushed his thumbs over the tightly-beaded nipples, and she gasped. He captured her mouth again, his tongue sliding between her lips, tangling with hers. Her hands were in his hair now, and the way she was kissing him back and pressing against him left him in absolutely no doubt that she wanted the same thing he did.

There was no one else around. Alonzo had gone, the door was locked, and the blinds were drawn on all the windows. There was no danger of anyone seeing inside, no fear of anyone interrupting them, and he needed her desperately.

But he'd been careless with her before. So focused on his own wants that he'd barely considered hers. He'd been so hot for her that he'd taken her virginity in the backseat of his car. He had more finesse now, and a hell of a lot more self-control. Usually.

Somehow being with Gabriella undermined all of his best intentions. She made him forget that he wanted to do the right thing this time and simply made him want. But he wasn't going to take her standing up against an old jukebox. Or laid out on top of a checkered tablecloth. He reprimanded himself for the alternate suggestion that immediately sprang to mind. And so, with unbelievable reluctance, he lifted his head from her breast and refastened the clip at the front of her bra.

"Gabriella—"

She pulled away from him, her fingers trembling as she pulled at the ties of her dress. "Don't say it."

"Say what?"

"Anything." She tugged at the bodice, settling the material back into place, and shook her head. "I can't believe how pathetic I am."

He heard the tears in her voice, as baffling as her words.

"What are you talking about?"

"Your mother was right—I am a slut. Maybe I've never slept around, but I've never been able to control my responses to you, either."

He stared at her, stunned not by what his mother had said but that she could possibly believe it. "*Mi Dios,* Gabriella. Allowing yourself to feel passion doesn't mean you're a…"

He trailed off, unable to even say the word. "It doesn't mean you're indiscriminate, it only means you're human."

"I almost let you seduce me in the middle of a restaurant." She had tears on her cheeks now and her eyes were filled with misery. "Is that why you brought me here?" she asked him now. "Did you figure I'd put out as easily now as I did seventeen years ago?"

"I didn't plan for this to happen," he told her.

She made a sound of disbelief as she finished tugging her skirt into place.

"But I'm not sorry. Because what just happened proves that the chemistry between us is as volatile now as it was seventeen years ago."

"It's not chemistry, it's hormones," she said derisively, but he sensed that she was more angry with herself than with him.

"Why are you so determined to fight this?" he asked gently.

"Because I don't do things like this." She swiped impatiently at another tear that slid down her cheek.

He tucked a lock of hair behind her ear. "Things like what?"

"Let myself be overcome by lust," she snapped at him.

She was trying to make the intimacy they'd just shared into less than it was, but he wasn't going to let her. "It's not about 'letting' when the attraction between two people is as strong as it is between us." He touched a hand to her face. "I've never felt this way with anyone else—before or after you."

"Are we done here?" she asked him.

He sighed. "And you're never going to give me another chance, are you?"

"Another chance for what?"

"To make a relationship between us work."

"We never had a relationship, we had sex."

"I loved you."

"Yeah, you made that clear when you dumped me after the weekend we spent together."

"I was young and stupid—"

"It doesn't matter," she said wearily. "Not the when or the why, because the truth is, the break-up was inevitable. Aside from the fact that we were both too young to have a clue about what we were doing, you're a blue-blood royal and I'm a working-class single mother."

"The mother of *my* child."

"Which might be my ticket to five minutes of fame but isn't going to lead to some kind of happily-ever-after."

"Not if you refuse to even consider the possibility."

She folded her arms over her chest, the action telling him more definitively than any words that she wouldn't be swayed, but she only said, "I need to be home before midnight."

"I'll have Lucien bring the car around."

Chapter Thirteen

Gabriella was on the back porch, watching the stars, when Sierra got home. While the midnight curfew was a matter of frequent debate between them, her daughter didn't seem to be holding a grudge tonight. Instead of ignoring her mother and going straight to her room, as she had a habit of doing when she was annoyed, she sat down on the step beside her.

"How was your date?" she asked.

"It was…" Gabriella wasn't quite sure how to respond. Both "wonderful" and "awful" were appropriate answers to the question, but either one would inevitably lead to more questions that she wasn't prepared to answer. So she only said, "Fine."

"Fine?" Sierra's brow furrowed. "Mom—if he can't do better than "fine," then you're wasting your time."

"Okay, it was better than fine," she allowed, not daring to let herself think about how much better specific parts of the evening had been. Specifically when her parts had been in close contact with his parts—

No, not going to think about those parts, she reminded herself sternly.

"Are you in love with him?"

Sierra's question startled her out of her reverie. She managed a laugh. "Love? Sierra, I've only been seeing him for a few weeks."

"But you've known him a long time, right?"

She nodded, because it was easier than explaining that she wasn't sure if she'd ever really known him at all.

"Did you date him?" Sierra prompted. "You know, when you knew him before?"

"Yes," Gabriella admitted, because while she'd never volunteered much information about her past, she'd never lied to Sierra, either. "For a little while."

"What went wrong?"

And how to answer that question without opening the floodgates? she wondered.

But maybe it was time to stop worrying about protecting Sierra and finally tell her the truth—to tell her that Prince Cameron Leandres of Tesoro del Mar was her father.

"We wanted different things from one another," she began, trailing off as she heard the sound of footsteps on the gravel driveway.

She glanced at her watch, noted that it was half past midnight. Sierra, obviously having heard the footsteps, too, was frowning. And they both jolted when a figure came around the side of the house.

Katarina stopped with her foot on the bottom step, her eyes wide. "What are you two doing out here at this time of night?" she demanded imperiously.

"I'd say the real question is what are *you* doing coming home at this time of night?" Gabriella countered. "Your car was in the driveway—I assumed you were home and in bed."

Katarina tilted her chin. "Well, you assumed wrong. As it turns out, I had a date tonight, too."

"With whom?" Gabriella demanded.

"With Dominic Donatella. Because I decided that I wasn't going to let him seduce the secrets of my buttercream icing out of me but I didn't mind if he seduced *me*."

"Go, Grandma," Sierra said approvingly.

Gabriella just shook her head. "Go to bed, Sierra."

Her daughter exhaled a long-suffering sigh, but she pushed herself to her feet, dropping a kiss first on her mother's cheek, then her grandmother's.

"Details over breakfast?" she whispered to Katarina.

"Not likely," her grandmother replied, but with an indulgent smile.

"I think I'm going to go to bed, too," Gabriella said, following her daughter toward the house.

"Have a cup of tea with me first," her mother urged. "I'm too wired to sleep right now."

Gabriella held up a hand. "Please, spare me the details."

Katarina picked up the kettle from the stove, filled it from the tap. "Obviously your date wasn't as…satisfying…as mine," she teased.

"No, I only *almost* had sex," Gabriella grumbled.

"That would explain your lousy mood," Katarina acknowledged.

"I should never have agreed to this dating charade. At first, it seemed like a legitimate way to explain why Cameron was hanging around while giving him some time to get to know Sierra. I didn't really think there would be any dating involved."

"And now you're worried that the lines between reality and fantasy are getting blurred," her mother guessed, all teasing forgotten.

Gabriella sighed, nodded.

"How do you feel about him?"

"I don't know. I don't know anything anymore."

"He's an attractive man," Katarina acknowledged. "A prince. And you were in love with him once before."

"A long time ago."

"Are you saying that you don't still have feelings for him?"

"I don't know. I mean, when I'm with him, he stirs up all kinds of feelings that I'd thought were dead and buried. I'm attracted to him," she admitted, although it made her blush to say the words aloud to her mother. Ridiculous, she knew, considering that her fifty-seven-year-old mother apparently didn't have any qualms about sharing the details of her sex life.

"But?" Katarina prompted.

Gabriella sighed. "But I don't know if I'm making those feelings into more than they are because I'm afraid of losing Sierra."

Her mother poured boiling water into the pot. "You're going to have to connect the dots for me."

"At first I was just going through the motions—letting Cameron hang around because I was sure that he would lose interest in playing daddy. But I've realized that he is serious about wanting to acknowledge Sierra as his daughter, and it's only a matter of time before he does so publicly. And when that happens, everything will change—for all of us, but mostly for Sierra. She will be a princess with royal duties and responsibilities, and I won't be able to help her with any of that. But if I'm with Cameron, well, it would ensure that I was able to stay close to her."

"Do you really think you could be that calculating?"

"Haven't I already proven that I will do anything for my daughter—even going so far as to keep her existence a secret from her own father for sixteen years?"

"Because the princess royal gave you no choice. Sierra

needed surgery, and she would only pay the hospital bills if you promised not to tell the prince about his child."

Gabriella nodded. "That's how I justified it to myself," she agreed. "But maybe it wasn't that simple. Maybe not telling Cameron about Sierra was a way of punishing him for dumping me."

"No one could blame you for being hurt or angry."

"But that doesn't justify using him for my own purposes now."

Katarina reached across the table to cover her daughter's hand with her own. "Are you really afraid that you're using him—or more afraid that you're not?"

"I can't fall for him again." Gabriella shook her head. "I won't."

"You say that with such conviction, as if you believe it."

"Because I do. Because it's true."

"Then you haven't learned anything at all in the past seventeen years," Katarina told her. "Because the mind does not and cannot control the heart."

Elena was growing weary of these late-night meetings, not so much the hour as the lack of results. In fact, she'd been more than a little tempted to cancel this one when she'd received Reynard's text message. "I think I've got something."

Elena had been as annoyed as she'd been intrigued. Her chief of security had been with her a long time, and he knew that she wanted results, not vague promises. Either he had something or he didn't—she wasn't interested in his thoughts.

Still, she was curious enough to keep the meeting, and she was waiting when Reynard appeared at the door precisely on schedule.

He knew her well enough not to waste any time on small talk, and as he made his way toward her desk, she could see that he had a small recording device in his hand. A touch of his thumb to one of the buttons and voices filled the silence.

Elena listened, definitely more intrigued than annoyed now. And when the playback finally ended, she nodded. "Yes, that should serve my purposes."

"Shall I arrange for a copy to be sent to his office?" Reynard asked.

She considered the idea for only a brief moment before discarding it. There wasn't a lot of time—with each day that passed, Gabriella was sinking her claws deeper and deeper into Cameron. Even though Elena had tried to warn her son about the kind of woman he was keeping company with, he'd refused to listen. His refusal had left Elena with no choice. She would do what was necessary to pull those claws free and if Cameron was left with scars, well, he would have no one to blame but himself.

"No," she finally responded to Reynard's question. "I'll deliver it to him personally."

Gabriella sat alone, thinking over her mother's words long after Katarina had gone up to bed.

She was right, of course. Not just about the fact that Gabriella couldn't stop herself from falling in love with Cameron again, but that the real root of her fear was the knowledge that she was already more than halfway there.

She should know better. She should have learned her lesson. But even if she didn't believe his claim that he'd loved her seventeen years ago, she did believe that he wasn't the same man now that he'd been then. And maybe, if he really did want a second chance and was willing to try to make a relationship between them work, Gabriella could make the effort, too.

She was scared, because there was so much more at stake now than just her heart. There was Sierra to think about—their daughter who didn't yet know that Cameron was her father.

There's no reward without risk, she reminded herself, and picked up the phone.

She faltered when she heard his voice on the other end. She hadn't expected him to answer, had anticipated leaving a message on his voice mail.

"I know it's late," she said.

"It's okay," he assured her. "I was still awake."

"Okay. Well, I, uh, wanted to apologize, for some of the things I said tonight."

"That's not necessary," he told her.

"It is," she insisted. "I was feeling emotional and vulnerable, and I lashed out at you."

"And I was pushing for too much too soon," he acknowledged.

"Maybe. A little." She blew out a breath. "Anyway, I thought maybe I could make it up to you, by inviting you to come over here for dinner. Tomorrow night."

"I thought you didn't cook."

"I didn't say I would cook, I said I would provide dinner. Actually, I thought I might be able to cajole my mother into cooking," she admitted. "But she's going away for the weekend, which means that I'll probably get takeout."

"Well, that's an intriguing offer," he said.

But he didn't immediately accept or decline, and Gabriella found herself babbling again. "It's short notice, I know. I should have realized that you probably already have plans. Or a date."

He laughed, although it sounded more strained than amused. "*Dios,* Gabriella, I don't have a date."

"Oh. Well."

"I was just…caught off guard by your invitation."

"It was an impulse," she admitted. "Probably a bad idea. Maybe we should just forget that I called."

"No way," he told her. "Just tell me what time tomorrow and I'll be there."

"Six? Seven? Whatever works for you," she said. "Although Sierra's going to a party with some friends tomorrow night, so if you want to see her, maybe you should come a little earlier."

"Earlier than six?"

"No, six would be fine."

"Then I'll see you at six," he promised.

"Okay."

She hung up the phone and wiped her damp palms on her skirt. She'd sounded like an idiot—worse, a babbling incoherent idiot. And yet, she had another date for tomorrow night.

She drew out a shaky breath and pressed a hand to her hammering heart. She was excited and terrified and determined. If this was her second chance, she was going to grab hold of it with both hands.

Cameron wasn't sure what had precipitated Gabriella's phone call, and he didn't care. He was just grateful that they seemed to have turned a corner, that she was finally willing to give him a second chance. He woke up the next morning with a smile that carried him through most of the day. The only snag was an early-afternoon visit from his mother.

There had been a time when he'd believed that Elena wanted only the best for him. He was no longer as trusting or naive, and he understood now that every action the princess royal performed and every word she spoke were carefully calculated to promote her own agenda. As she demonstrated with the recording she'd delivered to him that afternoon in an attempt to alter his intentions with respect to Gabriella and Sierra.

He'd been shocked to hear Gabriella's voice—and stunned by the words she spoke.

I will do anything for my daughter, even letting Cameron hang around. But I'm using him for my own purposes now, punishing him for dumping me. I won't fall for him again.

Elena claimed that Gabriella had spoken those words during a conversation with her mother, and listening to his own mother, he'd actually felt physically ill. Not because he believed what she was telling him, but because he was appalled by her actions. She insisted that she was only trying to protect him, but he saw the truth now: she was trying to control him, and she didn't give a damn about anyone else who might get hurt in the process.

She'd decided—for whatever reason so many years ago—that Gabriella wasn't a suitable partner for her son and she was going to do everything in her power to keep them apart. Apparently that included planting audio surveillance devices in Gabriella's home. When he confronted her, she neither denied nor apologized for her actions, insisting that she only wanted him to know what kind of vengeful, vindictive woman Gabriella really was.

Cameron had snapped the disk in half and told his mother to get out of his house. Then, when he'd verified that Gabriella and her mother and daughter were all out for the afternoon, he'd sent his own security team over to locate and remove the bugs. They'd found one in the kitchen, one in the living room, and one in Gabriella's bedroom.

On his way to Gabriella's house later that day, he tried to push all thoughts of Elena's lies and machinations from his mind. When Sierra opened the door and greeted him with a tentative smile, his heart actually felt as if it was expanding inside his chest.

And he finally realized that Gabriella was right—that the mistakes of the past didn't matter half as much as the gift of the present. Even though it was apparent that Sierra was ready to walk out the door as he was coming in, her smile confirmed that he was making progress with his daughter, and that was enough for now.

"Hi, Cameron. Bye, Cameron." She smiled again, then kissed her mother's cheek. "Bye, Mom."

But Gabriella held up a hand, halting her daughter's movement toward the door. "What's in the backpack?"

"My pajamas, toothbrush, a change of clothes."

"Because?"

"I'm staying at Jenna's tonight, remember?"

"I remember you asking if you could stay at Jenna's," Gabriella acknowledged. "And I remember telling you that I didn't think it was a good idea."

"Come on, Mom." Sierra cast a glance in Cameron's direction, as if to remind her mother that he was there, probably hoping she wouldn't want to argue in front of her guest.

But Gabriella shook her head. "Not tonight."

"Why not?"

"Because I wouldn't have any way of knowing what time you got back to Jenna's—or even if you did."

"I'll call you at midnight."

"No, you'll be back here by midnight," Gabriella insisted.

"You don't trust me," Sierra accused.

"If I didn't trust you, you wouldn't be going to the party at all," her mother told her.

"This is so unfair."

"Twelve o'clock," Gabriella said again.

"Do you realize that I'm the only one who has to be home by midnight?"

"Do you realize that I don't care what rules other parents set for their children? I only care about you."

"My life sucks," Sierra grumbled.

"I'm sure, from your perspective, it does," Gabriella agreed. "But for tonight, you have one of two choices. You can go to the party and be home by midnight, or you can not go to the party at all."

Sierra dumped her backpack on the ground. "Yeah, like that's really a choice."

"If you want to invite Paolo to come back here with you, I'm okay with that."

"Because Paolo's really going to want to leave the party at midnight."

"Obviously that's his choice."

"Yeah—*his* choice," Sierra repeated. "Because his parents don't treat him like a child."

"Maybe because he's eighteen years old and doesn't have temper tantrums like a child."

Sierra's eyes narrowed on her mother. She looked both angry enough and tempted to stamp her foot, but of course, that would only prove Gabriella right. Instead, the teenager turned on her heel and slammed the door as she went out.

Gabriella sighed, then turned to him with a rueful smile. "And that was the entertainment portion of the evening," she said lightly.

"Entertaining and enlightening," he said, matching her tone.

"Does it make you have second thoughts about wanting to take on the task of parenting a sixteen-year-old girl?"

"No," he said. "It only makes me admire you all the more."

"You're kidding."

He shook his head. "Every time I look at her, I'm absolutely awed and amazed to think that I had any part in her creation. But all I did was contribute to her DNA. And as stubborn and willful and downright scary as she can be at times, she's also a great kid, and that's entirely your doing."

Her smile wobbled, just a little. "Thanks. It's hard, sometimes, trying to enforce boundaries for her own protection when she insists on pushing against them."

"Do you really think her request to spend the night at her friend's house was just a ruse?"

"I know it," she said. "Because I was a teenager once, too, and I came up with all kinds of excuses to stay out past my curfew or spend the night with a friend in order to be with you."

He frowned. "How old were you, exactly?"

"Seventeen."

He scrubbed his hands over his face. "You were barely older than that child who just walked out the door."

"I was old enough to know what I wanted," Gabriella assured him. "And you were everything to me. I would have done almost anything to be with you."

"I don't think I'd ever been as completely infatuated with anyone as I was with you," Cameron confided. "From the very first time my friends and I went into Marconi's and you walked out of the kitchen, weaving your way between the tightly packed tables with a pizza tray held over your head, I was smitten."

"You were obnoxious."

"Andre was obnoxious," he reminded her. "I was just desperate to get your attention."

She smiled at the memory. "You succeeded."

"I ate a lot of pizza over the next few weeks, just so that I'd have an excuse to see you and talk to you."

"I didn't mind—you never skipped out on your bill and always left a decent tip."

"And still, you kept refusing to go out with me."

"I didn't understand why you kept asking," she admitted. "It was so obvious to me that you were way out of my league."

"You were so beautiful." He stroked a hand over her hair, let his fingers sift through the silky ends. "You *are* so beautiful."

"And you're still way out of my league," she said, sounding regretful.

"Don't you remember how good we were together?"

"Good is a valuation," she hedged. "And I didn't have any experience to judge it against."

"Then you'll have to trust my judgment, and believe me when I say that we had fabulous chemistry."

"We're not kids anymore," she said. "And now we have a kid to think about, which makes this a lot more complicated now than it was all those years ago."

"So tell me to go." He dipped his head and brushed his lips against hers, softly, fleetingly. "Tell me to go, and mean it, and I'll turn around and walk right out that door."

The tip of her tongue touched her bottom lip. "I invited you to come for dinner," she reminded him. "It would be rude to tell you to go without even feeding you."

"I don't care about dinner."

"I was going to order Thai."

"Tell me to go," he said again. "Or ask me to stay. But be sure you know what you want."

He saw the indecision in her eyes. Desire warring with caution; hope battling with fear. He understood her hesitation. They were at a crossroads, and if they went forward from here, there would be no going back.

She lifted a hand, laid her palm over his chest where his heart was beating fast and hard against his ribs.

"You," she finally said. "I want you."

Then her hand slid up to cup the back of his head, drawing his mouth down to hers so that she could whisper against his lips, "Stay."

Chapter Fourteen

Cameron's heart pounded hard against his ribs. Once, twice, as his mind absorbed her response. "You're sure?"

He couldn't believe he was asking the question. But the first time, he hadn't given her a choice. He'd seduced her thoroughly and completely, so that she'd been incapable of refusing what he wanted, what he needed.

He needed her no less now, but he also needed to know that the choice was hers and one made freely and without hesitation.

"I'm sure," she promised, and held out her hand.

He linked his fingers with hers and let her lead him up the stairs to her bedroom. The door was open, as were the pair of windows that flanked the gaslight-style double bed, and light, gauzy curtains waved in the gentle breeze. On the opposite wall, there were two mismatched dressers, with photos of Sierra hanging above. He didn't take in any other details—he was focused only on Gabriella.

She'd paused in the center of the room, and was looking

at him uncertainly. He raised their still-joined hands to press his lips to her palm, and felt her tremble.

"I feel like I'm seventeen again," she said, her voice little more than a whisper. "The way my heart is pounding and my knees are shaking."

He pressed her palm to his chest again, so that she would know that his heart was pounding, too. "I feel as if I've been waiting for you forever."

His lips brushed over hers, softly, testing.

Her eyelids drifted down on a sigh.

He took his time. Even if this was what they both wanted, he didn't want to rush. Not this time. Instead, he lingered on her mouth, sampling, nibbling, savoring her uniquely exotic flavor. When he finally slid his tongue between her lips, a low hum of pleasure sounded in her throat, and he took the kiss deeper.

It was only when his hands moved to the top button of her blouse that she started to draw back.

"I should pull down the shades," she said.

"Why?"

"Because it feels strange to be taking my clothes off with the sun streaming in the window."

"You don't have any neighbors close enough to peek in," he said, brushing his lips against hers again. "And I want to see you. Every inch of you. Gloriously naked."

"Now I'm really nervous," she admitted.

"Only because you're thinking. So stop thinking," he instructed, and kissed her again.

It was a long, deep kiss that completely and effectively wiped all thought from her mind. She wasn't thinking anymore, she wasn't capable of thinking anymore, only feeling. She could feel her heart pounding, she could feel the heat that pulsed in her veins, and she could feel the desperate, aching need that spread through her body.

This time, when he started to unfasten her buttons, she didn't even think of stopping him. When he pushed the blouse off of her shoulders, the balmy air caressed her skin, raising goosebumps on her flesh. Then he wrapped his arms around her waist, pulling her tight against his body, and all she felt was heat.

He ran his hands over her shoulders, down her arms. She tugged his shirt out of his pants, anxious to touch him as he was touching her. Her hands fumbled, just a little, as she worked at his buttons. When she had most of them unfastened, he tugged it over his head and tossed it aside.

Her hands splayed over his chest, relishing the feel of solid, warm flesh beneath her palms, and the strong, steady beat of his heart. Her hands slid lower, tracing the hard ridges of his abdomen, then lower still.

Within minutes, they were both naked, but as eager as she was for the joining of their bodies, she didn't want to rush a single moment of their time together. Cameron must have felt the same way, because he didn't immediately move toward the bed but seemed content to keep kissing her, touching her, teasing her.

When he finally lowered her onto the bed, the old mattress protested with a creak and a groan that jolted Gabriella back to reality. What was she thinking—making love with him here? He was used to being with glamorous women in exclusive penthouse hotel rooms, making love on top of sheets that probably cost more than all of her bedroom furniture combined. He was a prince and she—

The thought drifted away as his hands stroked over her, shooting arrows of pleasure streaking across her skin. Yeah, he was a prince, but he was here with her now, and that was all that mattered.

He worked his way from the top of her head to the tips of her toes, exploring and arousing every single inch of her. He used his hands and his lips and his body until she was panting with want, aching with need, and willing to beg. He took her to the sharpest edge of pleasure and then, finally, over. Her body was still trembling with the aftershocks when he drove into her, sending a whole new wave of sensation crashing through her system. Her hands clutched at his shoulders, her legs anchored around his hips. She felt as if she could drown in the pleasure he was giving her, and she gloried in it.

She cried out, her nails digging into his flesh as her body tightened around him, dragging him into the storm of sensation along with her.

He held her in his arms. As the last of the sun's rays faded from the sky, plunging the room into darkness, he continued to hold her. Her head was nestled against his shoulder, her arm draped across his belly—until his stomach grumbled, loudly.

"We skipped dinner, didn't we?"

"I wasn't hungry before," he said, his hand stroking down her back. "Except for you."

She tilted her head back to look at him. "And now?"

"Now, I'm starving," he admitted.

So they ordered the Thai food she'd promised him earlier. Then, refueled and re-energized, they went back to her bedroom and made love again.

"I missed you," he said, somehow finding it easier to speak the truth in the darkness. "I don't think I realized how much until I saw you again."

"While I appreciate the sentiment—"

"You don't believe me," he guessed.

"Cameron, I went to see you less than a month after the weekend we spent together and you didn't even remember my name."

"That's not true," he told her. "I only pretended not to remember your name."

"Why would you do something like that?" He heard the skepticism in her tone and ached for the hurt he'd caused.

"Because I didn't want to admit—even to myself—how much you meant to me. In only a couple of months, you'd gotten under my skin, wholly and completely. When I got home after saying goodbye to you at the end of that weekend, all I could think about was seeing you again."

"And I'm supposed to believe that's why you never called?" she asked dubiously.

"I know it sounds crazy—"

She didn't deny it.

"—but you have to understand how unusual that was for me. I was a royal—and I'd become so accustomed to having women throw themselves at me, I felt as if that was a birthright as much as my title.

"You were different, right from the start. I'd never felt about anyone else the way I felt about you, and the depth of those feelings terrified me. I was sure that if I just took a step back, I'd realize you weren't any different from any other girl I'd been with."

"That's flattering," she said dryly.

"But I was wrong," he told her. "The longer I stayed away, the more I missed you. And the harder I tried to deny my own feelings. When you showed up at the college that day—I was so thrilled to see you, and equally determined to play it cool. And then, when you told me you thought you might be pregnant...well, that panic was very real."

"I was feeling a little panicked myself."

He stroked his hand over her hair. "I'm so sorry."

"I'm not," she said. "I was hurt and angry for a long time, but once I got past that—or mostly past it, anyway—I was more grateful than anything else. Because Sierra truly was a blessing. I was young and alone and terrified, but I knew I had to get it together for her. She gave my life a focus—everything I did, I did for her."

"You put your own life on hold to raise our daughter while I was raising hell around the globe," he realized.

"We each have our hobbies," she said lightly.

He brushed a strand of hair off of her cheek. "When is it going to be time for you?"

"Well, I kind of think *this* was for me," she teased, trailing a finger down his chest, then beneath the covers and lower still.

She closed her fingers around him, and his eyes nearly crossed. "Yeah, that's definitely for you," he told her.

"Show me," she whispered against his lips.

It was a request he couldn't—and didn't want to—refuse.

A sound from downstairs stirred Gabriella from the depths of slumber. Her eyes went automatically to the clock on the small table beside her bed, though she had to squint to focus on the glowing numbers. When the time finally registered, she jolted from half-asleep to wide-awake in two seconds, but it was two seconds too late.

"Mom?" Sierra's voice was followed immediately by her footsteps.

Gabriella swore and pushed back the covers. Her clothes were still scattered on the floor, so she grabbed her robe off the hook on the back of her door.

"I'll just be—"

She was going to say "a minute" but Sierra, accustomed to an open-door policy, didn't wait for the rest of her response but stepped into the room.

Gabriella had just finished fastening the belt on her robe, and her daughter automatically apologized. "I didn't think you'd be asleep already."

"I wasn't asleep. Not yet." She tried to move out of the room, to steer her daughter back into the hall before her eyes adjusted to the dark enough to realize that there was someone still in her mother's bed.

She didn't know if Cameron had awakened, but if he had, she trusted that he would quickly assess the situation and stay quiet until Sierra was out of the room. She didn't anticipate an untimely phone call.

"What was that?" Sierra asked, obviously not recognizing the ring-tone.

She blew out a breath. "Cameron's cell phone."

Sierra's jaw dropped open. "Cameron's here?"

Gabriella took her daughter firmly by the shoulders and steered her out into the hall.

"Oh. My. God." Sierra stared at her, obviously stunned and hurt and furious. "You are *such* a hypocrite."

"I'm an adult," Gabriella said sharply. "And I don't have to explain myself to you."

"So it's okay for you and Cameron to spend the night banging the headboard against the wall while I'm watching the clock at the party to ensure I'm home by my twelve-o'clock curfew because *you* don't trust *me* to stay out with my boyfriend any later than that?"

"That's enough, Sierra." It was Cameron who spoke this time, and there was steel beneath his quiet tone.

Sierra spun to face him. "This is between me and my mother. You have no right—"

"I have more rights than you know," he told her.

"Because you're a prince?" She practically sneered the question at him.

He met her gaze evenly. "Because I'm your father."

Sierra felt as if all the air had been sucked out of her lungs.

She stared at him, unable to think or breathe. She couldn't believe it—it couldn't be true. She looked to her mother, silently seeking confirmation—or maybe she was hoping that Gabriella would deny his outrageous statement.

"Is it—" She had to swallow. "Is it true?"

Gabriella glanced at Cameron. Sierra had been on the receiving end of that look often enough to know what it meant—it was a silent reprimand to him, and a wordless confirmation for her.

"Oh. My. God." She had to lean back against the wall because her knees were suddenly feeling too weak and trembly to support her.

"Why don't we go downstairs to talk about this?" Gabriella suggested.

Sierra didn't want to go downstairs. She didn't want to talk about it. She didn't want it to be true. And yet, while her brain scrambled desperately for any other explanation, the heart that had always ached for a father urged her to believe.

Gabriella put a hand on her daughter's shoulder. "Sierra?"

She pushed away from the wall and started down the stairs.

While Gabriella busied herself making tea, Sierra tried to wrap her head around the possibility that Prince Cameron Leandres might actually be her father. She shook her head. It was too outrageous to believe.

She waited until her mother had brought the pot and cups to the table, then she asked, "Are you sure?"

Gabriella's cheeks flooded with color. "Of course, I'm sure. I was never with anyone else."

She turned to Cameron. "So you seduced a virgin and then abandoned her when she got pregnant?"

"I wouldn't have described the situation exactly like that," he said, "but that's essentially the truth."

She was surprised that he didn't try to paint the facts to present his actions in a more favorable light. Surprised and wary. "So why are you here now? It's been sixteen years."

"Because I want a chance to get to know you, to be a father to you."

"And how is sleeping with my mother supposed to accomplish that?"

"Sierra." Her mother's tone was sharp, and the glance she sent in Cameron's direction this time was apologetic.

"Well, at least I know now why you were always so tight-lipped when I asked any questions about my father," Sierra said to her. "It would have been embarrassing for you if I'd gone to school in the second grade and told my friends that my father was a prince. I mean, who would have believed it?"

"I've always tried to be honest with you," Gabriella said.

"If you'd really wanted to be honest, you would have told me who my father was when I asked. Instead, I got a song and dance about how he was someone you'd known a long time ago, someone you really cared about but who wasn't ready to be a father."

"All of which was true," her mother insisted.

"And suddenly he's ready and I'm supposed to be the happy, dutiful daughter? Well, you can forget that," she said. "I don't want or need a father now."

"Whether you like it or not, I am your father," Cameron told her.

"I don't like it," she decided. "And the way I see it, you weren't really anything more than a sperm donor."

His eyes narrowed dangerously, and Sierra shifted in her seat, suddenly nervous that she might have pushed him too far.

That she might have pushed him away.

"I think it might be a good idea to continue this discussion another time," Gabriella interjected. "Maybe in a few days…"

"Maybe in a few years," Sierra muttered.

Gabriella sighed. "Why don't you go up to bed? We'll talk in the morning."

Sierra wasn't sure how she felt about being so obviously dismissed, but she was grateful for the opportunity to escape.

She needed time and space to get her head around everything. But as she moved into the hall, she heard Cameron say, "I'm leaving for Rome tomorrow."

"Rome?"

Sierra hesitated, because in her mother's single-word response, she heard both surprise and suspicion.

"That was my secretary on the phone earlier," he explained. "I had some meetings scheduled for the end of the month that needed to be brought forward to accommodate the prime minister's vacation."

"And he called you after midnight on a Saturday to apprise you of the details?" Gabriella asked skeptically.

Sierra was blatantly eavesdropping now, but she didn't care.

"I told him to let me know as soon as the plans had been finalized," Cameron explained.

"Well, then." Sierra heard the scrape of chair legs on the tile floor, could picture her mother pushing away from the table. "You should be getting home to pack."

"I'm sure my valet has taken care of that already."

"Of course," she acknowledged coolly. "I should have realized you'd have someone to take care of those kinds of details for you."

Cameron finally seemed to clue in that something was up. "Why are you mad at me?"

"I'm not mad at you," Gabriella said wearily. "I'm kicking myself for being an idiot. Again."

"You think I'm going to Italy because we slept together? I got what I wanted and now I'm leaving the country to get away from you?"

"It wouldn't be the first time."

"I thought we'd moved past this, Gabriella. Yes, I treated you badly. I was a selfish and self-centered twenty-year-old who didn't think about anyone else. As a result, I missed out on the first sixteen years of my daughter's life, and it's quite possible she will never forgive me for that. But right now, I'm trying to focus on the future rather than the past—a future that I want to spend with you."

Gabriella's only response was to ask, "How long will you be gone?"

He blew out a breath. "Three weeks. After Italy, I'm going to France then Germany and Switzerland."

Sierra took a step forward. She was still hidden in the shadows but could partly see into the room, and she saw Cameron take her mother's hands in his.

"Come with me," he said.

Gabriella blinked, clearly stunned by the invitation. "What?"

"Come with me," he said again. "We could ride in a Venetian gondola and climb to the top of the Eiffel tower, catch a performance at the Frankfurt Opera and visit the Palais des Nations in Geneva."

"I thought it was a business trip."

"If you came, it would be business and pleasure."

She shook her head. "I have responsibilities here, I can't just take off on a whim—"

"If you really wanted to, we could make it work," Cameron insisted.

She didn't respond.

He made his way to the door, paused with his hand on the knob. "Maybe I am the one who's leaving, but you're the one who's running this time."

Gabriella stared at the door for a long moment after he'd gone. When she finally turned away, Sierra fled, silently tiptoeing up the stairs, trying not to think about the tears she'd seen shimmering in her mother's eyes.

Elena had a copy of Cameron's itinerary on top of her desk, so she knew that he was already on his way to Rome. He had a welcome dinner with the prime minister later tonight and meetings scheduled for the next several days after that.

She had hoped that it wouldn't come to this, but her son had left her no choice. She picked up the phone and called Reynard.

"It's time to get this started."

Chapter Fifteen

Sierra hid out in her room most of Sunday. Katarina came home from her weekend with Dominic later that evening, and Gabriella stayed awake all night second-guessing her refusal to go to Italy with Cameron.

She'd never been to Italy. Actually, aside from one trip to New York City with Rafe, she'd never been outside of Tesoro del Mar. She frowned at the thought, surprised by the realization that it was the first time she'd thought of Rafe since she'd said goodbye to him more than three weeks earlier. She'd thought she was in love with him, she'd even considered marrying him, and less than a month later, she was twisted up in knots over some other guy.

Okay, so Cameron was more than that. He'd been her first lover, the first man she'd ever loved, maybe the *only* man she'd ever loved. And the man she *still* loved.

She dropped her head down on her desk, banged it against the wood, as if the action might knock some sense into her. How was that possible? How could she still love him? And how could she have only realized it now, after she'd sent him away?

If she'd had qualms about her decision on Sunday, it was nothing compared to the fears and uncertainties that began to nag at her when she saw the photo of Cameron and Bridget Dewitt in the paper on Tuesday.

She waited for him to call, but he didn't, and she wasn't sure what to make of his silence. He'd invited her along on his trip, she'd said no. Maybe he felt that they'd said everything there was to say. But dammit, they'd slept together the night before he'd left. He should have at least called to explain why he was cuddled up with some other woman less than forty-eight hours after he'd left her bed.

She knew that she was being irrational. If she really wanted to talk to him, to demand an explanation, she could call him. But of course she didn't.

She was relieved when he finally left Rome on Thursday. And then she saw the paper on Friday.

This time he'd been photographed at a cocktail reception for international delegates attending the trade summit in France. There were several recognizable faces in the picture—political leaders and international financiers—but her gaze was drawn immediately to Cameron and the statuesque blonde by his side.

If she didn't know better, she'd think he was courting the press, that he was angry with her for turning down his invitation and wanted her to know where he was and who he was with. Except that he didn't look like he was angry. He looked like he was immensely enjoying the company of the gorgeous woman by his side.

She tossed the paper aside and took her mug of coffee into her office.

She tried to put the photo out of her mind and concentrate on her column, but the words wouldn't come. Every response she tried to write sounded false, and she knew why. Because a woman who could screw up her own life so completely had no business trying to advise others about theirs.

The tap at the door was a welcome reprieve, and she smiled when Sierra poked her head into her office.

"Busy?"

Gabriella shook her head.

"Have you seen this?" Her daughter held up the morning newspaper as she stepped cautiously into her mother's office.

She nodded and lifted her mug to her lips, wincing as she sipped her now stone-cold coffee.

"Aren't you mad?"

"At whom?"

"Cameron," Sierra said, as if the answer should have been obvious.

Gabriella noted that her daughter had yet to refer to her father by anything other than his given name or his formal title. Obviously she was going to need some time to accept the familial relationship between them, and she silently cursed the inopportune timing of the prince's trip. Sierra was still reeling from the news that Cameron was her father, and Gabriella believed her daughter would have benefited from having him around to answer her questions, assuage her doubts.

"Honey, I know this is all new to you, but your—*Cameron,*" she hastily amended, "has lived his entire life in the public eye. For a lot of women, being seen with a prince, having her name linked with his—however temporarily—is an enormous thrill."

"So it doesn't bother you that he was photographed with a redhead in Rome and a blonde in Bordeaux?"

Of course it bothered her. Enough that she'd taken the time to do some quick internet checking herself, which gave her the information to answer her daughter's question.

"He's on a business trip," she reminded Sierra. "The blonde happens to be an American ambassador also in France for meetings, and the redhead is an internationally-known model currently dating the youngest son of the Italian prime minister."

Sierra was silent, as if absorbing this information.

"You used to badger me with questions about your father," Gabriella reminded her. "If there's something you want to know now, just ask me."

"I guess I was just wondering…or maybe remembering. When I was little and asked you about my dad, you always told me that you'd loved him very much."

Gabriella nodded.

"Was it true?"

"Yes," she admitted. "I might not have given you a lot of information about your father, but what I did tell you was always the truth."

"Are you still in love with him?"

And because Gabriella didn't like to be dishonest with her daughter, even if she'd only recently acknowledged the truth to herself, she nodded again.

"So why didn't you go with him?"

She narrowed her gaze. "What makes you think he asked?"

"I heard him," she admitted. "When you told me to go to bed, I stayed in the hallway, listening to your conversation, and I heard him ask you."

There was no point in lecturing Sierra about eavesdropping on other people's conversations. What was done was done. So she only said, "Then you heard me tell him that I couldn't go because I have responsibilities here."

"That's a cop-out," Sierra said. "You know it and he knows it, too."

"I'm willing to answer any of your questions about Cameron but not about my personal relationship with him."

"Do you still have a personal relationship with him?" Sierra challenged.

Gabriella didn't have a ready response to that one.

* * *

Sierra hated keeping secrets from Jenna.

What was the point of having a BFF if she couldn't talk to her? But Gabriella had been adamant that she couldn't tell anyone about her father. Not even Jenna. Not yet.

But she had to talk to someone. And there was no one that she trusted more than Jenna. And she knew that she could trust her, because she'd told Jenna about the night she'd snuck out to meet Paolo, and Jenna hadn't whispered a word to anyone, not even Rachel or Beth.

So when she got home after her doctor's appointment Friday afternoon—without her cast finally—she picked up her phone and texted Jenna.

Can you get away? Need 2 talk 2 u.

And Jenna, because she was her BFF, texted back right away:

Where?

Half an hour later, they were sipping iced cappuccinos down at the waterfront.

It was only the beginning of the second week of a three-week trip, and Cameron already wanted to go home.

Usually he enjoyed the travel that was an essential aspect of his job, the opportunity to visit new places and meet new people. But in the short time that he'd been away, he'd realized that there wasn't anywhere in the world that he wanted to go unless it was with Gabriella and Sierra.

By the time he got to Germany, he was feeling edgy and impatient to be home. He thought about calling Gabriella. In fact, not a day had gone by since he'd left Tesoro del Mar that he hadn't picked up the phone at least half a dozen times to dial to her number. But each time, he'd set it down again. He wanted her there with him, but she'd refused. Of course, he'd been too stubborn and proud to beg, and now he was alone.

Well, not exactly alone. He was on his way to meet Dieter Meier for dinner. Dieter was the president of a major manufacturing firm in Nuremburg and an old friend from Cambridge, and Cameron was looking forward to catching up with him. But he promised himself that he would call Gabriella after his dinner with Dieter.

Except that when he got back to his hotel, there was a woman in his room. And not the woman he'd been missing.

"How did you get in here?" he demanded.

Chantal St. Laurent's glossy, painted lips curved. "I know the manager."

"Okay—what are you doing here?"

She rose to her feet, somehow balancing on four-inch ice-pick heels, and crossed the room to where he'd stopped, just inside the door. She'd poured herself into a short spandex dress that was the same color blue as her eyes. There were diamonds at her ears and her wrists, so that she glittered with every step and every turn. She looked good, spectacular even, but her presence stirred only basic male appreciation—and more than a little suspicion.

She ran a manicured nail down the front of his shirt, tracing the buttons. "Hoping to catch up with an old friend."

They used to run in the same circles, but he wouldn't have said they were friends. For a brief time they'd been lovers, but even then, they'd never been particularly friendly toward one another.

She slid her fingertip beneath the fabric, lightly scraped her nail against his bare skin. He grabbed her hand, pulled it away.

"I don't have time for your games, Chantal."

She pouted. "You just don't remember how much fun my games are."

"I do remember," he assured her. But mostly what he remembered was that she had a red-hot body and an ice-cold heart. "I specifically remember that you screwed me over more than you ever screwed me, and that wasn't a lot of fun."

"Let me make it up to you."

She tried to reach for him again, but he caught both her wrists and held her away.

"You can make it up to me by leaving this room. Now."

He dropped her wrists, but instead of going to the door, she moved toward the bar. She took her time selecting a glass, added a few cubes of ice from the silver bucket, then poured a generous splash of scotch over them.

She swirled the liquid around in the glass, then looked up at him with those big blue eyes that had brought legions of men to their knees. "Please don't send me away, Cameron. Not when I came all the way from St. Moritz to be with you."

He didn't ask what she'd been doing in St. Moritz. Truthfully, he didn't care. But he did wonder, "How did you even know I'd be here?"

"I've been following your career through the newspapers, hoping that our paths would cross again." She took a long sip of the scotch. "I've missed you, Cameron."

"Was I ever gullible enough to believe the lies that trip so easily off of your tongue?"

She set the glass down again with a snap. "You're not the man I remember."

"You have no idea how pleased I am to hear that," he told her.

"You'll regret turning me away," she promised him.

"I regret that you aren't already gone."

She picked up her glass again, tossed the last of her drink in his face.

He should have anticipated the attack. Unlike Allegra, Chantal had always been impulsive, her moods mercurial, and he'd baited her. Not because he wanted a reaction, but because he wanted her gone.

He was still blinking away the alcohol that stung his eyes when he heard the door slam. Well, he'd got what he wanted in that regard, anyway.

He flipped the security lock and went to the bathroom to shower off the remnants of expensive scotch and cheap memories.

Gabriella awakened to the sound of someone knocking on her door. No, it was more of a pounding, and the impatient, incessant hammering made her heart jolt painfully in her chest. It wasn't quite 4:00 a.m., and nothing good ever came from someone at the door at 4:00 a.m.

She pushed out of bed, yanking on her robe as she made her way down the stairs. She grabbed the phone from the charger on the way to the door, in case she needed to call 9-1-1. A flick of the switch had light flooding the front porch and revealing the identity of the late-night visitor.

She flipped the lock and yanked open the door.

"Alli? What on earth are you doing here?"

"I came to save you from the media hounds that will be on your doorstep before sunrise."

"What are you talking about?"

"The news just came across the wire," her editor warned her. "Alex saw it and immediately called me at home."

Her heart jolted again. "What news?"

"About Sierra."

"What about Sierra?" Katarina demanded.

Gabriella and Alli both turned to find Katarina on the stairs, Sierra behind her.

Alli glanced past Gabriella. "That she's Prince Cameron's daughter."

Gabriella didn't waste her breath swearing. She'd known the

truth would come out eventually and while she wasn't happy about the timing, she didn't think it was cause to panic— although apparently her editor did.

"The presses are running overtime," Alli told her. "But the print media's only part of it. The story's already all over the internet. There are photo montages on YouTube and blog posts about your affair."

Okay, so she hadn't expected the truth to come out quite like this. She swallowed, hard, as her stomach muscles cramped into painful knots.

"What can I do?" she asked.

"Go pack a suitcase," Alli advised, her gaze shifting to encompass both Katarina and Sierra in her instruction.

"I'm not letting the paparazzi chase me from my home," Gabriella's mother said.

"Hopefully it will only be for a few days," Alli soothed.

"And where are we supposed to go?" Sierra demanded.

"There's nowhere we can go that the reporters and photographers won't find us if they're determined to do so," Gabriella acknowledged dully.

"Actually, there is one place," Alli said.

"Where?"

"The royal palace."

Gabriella stared at her, certain her friend had lost her mind. "Okay," she said, playing along. "Let me just call the prince regent to see if there are any vacancies in the castle."

"No need," Alli told her. "I already did."

"You can't be serious."

"Prince Rowan and I go way back…to the beginning of June when you wrote that story about his cousin and the daughter of the King of Ardena, anyway."

"You really called him?"

"He's sending a car and bodyguards to make sure you get from here to there without incident."

"Well, then, we should get dressed," Katarina suggested, finally starting back up the stairs. "We can't go to meet royalty in our pajamas."

It was impossible not to be impressed by the royal palace. But as her daughter goggled over the marble floors and crystal chandeliers and her mother inspected the heirloom vases overflowing with fresh flowers and family portraits in ornate frames on the walls, Gabriella found herself even more impressed by the graciousness of Rowan Santiago, the prince regent, and Princess Lara, his wife, who both came to the foyer to greet them when they arrived.

Gabriella automatically dipped into a curtsy, and her mother and daughter followed suit.

"Please," Lara said, taking her hand. "It's an ungodly hour to worry about such formalities."

"It's an ungodly hour to be anywhere other than bed," Rowan added, "and your rooms are ready for you."

"Thank you, Your Highness," Katarina said gratefully.

"Hannah—" he gestured to the woman who hovered in the background "—will show you the way."

Sierra stifled a yawn as she fell into step beside her grandmother. Gabriella stayed back.

"I don't imagine sleep will come easily with everything that's on your mind," Lara said gently to her. "But you should try to get some rest."

"I will," she agreed. "I just wanted to thank you. I know those words are grossly inadequate, and I'm sorry that we showed up at your door under such circumstances, and so very grateful that you've opened your home to us."

Rowan put an arm across his wife's shoulders, a casual gesture of comfort and affection. "She's going to change her mind in a few hours."

The knots of anxiety that had begun to loosen when the driver pulled through the palace gates tightened in Gabriella's stomach again, but she forced herself to ask, "What's going to happen in a few hours?"

Lara smiled. "The kids will be awake."

The sun was high in the sky and the vultures were circling when Cameron's plane landed at the Port Augustine airport.

He was surrounded by bodyguards as he made his way from the plane to the car, but still he felt the press of the paparazzi pushing in on him. He ignored the shouted questions, the deliberately provocative comments and the blinding flash of cameras. He had only one focus: getting to Gabriella and Sierra.

He knew they were at the royal palace, and that they were safe there. But he didn't know if they had seen *El Informador.*

His secretary had handed him a copy of the paper as he'd stepped onto the plane, and after he'd read and reread the outrageous article, he'd spent the remainder of the almost three-hour flight thinking about how badly he'd screwed everything up.

As he ducked into the back of the black Mercedes SUV and the vehicle slowly began pulling away from the media mob, he accepted that Gabriella would have seen the article. It was inevitable, really. What worried him was that she might believe it.

Rowan and Lara's two sons were very spirited and utterly adorable. Matthew was six-and-a-half, William was almost four, and when the three generations of Vasquez women met them at breakfast the next morning—along with seventeen-year-old Princess Alexandria and thirteen-year-old Prince Damon—they were all immediately charmed. Prince Christian had eaten with Rowan much earlier, Lara informed her guests, so that they could indulge in a morning ride before the demands of the day caught up with them.

The boys chatted up a storm while Gabriella nibbled on a piece of toast and sipped her coffee, and for a few blissful minutes she let herself forget why she was hiding out at the palace and simply enjoyed being there.

When Lara slipped away to take a phone call, Katarina excused herself to head out to the gardens and Lexi invited Sierra to join her for a swim, leaving Gabriella with three very handsome—and very young—members of the royal family. By the time Lara returned, the boys had finished their breakfasts and gone down to the stables and Gabriella was indulging in a second cup of coffee.

"Should I apologize for everyone abandoning you or are you savoring a few quiet minutes?" the princess asked.

"I'm savoring," Gabriella admitted. "Probably because I know it's the calm before the storm."

"Did you manage to get any sleep last night?" Lara asked gently.

"Some," she said. "Enough that I'm thinking a little more clearly this morning and wondering if it wouldn't just be better to face the press and get it over with so that they move on to something else? And I think, if I was the only one who would face the backlash, I would do it."

"You're worried about your daughter," Lara guessed.

She nodded.

"I hope she doesn't mind staying here for a few days. I know kids—teenagers in particular—can be particular about their own space."

"Mind?" Gabriella smiled. "She said she feels like a princess."

"She is a princess," Lara reminded her.

"I know," she admitted. "But I'm not sure Sierra has let herself acknowledge that fact."

"Because it would mean accepting that Cameron is her father," the princess guessed.

Gabriella nodded. "It hasn't been an easy time for Sierra.

She hasn't known about Cameron very long—I thought I was doing her a favor, by keeping the identity of her father a secret. Because I knew that if anyone found out she was his daughter, her life would change." Her smile was wry. "Obviously I screwed up there."

"No one can blame you for wanting to protect your child," the princess said. "Although I don't know if it's fair—or even possible—to protect her from her birthright."

Gabriella sighed. "I know."

"But speaking of Cameron—he should be arriving here shortly."

"He's back from Germany?"

"His plane landed about twenty minutes ago."

Gabriella winced. "I can't imagine he's pleased to have his trip interrupted to deal with this media frenzy."

"I wouldn't worry," Lara said. "I'm sure Cameron is more accustomed to seeing his name in the headlines than most people."

"Does that mean… Is it in the headlines today?"

The princess nodded and passed her a copy of *El Informador.*

"*La Noticia* covered the basic story, too," Lara told her. "They couldn't very well be the only newspaper in Europe that ignored it, but they reported only the facts that had been independently confirmed."

Gabriella didn't reply, her attention already snagged by the harsh words spread across the top of the front page.

Chapter Sixteen

Prince Cameron's Mistress Exposes Truth About His Secret Love Child With Another Woman

Former international supermodel Chantal St. Laurent, recently spotted snuggling with the Tesorian prince in Germany, stormed out of his hotel room in Munich early this morning after learning that her lover is the father of an illegitimate teenage daughter with newspaper columnist Gabriella Vasquez.

"I was shocked when he told me," she later confided to a friend.

Independent investigation has confirmed that Gabriella Vasquez is the mother of a sixteen-year-old daughter named Sierra, but the prince is not named as the father on the child's certificate of birth. In fact, the official document lists the father as "unknown." Sources close to

Ms. Vasquez at the time of her child's birth agreed that
she was uncertain about who had fathered her child.

Gabriella pushed the paper aside, unable to read any further. And the thought of Sierra being exposed to such ugly
lies and rumors—she felt sick just thinking about it.

"It's a gossip rag," Lara said gently. "And Chantal St. Laurent will say or do anything to see her name in print. I don't
know how she happened to be in Germany at the same time
as Cameron, but I promise you it wasn't a coincidence."

"You think she set him up?" she asked hopefully.

"I think she's spewing venom and lies," Lara said. "I can't
imagine what she thinks she'll gain from any of this, but I
don't doubt for a minute that she made up the whole thing."

"Even the part about being in his hotel room?" she asked
hopefully.

"No, she was there."

Cameron acknowledged the fact wearily as he stepped into
the room.

He looked exhausted, as if he'd been up all night. Exhausted but still so handsome, and Gabriella wanted to rush
into his arms. She wanted him to hold her and reassure her
that everything was going to be okay. But she knew that he
couldn't make that kind of promise and it was foolish and
naive to wish that he could—especially when he'd just admitted that the woman who'd sold out Sierra to the media had
been in his hotel room. With him.

"I was out for dinner with a friend," he explained, "and
when I got back to my hotel room, Chantal was there."

"*In* your room?"

He nodded. "She wasn't there very long—probably not
more than ten minutes. Just long enough to ensure that the
photographer was in place to snap the photo of her leaving
again."

"And long enough for you to tell her about Sierra,"

Gabriella said, though she was still trying to fathom why he would do so.

"I didn't say a word to Chantal about Sierra," he said.

"Then how—" Gabriella faltered, as the pieces finally clicked into place in her mind.

Cameron nodded. "I knew you'd figure it out."

Lara picked up her coffee cup. "Is anyone going to fill me in?"

But Gabriella shook her head, wanting to deny it. "I know she hates me, but this—the lies and innuendos—they're going to hurt you and—" she blinked back the tears, because she knew that if she let even a single one fall, she wouldn't be able to stop the flood "—Sierra as much as they hurt me."

"Collateral damage," he said easily. "The princess royal wouldn't concern herself with that so long as she got what she wanted."

Lara stared at Cameron. "You think *your mother* set this whole thing in motion?"

"She didn't want Cameron to ever know about Sierra," Gabriella told her.

"And since you failed to keep that information from me, she used it to hurt you."

"Wait a minute—" the princess turned to Gabriella "—are you saying that Elena knew about Cameron's child and didn't tell him?"

"Yes, she knew," Cameron admitted.

Lara shook her head and pushed away from the table. "Apparently you two have bigger issues than the paparazzi to work through, so I'll leave you to it."

Cameron sat down at the table across from Gabriella.

"Are we going to be able to work through them?" he asked softly.

She wanted to say "yes." She wanted to believe it was true. But she wasn't as naive or idealistic as she used to be and she knew that the odds were stacked against them. It wasn't just that he was a royal and she was a commoner; it wasn't even that their fledgling relationship was suddenly under very public scrutiny. It was so many different things, but mostly it was the acceptance that no matter how much she loved him, love wasn't always enough.

And so, when she finally responded to his question, it was to say, "I honestly don't know."

It wasn't the answer he wanted, but Cameron couldn't blame Gabriella for being cautious.

One step forward, two steps back, he thought wearily. Their relationship had finally been moving in the right direction, until he'd left the country with a lot of questions and uncertainties still between them.

"Are you…" she hesitated, almost as if she was afraid of the answer he would give to her question. "Is it true—" she started again "—about you and Chantal being lovers?"

"No," he said. "*Dios,* no." And it was the truth, but not the whole truth, and he knew that he couldn't hold anything back from Gabriella now. If they were going to move forward, they couldn't do so with any more secrets between them. "Not anymore."

"So you were," she murmured.

"A long time ago."

She nodded.

She didn't look surprised or even disappointed. Obviously his confirmation was no more than she'd expected, and why wouldn't it be? For a lot of years, he'd been known as the partying prince—a favorite of the paparazzi because he was always out on the town, always with a different woman, always having fun. He'd grown weary of the scene long before he'd managed to extricate himself from it, and though he'd done so more than half a dozen years earlier, the reputation continued to haunt him.

"If it was over a long time ago, why would she do this?" Gabriella gestured to the paper.

He had several theories about the unlikely partnership between his mother and his former lover. It was possible that Elena had bribed or blackmailed Chantal to ensure her complicity. It was just as likely that Chantal had jumped at the opportunity to be involved—just for fun. "Because Chantal's never as happy as when she's in the middle of a scandal."

Gabriella shook her head. He knew she didn't understand people like Elena and Chantal, people who could find pleasure in using their power to hurt others. Her basic honesty and goodness had appealed to him from the start. And even when he'd been furious with her for keeping his daughter a secret, he'd known that it hadn't been easy for her.

Elena, on the other hand, wouldn't have lost a wink of sleep over the role she'd played in the deception. More likely, she'd have taken pride in the display of her power. It was what she did—manipulating others so that she could feel important. He'd long since figured out that her behavior was rooted in her own childhood, in the feeling that she was insignificant and powerless because she was a female child born to a ruler who already had a male heir. But the fact that he'd come to understand the reasoning behind her behavior didn't mean it sickened him any less.

Gabriella turned the paper over, so that she didn't have to see the headline staring at her. "Sierra's going to be devastated when she sees this."

Cameron wasn't so sure. Oh, he knew that Sierra would be hurt, that she'd wonder if there was any truth in the midst of all of the lies. But the fallout for her would be minimal. Regardless of what anyone believed about her father or her mother or the circumstances of her conception, she was the innocent in all of this. Right now he was more concerned about Gabriella.

"Rowan suggested a press conference, and I agree that it's probably the best way to handle this," he told her.

"Why don't I just walk outside the palace gates with a target on my chest instead?"

He reached across the table to touch her hand. He half-expected her to pull away, and when she didn't—when she actually turned her hand to link their fingers together—the relief he felt was almost overwhelming.

"We're going to present a united front," he promised her. "Me and you and our daughter. We'll read a prepared statement and formally introduce Princess Sierra and we won't answer any questions."

"That won't stop them from asking."

He nodded, acknowledging the fact.

"Okay." She drew in a deep breath. "When are we going to do this?"

They decided that the press conference would be held at Waterfront Park at nine o'clock the next morning. The exact location wasn't too far from where Cameron had initially confronted Gabriella about Sierra's paternity, although that was by coincidence rather than design. Rowan's advisors had suggested the outdoor stage where summer concerts often took place as a suitable venue to ensure access to all the media who chose to attend. Cameron had some concerns about providing security for Gabriella and Sierra in such an open space, but the prince regent promised that the royal security detail would be there to look out for them.

Gabriella had hoped that the paparazzi would back off when the date and time of the conference were announced. As grateful as she was to Rowan and Lara for allowing them to stay at the palace, she wanted to be back in her own home, she wanted to pretend that things were normal. But the media vans remained just outside the palace gates, trapping her inside.

When she'd ducked out of her house under cover of darkness

so many hours earlier, she hadn't thought about what she was throwing into the bag she brought with her. She certainly hadn't packed anything that would be appropriate to wear to a press conference. She had no sooner expressed this concern to Lara than the princess asked if she wanted to make a list of items for someone to pick up from the house or do some online shopping. Though she was tempted by the shopping, she opted to make a list. She already owed the princess far more than she could ever repay.

An hour later, she was sorting through the suits and blouses she'd selected. She managed to narrow it down, but continued to waver between the taupe and the red.

"Definitely the red," Lara said, when she'd finally got up the nerve to ask the princess for her opinion. "Even if you wear the taupe, you won't be able to escape the spotlight but it'll look like you tried. Also, Sierra's wearing red. Red and white, actually, but you'll coordinate nicely. And red is definitely your color."

So the next morning, Gabriella got dressed in the red, then she went to see what her daughter was wearing.

She halted in the doorway of Sierra's room and absorbed the twinge of regret that stabbed at her heart when she couldn't see any sign of her little girl anywhere. Instead, there was a poised and beautiful young woman in front of her, dressed in a simple but elegant white sundress with red poppies dancing along the hemline, red peep-toe pumps on her feet and a wide-brimmed red hat on her head.

"It was Lexi's idea," she said. "The hat. She said it would make me look more mysterious."

"I almost didn't even recognize you," Gabriella said with a smile.

She was pleased that Alexandria and Sierra had hit it off so quickly. Lexi had been raised as a princess from birth, so she knew everything there was to know about the duties and responsibilities of a royal and had already proven herself an invaluable support to Sierra.

"You look fabulous."

She smiled shyly. "I feel strange. I mean, I like the outfit, it's just so different from my usual style. But Lexi said it set the right tone between formal and casual."

"It's perfect," Gabriella assured her.

Sierra nodded. Then she took a deep breath and blurted out. "I told Jenna. About Cameron being my father."

And Gabriella suddenly realized why her daughter had been so uncharacteristically quiet and withdrawn over the past two days—not just because she was feeling overwhelmed by everything that was happening, but because she was feeling guilty.

"She's my best friend," Sierra continued. "And I didn't think she'd tell anyone—"

"She didn't," Gabriella interrupted. She took her daughter's hands, squeezed gently. "The leak didn't come from Jenna."

"You're sure?"

She nodded. "There were…details given to the media that Jenna couldn't have known, that you didn't know."

Sierra exhaled a heartfelt sigh of relief. "I thought this was all my fault."

"Oh, Sierra." She hugged her daughter tight. "None of this is your fault, honey. If anyone's to blame, it's me. If I'd told you the truth—if I'd told Cameron the truth—a long time ago, we might have avoided this now. Or at least been more prepared for it."

"Well, I'm as prepared as I'm going to be," Sierra told her. "So let's get it over with."

The park was packed. Somehow word had got out that Prince Cameron's daughter was going to be in attendance and the citizens of Tesoro del Mar flocked to the park, anxious to finally set eyes on Princess Sierra. A lot of Sierra's friends were there, too. Aside from Jenna, no one had known that her father was a prince until they'd read it in the papers or seen it on television, and they were all curious to know if the prince's daughter really was the same Sierra Vasquez that they knew.

Gabriella wasn't surprised by the turnout. She'd known there would be more curiosity-seekers than media personnel, but she'd still tried to discourage her mother from attending, worried that Katarina would be an easy target for the paparazzi. But Katarina had insisted on being there to support her daughter and granddaughter, and Gabriella saw that she wasn't alone. In fact, she was flanked on all sides by members of Cameron's family. Rowan and Lara and Matthew and William; Christian and Lexi and Damon; Eric and Molly and Maggie and Joshua. Even Cameron's sister, Marissa, was there, with her other brother's daughter.

Only the princess royal was absent—apparently having left the country on short notice to visit an ailing friend in Corsica. Gabriella knew that explanation was nothing more than an excuse, but she was nevertheless as grateful for Cameron's mother's absence as she was everyone else's support.

As a child, Sierra had relentlessly hounded Gabriella for a sister or a brother, and Gabriella's heart had ached that she couldn't give her little girl what she wanted. What Gabriella, too, had always wanted. Because from the time she'd been a child, she'd dreamed of someday having a big family—including at least half a dozen kids running around the yard.

Of course, in that scenario she'd also imagined that she would have a husband—someone who went out to work at a respectable but normal nine-to-five job every day and came home to his wife and family every night. Falling in love with a prince had totally screwed up all of her plans, and while she could maybe forgive herself for the youthful fantasies that had allowed it to happen when she was seventeen, she should have known better this time around.

...the mind does not and cannot control the heart.

She no longer doubted the truth of her mother's words, but as she looked out at the familiar faces in the front row, she could at least be happy that she'd finally given her daughter the family that she always wanted.

Rowan's secretary stepped up to the microphone first, drawing her attention back to the purpose of the assembly. He introduced himself to the crowd, thanked everyone for coming, and announced that Prince Cameron had a statement to make.

Though neither Gabriella nor Sierra was expected to say anything, it was agreed that they would stand with Cameron, demonstrating their support of him and agreement with the official statement he would deliver.

"Over the past couple of days, the media has been inundated with rumors regarding my history with Gabriella Vasquez and the paternity of Gabriella's daughter, Sierra. I'm here today to separate the fact from fiction…"

Gabriella didn't listen to any more of his speech. They'd gone over it together the previous afternoon, so she knew exactly what he intended to say. Instead, she focused on the sound of his voice, allowing her frayed nerves to be soothed by the smooth cadence.

As he spoke, she held Sierra's hand in her own. Her daughter's icy fingers were the only outward indication of her trepidation. She had to know that everyone was staring at her, but she stood tall with her head held high, looking every inch the princess, and Gabriella had never been more proud.

There was a brief silence after Cameron finished speaking—probably not more than a few seconds—and then the real uproar began. There were so many questions that it was almost impossible to decipher any individual words, until someone shouted: "Prince Cameron, are you going to marry Gabriella?"

And Gabriella's heart actually stopped for the space of several beats.

She and Cameron had talked about this scenario and they'd agreed that they wouldn't respond to any questions or statements from the crowd. But this one seemed to linger in the air for a moment, as if everyone was waiting for an answer. As Gabriella held her breath, waiting for the same thing.

Cameron had heard the question. She had no doubt about that. And he even paused, as if considering his response. But in the end, he only said, "Thank you all for your time."

And then he turned away from the microphone.

Sierra immediately fell into step behind him, obviously eager to get off the stage and away from the endless flash of bulbs, and Gabriella followed her. There were still questions being shouted, but Gabriella was only aware of the one that had gone unanswered.

What did you think—that he'd want to put a ring on your finger? Wake up, Gabriella. You're a nobody from nowhere and he'll never marry you.

The words that echoed in her mind now weren't those of her mother but his, and the scornful tone with which they'd been delivered had cut her to the quick. Because she'd believed him when he'd told her he loved her, and she'd been foolish enough to think that a man who loved her would want to marry her.

She wasn't seventeen anymore, and yet, she'd let herself get caught up in the fairytale all over again. She'd fallen in love with Cameron and she'd trusted him when he'd told her that he wanted a future for them together. She'd believed that he was committed to her and their relationship, but his silence on the subject of marriage spoke volumes.

Behind the scenes, the security force was filling vehicles for the return trip to the palace. Sierra rode with Lexi and her brothers, and Katrina had climbed into a vehicle with the prince regent and his family, leaving Gabriella to ride with Cameron.

She settled back against the plush leather seat with dark-tinted windows and finally let herself breathe. No one could see her in here. No one could know that her heart was breaking. No one except Cameron—but he'd seen it all before.

She didn't realize the tears had spilled over until she felt the brush of Cameron's knuckle on her cheek, wiping them away. His touch was gentle but she felt as if a fist was squeezing around her heart, and the ache was both painful and real.

"Are you okay?" he asked.

She nodded. "I'm just relieved it's finally over so I can go home." Back to her own house, her own life. Reality.

"It wouldn't hurt to stay at the palace a few more days," Cameron said. "You heard the questions the reporters were shouting—they don't have all the answers they want yet."

"Yes, I heard the questions," she agreed.

"We knew it was going to be like that," he reminded her. "No matter how much information we gave them, it wouldn't be enough."

She nodded. "I know. It wasn't the questions that bothered me—not really."

"Then what was it?"

He sounded as if he really didn't know, and she had no intention of enlightening him. "I understand that the media attention is a fact of life for you, and I know it will be for Sierra, too, but I can't live like that."

"What, exactly, are you saying?"

She drew in a deep breath. "That I don't want a life in the spotlight so we should stop pretending that a relationship between us could ever work."

His gaze narrowed on her. "At seventeen, you were pregnant and washing dishes in a restaurant kitchen so that you could afford to buy a crib for your baby. After you had the baby, you took night courses and you worked your way up from the circulation desk to columnist at *La Noticia*. I think you've already proven that you can do just about anything you want to, so if you think you can't handle a few skirmishes with the media, maybe the truth is that you don't want to," he accused.

"Maybe I don't," she agreed. "Or maybe I just don't want to handle it all by myself."

He scowled. "What are you talking about? You weren't by yourself. I was right there—"

"Standing on the opposite side of Sierra." She felt tears stinging her eyes again. "As if she was the only connection we had."

"What was I supposed to do—announce to the crowd that we're lovers?"

The words were a knife straight through her heart, the final, fatal strike to her illusions. She'd thought they were so much more than lovers. She'd thought they were in love, planning a future together, building a family.

"No," she finally said. "You weren't supposed to do any-thing."

Cameron followed her out of the SUV and up to her room, where she immediately began tossing her things into a suit-case. "If you're going to be mad, you could at least tell me why."

"I'm not mad."

It was obviously a lie, but he knew better than to call her on it. "Okay, then tell me how to fix whatever it is that I screwed up."

"There's nothing to fix," she said. "I've just decided that I won't be your dirty little secret anymore."

"What the hell are you talking about?"

"That's how Chantal referred to Sierra, but the truth is, our daughter was simply the result of your youthful indiscretion. You have absolutely nothing to be ashamed of there.

"But it's not quite so easy to explain me, is it? And that's why you haven't even tried. That's why you're so careful not to be seen in public with me, and why, even today, you kept six feet of space between us."

"How can you blame me for trying to shelter you from the media when you said you didn't want your name linked with mine in the tabloids?"

"That was before we were sleeping together."

"Well, obviously I didn't get the memo about the rule change."

"You had a chance to stand with me today," she told him. "To show the world that you wanted to be with me, to tell them 'yes—I do plan to marry her.'"

He couldn't help it. Afterward, he would agree that was no excuse for his action, but it was purely reflexive, completely instinctive—he stepped back.

She turned away to zip up her suitcase.

"Come on, Gabriella," he said reasonably. "We've only been together for a few weeks."

She looked right at him, baring her true feelings. "I know. But I've loved you for seventeen years."

I've loved you… If you loved me… The words spun in circles in his mind, making him dizzy.

He didn't want to believe that she was trying to manipulate him. He knew that she wasn't like that. And yet, he'd listened to those words too many times, and hearing them fall from her lips now, he froze.

"Are you giving me an ultimatum?" he asked coolly, waiting for her to spell out her terms. Waiting for her to look at him, her eyes filled with pleading/fury/tears, and finally tell him what she wanted. What he needed to do to prove that he loved her.

But she didn't look at him at all. She only picked up her suitcase and said, "No, I'm leaving."

Chapter Seventeen

It was rare for Cameron to have visitors at his office. And his days were usually so tightly scheduled that he wouldn't have time to spend with anyone who just happened to drop by, anyway. But since he wasn't yet supposed to be back from his trip, he had large blocks of unscheduled time—most of which he spent thinking about Gabriella and how thoroughly he'd ruined everything.

So when his secretary buzzed through on Tuesday afternoon to tell him that someone was there to see him, Cameron was grateful for the reprieve. Even more so when he realized that his visitor was Sierra. He hadn't seen her since the day of the press conference—the day that Gabriella had walked out on him.

He hadn't seen Gabriella, either, but only because he had yet to figure out the best way to grovel for her forgiveness.

"Lexi told me that it would be okay if I stopped by," Sierra said. "She didn't tell me I'd have to present three pieces of ID and be subjected to a body scan in order to get past the front door."

"I'll make sure you get security clearance so you can come here any time you want without going through all of that again," Cameron told her.

"That might be a good idea," she agreed. "Since I've decided that I should probably get to know you a little better—because of the family connection thing."

"I'd like that," he said.

"But it would be a lot more convenient for me if you came around to the house again," she told him.

"I could talk to your mother about the possibility," he said cautiously.

"Or you could just show up," she suggested. "I know she'd be happy to see you."

"Well, I'm not so sure about that."

She huffed out a breath. "Are all guys so dense?"

"I'll assume that's a rhetorical question," he said dryly.

"Okay, answer this one—are you in love with my mother?"

"Yes."

She blinked. "Wow. Not even a moment's hesitation."

"I would have told her the same thing, if she'd given me a chance." At least, he wanted to believe he would have told her, but she'd started talking about commitment and he'd started feeling backed into a corner.

He'd lived his whole life with his mother pulling his strings until he'd finally severed them. And then he'd been both relieved and determined that no one else would ever have that power over him again.

Unfortunately, it wasn't until Gabriella had gone and he'd listened to himself pouring his heart out to Lara that he realized Gabriella had never tried to bend him to her will. She wasn't looking for a commitment at any cost. She only wanted him if he wanted her, too.

And he did want her—more than anything else in the world.

"That's good, but the words aren't going to be enough," Sierra warned him. "She needs to know that you're going to stick."

"What do you mean?"

"You've got a history, right? She fell in love with you when you were younger, you said you loved her, too, and then you were gone. Fast-forward sixteen years and some months, and you're back again, saying you love her, blah-blah-blah."

"Blah-blah-blah?"

"I'm trying not to think too much about the details," she told him. "It's kind of weird, you know, with her being my mom and you being my dad."

She said it casually, as if it was no big deal, but to Cameron, it was a very big deal. It was the first time she'd explicitly acknowledged their father-daughter relationship, and while he was tempted to haul her in his arms and hug her so tight she could barely breathe, he managed to restrain himself.

"Your point?" he prompted instead.

"It's easy to say you love her, but she needs you to prove that you mean it."

"And how, exactly, am I supposed to do that?"

Sierra smiled. "Why are you asking me for advice when you could go straight to the relationship expert?"

Dear Gabby,

I'm writing to you in the desperate hope that you can help me convince the woman I love of my feelings for her.

I'm a thirty-six-year-old man who has fallen in love only twice—both times with the same woman. The first time, I was barely twenty years old, too young to understand the depth of my feelings and too immature to appreciate how truly rare and special our love was.

The second time was much more recent. After more than sixteen years apart, our paths happened to cross again and I realized that the feelings I had for her so long ago had never gone away.

I've tried to show her how I feel, but I think she's afraid to believe it, afraid that I'll hurt her again.

I'm more than willing to put my heart on the line. I'd happily hire skywriters or put a message on the big screen at a baseball game—whatever it takes to let her know that I'm going to stick around this time... forever.

Should I set my plans in motion—or do you think a man who royally screwed up once doesn't deserve a second chance?

Signed,

Lost in Love

Gabriella reread the letter twice. At first, she hadn't let herself believe Cameron had written it, but there were too many specific details to be able to disregard. And while hope flared in her heart, she forced herself to tamp it down. Because despite what he said in the letter, nothing had changed.

Or maybe everything had changed. The princess royal had told her that Cameron would never marry her, but this letter suggested not only that he would but that he wanted to, that he really wanted to be with her forever.

With that cautious hope in her heart, she settled her hands on the keyboard and began to type.

Dear Lost,

While I believe that everyone makes mistakes and everyone deserves second chances, I'd hold off on hiring the skywriters. Your willingness to put your heart on the line in a very public way is admirable, but not every woman wants or needs such a big statement. In fact, some women might worry that a man who goes to such extremes might be more flash than substance.

Instead of shouting your feelings from the rooftops, take the time to show her what's in your heart. As cliché as it sounds, it's often the little things that mean the most. Pick her a bouquet of flowers. Hold hands. Walk with her in the rain. Cook her favorite meal. Call her at bedtime, just to say good-night.

Give her some time to see and believe that you intend to stick around forever. It's not easy to let go of past heartaches, so be patient, be understanding, and be there for her.

Good luck,

Gabby

It happened to be raining the day that his letter and her response appeared in the newspaper, so Cameron snuck out of the office during his lunch and dropped by Gabriella's house. His wipers were on full-speed to clear the water from his windshield, giving him a moment's doubt about his plan, but he didn't change his course.

Gabriella was obviously surprised to see him, and more than a little wary when he suggested that she should put her coat and shoes on. But when she finally did, he took her by the hand and walked with her in the rain. They didn't go far but they still ended up soaked through to the skin.

He called her later that night, to see if she'd managed to dry out yet and to say good-night.

The next night, he called her again. And then again the night after that. He never kept her on the phone for more than a few minutes—just long enough for him to let her know that he was thinking about her and, he hoped, to make sure that she was thinking about him.

On the fourth night, he invited her to dinner. And after only a moment's hesitation, she accepted.

* * *

Gabriella was a nervous wreck as she got ready for her date with Cameron. Of course, it didn't help that both her mother and her daughter were hanging out in her room, critiquing every outfit that she tried on. Too sexy. Too frumpy. Too young. Too old. Finally Katarina left to go to her hot yoga class, and when Jenna called to see if Sierra wanted to go out for an iced capp, Gabriella was relieved to shove her daughter out the door, too.

Cameron showed up a short while later, with an enormous bunch of flowers in his hand. There were tall spikes of lavender, cheery pink anemones, fat white lilies and bobbing Spanish bluebells. But what she noticed, after the gorgeous array of colors, was that the stems of the flowers were uneven and broken…almost as if he'd picked them.

"They're beautiful," she said, filling a vase with water. "But I'm not sure why you're doing this."

"Doing what?"

"Bringing me flowers. Taking me to dinner."

"Because I don't cook, either," he told her. "I wanted to make your favorite meal, but I only know how to make reservations."

She smiled at that. "It wasn't intended to be a checklist, you know, just a few suggestions."

"But those suggestions made me realize that we'd missed a lot of those basic getting-to-know-you rituals and I thought it was time we started following some more traditional conventions."

"Such as?"

"Well, dating usually precedes courtship which precedes marriage."

The vase slipped out of her hands and clattered into the sink, splashing water all over the counter and Gabriella.

He handed her a towel. "And marriage, of course, precedes children. Obviously, we've done some things backwards."

She dabbed at the wet splotches on the front of her dress. "Backwards implies a reverse order, but we actually skipped a couple of those steps."

"We'll get to them," he promised.

"Is that was this is about? Are you...courting me?"

"And apparently not doing a good job of it, if you have to ask."

She looked at the flowers again. She could only imagine where he'd picked them—probably from a stranger's garden—and her heart completely melted. "Actually, I think you're doing a wonderful job."

"Really?" he asked hopefully.

"Really." She set the vase on the counter, then turned to touch her lips to his cheek. "Thank you for the flowers."

"You're welcome," he said, and kissed her again.

It was a kiss filled with hunger and frustration and longing, and Gabriella responded with her whole heart.

After what seemed like an eternity and yet not nearly long enough, he eased away. He brushed his thumb over her bottom lip, a slow sensual stroke that made her tremble. His eyes darkened and, for just a moment, she thought he was going to kiss her again.

Instead, he took a step back. "We should get going. We have a reservation at Tradewinds."

She drew in a long, slow breath and nodded. "Right. We wouldn't want to miss our reservation."

But neither of them moved.

"Although we've never worried much about conventions," she reminded him.

"No," he agreed.

"So maybe, instead of sitting through dinner wondering if the evening will end with sex, why don't we start with sex and wonder if we'll make it to dinner?"

He drew her back into his arms, which was exactly where she wanted to be. "I really like the way you think."

* * *

It was a long time later that he looked at the clock beside her bed and said, "We missed our dinner reservation."

She sighed contentedly. "We could order pizza."

"Okay." He kissed her. "One question first."

"Pepperoni," she told him, belting her robe.

He rummaged around on the floor, looking for his pants. "That wasn't the question."

"Okay, what's the question?"

He found his pants and put them on. Apparently whatever the question was, he didn't want to ask while he was naked. Then he shoved his hand into the pocket and pulled out a small, square box. Her heart began to pound furiously inside her chest.

"Compared to the sixteen years that we were apart, we've only been together for a short while," he said. "But the past two weeks without you have been the longest weeks of my life and I don't want to live another day without you by my side."

She blew out an unsteady breath. "You sure moved through that courtship stage fast."

"Because I finally realized what I want. And that's to marry you, build a life and share a family with you, Gabriella."

She desperately wanted to throw her arms around him and tell him that she wanted that, too. But while her heart was already committed, a tiny part of her brain continued to urge caution.

"Your mother hates me," she reminded him. "And to be honest, I'm not too fond of her either."

"I've gone through this scenario a few times in my mind," he admitted. "And never once did I imagine you wanting to talk about my mother."

She managed a smile, though everything inside of her was a quivering mass of nerves and uncertainties. "She's not my favorite topic of conversation, but she's your mother—your family—and you have to know that she won't be happy about this."

"She'll adjust," Cameron insisted. "Because she knows that I won't tolerate her interference in my life ever again. She'll even come to the wedding and smile, because she's a princess and she understands the importance of duty."

The steel in his voice was reassuring, but she still felt compelled to ask, "Is that why you're doing this? Because you think that marrying the mother of your child is your duty?"

"I'm asking you to marry me because I love you," he said. "Because I've always loved you, even when I was too much of an idiot to realize it. And because I want you to be my family—you and Sierra…and maybe another baby."

Her heart stuttered. "A baby?"

"If that's what you want," he hastily amended. "If you don't want to do it again, that's okay. But—"

"I'd love to have another baby," she told him.

"Really?"

"Maybe it's crazy, considering that I'm now twice the age that I was when I had Sierra, but yes, really."

"Does that mean you'll marry me?"

"I haven't actually heard a proposal," she said.

So he went down on one knee beside the bed and flipped open the box. "Will you marry me, Gabriella?"

She didn't even look at the ring—she didn't need to. The love that she saw shining in his eyes was all that she needed to see. "Yes, Cameron, I will absolutely marry you."

He slipped the ring on her finger. "You realize that after we exchange vows you'll become a 'princess' and living outside of the spotlight will no longer be an option?"

"I can handle it." She wrapped her arms around his neck. "I can handle anything as long as you're by my side."

"Then that's where I'll be," he promised her. "Forever."

Epilogue

*PRINCE CAMERON TO WED THE MOTHER OF HIS
CHILD?*
by Alex Girard

That's what everyone has been asking since the prince publicly confirmed he was the father of Gabriella Vasquez's sixteen-year-old daughter, Sierra, earlier this month. The question was finally answered on Saturday night in a beautiful candlelight ceremony at the royal palace.

The bride wore a simple but elegant Nicole Miller floor-length gown of ivory silk and carried a hand-tied bouquet of white gerbera daisies. The groom was outfitted by Savile Row in traditional black tie with royal decorations. The couple exchanged vows before an intimate gathering of family and close friends in the rose garden.

At the conclusion of the ceremony, the prince and his bride joined their hands together to cut into the gorgeous three-tier wedding cake created by the mother-of-the-bride (and having indulged in a taste of that exquisite cake, I now understand why Dominic Donatella wants to get his hands on her recipe!).

As the guests ate cake and drank champagne, Princess Sierra offered a first toast to the newlyweds, wishing them a long, happy life together—and wanting to know if they were *ever* going to give her a brother or a sister.

While the blissful couple left that question unanswered, at least for the moment, there is no doubt that their daughter's other wishes for them will come true.

* * * * *

THE RETURN OF
THE SHEIKH

KRISTI GOLD

One

The moment Madison Foster exited the black stretch limo, a security detail converged upon her, signaling the extreme importance of her prospective client. The light mist turned to rain as she crossed the parking lot. One massive guard was on her right, a somewhat smaller man at her left, while two other imposing goons dressed in dark suits led the way toward the Los Angeles high-rise. A few feet from the service entrance, she heard a series of shouts and camera shutters, but she didn't dare look back. Making that fatal error could land her on the cover of some seedy tabloid with a headline that read The Playboy Prince's Latest Paramour. And a disheveled presumed paramour at that. She could already feel the effects of the humidity on her unruly hair as curls began to form at her nape beneath the low ponytail. So much for the sleek, professional look. So much for the farce that it never rained in sunny Southern California.

When the guards opened the heavy metal door and ushered her inside, Madison stepped carefully onto the damp tile surface as if walking on black ice. Couldn't they see she was wearing three-inch heels? Clearly they didn't care, she realized as they navigated the mazelike hallway at a rapid clip. Fortunately they guided her into a carpeted corridor before she took a tumble and wounded her pride, or worse. They soon reached a secluded elevator at the end of the passage where one man keyed in a code on the pad next to the door.

Like a well-oiled human machine, they moved inside the car. Madison felt as if she were surrounded by a contingent of stoic man-crows. They kept their eyes trained straight ahead, not one affording her even a casual glance, much less a kind word, on the trip to the top floor.

The elevator came to a smooth stop a few moments later where the doors slid open to a gentleman dressed in a gray silk suit, his sparse scalp and wire-rimmed glasses giving him a somewhat scholarly appearance. As soon as Madison exited the car, he offered his hand and a hesitant smile. "Welcome, Miss Foster. I'm Mr. Deeb, His Highness's personal assistant."

Madison wasn't pleased with the "Miss" reference, but for the sake of decorum, she shook his hand and returned his smile without issuing a protest. "It's nice to meet you, Mr. Deeb."

"And I you." He then stepped aside and made a sweeping gesture to his right. "Come with me, please."

With the guards bringing up the rear like good little soldiers, they traveled down the penthouse's black marble vestibule beneath soaring, two-story ceilings. As a diplomat's daughter and political consultant, she'd been exposed to her share of opulence, but she wasn't so jaded she couldn't appreciate good taste. A bank of tall windows revealing the Hollywood Hills drew her attention before her focus fell on the polished steel staircase winding upward to the second story. The clean lines and contemporary furnishings were straight out of a designer's dream, but not at all what she'd expected. She'd envisioned jewels and gold and statues befitting of royalty, not a bachelor pad. An extremely wealthy bachelor's pad nonetheless. Only the best would do for Sheikh Zain ibn Aahil Jamar Mehdi, the crown prince of Bajul, who'd recently and unexpectedly become the imminent king, the reason why she'd been summoned—to restore the tarnished reputation of the man with many names. In less than a month.

After they passed beneath the staircase and took an immediate right, Madison regarded Mr. Deeb, who also seemed bent on sprinting to the finish line. "I'm surprised the prince was willing to meet with me this late in the evening."

Deeb tugged at his tie but failed to look at her. "Prince Rafiq determined the time."

Rafiq Mehdi, Prince Zain's brother, had been the one who'd hired her, so that made sense. Yet she found Deeb's odd demeanor somewhat disturbing. "His Highness is expecting me, isn't he?"

They stopped before double mahogany doors at the end of the hall where Deeb turned to face her. "When Prince Rafiq called to say you were coming, I assumed he had spoken to his brother about the matter, but I am not certain."

If Rafiq hadn't told his brother about the plan, Madison could be tossed out before her damp clothes had time to dry. "Then you're not sure if he even knows I'm here, much less why I'm here?"

Blatantly ignoring Madison's question, Deeb pointed to a small alcove containing two peacock-patterned club chairs. "If you wish to be seated, I will come for you when the emir is prepared to see you."

Provided the man actually decided to see her.

After the assistant executed an about-face and disappeared through the doors, Madison claimed a chair, smoothed a palm over her navy pencil skirt and prepared to wait. She surveyed the guards lined up along the walls with two positioned on either side of the entry. Heavily armed guards. Not surprising. When a soon-to-be-king was involved, enemies were sure to follow. She'd initially been considered a possible threat, apparent when they rifled through her leather purse looking for concealed weapons before she'd entered the limo. She highly doubted she could do much damage with a tube of lipstick and a nail file.

Madison suddenly detected the sound of a raised voice, though she couldn't make out what that voice might be saying. Even if she could, she probably wouldn't understand most of the Arabic words. Yet there was no mistaking someone was angry, and she'd bet her last bottle of merlot she knew the identity of that someone.

Zain Mehdi reportedly didn't know the meaning of restraint, evidenced by his questionable activities. The notorious sheikh had left his country some seven years ago and taken up residence in the States. He'd often disappeared for months at a time, only to surface with some starlet or supermodel on his arm, earning him the title "Phantom Prince of Arabia."

That behavior hadn't necessarily shocked Madison. Many years ago, she'd met him at a dinner party she'd attended with her parents in Milan. Back then, he'd been an incurable sixteen-year-old flirt. Not that he'd flirted with her, or that he would even remember her at all, a gawky preteen with no confidence. A girl who'd been content to blend into the background, very much like her mother.

She didn't do the blending-in thing these days. She intended to be front and center, and if she managed to succeed at this assignment, that would prove to be another huge feather in her professional cap.

When the doors opened wide, Madison came to her feet, adjusted her white linen jacket and held her breath in hopes that she wouldn't be dismissed. "Well?" she asked when Deeb didn't immediately speak.

"The emir will see you now," he said, his tone somewhat wary. "But he is not happy about it."

As long as she had the opportunity to win him over, Madison didn't give a horse's patoot about the prince's current mood. "Fair enough."

Deeb opened the door and followed her inside the well-appointed office. But she didn't have the time—or the inclination—to study the room further. The six-foot-plus man leaning back against the massive desk, arms folded across his chest, his intense gaze contrasting with his casual stance, now captured her complete attention. Publicity photos—or her distant memories—definitely didn't do Zain Mehdi justice.

With his perfectly symmetrical features, golden skin and deep brown eyes framed by ridiculously long black lashes, he could easily be pegged as a Hollywood star preparing to play the role of a Middle Eastern monarch. Yet he'd forgone the royal robes for a white tailored shirt rolled up at the sleeves and a pair of dark slacks. He also wore an expression that said he viewed her as an intruder.

Madison tamped down her nerves, shored up her

frame and faked a calm facade. "Good evening, Your Highness. I'm Madison Foster."

He studied her offered hand but ignored the gesture. "I know who you are. You are the daughter of Anson Foster, a member of the diplomatic corps and a longtime acquaintance of my father's."

At least he remembered her father, even if he probably didn't remember her. "My sincerest condolences on your loss, Your Highness. I'm sure the king's sudden passing came as quite a shock."

He shifted his weight slightly, a sure sign of discomfort. "Not as shocking as learning of his death two weeks after the fact."

"The emir was traveling when his father passed," Deeb added from behind Madison.

The sheikh sent his assistant a quelling look. "That will be all, Deeb. Ms. Foster and I will continue this conversation in private."

Madison glanced over her shoulder to see Deeb nodding before he said, "As you wish, Emir."

As soon as the right-hand man left the room, the sheikh strolled around the desk, dropped down into the leather chair and gestured toward the opposing chair. "Be seated."

Say please, Madison wanted to toss out. Instead, she slid into the chair, set her bag at her feet and made a mental note to work on his manners. "Now that we've established you know who I am, do you understand why I'm here?"

He leaned back and streaked a palm over his shadowed jaw. "You are here at my brother's request, not mine. According to Rafiq, you are one of the best political consultants in this country. *If* your reputation holds true."

If his reputation held true, she had her work cut out for her. "I've worked alongside political strategists in successfully assisting high-profile figures with public perception."

"And why do you believe I would need your assistance with that?"

Okay, she'd draw him a picture, but it wouldn't be pretty. "For starters, you haven't been back to Bajul in years. Second, I know there's concern that you won't be welcomed with open arms when you do return to assume your position as king. And last, there is the issue with the women."

He had the gall to give her a devil-may-care grin. "You cannot believe everything you hear, Ms. Foster."

"True, but many people believe what they read. Therefore, it's imperative we convey that you're focused on being an effective leader like your father."

His smile disappeared out of sight. "Then I am to assume you wish to mold me into the image of my father."

She found the comment to be extremely telling. "No. I want to help you build a more favorable image of yourself."

"And how do you propose to do that?"

Very carefully. "By reintroducing you to your people through a series of public appearances and social events."

He inclined his head and studied her straight-on. "You intend to invite the entire country to a cocktail party?"

She could now add *sarcastic* along with *sexy* to his list of attributes. "The social events would be private. I'll include only those in your close circle of friends and your family, as well as members of the governing council. Possibly a few foreign dignitaries and politicians and perhaps some investors."

He grabbed a pen from the desktop and began to turn it over and over. "Go on."

At least he seemed mildly interested. "As far as the public appearances are concerned, I have a lot of experience with speech writing," she said. "I'd be happy to assist you with that."

He frowned. "I have a graduate degree in economics from Oxford and I am fluent in five languages, Ms. Foster. What makes you think I cannot compose my own speeches in an articulate manner?"

Nothing like stepping on his royal pride. "I'm sure you're quite capable, Your Highness, which is why I said I'd *assist* you. What you say and how you say it will be extremely important in winning over the masses."

He tossed the pen aside and released a gruff sigh. "I have no reason to engage in political maneuvering. In the event you haven't heard, my position is already secure. I was chosen to be king, and my word is the law. I *am* the law."

"True, but when people are happy with their leader, that makes for a more peaceful country. And we have less than a month before your official coronation to change your country's opinion of you. During that time, we'll cover all the details, from the way you speak and act to the way you dress."

He sent her a sly, overtly sensual smile. "Will you be dressing me?"

The sudden images flitting around Madison's mind would be deemed less than appropriate. They even leaned a little toward being downright dirty. "I'm sure your staff can assist you with that."

"It's unfortunate that's not among your duties," he said. "I would be more inclined to agree to your plan."

As far as she was concerned, he could put that charisma card right back into the deck. "Look, I realize you're used to charming women into doing your bidding, but that tact doesn't work with me."

He gave her a skeptical look. "If I decide to accept your offer, would you be willing to stay on after the coronation?"

She hadn't expected that question. "Possibly, if you could afford to keep me on staff. My services aren't cheap."

He released a sharp, cynical laugh. "Look around, Ms. Foster. Does it appear I'm destitute?"

Not even close. "We can discuss the possibility later. Right now, we need to concentrate on the current issue at hand, if you're willing to work with me."

He studied the ceiling for a moment before bringing his gaze back to hers. "The answer is no, I am not willing to work with you. I am quite capable of handling my own affairs."

She wasn't ready to give up without pointing out the most major concern. "Speaking of affairs, I'm also skilled when it comes to dealing with scandals, in case you have any of those little sex skeletons hiding in a closet."

His expression turned steely as he stood. "My apologies for wasting your time, but I believe we are finished now."

Apparently she'd hit a serious nerve, and yes, they were definitely finished.

Madison came to her feet, withdrew a business card from her bag and placed it on the desk. "Should you change your mind, here's my number. I'll let you break the news to your brother."

"Believe me, I have much to stay to my brother," he said. "That is first on my agenda when I return to Bajul."

She'd like to have front row seats to that. She'd also like to think he might reconsider. Unfortunately, neither fell into the realm of possibility at the moment. "I wish you all the best for a smooth transition, Your Highness. Again, let me know if you decide you need my services."

After slipping the bag's strap back on her shoulder, Madison covered her disappointment with a determined walk to the door. But before she made a hasty exit, the sheikh called her back. "Yes?" she said as she faced him, trying hard not to seem too hopeful.

He'd rounded the desk and now stood only a few feet away. "You've changed quite a bit since we first met all those years ago."

The fact he did recall the dinner party, and he hadn't bothered to mention it before now, thoroughly shocked her. "I'm surprised you remember me at all."

"Very difficult to forget such an innocent face, ocean-blue eyes and those remarkable blond curls."

Here came the annoying blush, right on cue. "I wore glasses and braces and my hair was completely out of control." Which had all been remedied with laser eye surgery, orthodontists and flat irons.

He took a few steps toward her. "You wore a pink dress, and you were very shy. You barely glanced my way."

Oh, but she had. Several times. When he hadn't been looking. "I've since gotten over the shyness."

"I noticed that immediately. I've also noticed you've grown into a very beautiful woman."

Madison barely noticed anything but his dark, pensive eyes when he walked right up to her, leaving little space between them. "Now that we've established my transformation," she said, "I need to get to the airport so I don't miss my flight to D.C." She needed to get away from him before his extreme magnetism commandeered her common sense.

"I do have a private jet," he said, his gaze unwavering. "You are welcome to use it whenever it is available. If you plan to travel to the region in the future, feel free to contact me and I'll arrange to have you transported to Bajul. I would enjoy having you as my guest. I could show you things you've never seen before. Give you an experience you will not easily forget."

She'd enjoy being his guest, perhaps too much. "You mean an evening trek by camel, or perhaps on the back of an elephant, across the desert? You'll feed me pomegranates while we're entertained by dancing girls?"

He looked more amused than offended by her cynicism. "I prefer all-terrain vehicles to camels and pachyderms, I detest pomegranates, but dancing would be an option. Between us, of course."

She didn't dare dance with him, much less take a midnight ride with him in any form or fashion. "As fascinating as that sounds, and as much as I appreciate the offer, I won't be traveling outside the U.S. now that I won't be working with you. But thank you for the invitation, and have a safe trip home."

This time when Madison hurried away, the future king closed the doors behind her, a strong reminder that another important career door had closed.

However, she refused to give in to defeat. Not quite yet. As soon as the sheikh returned home, he might decide he needed her after all.

He greatly needed an escape.

The absolute loss of freedom weighed heavily on Zain as the armored car navigated the steep drive leading to the palace. So did the less-than-friendly reception. A multitude of citizens lined the drive, held back by the guards charged with his protection. Some had their fists raised in anger, others simply scowled. Because of the bulletproof glass, he couldn't quite make out what they were shouting, yet he doubted they were singing his praises.

Rafiq had suggested he return at night, yet he'd refused. He might be seriously flawed, but had never been a coward. Whatever he had to endure to fulfill his obligation, he would do so with his head held high and without help.

He thought back to Madison Foster's visit two days ago, as well as her intimation that he might be considered a stranger in a familiar land. He'd come close to accepting her offer, but not for those reasons. She'd simply intrigued him. She'd also forced him to realize how long it had been since he'd kept company with a woman. Yet she would have proven to be too great a temptation, and he could not afford even a hint of a scandal. If they only knew the real scandal that had existed within the palace gates, a secret that had plagued him for seven years, and the primary reason why he'd left.

As the car came to a stop, Zain quickly exited, but he couldn't ignore the shouts of *"Kha'en!"* He could not counter the claims he'd been a traitor without revealing truths he had no intention of disclosing.

Two sentries opened the heavy doors wide, allowing him to evade the crowd's condemnation for the time being. Yet the hallowed halls of the palace were as cold as the stone that comprised them. At one time he'd been happy to call this place home—a refuge steeped in lavish riches and ancient history. Not anymore. But he did welcome the site of the petite woman standing at the end of the lengthy corridor—Elena Battelli, the Italian au pair hired by his father for his sons, despite serious disapproval from the elders. Elena had been his nursemaid, his teacher, his confidante and eventually his surrogate mother following his own mother's untimely death. She'd been the only person who understood his ways, including his wanderlust.

As soon as Zain reached her, Elena opened her arms and smiled. "Welcome back, *caro mio.*" She spoke to him in English, as she always had with the Mehdi boys, their "code" when they'd wanted to avoid prying ears.

He drew her into an embrace before stepping back and studying her face. "You are still as elegant as a gazelle, Elena."

She patted her neatly coiffed silver hair. "I am an old gazelle, and you are still the charming *giovinetto* I have always adored." A melancholy look suddenly crossed her face. "Now that your father has sadly left us, and you are to be king, I shall address you as such, Your Majesty."

"Do not even think of it," he said. "You are family and always will be, regardless of my station."

She reached up and patted his cheek. "Yes, that is true. But you are still the king."

"Not officially for another few weeks." That reminded him of his most pressing mission. "Where is Rafiq?"

She shrugged. "In your father's study, *caro.* He has spent most of his time there since..." Her gaze wandered away, but not before Zain glimpsed tears in her eyes.

He leaned and kissed her cheek. "We shall have a long talk soon."

She pulled a tissue from her pocket and dabbed at her eyes. "We shall. You must tell me everything you have been doing while you were away."

He didn't dare tell her everything. He might be an

adult now, but she could still make him feel like the errant schoolboy. "I look forward to our visit."

Ignoring his bodyguards and Deeb, Zain sprinted up the stone steps to his father's second-floor sanctuary and opened the door without bothering to knock. The moment he stepped inside, he thought back to how badly he'd hated this place, plagued by memories of facing his father's ire over crossing lines that he'd been warned not to cross. King Aadil Mehdi had ruled with an iron hand and little heart. And now he was gone.

Zain experienced both guilt and regret that their last words had been spoken in anger. That he hadn't been able to forgive his father for his transgressions. Yet he could not worry about that now. He had more pressing matters that hung over his head like a guillotine.

His gaze came to rest on his brother predictably seated in the king's favorite chair located near the shelves housing several rare collections. The changes in Rafiq were subtle in some ways, obvious in others. He wore the kaffiyeh, which Zain refused to wear, at least for the time being. He also sported a neatly trimmed goatee, much the same as their father's. In fact, Rafiq could be a younger version of the king in every way—both physically and philosophically.

Rafiq glanced up from the newspaper he'd been reading and leveled a nonchalant look on Zain. "I see you have arrived in one piece."

He didn't appreciate his brother's indifference or that he looked entirely too comfortable in the surroundings. "And I see you've taken up residence in the king's official office. Do you plan to stay here indefinitely?"

Rafiq folded the paper in precise creases and tossed it onto the nearby desk. "The question is, brother, do you intend to stay indefinitely, or will this be only a brief visit?"

Zain's anger began to boil below the surface as he attempted to cling to his calm. "Unfortunately for you, as the rightful heir to the throne, I'll be here permanently. I've been preparing for this role for years."

"By bedding women on several continents?"

His composure began to diminish. "Do not pretend to know me, Rafiq."

"I would never presume that, Zain. You have been away for seven years and I only know what I have read about you."

At one time, he and Rafiq had been thick as thieves. Sadly, that had ended when his brother had sided with their father over their differences, leaving brotherly ties in tatters. "I left because our father placed me in an intolerable position."

"He only wanted you to adhere to the rules."

Outdated rules that made no sense in modern times, yet that had only been a small part of his decision. If Rafiq knew the whole story, he might not be so quick to revere their patriarch. "He wanted me to be exactly like him—unwilling to move this country into the millennium because of archaic ideals."

Rafiq rose slowly to his feet and walked to the window to peer outside. "The people are gathered at the gates, along with members of the press. One group demands an explanation as to why their new king deserted them years ago, the other waits for the wayward prince to explain his questionable behavior. Quite the dilemma."

"I will answer those questions in due time." Those that needed answering.

Rafiq turned and frowned. "Are you certain you can handle the pressure?"

If he didn't leave soon, he could possibly throw a punch, producing more fodder for the gossip mill. "Your lack of faith wounds me, brother. Have you ever known a time when I failed to win people over?"

"We are not children any longer, Zain," he said. "You can no longer brandish a smile and a few choice words and expect to prove you are worthy to be king."

He clenched his fists now dangling at his sides. "Yet our father chose me to be king, Rafiq, whether you agree or not."

"Our father believed that designating you as his successor would ensure you would eventually return. And in regard to your current status, you have yet to be officially crowned."

Zain wondered if his brother might be hoping he would abdicate before that time. Never in a million years would he do that. Especially now. "That should be enough time for a seamless transition." If only he felt as confident as he'd sounded.

"There will be serious challenges," Rafiq said. "Our father worked hard to maintain our status as a neutral, autonomous country. Our borders are secure and we have avoided political unrest."

"And we will continue to do so under my reign."

"Only if you can convince your subjects that you have their best interests at heart. Any semblance of unrest will only invite those who would take advantage of the division. That is why I urge you to consider working with Madison Foster."

He should have known it would come back to her. He'd had enough trouble keeping his thoughts away from Madison without the reminder. "Why do you believe her input would be so invaluable?"

"She has been extremely successful in her endeavors," Rafiq said. "She has taken men with political aspirations and serious deficits and restored their honor."

He was growing weary of the insults. "So now my honor is in question?"

"To some degree, yes," Rafiq said as he reclaimed the chair. "What harm would there be in utilizing her talents? Quite frankly, I cannot believe you would refuse the opportunity to spend time with an attractive woman."

As always, most people assumed he had no other concerns than his next conquest. Of course, he couldn't deny that he'd considered the advantages of having Madison involved in his daily routine. Yet that might be dangerous in the long term, unless he wanted to prove everyone right that he could not resist temptation. "Again, I do not wish or need her help."

Rafiq blew out a frustrated sigh. "If you choose the wrong path, Zain, there will be no turning back. If you fail to win over your subjects, you will weaken our country, leaving it open to radical factions bent on taking advantage of our weakness. Is your pride worth possible ruin?"

Zain thought back to the angry voices, the accusations he'd endured moments ago. He hated to concede to his brother's demands, but he did recognize Rafiq's valid concerns. He would find a way to maintain his pride and still accept Madison's assistance—as long as she understood that he would remain completely in charge. Considering the woman's obvious tenacity, that could be a challenge. But then he had always welcomed a good challenge.

If bringing Madison Foster temporarily into the fold kept Rafiq off his back, he saw no harm in giving it a try. "All right. I will give it some thought, but should I decide to accept her assistance, I will only do so if it's understood that I'll dismiss her if she is more hindrance than help."

"Actually, the agreement is already in place, and the terms of her contract state she cannot be dismissed on the grounds of anything other than gross misconduct. That would be my determination, not yours."

Contract? "When did she sign this document?"

"After she contacted me to report on your initial meeting. She is bound to stay until after your coronation, but she insisted on a clause that allows her the option to leave prior to that time should she find the situation intolerable."

His own brother had tied him to a liaison against his will. However, that did not mean he had to be cooperative. "Since you leave me no choice, my first official edict states you will be in charge of the arrangements to bring her here."

Rafiq sent him a victorious smile. "You may consider it done."

As fatigue began to set in, Zain loosened his tie and released the shirt collar's top button. "We'll continue our conversation over dinner." He suddenly remembered he hadn't seen any sign of his youngest brother. "Will Adan be joining us?"

"Adan is currently in the United Kingdom for flight training. He will be returning before the coronation."

Zain couldn't mask his disappointment. "I've been looking forward to seeing him and catching up on his accomplishments. But it's probably best we have no distractions when you bring me up to speed on the council's most recent endeavors."

Rafiq cleared his throat and looked away. "We will not exactly be dining alone."

"Another member of the council?"

"No. A woman."

Zain suspected he might know what this was all about. "Is this someone special in your life?"

"She has no bearing on my life."

He internally cringed. "If this is the beginning of the queen candidate procession, then I—"

"She is not in the market to be your wife."

He did not appreciate his brother's vagueness. "Then who is she, Rafiq?"

"Madison Foster."

Two

"Do you always insist on having your way?"

Startled, Madison shot a glance to her right to discover Zain Mehdi standing in the doorway, one shoulder leaned against the frame, his expression unforgiving on that patently gorgeous face. "Do you always barge in without knocking?" she asked around the surprise attack.

"The door was ajar."

She turned from the bureau, bumped the drawer closed with her butt and tightened the sash on the blue satin robe. "Really? I could have sworn I closed it before I took my shower. But I suppose it could have magically opened on its own, since Arabia is well-known for its magic."

He ignored her sarcasm and walked into the room without an invitation, hands firmly planted in the pockets of his black slacks. With those deadly dark eyes and remarkable physique, the Arabian king could pass for an exotic male model—a model who sorely lacked good comportment.

He strolled to the open armoire to inspect the row of suits, skirts and slacks that Madison had hung only moments before. "As I predicted. Conventional clothing."

His audacity was second only to his arrogance. "It's known as business attire."

"Attire that conceals your true nature," he said as he slid his fingertips down the side of one beige silk skirt.

She couldn't quite explain why she shivered over the gesture, or the sudden, unexpected image of experiencing his touch firsthand. "What do you know about my true nature?"

"I know your kind." He turned and presented a seriously sexy half smile. "Beneath the conservative clothes you wear colorful lingerie."

Lucky guess. "That's a rather huge assumption."

"Am I wrong?"

She refused to confirm or deny his conjecture. "Don't you have some royal duty to perform? Maybe you should have all the locks checked on all the palace doors."

He took a few slow steps toward her. "I'll leave as soon as you tell me why you're here when I made it quite I clear I do not need your help."

She was starting to ask herself the same question. "Your brother's convinced that you need my help."

"Rafiq isn't in charge of my life, nor is he in charge of the country. I am, and I can handle the transition on my own without any assistance."

Oh, but he did need her help, even if he wouldn't admit it. Yet. "From what I witnessed during your arrival, it appears the people aren't welcoming you with open arms."

His expression turned to stone. "As I told you before, Ms. Foster, they have no choice. I am this country's rightful leader and they will have to learn to accept it."

"But wouldn't it be more favorable if you had the blessing of your country's people?"

"And how do you propose to assist me in winning their approval? Do you plan to throw me a parade along with the international cocktail party?"

She mentally added *cynical* to the *sexy* thing. "I suppose we could try that, but a parade isn't successful unless someone shows up. I have several ideas and I hope that you'll at least give me the opportunity to explore those options with you."

"Ah, yes. The social gatherings where you'll be parading me in front of dignitaries."

"We nixed the parade, remember?"

Amusement called out from his dark eyes. "I am still not convinced that you will make an impact on my acceptance."

Time to bring out the legal implications. "As I'm sure your brother told you, the contract states I'll be here until the coronation, whether you choose to work with me or not. Of course, I can't force you to cooperate, but it would be worth your while to at least make the effort."

He seemed to mull that over for a minute while Madison held her breath. "All right. Since you are protected by a legal document, and I've been stripped of my power to dismiss you, I will cooperate on a trial basis. But that cooperation hinges on your ability to meet my terms."

She should have known he'd have an ulterior motive behind his sudden change of heart. "And what would those be?"

His smile returned, slow as a desert sunrise. "I'll let you know in the upcoming days."

Something told Madison his terms could be somewhat suspect. Still, she was more than curious, as well as determined to win him over. "Fine. We can begin tomorrow morning."

"We can begin tonight after dinner," he said, followed by a long visual journey from her neck to her bare feet. "I personally have no objection to your current attire, but something a little less distracting might be more appropriate."

She'd basically forgotten what she was wearing—or wasn't wearing for that matter. "Since I've spent a good deal of time attending state dinners, I know how to dress properly."

He rested one hand on the ornately carved footboard. "This isn't a diplomatic affair, Ms. Foster, only a casual meal."

She felt somewhat uncomfortable having him so close to the bed. "Will both your brothers be dining with us?"

"Only Rafiq. Adan's currently away on a mission."

She was disappointed she wouldn't meet the youngest Mehdi son. "Diplomatic assignment?"

"Military. He's testing a new aircraft."

"That's right. I'd read somewhere he's a pilot."

"Adan's affinity for danger is second only to his appreciation of beautiful women," he said. "He will be greatly disappointed if he does not have the opportunity to meet you."

Maybe it was best if baby brother stayed away for as long as possible. Two womanizers under one roof could be too much to handle. "Will he be back for the coronation?"

Zain pushed away from the bed, allowing Madison to breathe a little easier. "As far as I know."

She hugged her arms closer to her middle. "I'll meet him then."

"If you are still here," he said.

He wasn't going to get rid of her that easily. But she did plan to dismiss him for the time being. "Since it's getting late, I should probably get dressed now."

"Yes, I suppose you should," he said, a hint of fake disappointment in his tone. "I wouldn't mind seeing you in the black dress you have hanging behind your business suits."

He'd been more observant than she realized. "I'll decide what I'm wearing after you're gone."

"You should definitely consider the red lingerie."

Madison didn't understand his fascination with her underwear, or how he'd correctly guessed her fondness for red silk, until she followed his gaze to some focal point at her hip. When she looked down, she saw her bra strap hanging from the closed drawer like a crimson snake in the grass. She quickly stuffed it back inside before pointing toward the door. "Out. Now."

"Dinner is at five-thirty sharp. Do not be late," he said as he walked out the door and closed it behind him.

The man's overbearing behavior equaled his fortune, but he had a thing or two to learn about Madison's determination. She didn't appreciate his observations, even if he had been on target when it came to her clothing. Still, no sexy, bossy sheikh—even if he happened to be a king and her current employer—would dictate her choice in panties. In fact, Zain Mehdi would have nothing whatsoever to do with her panties. And the next time she had him alone, she planned to set him straight about what she expected from him. Namely respect.

The sudden knock indicated she could have an immediate opportunity to do that very thing. On the heels of her frustration, she strode across the room, flung open the door and greeted the offending party with, "More commentary on my underwear?"

When she saw the demure lady with silver hair and topaz eyes standing in the hallway, Madison realized she'd made a colossal mistake. Yet she couldn't seem to speak around her mortification.

"I'm Elena Battelli," the woman said as she extended her hand. "And I am not concerned with your undergarments."

She accepted the gesture and attempted a self-conscious smile. "I'm Madison Foster, and I'm so sorry. I thought you were—"

"Prince Zain, of course."

Realizing her state of undress had only compounded the erroneous assumptions, Madison hugged her arms tightly around her middle. "I know how this must look to you, but His Highness accidentally walked in on me."

The woman sent her a knowing look. "Prince Zain never does anything accidentally."

She wouldn't dispute that point. "Regardless, nothing inappropriate occurred."

"Of course," Elena said, her tone hinting at disbelief. "Do you find your accommodations satisfactory?"

Who wouldn't? The massive marble jetted tub alone was worth any grief Zain Mehdi could hand her. "Very much so, thank you."

She took a slight step back. "Good. Dinner's at six."

"Prince Zain told me five-thirty."

"I am afraid you've been misled," Elena said. "Dinner is always served at 6:00 p.m. That has been the designated time since I've been an employee."

Madison saw the woman as the perfect resource for information on the future king. "How long ago has that been?"

She lifted her chin with pride. "Thirty-four years. I arrived before Prince Zain's birth to assume my role as his *bambinaia,* or in English, his—"

"Nanny," Madison interjected, then added, "I speak Italian. I studied abroad in Florence my sophomore year in college."

Elena's expression brightened. "Excellent. I am from Scandicci."

"I visited there a few times. It's a beautiful place. Do you go back often?"

All the joy seemed to drain from Elena's face. "Not as often as I would like. My life is here with the royal family."

A royal family with adult sons who no longer needed a nanny. A keeper, maybe, but not a nursemaid. "How do you spend your days now that the princes are grown?"

"I am basically in charge of running the household while waiting for my opportunity to raise another generation of Mehdi children."

Madison didn't quite see Zain as father material, an opinion she'd keep to herself. "I'm sure you gained invaluable experience with Prince Zain."

"Yes, yet clearly I failed to impress upon him the merits of self-control when it comes to the opposite sex. Otherwise, he would not be interested in your undergarments."

They shared in a brief laugh before Madison revealed her opinion on the subject. "I assure you, Prince Zain will not be commenting on my personal effects if I have any say in the matter."

Elena presented a sly smile. "A word of advice. Prince Zain is a good man, yet he is still a man. What he lacks in restraint, he makes up in charm. Stand firm with him."

With that, she walked away, leaving Madison to ponder exactly what the future king might have up his sleeve when he'd told her the incorrect time for dinner. She highly doubted he'd forgotten standard palace protocol in spite of his lengthy absence. Perhaps he was simply trying to throw her off balance in order to be rid of her.

Too bad. She would definitely stand her ground with him from this point forward. And as far as dinner went, she'd ignore his edict and show up when she darn well pleased.

She was fifteen minutes late, yet Zain wasn't at all surprised. Madison Foster possessed an extreme need to be in control. Granted, he had the means to break down her defenses, and he was tempted to try. Nothing overt. Nothing more than a subtle and slight seduction designed to make her uncomfortable enough to bow out and return to the States where she belonged.

However, she could very well turn the tables by responding to his advances. Possible, but not likely, he decided when she entered the dining room wearing a slim black skirt that came right above her knees, conservative heels and a simple white blouse. A blouse sheer enough to reveal the outline of an equally white bra, most likely in an effort to prove her point. But he knew better. That professional, prim and proper persona only served to conceal the daring beneath her cool exterior. He'd wager the kingdom she had on a pair of brightly colored panties. Red panties.

A richly detailed fantasy assaulted him, one that involved sitting beside her and running his hand up the inside of her thigh and—

"Where would you like me?"

He thought of several answers, none of them appropriate. He chose the least suggestive one. "Are you referring to the seating arrangements, or do you have something else in mind?"

She approached the table and sent him a false smile. "Let me rephrase for the sake of clarity. Where do you want me to be seated?"

Zain gestured to the right of where he was positioned at the head of the lengthy table. "Here." He waited for her to slide into the chair before he launched into his reprimand. "You're late."

She made an exaggerated show of checking her watch. "Actually, I'm fifteen minutes early, since it seems, according to Elena, dinner is and always has been at six."

He'd been betrayed by his former governess and long-time confidante. "Now that I will soon assume my rightful role as king, dinner will be at five-thirty."

She folded her hands atop the table, her gaze unwavering. "I suppose having your first royal edict involving dinnertime is preferable to, oh, say, changing the entire governmental structure."

"That will be my second royal edict."

She looked sincerely confused. "Are you serious?"

He smiled. "Not entirely, but I do plan to implement some much-needed change."

"Change cannot occur until you are officially crowned, brother."

Zain pulled his gaze from Madison to see Rafiq claiming his place at the opposite end of the table. "As disappointing as it might be to you, *brother,* that will happen in a matter of weeks. In the meantime, I plan to outline those changes to the council later this week."

Rafiq lifted his napkin and placed it in his lap. "I have no designs on your position, Zain. But I do have a vested interest in the direction in which you plan to take my country."

He fisted his hands on the heels of his anger. "*Our* country, Rafiq. A country that I plan to lead into the twenty-first century."

Madison cleared her throat, garnering their attention. "What's for dinner?"

"Cheeseburgers in your honor."

When he winked, she surprisingly smiled. "I was truly looking forward to sampling some Middle Eastern fare," she said.

"We're having the chef's special kebabs," Rafiq said. "You will have to excuse my brother's somewhat questionable sense of humor, Ms. Foster."

After shooting Rafiq an acid look, Zain regarded Madison again. "I believe you'll agree that a questionable sense of humor is better than no sense of humor at all."

She shifted slightly in her seat. "I enjoyed meeting Elena. Will she be joining us?"

"Not tonight," Rafiq said as one of the staff circled the table and poured water. "She has some work to attend to, but she sends her apologies."

"She works much too hard," Zain added. "I plan to put an end to that and soon."

Rafiq leaned back in his chair. "I am afraid her work will not let up until after the coronation and the wedding."

"Wedding?" Madison asked, the shock in her tone matching Zain's.

"And who is the lucky bride?" Zain asked, though he suspected he knew the answer.

"Rima Acar, of course," Rafiq said. "We will be married the week before the coronation."

Zain wasn't at all surprised by the news his brother was going through with the long-standing marriage contract. He was surprised—and angry—over the timing.

"Is this wedding a means to detract from my assuming my rightful place as king?"

"Of course not," Rafiq said. "This wedding has been in the planning stages for years. Almost twelve if you consider when Father and the sultan came to an agreement."

"Ah, yes, the age-old tradition of bride bartering." Zain turned his attention back to Madison, who seemed intent on pushing fruit around on her plate. "We are destined to choose a wife from the highest bidder. Someone who will give us many heirs, if not passion."

"As you, too, had your bride chosen for you," Rafiq added.

Madison's blue eyes went wide. "You're engaged?"

"Not any longer," Rafiq said. "Zain's intended grew tired of waiting for his return and married another."

He had thanked his good fortune for that many times over. "Her decision was for the best. I refuse to wed a woman whom I've never met, let alone kissed." He leaned forward and leveled his gaze on his brother. "Have you kissed Rima? Have you determined there will be enough passion to sustain your marriage? Or do you even care?"

He could see the fury brewing in Rafiq's eyes. "That is none of your concern. Passion is not important. Continuing the royal lineage is."

"Procreating would be rather difficult if you cannot bear to touch your wife, brother. Or perhaps you will be satisfied with bedding her only enough times to make a child, as it was with our own parents."

"Do not believe everything you hear, Zain. Our parents had a satisfactory marriage."

Rafiq—always their father's defender. "Satisfactory?

Are you also going to dispute that the king played a part in our mother's—"

Rafiq slammed his palm on the table, rattling the dinnerware. "That is enough."

Zain tossed his napkin aside and ignored the woman setting the entrée before him. "I agree. I have had enough of this conversation." He came to his feet and regarded Madison. "Ms. Foster, my apologies for disrupting your meal."

Without even a passing glance at his brother, Zain left the room and took the stairs two at a time. He had no doubt that after the display of distasteful family dynamics, he would have no need to seduce Madison Foster. She would most likely be taking the first plane back to America.

With a plate balanced in her left hand, Madison knocked with her right and waited to gain entry, affording the king the courtesy he hadn't shown her earlier that afternoon.

"Enter" sounded from behind the heavy wooden door, the gruff, masculine voice full of obvious frustration.

Madison strode into the room, head held high, determined not to show even a speck of nervousness, though admittedly she was a little shaky. More than a little shaky when she met his stern gaze and realized he didn't look at all thrilled to see her.

She set the plate on the desk and sat across from him without waiting for an invitation. "Elena sent you some pasta and the message that if you don't eat, you'll be too weak to rule."

He didn't bother to stand. Instead, he stared at her for a few moments before he pushed the offering away. "You may tell Elena I will eat when I'm hungry."

She'd been stuck in the middle of one argument too many today. "You can tell her. Right now, we need to discuss your upcoming plans."

He leaned back in the brown leather chair and tented his hands together. "I assumed you would be well on your way home by now."

"You assumed wrong. I'm determined to see this through."

"Even after we aired our family grievances at dinner?"

He had a lot to learn about her tenacity. "I've heard worse, and now I'd like to ask you a few questions."

"Proceed."

She would, with caution. "Do you have a strategy for overcoming your playboy reputation?"

"My reputation has been overblown, Ms. Foster."

"Perception is everything when it comes to politics, Your Highness. And believe what you will, you're in a political battle to restore your people's faith in you. You've been gone almost ten years—"

"Seven years."

"If you were a dog, that's equivalent to almost fifty years." And that had to be the most inane thing she'd said in ages, if ever. "Not that you're a dog. I'm only saying that seven years is a long time in your situation."

He hinted at a smile. "Do you own a dog?"

"Yes, I do. I mean, I did." Clearly he was trying to divert her attention from more pressing concerns by using her former pooch. "Could we please get back on point?"

"Yes," he said. "The point is I am quite capable of overcoming my exaggerated reputation by demonstrating there is more to my character."

He was so sure of himself. So sexy in his confidence, and she hated herself for noticing. Again. "Can you really do that? Can you persuade the world you're a serious leader when you can't even convince your own brother you're committed to your duty?"

His dark eyes relayed an intense anger. "What did Rafiq tell you when I left the table?"

Not as much as she would've liked. "He only said that he's worried you'll take off again if the pressure becomes too great."

"Despite what my brother believes, I am not a coward."

"I don't think anyone is calling you a coward." She sighed. "Look, I realize you have a lot of pride, but you might want to give up a little and realize you need someone in your corner. Someone who can serve as a sounding board during this transition."

"And you are that someone?"

"I can be. And if you'll allow me to use my connections, I can help establish some allies, and every country needs those. Even small, autonomous countries. I also still contend that you could use some help with your public addresses." When he started to speak, she held up her hand to silence him. "I know, you have a degree and you're intelligent and articulate, but I don't see the harm in brainstorming content."

"I still see no reason why I would need to consult anyone on what I wish to say or how I wish to say it."

She was making no headway whatsoever. "What about the press? Wouldn't you like to have someone serve as a buffer to make certain they convey the proper message?"

"I have Deeb for that."

Deeb had about as much personality as a paperweight. "But if you show the world that you have a woman at your side, and one you're not engaging in a torrid affair, that would send a clear message you're not the player everyone believes you to be."

He studied the ceiling and remained silent for a few seconds before he brought his attention back to her. "Should we proceed, I have to be assured that whatever you might hear or might learn within these sacred walls will not be repeated."

Madison sensed impending victory, and possibly some serious secrets. "You can trust me to maintain confidentiality at all costs. But I have to know if there's a scandal that could surface in the foreseeable future."

"Not if I can prevent it. And at the moment, that is all you need to know."

Madison could only hope that he might eventually trust her enough to confide in her. Otherwise, she couldn't prepare for the worst-case scenario. "Fine. Then you agree to accept my help?"

He streaked a palm over his shaded jaw. "For the time being, and as I stated earlier, you must agree to my terms."

Clearly he needed to maintain control. She'd give him a little leeway for now. "Fine. Perhaps now would be a good time to spell out your terms."

"If I disagree with your advice, you'll refrain from arguing," he said.

That could prove to be a challenge. "Okay."

"You will consult me before you plan your soirées, and you will let me approve the guest lists."

Considering his lack of popularity, it could prove to be a short list. "Fair enough."

"And you will adhere to my schedule, which means I will decide the time and the place for our meetings."

"I assumed your study would be the most appropriate meeting place."

"It might be necessary to find a more private venue."

Now she had her own terms to present. "As long as it's not your bedroom."

He smiled. "You're not the least bit curious about my royal quarters?"

Oh, yes, she was. "No. Anything else?"

He feigned disappointment. "I'll let you know as soon as I've determined what I expect beyond what we've already discussed."

Talk about being vague. But she'd accept vague as long as she could continue as planned. "We'll go over your upcoming schedule in the morning, Your Highness, and plan accordingly."

"Call me Zain."

Her mouth momentarily dropped open over the request. "That's a bit too informal, don't you think?"

"When we're alone, I want you to call me by my given name. Otherwise, our agreement terminates immediately."

What kind of game was he playing? Only time would tell, and Madison hoped she didn't find herself on the losing end.

She came to her feet and tugged at the hem of her blouse. "Whatever floats your boat, *Zain*. Now if you'll excuse me, I'm going to my room to relax."

"You are excused. For now."

Madison had only made it a few steps toward the door before Zain uttered the single word. "Black."

She turned and frowned. "Excuse me?"

"You're wearing black lingerie."

Did the man have X-ray vision? "Why are you so fascinated with my underwear?"

His grin arrived slowly. "Am I correct?"

She folded her arms beneath her breasts. "That's for me to know—"

"And for me to find out?"

She should've known he'd been in America long enough to learn all the little sayings. "That's for me to know, period. Anything else? Or would you like to discuss *your* royal underwear?"

His grin deepened. "I have nothing to hide."

That remained to be seen. She intended to leave well enough alone before she was tempted to abandon the good-sense ship. Before she gave in to the tiny little spark of awareness or the slight full-body shiver brought about by his deadly smile. "I'm going now."

He finally rose from the chair. "I suggest you watch the sunset from the terrace outside your room. I'll have Elena send up some of her special tea to help you relax."

She'd be more relaxed as soon as she got away from all his charisma. "What kind of tea?"

"I'm not certain," he said as he strolled toward her and stopped only a foot or so away. "I've never tried it. I do know it is formulated to help a person sleep."

She'd probably have no trouble sleeping the moment her head hit the pillow. "Thank you, and I'll see you in the morning."

"You're welcome." He reached out and pushed a strand of hair behind her ear. "If the tea doesn't help you sleep, my room is next door to yours. Feel free to wake me."

"What for?" As if she really had to ask.

"Whatever you need to help you relax."

She suddenly engaged in one heck of a naked-body fantasy that made her want to run for cover. "I assure you I won't need anything to help me relax."

"Let me know if you change your mind."

"I won't be changing my mind." She turned toward the door then faced him again when something dawned on her. "By the way, if all this innuendo is some ploy to scare me off, save your breath. I've been propositioned by the best." And the worst of the worst.

He looked almost crestfallen. "I'm wounded you would think I would resort to such underhanded tactics."

Maybe she had overreacted a tad. Some men just happened to be blessed with the flirtation gene. "My apologies if I'm wrong about your motives."

"Actually, you are correct," he said. "That was my original plan. But you have bested me, so I promise to behave myself from this point forward."

She had a hard time believing that. "Well, in case you should get any more bright ideas, just know it will take more than a few well-rehearsed, suggestive lines to send me packing. I've spent many years studying human nature, and I know what you're all about."

He braced a hand on the doorframe above her head. "Enlighten me, Madison."

The sound of her name rolling softly out of his mouth, his close proximity, was not helping her concentration. "You use your charm to discourage perceived threats to your control, and to encourage the results you wish to achieve, namely driving people away. But beneath all that sexy macho bravado, I believe you're a man with a great deal of conviction when it comes to his country's future. Am I correct?"

"Perhaps you are only projecting your need for control on me. I believe at times giving up control to another is preferable. Have you never been tempted to throw out logic and act on pure instinct?"

Her instincts told her he wasn't referring to a professional relationship. "Not when it comes to mixing business with pleasure, if that's what you're asking. Don't forget we're trying to repair your reputation, not enhance it."

He had the nerve to show his pearly whites to supreme advantage. "Sometimes the pleasure is worth the risk."

"I thought you promised to behave."

He straightened and attempted to look contrite. "My apologies. I was momentarily struck senseless by your analysis."

Before she was momentarily struck stupid and kissed that smug, sexy smile off his face, Madison made a hasty exit.

She hadn't lied when she'd admitted she'd been propositioned before. She *had* lied when she'd claimed she hadn't been tempted to cross professional lines, because she had—the moment she'd reunited with Zain Mehdi.

Three

Perception is everything...

Zain had to agree with Madison on that point. He'd always been perceived as a man with a strong affinity for attractive women, a fact he could not deny. Yet that standing had provided the means to carry out his covert activities over the past seven years, and earned him the Phantom Sheikh title. His absence had always been blamed on a lover, and most of the time that had been far from the truth. *Most* of the time. He hadn't been celibate by any means, but he had not had as many affairs as what the media had led people to believe. If he had, he would have been perpetually sleep deprived.

He also recognized that giving in to temptation with a woman like Madison Foster—an intelligent, beautiful and somewhat willful woman—could possibly lead to disaster. Still, he wasn't one to easily ignore temptation, even if wisdom dictated that he must. And at the moment, Madison looked extremely tempting.

Zain remained in the open doorway to his suite in order to study her. She stood at the veranda's stone wall, looking out over the valley below, her golden hair flowing down her back. She'd exchanged her conservative clothing for more comfortable attire—a casual gauze skirt and a loose magenta top that revealed one slim, bare shoulder. He didn't need to venture a guess as to the color of her bra, since she didn't appear to be wearing one. That thought alone had him reconsidering the merits of wisdom.

Zain cleared his throat as he approached her, yet she didn't seem to notice his presence. Not until he said, "It's a remarkable view, isn't it?"

She sent him a backward glance and a slight scowl. "Why do you keep sneaking up on me?"

He moved beside her, leaving a comfortable distance between them. "My apologies. I did not intend to startle you. I only wanted to make certain you have everything you need from me."

She faced him, leaned a hip against the wall and rolled her eyes. "Are we back to that again?"

"My intentions are completely innocent." Only a half-truth. He'd gladly give her anything she needed in a carnal sense.

She took a sip from the cup clutched in her hands. "Sorry, but I'm having trouble buying the innocent act after your recent admission."

That came as no surprise to Zain, and he probably deserved her suspicions. "I will do my best to earn your trust." He nodded toward the cup. "I gather that's Elena's special tea."

"Yes, it is, and it's very good."

"Do you have any idea what might be in it?"

She lifted that bare shoulder in a shrug and took a sip. "I suspect it's chamomile and some other kind of herb. I can taste mint."

He turned toward her and rested one elbow on the stone barrier. "Take care with how much you drink. It could be more than tea."

"Too late. This is my third cup, and do you mean alcohol?"

"Precisely."

"Is that allowed?" she asked.

"Elena is free to do as she pleases, as is everyone else in the country, within reason. We've always had a spiritually, economically and culturally diverse population, due in part to people entering the borders seeking—"

"Asylum?"

"And peace."

She turned back to the view and surveyed the scene. "Then Bajul is the Switzerland of the Middle East?"

"In a manner of speaking. I might not have agreed with all my father's philosophies, but I've always admired his determination to remain neutral in a volatile region. Unfortunately, the threat to end our peaceful co-existence still exists, as it always has. As it is everywhere else in the world."

She took another drink and set the cup aside. "The landscape is incredible. I hadn't expected Bajul to be so green or elevated."

"You expected desert."

"Honestly, yes, I did."

Another example of inaccurate perception. "If you go north, you'll find the desert. Go south and you'll find the sea."

She sighed. "I love the sea. I love water, period."

He took the opportunity to move a little closer, his arm pressed against hers as he pointed toward the horizon. "Do you see that mountain rising between two smaller peaks?"

She shaded her eyes against the setting sun. "The skinny one that looks almost phallic?"

That made him smile. "It is known as Mabrúruk, our capital city's namesake. Legend has it that Al-'Uzzá, a mythological goddess, placed it there to enhance fertility. Reportedly her efforts have been successful, from crops to livestock to humans."

"Interesting," she said. "Do people have to go to the mountain to procreate, or does it have a long radius?" She followed the comment with a soft, sensual laugh. "No pun intended."

Discussing procreation with her so close only made Zain's fantasies spring to life, among other things. "I suppose it's possible, but that's not the point I was trying to make."

She turned and leaned a hip against the wall. "What point were you trying to make, Your Highness?"

She seemed determined to disregard his terms. "Zain."

Madison blew out a long breath. "What were you going to say before the topic turned to the baby-making mountain, *Zain?*"

He liked the breathless way she said his name. He liked the way she looked at the moment—slightly disheveled and extremely sensual. "I was going to point out that beyond the ridge there are two lakes. Perhaps I'll take you there in the near future."

"That would be nice, as long as you don't expect any baby making."

He certainly wouldn't mind making love to her in the

shadow of the mountain, or perhaps in the lake. Without the resulting baby, of course.

He forced his thoughts back to business matters. "My intent would be to show you the key to Bajul's future."

"What would that be?"

"Water."

She appeared to be confused. "For a fishery?"

"Food and water are commodities in the region," he explained. "We have more rain than most, and our lakes have deep aquifers. They also have the capacity to sustain our land for many years to come, and that means bountiful crops and livestock. Those commodities could serve as an export for countries that suffer shortages as long as we make certain we protect our resources. My plans include exploring innovative and eco-friendly ways to treat and preserve the water from the lakes."

She laid her palm on his arm. "That sounds like a wonderful plan, Zain."

The simple touch sent a surge of heat coursing through his body. "That plan will not come to fruition unless I can convince the council it's our best recourse as opposed to oil."

She unfortunately took her hand away. "But you'll have your brother's support, correct?"

If only that were true. "He'll be the hardest to convince. He will most likely side with the council and suggest drilling as soon as possible. I refuse to allow that unless we have exhausted all alternatives."

"I don't understand why the two of you seem to butt horns at every turn."

This would require more than a brief explanation, yet he felt she had the right to know. "Most believe that the crown automatically passes to the firstborn son. In my family's case, the reigning king can designate a successor, and he designated me, not Rafiq. My brother has resented that decision for years."

She shook her head. "I guess I assumed Rafiq was younger, although he does seem older in many ways. Not in appearance, because the resemblance between the two of you is remarkable. But he's very stoic."

"He's thirteen months older," he said. "And he is serious about preserving traditions that should be deemed obsolete in this day and time."

"I take it you're referring to arranged marriages."

Unfortunately, that was one change he wasn't prepared to make, even if it impacted his own future. "The tradition of selecting a bride with a royal heritage is necessary. Only a member of royalty can understand the royal life."

"Of course, and keeping the blood blue must be very important."

He ignored the bitterness in her tone. "I know how antiquated it might sound, but yes, that does hold some importance."

"Then why did you give your brother such a hard time about it?"

"Because I do not believe in committing to someone if you haven't explored an intimate relationship prior to committing to marriage. I would never have bought my Bugatti without test-driving it first."

Her eyes went wide. "You're comparing a woman to a car?"

"No. I am only saying that sexual compatibility holds great importance in a marriage, or it should. How will you know you are compatible in that regard unless you experience intimacy before you make a commitment?"

She looked skeptical and borderline angry. "In my

opinion, sex shouldn't carry too much weight. As they say, passion does have a tendency to fade."

"You sound as if you speak from experience. Have you been married?"

"No, but I was in a long-term relationship, and he's the reason I no longer have my dog."

"So you parted because of a canine?"

She briefly smiled. "We were the cliché. He wanted a house and kids and to live in suburbia, while I wanted a career in the city."

"And you have no desire to have a family?"

An odd and fleeting look of pain crossed her expression. "I have no intention of giving up my career for a man. My mother fell into that trap with my father."

Her past obviously was as complex as his. "That wasn't the life she chose?"

She downed the rest of the tea. "Oh, she chose it, all right. She gave up a career as a medical researcher to globe-trot with her diplomat husband. I've never understood how someone could claim to love someone so much that they'd set their aspirations aside for another person."

"Perhaps it all goes back to shared and sustained passion."

She released a sarcastic laugh. "Sorry, but I just can't wrap my mind around that. In fact, I don't even want to think about passion and my parents in the same sentence."

Her skepticism both surprised and intrigued him. "Have you never experienced a strong passion for someone?"

"As I've said, it's overrated."

Apparently she hadn't been with the right man. A man who could show her the true meaning of desire.

He could be that man. He wanted to be that man despite his original intention to drive her away. And so went the last of his wisdom.

He surveyed her face from forehead to chin and centered on her mouth. "You've never been so attuned to someone that when you enter a room, that person is all you see? You've never wanted someone so desperately that you would risk everything to have them?"

She drew in a shaky breath. "Not that I recall."

"I cannot imagine you would have voluntarily missed out on all that lovemaking has to offer."

Her eyes took on a hazy cast. "What makes you think I have missed out?"

He traced her lips with a fingertip. "If you had, you wouldn't be so quick to dismiss the existence of phenomenal sex."

He expected her to argue the point. He predicted she would back away. He wasn't prepared when she gripped the back of his neck and brought his mouth to hers.

All her untapped passion came out in the kiss. He could taste the mint on her tongue, could sense any latent resistance melt when he tightened his hold on her. He had no doubt she could feel how much he wanted her when he streamed his hands to her hips and nudged her completely against him.

He should halt the insanity before he carried her to his bed, or dispensed with formality and took her down where they now stood. Yet stopping didn't appear to be an option—until she stopped.

Madison wrested out of his arms, looking stunned and well kissed and quite perturbed. "What was that?"

Zain leaned back against the wall and dared to smile. "That was uncontrolled passion. I suppose I shouldn't be surprised you didn't recognize it."

She backed up a few steps and tugged at the hem of her blouse. "I tell you what that was. That was a huge mistake on my part. That was too much talk about that darn baby-making mountain."

When she spun around and listed to one side, he clasped her arm to prevent her from falling. "Perhaps it was the tea," he whispered in her ear from behind her.

"Perhaps I'm just an idiot." She pulled away again and spun around to face him. "I'm going to bed now."

"Do you wish some company?" he asked as she backed toward her room.

"Yes… No, I don't wish any company."

With that, she turned and disappeared through the glass door, leaving Zain alone with a strong urge to follow her, and an erection that would take hours to calm.

Now that he'd sampled what Madison Foster had to offer aside from her political expertise, he didn't want her to leave yet. He wanted more. He wanted it all.

She wanted to scream. She wanted to pull the covers over her head and forget what had happened the evening before. She wanted to tell the person who was knocking to go away and come back in day or so. Maybe by then she would be over her mortification enough to make an appearance.

Instead, Madison shoved the heavy eggplant-colored spread aside, left the bed and put on her robe on the way to answer the summons. If she happened to encounter the reason behind her current distress, she just might have to give him another piece of what was left of her mind. Or invite him in…

She yanked open the door to discover Elena once again standing on the threshold, tray in hand and a cheerful smile on her face. "Good morning, Miss Foster. Did you sleep well?"

"Like a rock." Like the dead or better still, the drunk. "What was in that tea, Elena?"

She breezed into the room and set the tray on a table near the glass doors. "Chamomile and a few other things."

Madison tightened her robe. "What other things?"

Elena straightened and swept a hand through her silver hair. "Some herbs and honey and schnapps."

Schnapps. That explained a lot. "You should have warned me. I drank three cups and had to take a twenty-minute shower to sober up before I could find the bed."

"My apologies, *cara*. I only wanted to aid you in relaxing."

"I was definitely relaxed." So much so she'd melted right into Zain's mouth.

Elena pointed in the direction of Madison's chin. "I have a special balm that will help with that irritation."

Confused, Madison strode to the mirrored dresser to take a look. Not only was her hair a blond Medusa mess from going to bed with it wet, she had a nice red patch of whisker burn below her bottom lip. "I used something new on my face, so that must be it. I'll be avoiding it from now on." Avoiding Zain's seduction skills, even if she couldn't avoid him.

"Would this something new be tall, dark and have a heavy evening beard?"

She met Elena's wily smile in the reflection. She hated to lie, so she'd simply be evasive. Turning from the mirror, she gestured toward the tray holding a silver pot and a plate of pastries. "I hope that's not more tea."

Elena shook her head. "No. It's coffee. Very strong

coffee. I decided you would need some caffeine for your meeting with Prince Zain."

She didn't recall scheduling a specific time. Then again, last night's details were a bit fuzzy, except for the blasted kiss. "When does he expect me?"

"Now. He's is in the study, waiting. And he seems to be in a somewhat foul mood."

Lovely. "Do you know the reason behind his foul mood?"

Elena tapped her chin with a slender finger and looked thoughtful. "Perhaps it is because he has tried something new on his face and he would like more of the same."

Madison internally cringed. If she kept backing herself into corners, she'd soon be folded in half. "Elena, seriously, this is just a rash. I have very sensitive skin."

"Yes, *cara,* and I am the Queen of Italia. I can tell when a woman has been kissed, and kissed well. And of course, I know Prince Zain is the culprit. He is a charmer, that *diavoletto.*"

Little devil was an apt description of Zain Mehdi. *Sexy little devil.* "Okay, if you must know, we shared a friendly kiss. Thanks to your special tea, I had a temporary lapse in judgment."

Elena laughed softly. "Prince Zain's powers of persuasion are much stronger than my tea. I only caution you to take care with your heart."

Madison held up her hand as if taking an oath. "I promise you there will be no more kissing, friendly or otherwise. I'm not one to bend the rules, much less break them."

Elena smiled. "I wish you much luck with that." She headed for the door and paused with her hand on the knob. *"L'amore domina senza regole,"* she muttered before she disappeared into the corridor.

Love rules without rules.

Who said anything about love? She wasn't in love with Zain Mehdi. In lust maybe, but that fell far from love.

Regardless, she didn't have time to ponder the woman's warning or the kiss or anything else for that matter. She needed to prepare to see the future king.

After she completed her morning ritual, Madison applied some makeup and twisted and secured her crazy hair at her nape. She dressed in brown slacks and sleeveless beige silk turtleneck that she covered with a taupe jacket, intentionally making certain she bared no skin aside from her hands and face. Wearing gloves and a veil would probably be overkill. She chose to nix the pastry but paused long enough to drink a cup of black lukewarm coffee. Even if she was somewhat hungry, she didn't dare feed the butterflies flitting around in her belly.

Those butterflies continued to annoy her as she grabbed her briefcase and headed downstairs to the second-floor office. Surprisingly she found the door partially ajar, but no guards and no prince in sight when she entered the vacant study. Only a few seconds passed before Zain emerged from what appeared to be an en suite bathroom.

Aside from one wayward lock of dark hair falling across his forehead, he looked every bit the debonair businessman. He wore a pair of black wool slacks and a white shirt with a gray tie draped loosely around his neck. The light shading of whiskers surrounding his mouth led Madison right down the memory path toward that toe-curling kiss.

She shoved the thoughts away and put on a sunny smile. "Good morning."

Without returning the greeting, Zain crossed the room

to the coat tree to the right of the desk and took a jacket from one hanger. "Did you have breakfast?" he asked.

He was so absolutely gorgeous she'd love to have him for breakfast. And lunch. And dinner… "I didn't have time. But I did have the most important staple—coffee."

He turned, slipped the coat on and nailed her with those lethal dark eyes. "I'll have the chef prepare you something you can eat while you wait."

"Wait for what?"

"I am about to address my royal subjects."

Several key concerns tumbled around in Madison's mind. She'd begin with the first. "Best I recall, you're not scheduled to do that for another two days."

He slid the top button closed on his collar. "Apparently the masses did not receive the memo."

Apparently. "Where is this going to take place?"

He gestured to his right. "Outside on the terrace where my father and my father's father have always spoken to the people."

Madison set her briefcase on a chair and immediately walked to the double doors to peek through the heavy red curtains. She saw a substantial stone balcony containing a podium with a skinny microphone as well as several stern—and heavily armed—sentries standing guard. As she peered in the distance, she caught a glimpse of an iron fence, also lined with guards, holding back the milling crowd. And in that crowd stood a few respectable correspondents, along with more than a few pond-scum tabloid reporters.

After dropping the curtain, she faced Zain again. "Do you know what you're going to say?"

He rounded the desk, leaned back against it and began to work his tie. "I am your new king. Accept it."

Her mouth dropped open momentarily from shock. "You can't be serious."

"It is simple and to the point." His smile was crooked, and so was his tie.

"Perhaps a little too simple and too pointed."

"I am not yet prepared to speak on all my plans."

"But are you prepared for the questions that are going to be hurled at you by reporters?"

He buttoned his coat closed. "Rest assured I've handled the press before."

"Even paparazzi?"

"Especially paparazzi."

Considering his notorious way with women, she supposed he probably had encountered more than his share of media stalkers. However, she still worried he could get bombarded by a few queries that could trip him up. Hopefully he'd learned how to ignore those. Too bad his tie was too askew for her to ignore.

Without giving it a second thought, Madison walked right up to him to fix the problem. The memory of her mother doing the same thing for Madison's dad settled over her. Was she in danger of becoming her mother? Only if she professed her undying love to Zain and promised to follow him throughout the world. He wasn't the undying-love kind, but he certainly did smell great. Nothing overpowering, just a hint of light, earthy cologne. Or maybe it was the soap he'd used in the shower. Never before had she aspired to be a bar of soap, but at the moment she did. How nice it would be to travel down all that slick, wet, fantastic male terrain, over muscle and sinew and hills and valleys. Definitely hills…

"Are you finished yet?"

Zain's question jarred Madison back into the here and now. "Almost." She smoothed her hand over the gray silk tie and straightened lapels that didn't need straighten-ing. Just when she was about to step back, he captured her hands against his chest.

"I am curious about something," he said, his dark eyes leveled on hers.

"Sage-green satin. Matching bra, if you must know." Heavens, she was volunteering underwear info before he'd officially asked.

"Actually, I was about to inquire about your night and if you slept well."

Now she felt somewhat foolish and confused as to why she hadn't tried to wrest her hands away from his. "I slept well, thank you, although I did have a few odd dreams."

He raised a brow. "Sexual dreams?"

"Strange dreams. I was climbing up a mountain chas-ing a snake."

His smile caught her off guard. "Some believe climb-ing denotes a craving for intercourse. Need I say what the mountain and snake symbolize?"

That phallic mountain would be her Waterloo if they didn't stop discussing it. "Spoken like a man. I'm sure you could make a dream about doing laundry all about sex."

"Perhaps if it involved washing your lingerie."

She tried to hold back her own smile, without suc-cess. "Right now you should be concentrating on your speech, not sex dreams."

He raised her hand and kissed her palm before set-ting it back against his chest. "It's difficult to concentrate with this ongoing chemistry between us."

She couldn't argue that, although she would. "Don't be ridiculous."

"Don't be naive, Madison. You feel it now."

She admittedly did feel a bit warm and somewhat tingly. Maybe a little lightheaded, but then that could be some lingering effects of the tea. She managed to slip from his grasp and take a much-needed step back. "If you're referring to what happened last night, that was a mistake."

"You're going to deny that you wanted to kiss me? That you want to kiss me now?"

She could deny—and lie—in the same breath. "I want to get back to the issue at hand, namely your speech. In my opinion, it's important that you appear to be a strong yet compassionate leader. Be decisive but not forceful."

"I have come to one important decision now."

She folded her arms beneath her breasts. "What would that be?"

He moved closer, rested a hand on her shoulder and brought his lips to her ear. He whispered soft words that sounded lyrical, sensual, though she couldn't begin to comprehend the message, at least not literally. She could venture a guess that the missive was sexual in nature.

When Zain pulled back and homed in on her gaze, she released a slow, ragged breath. "Do you care to interpret what you just said to me?"

"Later, when we have complete privacy."

That sent Madison's imagination straight into overdrive and would have quite possibly, had it not been for the rap on the door, sent Madison straight into Zain's arms.

"Enter," he said, his voice somewhat raspy and noticeably strained.

Madison smoothed a hand down her jacket then over her hair as Deeb stepped in the room, looking every bit the humorless assistant. "You are cleared to proceed, Emir."

Zain rubbed a hand over his jaw. "The shooters are in place?"

"Yes. Four positioned on the roof, two in the tower."

The reality of Zain's importance suddenly hit home for Madison. So did the reality of what she'd almost done—kiss the king for the second time in less than twenty-four hours. Yet she didn't have time to think about it as two bodyguards swept into the room, pulled back the curtains and escorted Zain onto the terrace.

Madison stood to one side slightly behind the drapes while Mr. Deeb took his place beside her. When Zain positioned himself behind the podium, a series of shouts ensued above the murmuring crowd. "What are they saying?" she asked Deeb.

"They are calling him a turncoat."

Ouch. She wished she could see Zain's face, gauge his reaction, but she could only see his back and his hands gripping the edge of the wooden surface, indicating he could be stressed. But no one would know that, she realized, the moment he began to speak in words she couldn't begin to understand.

"What's he saying?" she asked Deeb who remained his usual noncommittal self.

"He is telling them he is honored to be their leader and he looks forward to serving them."

So far, so good. But then she heard the sounds of disapproval and didn't feel nearly as confident. "What now?"

"He claims he is not his father and that he will rule differently," Deeb said. "He is also speaking of positive changes he wishes to make, such as improvements to the hospital and the schools."

As Zain continued, Madison noticed the temporarily dissatisfied crowd had quieted and many people, particularly women, seemed to hang on his every word. And although she couldn't interpret his words, she could certainly appreciate his voice—a deep, mellow voice that went down as smoothly as a vintage glass of wine.

After an enthusiastic round of applause, she turned to ask for clarification from Deeb, only to hear someone suddenly shout in English, "Is it true you fathered a child with Keeley Winterlind?"

Though she'd been aware of Zain's liaison with the supermodel, Madison was seriously stunned by the query, and thoroughly appalled that someone would interrupt a king's speech in search of a sordid story. Worse, was it true?

Zain ignored the question and continued to speak to the throng that seemed to grow more restless by the minute. Then another reporter demanded he address the pregnancy issue, prompting shouts from the masses.

Although Madison still couldn't see Zain's expression, she did notice his hands fisted at his sides. She had no clue what he'd muttered, but it didn't sound at all friendly and, considering the crowd's angry reaction, it wasn't. Amid the show of raised fists and verbal condemnation, Zain turned and stormed back into the study. He didn't afford her or Deeb a passing glance, nor did he hesitate to make a swift exit, slamming the door behind him.

Madison waited for the sentries to leave before she sought confirmation or denial from her only immediate source of information. "Is it true about the baby?"

Deeb's expression remained emotionless, but she saw a flicker of concern in his eyes. "I am afraid, Miss Foster, you will have to ask the emir."

And that's exactly what Madison intended to do. First, she had to find him, and soon, before all hell broke loose.

Four

"Did you find your meal satisfactory, Your Wickedness?"

Zain looked up from his barren plate to see Maysa Barad—*Doctor* Maysa Barad—standing in the doorway wearing a bright purple caftan, her dark hair pulled back into a braid. He returned her smile, though that was the last thing he cared to do. But she was his friend, and she had opened her home to him as a temporary sanctuary. "It was very good. My compliments to your chef. He has a masterful hand."

"*She* is a master," Maysa said as she pulled back the adjacent chair and sat. "I made your dinner after I gave my chef the night off. However, since I still have household staff on the premises, we should continue to speak English to ensure our new king has his privacy."

At the moment he preferred not to be reminded of

his duty. "My position will not be official until the coronation."

"You were king the moment your father passed. My sympathies to you, though I know the two of you did not always see eye to eye."

That was an understatement. "Thank you for that, and for allowing me to arrive virtually unannounced."

"You are always welcome here, Zain." She rested her elbow on the table and supported her cheek with her palm, sending the heavy bangles at her wrists down her arm. "And you have always been the official king of mischief."

"And you are still as pretty as you were the last time I saw you."

Her smile expanded. "But are you still the little devil who attempted to frighten me with toads?"

She had been the sister he'd never had. "You were never really frightened, were you?"

"No. I was simply playing along until Rafiq came along to rescue me."

Zain had always suspected that to be the case. Maysa had been in love with his brother for as long as he could recall. He wondered if she still was. "Speaking of Rafiq, will you be attending the wedding?"

She straightened in the chair, her frame as rigid as the carved wooden table. "I received an invitation, but do not wish to witness that charade."

Yes, she was still in love with Rafiq. "I agree it might not be the best match."

"A match made in misery. Rafiq will never be happy with a woman whose heart belongs to another man."

"What man?"

Zain saw a flash of regret pass over her expression.

"I would rather not say. In fact, I have already said too much."

"Can you tell me if Rima has returned this man's affections?"

"Yes, she has."

He tried to contain his shock. "Does Rafiq know?"

She lifted her shoulders in a shrug. "If he does, he has chosen to ignore it. Regardless, it is not my place to tell him, and I would hope you keep it to yourself, as well."

He did not like the thought of concealing the truth from his brother, yet he doubted Rafiq would believe him. "It would not matter, Maysa. Rafiq is all about duty, regardless of the circumstance. He has every intention of honoring the marriage contract."

She flipped her hand in dismissal. "Enough talk about your brother and his bride. Tell me about California. I did not have the opportunity to visit there when I was in medical school in the States."

Los Angeles had only been his home base and little more. "I traveled a good deal of the time."

"Then tell me about that. I am sure you met many interesting people and saw many interesting sights."

He had seen devastation, drought, famine and disease. Sights he never cared to see again, especially in his own country. "I'm certain my experiences do not compare to yours as a physician."

She shook her head. "My experiences have been challenging since my return to Bajul. I am the only female doctor and the only one who will treat those who can pay very little, if at all. The others cater to the wealthier population."

That came as no surprise to Zain. "Your commitment is admirable, Maysa. Once I am fully in charge, I will make certain the hospital undergoes renovations and medical offices are added. Perhaps then you can receive pay for your services."

"I do not need the money as much as the people need my help," she said. "Fortunately, my father has allowed me to live in his palatial second home regardless that I have failed him as a daughter. He is also kind enough to provide the funds to keep the household going, though I despise taking even one riyal from him."

Zain could not imagine a father considering his daughter a failure after she had established a successful medical career. But then Maysa's father had always been an ass. "Does the sultan come to visit often?"

She released a bitter laugh. "Oh, no. He is either in Saudi or Yemen with my poor mother, building his fortune so that he may provide for his many mistresses."

Maysa had the same issues with her father as Zain had always had with his. "I believe I recall you were bound to a betrothal at one time. I take it that did not come to fruition."

"Actually, it did. Two weeks after the wedding, I realized that contrary to our culture, a woman does not need a man to survive. It took some effort to obtain a divorce, but I managed it. And Father has not forgiven me for it."

"I'm certain it hasn't been easy on you."

She shrugged. "I realized there would be those who would shun me because of my decision, yet I refused to let that deter me. No man will ever dictate my future."

Zain couldn't help but smile when he thought about Madison. She and Maysa were very much alike. Yet he felt more than brotherly fondness for Madison.

"Do you find me amusing, *Your Highness?*" Maysa asked.

"No. You reminded me of someone else I know."

"Someone special?"

Perhaps too special for his own good. "Actually, she is a political consultant Rafiq hired to save me from myself."

"She has a huge task ahead of her then."

"Believe me, she is up to the task. She is also very headstrong, and extremely intelligent. Fortunately, she has a sense of humor, as well. Sometimes I find her frustrating, other times extremely intriguing."

"Is she attractive?"

"Yes, but her attractiveness goes well beyond her physical appearance. She is one of the most fascinating women I have ever encountered."

She inclined her head and studied him. "You have feelings for her."

Maysa's comment took him aback. "She is an employee."

"An employee who has hypnotized you, Zain. Perhaps the sheikh has met his match in more ways than one."

"That is absurd," he said without much conviction. "I have only known her a few days."

"Yet it is those immediate connections that at times make a lasting impact on our lives."

From the wistfulness in Maysa's tone, Zain recognized she spoke from experience. "Even if I did develop these feelings you speak of, we both know a permanent relationship with an outsider could never happen."

She drummed her fingertips on the tabletop. "Ah, yes. We are back to the antiquated tradition of marrying our own kind. You have the power to change that."

"I have other changes to make that are more important. Changes that will affect the future of this country."

"And you are not concerned about your own future?" she asked. "Would you give up a chance at finding love for a tradition that should have died long ago?"

He was too tired to defend his decisions, which led to his next request. "Would you have an available room where I could stay the night?"

"I have twelve bedrooms at your disposal," she said. "But will you not be missed?"

He would, but he did not care. "Deeb knows where I am."

"Zain, although it is truly not any of my concern, you cannot hide away when times become difficult."

He tossed his napkin aside. "Then you've heard about the latest accusations."

"I was there when you spoke this morning. You had everyone in the palm of your hand until that *himar* intruded."

Zain had considered calling him something much worse than a donkey. "For your information, I am not hiding. I am only taking a brief sabbatical to gather my thoughts."

She frowned. "Forgive me for pointing this out, but you have always been one to withdraw from the world when you lose control. The role you will soon assume requires continuity. Are you certain you are willing to bear that burden?"

Though he did not appreciate her commentary, he reluctantly admitted she was partially right. "I have prepared for this opportunity for many years. Once I am established, I will commit fully to my duties."

She smiled and patted his hand. "I know you will. Now if you will follow me, I will show you to your quarters for the evening, where you can rest and fantasize about that special consultant who has obviously earned a little piece of the king's heart."

Maysa knew him all too well, yet she was wrong

about his feelings for Madison. She did not—nor would she ever—have any claim on his heart.

After Zain's twenty-four-hour absence, Madison finally located him on the palace's rooftop. He sat on the cement ground with his back against the wall, hands laced together on his belly, one long leg stretched out before him, the other bent at the knee. He seemed so lost in his thoughts, she questioned whether she should give him more alone time. Regrettably, time was a luxury they didn't have. Not when she required answers to burning questions in order to circumvent the gossip. Provided it *was* gossip.

Before moving forward, she paused a few moments to ponder his atypical clothing. The standard white tailored shirt, Italian loafers and dark slacks had been replaced by a fitted black tee, khaki cargo pants and heavy brown boots. He reminded her of an adventurous explorer ready for travel—and in some ways dressed to kill. His rugged appearance was unquestionably murdering her composure.

Madison shored up her courage, walked right up to him and hovered above him. "I see the sheikh has finally returned."

He glanced up at her, his expression somber. "How did you know where to find me?"

"Elena mentioned you might be here. She said you and your brothers used to hide from her up here when it was time for your lessons."

He smiled but it faded fast. "I should have known she would give my secrets away."

Madison wondered what other secrets he might be keeping. "Mind if I join you?"

He gestured toward the space beside him. "It's less than comfortable, but be my guest."

She carefully lowered herself to the ground and hugged her knees to her chest, taking care to make sure the hem of her dress was properly in place. "The next time you decide to do a disappearing act, do you mind letting me in on it?"

"I assure you, it will not happen again."

"I hope I can trust you on that. You wouldn't believe how frantic everyone was until Mr. Deeb told us you were safe."

"I was never in danger," he said as he continued to stare straight ahead. "I stayed with a friend at a house in the foothills."

She could only imagine what that might have entailed if that friend happened to be female. "How did you get there? And how did you manage to evade your bodyguards? Rafiq is still furious over that."

"I took one of the all-terrain vehicles, and Deeb was aware of my departure. Guards are not necessary when I take care to disguise myself."

She noticed a camouflage baseball cap resting at his side. "So that's the reason for the casual clothes?"

"They serve me well in hiding my identity."

They served him well in highlighting his finer points, and that sent her straight into a fishing expedition. "And this friend had no qualms about concealing the future king?"

"Maysa understands my need for privacy. She made certain I was not disturbed."

As she'd gathered—a woman friend. "Does this friendship come with or without benefits?" She hated that she sounded like some jealous lover.

"Without benefits," he said before adding, "although I do not expect you to believe me."

He sounded more frustrated than angry. "I never said I didn't believe you."

He sent her a sideways glance. "Then you are in the minority. Most people choose to believe the worst of me."

She lowered her legs and shifted slightly to face him. "Since it seems you don't have an official press secretary, I spent the day sending out releases stating you vehemently deny fathering Keeley Winterlind's child. The question is, did I lie?"

"No."

She released the breath she didn't know she'd been holding. "Not even a remote possibility?"

"No."

She truly wanted to believe him, but… "I do remember seeing photos of the two of you a couple years ago."

"That means nothing." Now he sounded angry.

"It means there's proof you had a connection with her."

"A platonic connection," he said. "I came upon her ex-lover threatening her at a social gathering and I intervened. We remained in contact because she needed someone to set her on the right path. However, she was young and impressionable and immature. The last I heard, she had reunited with the boyfriend because I could not convince her that the controlling bastard wasn't good for her."

If what he'd said was true, then in essence he was a champion of women. "Do you think she's the one claiming you're her baby's father?"

"No. She contacted me this afternoon and assured me she had nothing to do with the speculation, and I trust her. She also confirmed the ex is the father."

"I'm relieved I told the truth when I denied the speculation."

"As if that will do any good."

He seemed so sullen, Madison felt the need to lift his spirits. "Have you seen the news footage of your speech?"

"No, and I refuse to watch it."

No surprise there. "Well, you looked incredibly debonair and poised." And absolutely gorgeous. "I'm sure you'll start receiving requests for invitations from a slew of queen candidates."

"I highly doubt they would be interested in light of the recent attacks on my character."

Her efforts to cheer him up were on the verge of becoming an epic failure. "Hey, if they could see you in your adventurer's gear, they wouldn't care about your character."

She'd finally coaxed a smile from him. A tiny smile, but at least it was something. "I fail to understand how I could charm a woman with clothing not fit for a king."

"Then maybe you don't know women as well as you think you do. Of course, it doesn't hurt you're the ruler of a country, and your house isn't too shabby, either."

For the first time since her arrival, he gave her his full attention and a fully formed smile. "You are looking quite beautiful tonight."

She couldn't immediately recall the last time any man had called her beautiful. Her shapeless aqua sundress certainly wouldn't qualify. "Thank you, but this outfit is designed solely for comfort, not beauty."

"I was not referencing your clothing." He lightly touched her cheek. "You are beautiful."

When Madison contacted those dark, mysterious eyes, that spark of awareness threatened to become a flame. With little effort, it could blaze out of control. Yet she recognized Zain was only attempting to divert attention from the seriousness of the situation, and possibly cover his internal turmoil. She truly wanted to provide him with a diversion, but the last thing Zain needed was a potential scandal involving his political consultant. The last thing she needed was to venture into personal involvement with him. She'd already started down that slippery slope.

She shored up her wavering willpower. "Now that we have engaged in sufficient mutual admiration, we should probably go inside and discuss how we're going to handle any other problems that might arise. I'd also be happy to listen to what you have planned for the council meeting tomorrow."

"I prefer to stay here with you."

And she wanted to stay with him, honestly she did, but to what end? "If we stay much longer, we could make another mistake."

He searched her face and paused at her mouth before returning to her eyes. "I have made many mistakes in my lifetime, but spending time with you will not ever be a mistake."

Her foolish heart executed a little flip-flop in her chest. "Flattery will get you everywhere."

"Everywhere?"

One more sexy word out of his incredible mouth and she'd be too far gone to stop any madness that might occur. "The only place we should be going is into your office, and repairing your reputation is the only thing we should consider."

He studied the stars and sighed. A rough, sensuous and slightly irritated sigh. "You are right. Business should always come before pleasure, no matter how re-volting that business might be."

Madison was admittedly somewhat disappointed that he conceded so quickly. "You will get through this, Zain. It's only a matter of time before you earn your country's trust. You are destined to be a great leader."

"I sincerely appreciate your faith in my abilities."

He both looked and sounded sincere, causing her spirits to rise. "Now let's get some work done before dawn."

When Zain came to his feet and held out his hand to help her up, Madison wasn't quite prepared for the sharp sting of awareness as they stood. She wasn't exactly surprised when he framed her face in his palm. But the sudden impact of his mouth covering hers nearly buckled her knees. The kiss was powerful, almost desperate, yet she didn't have the will to stop him. Every argument she'd made against this very thing went the way of the warm breeze surrounding them.

She somehow wound up backed against the wall with Zain flush against her. Even when he left her mouth to trail kisses down her neck, lowered one strap and slid the tip of his tongue slightly beneath the scoop neck of her dress, she disregarded the warning bells sounding in her head. Even when he worked her hem up to her waist, slipped his hands down the back of her panties and clasped her bottom, she couldn't manage one protest. And as he kissed her again, pressed as close to her as he possibly could and simulated the act she'd been determined to avoid with both his body and tongue, stop became go and thinking became an impossible effort.

Separated only by silk and cotton, Madison felt the beginnings of a climax, prompting an odd sound bubbling up from her throat. She was vaguely aware of the rasp of a zipper, very aware the no-return point had arrived and extremely aware when Zain abruptly let her go.

She closed her eyes and waited until her respiration had almost returned to normal before she risked a glance to see him facing the wall, both hands raised above his head as if in surrender. "It appears we're suffering from restraint issues."

He straightened and redid his fly. "Suffering is an apt description."

She pushed the strap back into place while struggling for something more to say. "Out of curiosity, why did you stop?"

He leaned back against the stone and stared straight ahead. "You deserve better than frantic sex against a wall."

"Honestly, it was the hottest few moments of my life and frankly out of character for me."

"Leave, Madison."

The command caught her off guard. "We still have to go over—"

"We'll meet in the morning."

"But you need—"

"I need you to go before I am tempted to carry you to my bed and complete your climax before giving you another while I am inside you."

Madison understood that, loud and clear. She couldn't remember ever having such a heated physical reaction to a man's words. Then again, no man had ever said anything remotely close to that to her. "I'm not leaving until I make myself clear. Whatever this thing is between us, it's going to take a lot of strength to ignore it. I'm not sure that's going to happen, so we have two options. One, we accept we're consenting adults and just do it and get it out of our system. Or I bow out gracefully before I cause you more problems."

He finally looked at her. "The second option is out. The first will not be possible until I am assured you can give me what I need."

Surely he wasn't suggesting… "Are you questioning my lovemaking abilities?"

"No. I need to know I have your respect and above all, your trust."

With that, Zain turned and disappeared through the opening leading to the stairway.

Madison sank back onto the ground and pinched the bridge of her nose from the onset of a tremendous headache. She did respect Zain and his ideals. Did she trust him? At the moment, she wasn't sure.

"My apologies for disturbing you, Emir."

Zain tossed his notes onto the side table to acknowledge Deeb, who had somehow entered his suite without his notice. But then he'd been distracted since he'd left Madison on the rooftop an hour ago. "What is it, Deeb?"

"I wanted to know if you required anything before I leave for home."

He needed the woman in the bedroom next door, but he could not have her. Not yet. "You are dismissed."

Deeb nodded and said, "Have a restful evening, Your Highness."

That was not a likely prospect. When Deeb retreated toward the door, Zain reconsidered and called him back. "I have a few questions for you." Questions he had intentionally failed to ask for fear of the answers.

Deeb pushed the glasses up on his nose. "Yes?"

Zain shifted in the less-than-comfortable chair. "How long have you been employed by the royal family?"

"Fifteen years last December."

His thoughts drifted off topic momentarily. "And you never thought to marry during that time?"

"I am married. I have been for fifteen years."

He was surprised Deeb had not mentioned that before, but then he had never inquired about his private life. "Children?"

A look of pride passed over the man's expression. "I have six children, four boys and two girls. The oldest is nine, the youngest three months."

As far as Zain was concerned, that was quite a feat for several reasons. "You were with me in the States for seven years, so I find that rather remarkable."

"If you recall, you allowed me to return to Bajul during your travels."

Clearly the man impregnated his bride every time he'd been home. "And your wife did not take exception to your absences?"

Deeb hinted at a smile. "If that were true, we would not have six children."

Zain could not argue that. "Are you still happily wed?"

"Yes, Emir."

Zain tented his fingers beneath his chin. "To what do you attribute that happiness?"

"Patience and tolerance. Most important, sustained passion. When you choose your mate, it is best to always remember this."

He could not agree more, especially when it came to the passion. "I appreciate the advice."

"You are welcome, Your Highness. Now if that is all—"

"It is not." He had to pose one more question. An extremely difficult question. "Do you know if the rumors of my father's infidelity are true?"

Deeb tugged at his collar as if he had a noose around his neck. "I feel compelled not to betray the king's confidence."

As suspected, he did have information. "You need not conceal my father's secrets any longer, Deeb. You answer to me now." He despised sounding so harsh, but he was that desperate for confirmation.

"I know of only one woman," he said after a brief hesitation.

"Who is this woman?"

"I will only say that she is above reproach. She was only doing the king's bidding."

Zain sensed that Deeb was protecting more than the king's secrets. He could very well have a connection with the mistress, which led him to believe she could have been a former staff member. At the moment, he was too exhausted to press his assistant for more details. "That will be all, Deeb."

"As you wish." Deeb turned to leave before facing Zain again. "If I may speak candidly, I would like to add that some things are not as they seem."

He'd said that to Madison on more than one occasion. "Perhaps, yet you cannot deny that my father dishonored my mother?"

"Again, every situation is unique and at times not for us to judge."

Zain could not help but judge his father. The man had caused him to doubt himself on many levels, the least of which had to do with personal relationships. "Thank you for your candor. You may go now."

"Before I take my leave," he said, "may I speak freely?"

"You may." For now.

"If it is any solace, I firmly believe you are nothing like the king."

With that, Deeb left the room, leaving Zain in a state of disbelief. He learned tonight how little he knew about his assistant, yet the man seemed to know much about him.

Feeling restless, Zain paced the room for a few moments, growing angrier by the minute as he thought back to Deeb's confirmation of his father's infidelity. He strode to the shelf housing several books, picked up the photo of the king posing with a U.S. president and hurled it against the far wall. The glass shattered and rained down in shards to the carpeted floor.

Despite Deeb's insistence there were extenuating circumstances, Zain could never forgive his father. Not when his ruthless behavior had dealt his mother the worst fate. Death.

Five

The second she walked into the conference room, Madison felt as if she'd entered Antarctica. With their immaculate black suits and impeccable grooming, Rafiq and Zain Mehdi could be corporate raiders involved in a business debate, not two brothers engaged in an ongoing war of wills.

"Good afternoon, gentlemen," she said as she pulled out a chair across from Zain, sat and scooted beneath the massive conference table.

"Do you have anything to report on the latest scandal?" Rafiq asked, while Zain seemed more interested in the view out the window at Madison's back.

She set her briefcase at her feet and folded her hands on the table. "I do, actually." A report that wouldn't go over well with Zain. "I spent most of the morning on the phone tracking down Ms. Winterlind's publicist. I finally heard from her a few moments ago."

Zain finally looked at her when she hesitated. "And?"

"She told me that Ms. Winterlind did in fact leak the initial claim that you're the father of her baby."

Anger flashed in Zain's eyes. "Impossible."

"I'm afraid it's not. She did send her apologies to you through the publicist and is in the process of retracting the claim."

"It seems your faith in the model was misplaced, Zain," Rafiq said.

If looks really could kill, Zain had just delivered a visual bullet, right between his brother's eyes. "She had her reasons."

"What would those be, brother? She has her sights set on trapping a king?"

Zain muttered something acid and probably insulting in Arabic. "She is not like that, Rafiq."

Time for a much-needed intervention on Zain's behalf. "Actually, Prince Rafiq, she made the claim to protect her son from her ex, who is a known batterer. Fortunately, he's currently incarcerated on assault charges."

Zain's gaze snapped to hers. "Did he beat her?"

Evidently he still cared about the model, maybe even more than he'd let on in their previous conversations. "No. He beat up some guy in a bar and nearly killed him. He'll be going away for a long time."

"Good riddance," Zain muttered.

"Are there other women who will surface with similar claims?" Rafiq asked Zain, venom in his tone.

Zain's eyes narrowed. "The women with whom I have been intimately involved are trustworthy."

"I believe the model contradicts that assertion."

"I was not intimate with her."

Rafiq raised a brow. "Then it would seem those whom

you have bedded and spurned would be more likely to lie."

Zain looked as if he might bolt out of the chair. *"Izhab ila al djaheem, Rafiq."*

Madison had no idea what Zain had said to his brother, but she did feel she needed to defuse the situation, possibly at her own peril. "Look, Your Highness, Prince Rafiq does have a point. We need to know if there is even a remote possibility a woman might come forward with some scandalous claim, unfounded or not."

Zain's expression turned cold. "My former lovers should not be a concern, unless perhaps one is interested in the extent of my sexual experience."

His attitude, and the pointed comment, shredded her already thinned patience. "I don't need a list, only a number. Less than five? More than ten? Fifty?" Now *she* sounded like a scorned lover.

"I assure you, my past will not affect my ability to lead," he said. "Many married leaders worldwide have openly engaged in affairs and continued to rule."

Madison had known more than her fair share. Some came through it unscathed. Others had not. "Any scandal could influence your people's trust in you if it rears its ugly head again."

He kept his gaze centered on hers. "Does that include your trust in me, Madison?"

"Trust is earned, *Zain*."

She regretted the informality faux pas the minute she glanced at Rafiq and saw the suspicious look in his eyes. She could only imagine how the exchange sounded— like lovers engaged in a spat.

Rafiq checked his watch and stood. "The meeting begins in ten minutes. You can continue this discussion later."

Madison might receive an emphatic no, but she had to ask. "I'd like to sit in on the meeting."

Rafiq looked as though she'd requested to run naked through the royal gardens. "That is not permitted."

"I will allow it," Zain said. "You may observe from the gallery. I'll have Deeb interpret for you."

She wasn't sure if Zain had granted her request because he wanted her there, or because he wanted to one-up his brother. It didn't matter as long as she had a ringside seat where she could watch him in action.

When Zain failed to stand, Rafiq nailed him with another glare. "Are you coming now, or should I have the guards escort you?"

"I will be along shortly," Zain said. "I need to speak privately with Ms. Foster."

"I have no doubt you do." With that, Rafiq strode out of the room.

As soon as the door closed, Madison directed her attention to Zain. "This is exactly what I feared would happen. My stupid miscue with your name wasn't lost on your brother. There's no telling what he thinks is going on between us."

"Let him believe what he will," he said. "He would have assumed the worst whether I had touched you or not."

Oh, but he had touched her. "If you're not concerned about Rafiq, then why did you need to speak to me in private?"

He looked all too serious. "First, I want to apologize. My problem is with Rafiq's attitude, not yours. Second, I need to know if you're all right after last evening."

She shrugged. "I'm fine. It happened, it's done and it's over."

He inclined his head and studied her. "Is it truly over?"

If only she could say yes without any reservations. Trouble was, she couldn't. "Right now you need to concentrate on what you have to propose to the council."

He reached across the table and took her hand. "How can I concentrate when I know you're upset?"

"I told you, I'm fine." She came to her feet and grabbed her briefcase. "I'm sure you'll regain your full concentration once you're in the meeting. Now let's go before Rafiq calls out the guard."

As Zain stood, Madison started toward the door. But before she made it more than a few steps, Zain caught her arm and turned her to face him. "Do you recall what I said to you last night?"

She recalled every detail of last night. "Yes, and I meant what I said to you a few minutes ago. You're going to have to prove you're trustworthy."

"At times trust requires a leap of faith."

If she leaped too quickly, she could land in an emotional briar patch. "Faith has failed me before."

"You are not alone in that. Yet whatever my faults might be, I am a man of my word."

She really wanted to believe that. "Speaking of words, you've never told me what you said to me the day you addressed the crowd."

He rubbed his thumb slowly back and forth down her arm. Not only could she feel it through her linen jacket, she could feel it everywhere. "You really wish for me to tell you now?"

"Yes, I do." Although she had a feeling she might regret it.

As he had the first time he'd whispered words she

hadn't understood, he rested his lips against her ear. "You should never have kissed me."

He had to be kidding. "That's it? You're saying the kiss was all my fault?"

"No. It was my fault for baiting you. I simply did not believe you would take the bait. However, if we had never shared that first kiss, I would not be lying awake at night fantasizing about all the ways I would make love to you. I would not want you so badly that I would gladly reschedule this meeting and take you away from here."

He released her then, walked to the door and left the room, while she stood still as a statue, cursing Zain for his uncanny knack of keeping her off balance. She didn't move an inch until Deeb summoned her into the hallway.

Madison followed the entourage down the corridor, watching as Zain walked ahead with overt confidence. Several times she had to tear her gaze away after trying to sneak a peek at his notable royal butt. Once they reached the end of the hall, Zain walked through double doors while Deeb showed Madison to his right, where they descended a short flight of stairs, and into the glass-enclosed gallery.

Madison took a seat in the front row of chairs beside him and looked down on the scene. Several men were seated at a large round table—eleven by her count—all dressed in high-neck button-down white robes, various colored sashes draped around their necks, and white kaffiyehs with bands that matched the sashes. The chairs flanking either side of Rafiq were noticeably empty, one most likely reserved for Zain. She leaned toward Deeb and asked, "Who's missing, aside from His Highness?"

"The youngest emir, Adan," he said. "He is excused today due to the importance of his mission."

Madison doubted Zain would be afforded the same

courtesy if he'd decided not to appear. As the minutes ticked off, she began to worry he might have taken that route. And considering the way the council members kept looking around, she assumed they were worried, as well.

A few seconds later, the doors opened to the future king, prompting the men to stand. He wore the same white robe with a gold-and-black sash draped around his neck, but nothing on his head. She didn't know if he was intentionally bucking tradition, or if someone had forgotten his headdress. Frankly, that was fine by Madison. She'd hate to see even one inch of that pretty face concealed from her view.

When Zain lowered himself into the chair, the men followed suit while Deeb reached forward and flipped a switch to the intercom. Zain began to speak in a language that Madison regretted not learning. She'd only mastered a few official greetings and the all-important request for the ladies' room. Perhaps she would ask Zain to teach her more. She imagined he could teach her quite a bit from a nonlinguistic standpoint, and she would happily be a willing student.

Madison forced her attention back to the meeting and wondered what she'd hoped to gain by observing when she couldn't understand a word.

Deeb demonstrated that he understood her confusion when he said, "They are currently discussing economic concerns. Rafiq is the minister of finance."

"And Adan?" she asked.

"He is the head of the military."

That made sense. Unfortunately, nothing else did.

As the discourse continued, Madison became focused on watching Zain's hands move as he spoke. Strong, steady, expressive hands. Skilled hands. Her thoughts drifted back to the night before when she'd experienced those hands on her body. She'd wanted to experience more of them in places that he'd obviously avoided. The sudden, unexpected rush of heat caused her to cross her legs against the sensations. She felt as she might actually start to squirm if she didn't get her mind back on business. Easier said than done.

Hormone overload, pure and simple. What else could it possibly be?

You've never been so attuned to someone that when you enter a room, that person is all you see? You've never wanted someone so desperately that you would risk everything to have them?

Yes, she wanted Zain, with a force that defied logic. Even more now after what he'd said only minutes ago.

I would not be lying awake at night fantasizing about all the ways I would make love to you.

Graphic, detailed images of making love with Zain filtered into Madison's mind when she should have been focusing on the meeting. She shifted her crossed legs from restlessness and pure, undeniable desire for a man who shouldn't be on her sexual radar. But he was, front and center, sending out signals that she urgently wanted to answer.

The sound of raised voices jarred Madison out of her fantasies and back into reality. She regarded Deeb, who appeared impervious to the disruption.

"What's happening now?" she asked.

"The emir is explaining his water proposal. Sheikh Barad has taken exception to it."

"Which one is he?"

"To the right of Prince Rafiq."

Madison honed in on a fierce-looking man with a neatly trimmed goatee and beady eyes. "Is he a relative?"

"No. He is a childhood friend of Prince Rafiq's. His sister, Maysa, is a physician."

Maysa. The woman Zain had visited the other night. "He doesn't appear to care for Zain."

"He does not care for the emir's plan, nor does he care for the emir's demand that he halt any plans for drilling."

Obviously oil and water truly didn't mix in this case. "Is this going to be a problem for Zain?" Not again. "His Highness?"

Deeb didn't seem at all disturbed by her second informality screwup. "That depends on how he chooses to handle the matter."

Zain chose to handle it by rising from the chair and slamming his palm on the table. He then launched into an impassioned diatribe that seemed to silence everyone into submission.

"He is telling everyone that he is the king," Deeb began. "His word is the law, and those who go against him will be summarily dismissed and tried for treason."

Apparently Zain was dead serious. "What does that entail?"

"If found guilty, a firing squad."

Madison wondered if that held true for unsuitable women who overstepped their bounds and slept with the king. She preferred not to find out.

Zain reclaimed his seat but continued to speak, this time in low, more temperate tones. Deeb explained that he spoke of the people, their needs and the importance of their future, the evils of profiteering and raping the land, as well as his commitment to bringing the country into the twenty-first century. "If there are those who do not support his vision," Deeb continued, "they may relinquish their positions immediately."

As Zain continued to address the men, Madison found

his absolute control, his sheer air of power, as heady as a hot bath. Funny, she had never been turned on by authoritative men. Then again, she'd never met anyone like Zain before. Not even close. In the five years she'd lived with her former boyfriend, not once had Jay ever made her feel as if she might climb out of her skin if she didn't have him. Not once did she spot him across a crowded room and feel an overwhelming sense of passion.

Without warning, Zain abruptly stood, did an about-face and strode out of the room, leaving the men exchanging glances with each other, their mouths agape. Everyone but Rafiq, who looked more angry than shocked.

"I guess the meeting's over," Madison said as the rest of the members began to exit, one by one.

"Yes, it is," Deeb said solemnly. "Unfortunately, the emir's problems have only begun."

Madison understood that all too well. Her respect for Zain had risen tenfold, but so had the realization that his position required his undivided attention. He couldn't afford any distractions, and that included her.

Feeling a headache coming on, Madison left the gallery and headed straight for her quarters. She vowed that from this point forward, she would avoid being alone with Zain.

"I must commend you on your success, brother."

With only a brief glance at Rafiq standing at the study door, Zain tossed the robe onto the sofa and claimed the place beside it. "I am pleased you have finally realized I am quite capable of handling my duties."

Rafiq strolled into the room and took the opposing chair. "I am not referring to your duty. I am referring to Ms. Foster. It has taken you less than five days to bed her. However, that is still two days more than the new cook's assistant ten years ago."

He should have known his sibling would never congratulate him on his success with the council meeting. "And if my memory serves me correctly, you slept with the gardener's daughter the day you met her, brother."

Rafiq presented an acerbic smile. "True, but that young woman did not have the power to destroy my reputation."

"Neither does Ms. Foster, and for your information, I have not slept with her." Not beyond his fantasies.

"All signs point to the contrary."

"And your imagination is out of control."

"I did not imagine the way the two of you looked at each other earlier today," Rafiq said. "Nor did I imagine your talk of trust."

"She was referring to trust in regard to my recent disappearance." Only a partial truth. "You always have, and always will, assume that I have no self-control when it comes to the opposite sex."

"I would be joined by the rest of the world in that assumption."

With effort, Zain kept his anger in check. "Perhaps that is why you hired Ms. Foster. You were setting me up to fail because of the temptation she poses."

He presented a self-satisfied smile. "Then you admit you are tempted by her."

More than his brother knew. "And you are not?"

"I am to be married in two weeks' time."

"You are still a man, Rafiq, and you are marrying a woman who does not support your libido, only your foreign bank account."

Rafiq came to his feet. "I have no time for this. But mark my words, should you give in to temptation with

Ms. Foster, you are taking a risk that could destroy what little standing you have left among our people."

Zain refused to comment as his brother exited the room. Yes, Madison posed a tremendous temptation. And yes, any intimacy with her would come with considerable risk. But she had become one of his greatest weaknesses in the past few days. Perhaps one of his greatest weaknesses ever.

Feeling restless and ready to run, Zain decided he needed some space. He knew exactly where he wanted to go, and he did not intend to go alone.

"Change into some comfortable clothes and shoes, and come with me."

Madison remained at the open veranda door, determined to stand her ground with Zain. "After today, running off together is the last thing you need. In fact, I've decided it's best we aren't alone together again."

"We will not be alone for long on this journey."

Evidently they'd be accompanied by a contingent of guards, which would be for the best—if she decided to go with him. "Where exactly do you plan to take me?"

"It's a surprise."

She planted her fists on her hips and refused to budge. "I'm not too fond of surprises."

He leaned a shoulder against the doorframe. "You will enjoy this one. We do need to hurry to reach our destination on time."

"Which is?"

"On the outskirts of the village. It will take us a while to arrive there."

Could he be any more vague? "As far as I know, the village is only a mile or so from the palace, which is about a two minute drive. Are we going by camel?"

He had the gall to grin. "No. We are going by foot."

He'd evidently lost his royal mind if he honestly believed she'd agree to traipse down a mountain in the dark. She was basically a klutz on level ground in broad daylight. "You're proposing we walk down to the village at dusk."

"Yes, and if you will stop talking and start dressing, we might be there before dawn."

He apparently wouldn't give up until she gave in, and she wasn't quite ready to do that. "I refuse to go unless you give me details."

He streaked a hand over his chin. "All right. I want you to see the village with me serving as your guide. I want you to know the people and understand why my position as their king holds great importance."

"Why didn't you just say that in the first place?"

"Because you are quite beautiful when you are not in control."

And he was quite the cad. An incredibly sensual cad. "I'll go, but only on one condition."

He released a rough sigh. "What would that be?"

"You say please."

He took her hand and gave it a light kiss. "Would you please do me the honor of allowing me to show you my world?"

How could she refuse him now? "Fine. Just give me a few minutes."

"Wear a waterproof jacket, since rain is predicted for later tonight."

Great. "You expect me to walk back up the mountain in the dark all wet?"

He grinned. "There is no guarantee you will be wet, but chances are you very well could be, whether it rains or not."

The innuendo wasn't lost on Madison, or her contrary libido. "If you don't behave, I'm staying here."

His smile faded into a frown. "I will arrange transportation for our return if that will satisfy you."

"That will." She could only hope he made good on his word. "Wait here while I change."

"I may not come inside and wait?"

How easy it would be to say yes, but if she did, they might forgo their little expedition for a different kind of journey. In bed. "No, you may not wait inside."

"You still do not trust me."

"Not when my underwear happens to be involved."

After closing the door on him, Madison piled her hair into a ponytail then quickly changed into a T-shirt, jeans, her lone pair of sneakers and an all-weather lightweight coat. Probably not the best in the way of hiking clothes, but they'd have to do.

She returned to the veranda to find him leaning back against the wall, a military-green jacket covering his black tee and beige cargo pants, the camouflage baseball cap set low on his brow. For all intents and purposes, he could be an ordinary man on a mission of leisure. Yet there was nothing ordinary about those pensive dark eyes.

He held out his hand to her. "Are you ready for an adventure?"

That depended on what kind of adventure he had in mind. Only one way to find out. "As ready as I'll ever be."

After Madison clasped his offered hand, Zain led her down the side stairs leading to the labyrinth of courtyards on the ground level. He came to a small iron gate and opened it to a rock path that led away from the rear of the palace. The stone soon turned to dirt, and the trail soon took a sharp downward descent.

"Are you sure this is safe?" she asked when they reached a rocky place that looked way too precarious to go forward.

Zain released her, stepped down and then signaled her forward. "Take my hand and I'll assist you."

She would rather ride down on his back but that could be a bit awkward. "Okay, if you say so."

Slowly, steadily, they navigated the pathway until they finally reached firm footing, and not once had Zain let her go. She began to relax as they continued on, knowing he would do his best to keep her out of harm's way. But then he came to an ominous-looking boulder pile and started to climb.

"Follow me," he said over one shoulder.

Madison remained at the bottom and glared up at him. "Excuse me, but I thought we're supposed to be going down, not up."

"First, you must see the view from here before we continue."

Her gaze wandered up to the plateau. "You can describe it to me."

"You have to witness it firsthand."

"I can't see it if I break my neck."

He scurried down and gestured toward the formation. "I will be immediately behind you offering support should you need it. Trust me, I will not let you fall."

She did trust him, at least in this case. "Okay, I'll do it, as long as you keep your eye on the goal and not on my butt."

He smiled. "I cannot promise I will not look, but I will try to refrain from touching you."

And she'd try to refrain from requesting he touch her, though she couldn't promise that, either.

One foot in front of the other, she silently chanted as

she began the ascent. Truth was, she'd hiked before in similar terrain, just not in a long time. Yet her confidence grew knowing Zain would catch her if she stumbled. And with only moderate effort, she made it to the top just in time to catch the view of the valley washed in the final rays of the setting sun.

"Unbelievable," she muttered when Zain came up behind her. "I can see so much more here than on the veranda."

"I told you it was not to be missed." He rested his hands lightly on her shoulders. "If you look closely, you can see the lake right beyond the base of Mabrúruk."

She spotted a patch of cerulean-blue on the horizon. "I see it. Is that a hotel on the cliff above it?"

"A resort," he said. "It's owned by the Barad family and managed by Shamil Barad."

"Maysa's brother," Madison replied. "Mr. Deeb told me about him."

"Maysa is nothing like him." He sounded and looked irate. "Where she cares about the people, Shamil only cares about padding his fortune at any cost."

"Believe me, I've met his kind. And I'm positive you'll keep him in his place."

He leaned and kissed her cheek. "I truly appreciate your confidence in me."

As Zain continued to point out the landmarks, Madison found herself leaning back against him. And when he slipped his arms around her waist, she didn't bother to pull away. She simply marveled at the passion in his voice when he spoke about his people, and relished the way he made her felt so protected.

A span of silence passed before Madison looked up at him. "You really love your country, don't you?"

"Yes, I do," he said as he stared off into the distance.

"That is why I cannot fail, yet the burden to succeed at times seems too heavy for one man to bear. Especially a flawed man like myself."

She sensed making that admission had cost him, and that alone made her appreciate him all the more. She turned into his arms and gave him a smile. "But you will succeed, Zain. You have too much conviction not to see this through."

"I am certainly going to try." For a moment he looked as though he might kiss her but surprisingly let her go. "We'd best be on our way, otherwise we will be walking in the dark."

"If we must."

Zain led the way, his hand firmly gripping hers as they made their way down the slope. Once at the bottom, he took her by the waist, lifted her up and set her on her feet. "I am so glad I made it without breaking something," she said as she tightened the band securing her hair.

"I would never let you fall, Madison."

Oh, but she was in the process of falling for him, and he couldn't be her human safety net. In a matter of weeks, she would leave him behind, and she'd have only the memories of a man who was beginning to mean too much to her. So tonight, she would make more good memories that would remain long after they'd said goodbye.

Six

"How much farther is it?"

Zain glanced back at Madison, who was trudging up the drive slowly. "Only thirty meters or so."

"My metrics suck, Zain," she said, sounding winded. "And apparently so does my stamina. But at least you were kind enough to stop for food, however rushed the meal might have been."

He'd feared being identified in such a public place. Fortunately, they'd somehow escaped recognition. "We are almost there."

As they rounded the bend, the three-quarter moon provided enough light to illuminate the small flat-roofed structure that had been a second home during his youth. He paused and pointed. "It is right there."

She came to his side and squinted. "Who lives here?"

"My friend Malik. He owns the surrounding land and raises sheep."

Madison knelt to retie her shoe. "Does he know we're coming?"

"No, but he will be glad to see me." Or so he hoped. Seven years had come and gone since their last contact, but they had been the best of friends though they lived on opposite sides of the social dividing line.

She straightened and secured the band in her hair. "Let's get going, then, before my legs give out completely. If that happens, you'll have to carry me the rest of the way."

He saw no reason not to do that now. Without giving Madison warning, he swept her up, tossed her over his shoulder and started toward their destination.

"Put me down, you royal caveman."

Had she not been laughing, he would have complied due to the insult. "I am not a caveman. I am a gentleman."

"A gentleman Neanderthal."

"I am the Neanderthal who is coming to your rescue, therefore you should refrain from complaining."

"My hero."

Ignoring her sarcasm, he continued until he made it up the single step and onto the small porch before he slid her down to her feet. "Are you sufficiently rested now?"

She adjusted her clothing and sighed. "I'm probably a mess."

"You are a beautiful mess."

She smiled. "You are a wonderful liar."

He reached out and touched her flushed cheek. "It is unfortunate you do not realize the extent of your beauty, yet is it also refreshing. I have known too many women whose beauty is only superficial. Yours is far-reaching."

She laid her palm on his hand. "You are determined to say all the right things tonight, aren't you?"

He also wanted to do all the right things, avoiding any missteps along the way. That alone prevented him from kissing her now, though he desperately wanted to do that, and more. "I am only trying to give you an enjoyable evening."

"So far, so good, expect for the marathon walk. Now, do you think you might want to knock before your friend goes to bed?"

"That is probably a good idea." He reluctantly dropped his hand from her face and rapped on the door.

Several minutes passed before Malik answered the summons. "Yes?"

Zain removed his cap. "Do you have water for two weary travelers, *sadiq?*"

The initial confusion on his friend's face quickly dissolved into recognition. "Zain, is that you?"

"Have I changed that much?"

Malik greeted him with a stern expression. "No, you have not changed. You are still the *kalet* who always appears unannounced."

Sadly, he had mistakenly believed he would be welcome. "Perhaps I should return another time."

"I prefer not to wait another seven years before I can beat you at a game of Tarneeb." He opened the door wide and grinned. *"Marhaban, sadiq."*

The warm greeting lifted Zain's spirits and concerns. He entered the house and accepted his friend's brief embrace before he remembered Madison was still waiting outside.

He turned and gestured her forward. "Malik, this is Madison Foster. Madison, Malik El-Amin."

"It's a pleasure to meet you, Malik," Madison said as she offered her hand to Malik to shake.

"Come and sit." Malik gestured toward the familiar low corner sofa covered in heavy blue fabric.

Before they could comply, a dark-haired child bolted into the room and immediately hid behind Malik. She smiled up at Zain as she twirled a long braid and rocked back and forth on her heels.

"Who have we here?" Zain asked.

"This is Lailah," Malik said as he nudged her forward. "She is six and our oldest."

"She's beautiful," Madison said from behind Zain.

Malik smiled with pride as he swept Lailah into his arms. "She fortunately resembles her mother, as do the rest of our daughters."

When a sudden, bittersweet memory filtered into Zain's mind, he pushed it aside. Yet he couldn't quite dismiss the regrets over losing touch with his friend. "How many children do you have?"

"Three more," Malik said as he set Lailah on her feet, prompting her to exit as quickly as she'd come into the room. "Badia is five and Jada is four. Ma'ali is our youngest. She arrived three months ago."

Zain patted his back. "Congratulations. It appears Mabrúruk has been good to you."

Malik frowned. "Perhaps too good."

He looked around for signs of his friend's wife. "Is Helene so exhausted she has already retired for the evening?"

"She is putting the baby to bed."

"Unfortunately, I have not been successful in that endeavor."

Zain turned his attention to the former Helene Christos, who breezed into the room, her thick brown hair flowing over her shoulders, a swaddled infant nestled in the crook of her arm. He immediately went to her and kissed both her cheeks. "You have not changed since the day you wed Malik." A somewhat controversial wedding between an Arabic farmer and a Greek-American restaurant owner's daughter. Clearly they had survived that controversy.

She frowned. "And you are forever the royal charmer, Zain Mehdi. But then I suppose I should be calling you King now. Forgive me for not bowing. I have my hands full."

He decided not to point out he was not the official king yet. "Clearly Malik has his hands full as well, since you have given him four daughters. I suppose he deserves that much."

She patted his cheek. "As do you. I wish for you many daughters and much grief protecting them from rogues like you and Malik."

"I'll second that," Madison added.

Zain felt bad for not including Madison in the conversation. Without thought, he took her hand, pulled her forward and kept his palm against the small of her back. "This is Madison Foster."

Helene eyed her for a few moments before she handed the sleeping infant over to her husband. "Are you a souvenir Zain brought from Los Angeles?"

Madison shook her head. "Not hardly. I'm currently serving as a consultant during his transition from prince to king."

"Helene's family owns the restaurant where we dined tonight," Zain added.

"The tapas were wonderful," Madison said. "I haven't found anything remotely as good in the D.C. area."

Helene's expression brightened. "You're from D.C.? My family is originally from Baltimore, although I haven't lived there since my father saw an opportunity and opened his restaurant here fifteen years ago." She reclaimed the baby from Malik before gesturing toward the sofa. "Have a seat and tell me what's the latest in spring fashion in America."

When the women settled onto the sofa to converse, Malik nodded to his right. "Let us escape before we are asked our opinions on footwear."

Zain followed Malik into the modest kitchen that had been fitted with modern appliances. "I see you have made some improvements."

Malik leaned back against the counter and folded his arms. "After my mother passed four years ago, I felt the need to make Helene feel more welcome in our home."

"I was not aware of your loss." A loss to which Zain could relate. "My sympathies. She was a good woman."

"She was a hard-working woman. She was forced to be the sole support following my father's death. I do not wish Helene to endure such hardship if I can prevent it."

Yet Malik had turned down Zain's loan offer several years ago. "Is the farming going well?"

"It has been for the last few years. After I married Helene, we were shunned by a few traditionalists but fortunately accepted by those who have blended, multicultural families. Those people kept us afloat until we finally gained acceptance."

He felt a measure of guilt that he hadn't been around to offer moral support. "I am sorry it's been so difficult for the two of you, Malik. My wish is for your continued success and a prosperous future for your family."

"You can assist us with that, Zain."

Finally, the man would let go of his pride and accept help. "How much money do you need?"

"I am not speaking of money," Malik said. "The local madrasa is in great need of funds for supplies and books. We cannot afford a private school and we want our daughters to have the best education."

Only one more change he would need to make among many. "Consider it done. I will add that to the budget now under consideration." And hoped he would not face another battle with the council.

"I appreciate whatever you can do." Malik inclined his head and sent him a curious look. "What is your true relationship with this Madison Foster?"

That happened to be one question he wasn't prepared to answer, perhaps because he was still uncertain. "As we previously explained, she is a contracted employee."

"Is serving as your lover one of the requirements?"

The question took Zain aback. "She is not my lover."

"Yet that is precisely what you are wishing for, *sadiq.*"

"I did not say that." He sounded too defensive to support a denial.

Zain was certain Malik saw through his guise after his friend laid a hand on his shoulder. "When you escaped the palace to play with the local boys in the village streets on the day we met, I recognized you were destined for greatness. And when you became the chosen successor to the throne, I knew that would come to pass. Are you willing to give up your destiny for a woman who would not be deemed suitable?"

Zain tamped down his anger for the sake of friendship. "Are those not the words of a hypocrite, Malik? You did not let suitability sway you when you chose Helene."

"Yet I am not the king with an entire country following my every move."

He reluctantly acknowledged his friend had a point. "The people of this country should not be allowed to dictate my personal life or who I choose to be with."

Malik narrowed his eyes. "It is apparent this woman

means more to you than another conquest to add to all the others."

He felt the need to be truthful. "I am not certain what she means to me. I do know she seems to understand me in ways no one has before. When she's not in my presence, she is constantly in my thoughts. When I am with her, I dread the moment she has to leave me. Have you felt as if you had known someone your entire life, yet you've only known them for a few days?"

"Yes. Helene. And you, *sadiq,* are in the throes of love."

He had to believe that his current state was only the result of unrequited lust. "I cannot afford those emotions, Malik. I do know I can only consider the time we have now before she returns to America."

"And when will that be?"

"Following the coronation." The time had come to pose a request, one his friend could adamantly refuse. "Do you have a vehicle I could borrow for the evening? I will see that it is returned to you tomorrow morning."

"You did not arrive in an official car?" Malik asked.

"We walked into the village so that Madison could see the sights. Tonight I desire to be only a man with no responsibility other than being with a remarkable woman."

His friend scowled. "Yet you are a king with no car and obviously no guards."

"I do not need guards where I have been, or where I am going."

"Where would that be?"

"I wish to show Madison the lake."

Malik gave him a good-natured grin. "You wish to show her more than that, I fear. Perhaps you need protection not from guards, but from the powers of Mabrúruk."

"I only need a vehicle." In terms of lovemaking, the

protection issue would warrant discussion only if the situation arose once he had Madison alone. "Will you accommodate me, or will I need to go door-to-door to make the request?"

Malik walked to the back entrance, took a key hanging from the hook on the wall and returned to offer it to Zain. "This is to my truck. It is old and it has no rear seating, but it runs and it does have fuel, as well as two blankets for your comfort. Please return it in the same condition."

Zain pocketed the keys. "I am eternally in your debt."

"You may repay me by proceeding with caution. But then you have always been the master of escape, which leads me to believe you have a plan."

He planned only to leave as soon as possible before he had to endure more of his friend's counsel. "If you are finished with the advice, we need to be going before the night is over."

"I only have a few more words to say." When Zain opened his mouth to protest, Malik held up a hand to silence him and continued. "I understand your need to hurry, but I urge you to think before you head down the path of no return. And after some consideration, you may keep the blankets as a memento."

They shared in a hearty laugh as they returned to the living area to find the women still engaged in conversation. Zain was surprised to see Madison holding the baby against her shoulder and rocking slowly, back and forth.

She seemed very natural with the child, yet he saw a hint of sadness in her eyes when she glanced at him, and perhaps longing. That telling sign led Zain to believe she had not been honest when she'd firmly stated she had no interest in having a family. Perhaps she had not found the right man to father her children. He could be that man.

The thought came to him clear and concise, rendering him mentally off balance. He could not wish for the unattainable. He would not subject her to years of regret by wanting more from her than he could give her. But he could give her this night. A night she would not soon forget.

"Are you sure this thing is going to make it?" When Madison failed to receive a response from Zain, who had his eyes trained on the treacherous road, she gave up trying to talk to him. Between the vehicle's squeaks and groans, and the whistling wind, which had picked up steam, conversation was out of the question.

She'd climbed into the monstrosity on the assumption they were returning to the palace. She soon realized she'd been wrong when they headed away from the village and started toward the massive mountain.

Madison gripped the top of the windowless door as Zain guided the truck on a downward trek through a narrow passage comprised of boulders on both sides. She decided in this case ignorance was truly bliss and closed her eyes. She stayed that way until they came to a teeth-jarring stop.

The moon and the headlights provided enough illumination for her to view the shimmering lake spread out before them. Zain rounded the car, opened the passenger door, held out his hand and helped her climb down.

"So this is it?" she said as soon as she had her feet on solid ground. "I just wish I could see it better."

"I promised to bring you here before your departure, and with the upcoming chaos, I felt tonight would be the best time."

She didn't want to think about leaving Bajul, about

leaving him, so she wouldn't. "I'm glad we survived the drive so I could see it." Or see as much as she could.

She did spot a path leading to the shore, and immediately saw relief for her aching feet. Without another word, she took off toward the lake and, after arriving on the sandy beach, toed out of her sneakers and socks and rolled up her jeans. The minute her toes hit the cool water, she sighed at the sensations. A soothing balm for her sore soles.

"Take care of the piranha."

Madison spun around and did a little dance out of the water. When she heard the sound of Zain's laughter echoing over the area, she glanced up to see him standing above her. She considered sending him a dirty look but doubted he could see it, so she chose to give him a verbal lashing. "That was not funny at all, Zain Mehdi. It's bad enough that you took me on a dangerous joyride to get here, and now you're trying to scare me with killer fish."

He slipped his hands in his pockets. "My apologies for frightening you."

She snatched up her shoes and started toward him. "I take it there are no flesh-eating fish?"

"There are fish, but they do not crave flesh."

"Good to know, after the fact," she said when she reached him. "What now? Midnight scuba diving? Underwater basket-weaving?"

"Whatever you wish to do."

What Madison wanted to do and what she should do were two different animals. She stared up at the mist that had formed over the looming mountain, and the clouds gathering in the distance. "Since it looks like it's about to rain, we should probably head back to the palace."

"Are you afraid of rain?"

She turned her attention to Zain, specifically his eyes, which seemed darker than midnight. "I'm afraid of what might happen if we stay."

"You fear we'll make love."

"Yes, I do. I told myself I wouldn't be alone with you where anything was possible. And here we are."

He moved a little closer. "And I have told you I have certain conditions before that will happen."

"You want me to say I trust you." And if she didn't, that would be the end of it.

"Do you trust that I would never hurt you?"

Not physically, but he could hurt her in so many other ways. "I know that."

"Do you trust that what has been said about my relationships with women is not the truth?"

"Do I think your sexual exploits are overblown? Probably." Though she wasn't sure how exaggerated they might have been.

He reached out and touched her face. "Most important, you may trust that whatever happens between us tonight, I will not take it lightly. And I will not tell a soul. I only want to prove that you are a desirable, sensual woman. With that said, do you trust me?"

Call it instinct, call it crazy, but she did. "Yes, I do trust you. I'm not sure I trust myself around you."

He took her shoes, dropped them on the ground, slid her jacket away and tossed it down to join her sneakers. "I will teach you to trust your own sexuality." He shrugged out of his jacket and added it to the pile. "I only ask that you let go of your inhibitions."

That could be a test for her normally cautious self, and she wondered if going forward would be worth the risk. Yet when he pulled her into his arms and lowered his mouth to hers, she began to believe she could meet the challenge. He kissed her gently at first, just a light tease of his tongue against hers. Then he held her tighter, kissed her deeply, thoroughly, until her pulse started to sprint. The rain had begun to lightly fall, but she didn't care. Didn't care that before this was over, she would be soaked to the skin. Come to think of it, they could be down to only skin very, very soon.

Madison started to protest when Zain pulled away and stepped back. But all arguments died on her lips as he tugged his shirt over his head and tossed it aside. Due to the limited light, she could barely see the finer points of his bare chest. However, she could make out the width of his shoulders, the definition of his biceps and the light shading at his sternum. She was dying to touch him, investigate the extremely masculine terrain. As if he'd read her mind, he moved forward, leaving little space between them, and flattened her palms against his chest immediately below his collarbone. She took a downward path over his damp skin and when she circled his nipples with her fingertips, she heard the slight catch of his breath. When she slid her hands to his abdomen, she thought he might have stopped breathing. She kept going, using a fingertip to trace the thin trail of hair that disappeared into his waistband.

But that was as far as he allowed her to go. He clasped her wrists, lifted her hands and kissed each palm. Then without fair warning, he pulled her T-shirt up and over her head. She wore only jeans, a pink floral bra and a blanket of goose bumps that had nothing to do with the weather. She predicted he would soon relieve her of the rest of her clothes. Instead, he claimed a boulder to take off his boots and sent her a *What are you waiting for?* look.

"No inhibitions," he said when she failed to remove her bra.

The time had come to kick the self-consciousness to the curb. She sucked in a deep breath, undid the clasp, slipped the straps from her shoulders and added her bra to the clothes heap. "No inhibitions."

The words seemed to shred Zain's control, apparent by the way he pushed off the rock and engaged her in one deep, deadly kiss. After a few moments, he shifted his attention to the column of her throat with light kisses. When his mouth closed over her breast, Madison feathered her hands in his hair in order to stay somewhat steady against the sensual onslaught. So caught up in the pull of his mouth, the feel of his tongue swirling around her nipple, she was only vaguely aware that he'd unfastened her jeans. She became extremely aware when he pushed her pants down her hips, along with her underwear, until both dropped to her ankles.

"No inhibitions," he whispered. "No turning back."

She couldn't turn back if she wanted to, and she didn't. Not in the least. Taking his cue, she used his broad shoulders for support and stepped out of the jeans. Now she was completely naked, while he was still dressed from the waist down. Normally that might make her feel extremely uneasy. Instead, she was incredibly hot, especially when he kissed her again, his hands roving over her bottom, his fingers curling between her thighs.

She wanted him as naked as she was. She wanted him more than she'd wanted anything in quite some time. And it appeared she would get what she wanted when he swept her up into his arms, carried her to the ancient truck and set her on the tailgate. She glanced over her shoulder to discover the bed had been conveniently covered by a colorful quilt, but all her attention soon turned to Zain as he stood in front of her, his hand at his fly.

She was in the buff and barely breathing and drenched. Everywhere. She was also overcome with impatience when Zain failed to remove his slacks.

"Birth control," he grated out as he continued to lower his zipper.

She didn't want to reveal why it wasn't a problem, or burden him with the truth—the chance she could become pregnant was slim to none without medical assistance. This was not the time for sadness or regrets and, most of all, sympathy. "It's not an issue."

"Are you certain?" he asked.

"You're going to have to trust me on this."

That seemed to satisfy his concerns as he took little time shoving his pants down and kicking them away. Now they were both equally undressed and she was extremely impressed. Despite the fact that he'd left on the truck's parking lights, she still wished she could see him better. But even if the sun made an unexpected appearance, Zain wouldn't have given her the chance to assess the details. He hoisted himself onto the tailgate and in a matter of seconds, had her on her back on the makeshift bed.

He hovered above her, his hand resting lightly on her thigh, his gaze leveled on hers. "Do you still trust me?"

Right now, she'd say anything if he'd just get on with it. "Yes."

"Then roll to your side away from me."

Madison wasn't sure where this might be heading, yet she complied because she did trust him. Trusted him not to hurt her. Trusted him to take her on an unforgettable ride.

Zain fitted himself against her back, pushed her

damp hair aside and pressed his lips to her ear. "Clear your mind and think of nothing else but us together." He streamed his hand down her thigh and lifted her leg over his. "Enjoy these moments." He slowly slid his palm down her abdomen. "Pretend this is the only time you will feel this good—" he eased inside her "—again."

The moment Zain hit the mark, Madison shuddered from the sensations. He seemed to time his movement with the stroke of his fingertips, and she responded as if she never had felt this good, because she couldn't recall when she had. He kept a slow, steady pace with both his touch and his body, yet her own body reacted as if they were on a sexual sprint. If she could prolong the involuntary release, she would, but that all-important passion had led to this moment when her body claimed all control. The orgasm arrived quickly in strong spasms, wave after wave of pleasure that seemed to go on forever, though not nearly long enough.

Zain muttered something in Arabic that sound suspiciously like an oath, then pulled out and turned her onto her back. He entered her again, this time not quite as carefully as before, but as promised, he didn't hurt her. He did fuel her fantasies as he rose up on his arms and moved again, harder, faster, his dark gaze firmly fixed on hers. Madison found his powerful thrusts, the continuing rain and the fact they were out in the open highly erotic. And so was the way his jaw went rigid, his eyes closed and his body tensed with the force of his climax that soon came sure and swift.

When Zain collapsed against her, Madison savored the feel of his solid back beneath her palms, even his weight. She didn't exactly appreciate what he had done to her—coaxed her into crossing a line she had never intended to cross. A dangerous boundary that could cost them both if anyone found out.

But even in light of that possibility, she truly believed that this first experience with the king—the *only* experience she could afford—had been absolutely worth the risk.

Unfortunately, it was the last risk she would allow them to take.

Seven

Had it not been for the deluge, Zain would have made love to her again. And again.

Instead, he had carried Madison and set her in the cab. He re-dressed in soaked clothing and gathered hers, only to return to find her wrapped in the dry blanket. Not long after they'd left the lake, she'd settled against his side, her head tipped against his shoulder, and fallen fast asleep. Even when he navigated the rugged terrain, she hadn't woken. But during that time, and since, he had been very aware that she was still naked beneath the blanket. Whenever she stirred, his body did the same. Tonight's brief interlude had not been enough. If he had his way, they would enjoy more of the same, and often, in the upcoming days.

When Madison shifted slightly, Zain glanced at her to see she was still sleeping, looking beautiful and somewhat innocent. She brought out his protective side, though she did not need his protection. She was fiercely independent, fiery and intractable, everything he admired in a woman. Tonight she had proven she possessed an untapped passion that he needed to explore further. She also made him want to right his transgressions and prove to her he owned a measure of honor. He wanted to toss away convention and be with her after the coronation. And that was impossible. Eventually he would be required to marry, and he would not relegate Madison to mistress status. She deserved much better, and so would his future wife. So had his own mother.

That did not preclude him from being with her until the day she left.

When he hit a bump in the road, Madison raised her head and gave him a sleepy smile. "How much longer until we're at the palace?"

"Approximately ten minutes."

She straightened and sent him a panicked look. "You should have woken me earlier," she said as she sorted through the clothes at her side.

"Dressing is not necessary." He preferred she remained naked, as he planned to take her to his bed as soon as they arrived.

"I'm not walking into the royal abode wearing only a blanket." A blanket she tossed aside without regard to her nudity or his discomfort.

He became mesmerized when she lifted her hips and slid her panties into place, followed by her jeans. She picked up her shirt, shook it out, allowing him an extended look at her breasts, the pale pink nipples…

The sound of grating beneath the tires forced his gaze to the road that he'd inadvertently left during his visual exploration. He jerked the truck back onto pavement immediately before he ended up in some unsuspecting citizen's front yard.

"Are you trying to kill us, Zain?"

"I was avoiding a goat."

Madison laughed softly. "An imaginary goat."

He frowned. "It is your fault for distracting me."

"It's your fault for not keeping your eyes on the road."

"I am a man, Madison. You cannot expect me to ignore your state of undress. You should know that after what we shared tonight."

"You're right, and I'm sorry."

He sent another fast glance in her direction to find her completely clothed and smiling. "Are you more comfortable now?"

"I'm very wet."

That prompted a very vivid fantasy, and a return of his erection. "If you will remove your pants again and come over here, I will remedy that."

She shot him a sour look. "You are such a bad boy. No wonder all those women fell all over themselves to be with you."

"Two women."

"Excuse me?"

He finally recognized that she could trust him freely only if he freely gave her accurate information. "I was involved with two women during my time away."

Her blue eyes widened. "You're saying that out of all those highly publicized photos of you escorting various starlets and such, you were only involved with two?"

The disbelief in her voice and expression drove him to disclose the details. "The first woman was older," he continued. "I met Elizabeth through business contacts about a year after I arrived in L.A. My father released only limited funds to me and she assisted with my investments. I owe the majority of my second fortune to her."

"How long were you together?"

Too long for his comfort. "Almost three years."

"What about the second woman?"

This explanation would prove to be more difficult, and much more revealing. Yet for some reason, he wanted Madison to know the facts. Facts few people knew. "Her name was Genevieve. I met her in a café in Paris. I was there for business, she was on sabbatical."

"Then it was only a brief fling?"

"No. I joined her in Africa."

"Africa?" Madison sounded stunned by the revelation. "How long were you there? *Why* were you there?"

"Eighteen months in Ethiopia and, after a three-month break, fifteen months in Nigeria. Genevieve is a humanitarian aid worker. I assisted her with the relief effort by delivering supplies and building temporary shelter."

"Did anyone know your true identity?"

"Only Genevieve." He smiled with remembrance. "She introduced me as Joe Smith."

"That name definitely encourages anonymity," she said. "And to think that all this time, people believed you were holed up with some supermodel, while you were less than a thousand miles away from Bajul being a really stellar guy. Unbelievable."

"Genevieve convinced me I needed to learn the reality of the situation in order to be a better leader." And he had not been prepared for that reality. "I have never seen such desolation. Violence brought about by unrest and ignorance. Famine, starvation and disease brought about by drought and insufficient food and water distribution."

"And that's when you decided to develop your water conservation plans."

He started up the road leading to the castle, relieved that the conversation would soon have to come to an end. "I vowed when my opportunity to rule arrived, I would do everything in my power to prevent the possibility of that devastation in my country. I had not expected the opportunity to arrive so quickly. My plans were to return to Bajul to present my proposals when I received word of my father's death."

"So he never knew about your ideas."

"No." Even if he had, his inflexible father would have rejected them because he had the power to do so. "Regardless, I will never be able to repay Genevieve for forcing me to open my eyes to the possibilities. The experience changed me. She changed me."

"She sounds like a very special woman."

"She was caring and committed and possessed all the attributes I had never acquired." And she'd been much too good for a man whose character had been questionable up to that point in time.

Madison laid a hand on his arm. "But as you've said, you've changed for the better. Not many men in your position would have personally taken on those challenges, and dangerous ones at that. Most would have written a check and returned home."

He appreciated her praise. He greatly appreciated her willingness to listen without judgment. "At times I wish I could have accomplished more, especially when it came to the children."

She sighed. "I know. I remember traveling with my parents to some of the worst poverty-stricken places in the world. The children always suffer the most, even in America."

The memories came back to Zain with the clarity of cut glass. Memories he had never shared with one soul since his return. "I met a special child there. She was around four years of age and an orphan. The workers took charge of her care until a relative could be located. For some reason, she attached herself to me. We spoke different languages, yet we found ways to communicate. Perhaps she appreciated the treats I gave her."

"Or maybe she recognized someone she could trust."

The sincerity in Madison's tone temporarily lifted his spirits. "Her name was Ajo. It means *joyful,* and that suited her. Yet I saw no joy in her when they took her away." He would never forget the way she held out her arms to him, or her tears. The images still haunted him, and at times he felt he had abandoned her.

"Do you know what happened to her?" Madison asked.

He arrived at the gate and raised his hand at the confused guards who, after a slight hesitation, allowed him entry. "Genevieve has been kind enough to keep me apprised of her situation and to deliver the funds I send monthly for Ajo's care. Fortunately, her aunt and uncle see to it she is safe and secure."

"That's wonderful, Zain. But what about your relationship with Genevieve?"

A complex relationship that was never meant to be. "I returned to L.A. when she was reassigned. I had my responsibilities, and she had hers."

"Were you in love with her?"

He was surprised by the query, and uncertain how to answer. He'd cared a great deal for Genevieve, but love had not entered into it. "We both understood from the beginning that our relationship could only be temporary.

We agreed to enjoy each other's company while the opportunity existed."

Madison shifted back to his side and rested her head against his shoulder. "I'm sorry I misjudged you. I bought into the whole 'superficial, arrogant, rich playboy' assumption, just like everyone else did. It's nice to know that couldn't be further from the truth. Despite your issues with your father, it's clear he raised you to be an honorable man."

Anger broke through his remorse. Anger aimed at his patriarch, not at Madison. "My father knew nothing of honor, and he did little to raise me. You may thank Elena for that. I would never take a mistress and force my wife to have a child she did not want. As far as I am concerned, he was responsible for her death due to his careless disregard."

"What happened to her, Zain?"

The strong urge to halt the conversation overcame him. He had already said too much. But Madison's expectant look proved too much, as well. "She was found below the mountain, not far from the lake. Some believe she slipped and fell. Many believe she took her own life due to my father's infidelity. I suppose we will never know the truth."

"I'm so sorry, Zain."

So was he. Sorry that he had almost ruined the evening with regrets. That ended now.

He tipped her face up and kissed her. "We will return to the veranda the same way we left, only we will stay in my room tonight."

She pulled back and slid across the seat away from him. "We're going to walk in the front door, otherwise we'll look guilty. And we're going to stay in separate beds, tonight and every night until I leave."

That would not suffice. "I would prefer you sleep in my bed the majority of the night after we make love. As long as we've parted by morning, no one will be the wiser."

She folded the jacket's hem back and forth. "We can't take the risk that someone will find out. I had a wonderful time tonight, but we can't be together in that way again."

How many times in his youth had he said something of a similar nature to a woman? "That is unacceptable. How to you expect me to pretend I do not want you when I do?" More than she knew. More than he realized until he faced the prospect of not having her.

"We're going to limit our alone time together."

"You've said that before."

"This time I mean it, Zain. I am not going to be responsible for a scandal that could ruin all the work we're doing to restore your image."

Zain gripped the wheel and stared straight ahead. "Then you lied when you said you trust me."

"I do trust you, and so should your people. I admire and respect you even more now. But when I said I didn't trust myself, I wasn't talking about sex. I've already blurred the personal and professional lines and I can't afford to become more emotionally involved with you than I already am. Now we need to go inside before they come looking for us."

Before Zain could respond, she was out the door and walking toward the path leading to the front entrance. He left the truck and caught up with her in the courtyard flanking the front steps. After clasping her arm, he turned her to face him. "I will honor your wishes. I will allow you your blessed distance, but not before I give you this."

He crushed her against him and kissed her with all the desperation he experienced at the moment. He expected her to fight him, and when instead she responded, he realized she wanted him as much as he wanted her. As much as he needed her for reasons that defied logic. He agreed with her on one point—this was not only about sex.

Then she wrested from his grasp, looking as if he'd struck her. "Don't make this more complicated than it already is, Zain."

Madison hurried around the corner and by the time he reached the stone steps, she had already disappeared through the doors.

Once inside, he was met by a security contingent and Deeb. "You are all dismissed," he said in Arabic. "No harm has come to me to warrant this attention." Not the kind of harm they would assume.

He ascended the stairs only to have Deeb stop him on the second-floor landing. "Your brother asked me to summon you to his study upon your return."

Confronting Rafiq was the last thing he needed. "I have no desire to speak to him."

"What shall I tell him, Emir?"

Tell him to go to hell. "I will see him in the morning."

Zain arrived at the corridor leading to his quarters in time to see the door to Madison's room close, shutting him out.

Perhaps she could easily dismiss him and what they had shared tonight, but he would wager she would suffer for the decision to avoid him. So would he.

But he would do as he had promised and hoped she decided they should take advantage of what little time together they had left. In the meantime, he would prepare to spend the first of several long, sleepless nights.

* * *

Ten days had passed since Madison had enjoyed a decent night's sleep, and she had Zain to thank for that. Not only had he upheld his promise to give her space, he'd downright ignored her. He'd avoided all eye contact when they'd been together, and he'd only spoken to her when she had spoken first. The two times they'd briefly found themselves alone following one of his myriad meetings, not once had he mentioned their night together, nor had he delivered even the slightest innuendo. He hadn't joined her and Rafiq for dinner, but at least she'd had a chance to get to know the older brother, who was highly intelligent and not quite as serious as she'd once assumed.

She truly didn't know if Zain was simply pouting, or proving a point. Either way, she admittedly missed their intimate conversations. Missed kissing him, as well. She definitely missed her former common sense, which had apparently followed the rain out of town.

Zain had been right to remain in strictly business mode, and business was exactly what she needed to focus on today, and each day until the coronation.

Madison sought out Elena and found her in the kitchen, where the wonderful scents permeating the area caused her stomach to rumble even though she'd had enough breakfast to kill an elephant. Evidently she'd been making up for the lack of sex by eating her way through the kingdom.

"That smells marvelous," she said as she approached the metal prep table holding a platter full of puffed pastries.

Elena smiled and gestured toward the fare. "Please try one. The chef prepared the samples for Prince Zain's approval, but he refused. He said he did not care if they served water and wheat at the wedding reception."

Clearly His Royal Pain in the Arse had forgotten they'd added guests to the list, who could be beneficial to his reign. But hey, if he didn't want to try the goodies, she certainly would. "Thanks, I believe I will take a bite or two." Or three, she decided when the flaky crust and creamy filling practically melted in her mouth.

After Madison had consumed five of the canapés, she looked up to meet Elena's quizzical look. "Tell the chef he's hit a home run with this." As if the guy would understand a baseball analogy. "Better still, tell him they're perfect."

"I will pass that on," Elena said. "I will also tell him to prepare double for you."

Great. She'd demonstrated she had serious etiquette issues. "That's not necessary. I eat when I'm nervous, and this whole reception has me on edge. I hope we're doing the right thing by not having a separate gathering prior to the coronation."

"Have you consulted the new king about forgoing that honor?"

"Actually, it was his idea. He's not being all that cooperative these days. Maybe he's a bit anxious about officially becoming His Majesty in less than two weeks."

"Or perhaps he is being denied something he wants more than the crown."

Madison faked ignorance. "A new sports car?"

Elena raised a thin brow. "You may fool the rest of the household, *cara,* but you are not fooling me. I know you and Prince Zain stole away without notifying anyone of your departure, and returned in wet clothing."

The palace apparently had spies in place and gossip down to a science. "He wanted to show me the lake and we got caught in a storm." A firestorm. "That's all there was to it."

"Are you certain of that?"

She knew better than to try to lie to a wise bird like Elena. She also knew not to reveal too much, even if she thought she could trust her with the truth. "Wise or not, we have developed a friendship. He's even begun to confide in me about his past and, most important, his goals. That's been beneficial for me, since I've been preparing the speech he'll deliver next week." A speech he would probably reject.

She couldn't miss the concern on Elena's face. "What has he said about the king and queen?"

"Since he took me into his confidence, I don't feel I should say more." She'd already come down with foot-in-mouth disease to go with the voracious appetite.

"Anything you could say to me, *cara mia,* I have already heard in the many years I've been here. The staff talks about things they know nothing about, and most is not true."

She did have a point. "He mentioned something about the king having mistresses, and that he believes that was directly related to the queen's death."

Elena grabbed the platter and took it to the counter next to the massive industrial sink. "Go on," she said, keeping her back to Madison.

The fact Elena didn't deny the conjecture was very telling. "He also said that the queen was forced to have a third child against her will."

Elena spun around, a touch of anger calling out from her amber eyes. "That is not true. The queen would have done anything to have another child. And furthermore, the king was the one who only wanted two children, yet he was so devoted to her, he gave her what she desired. Sadly, Adan did not aid in her happiness."

"Was she so unhappy that she took her own life?"

"I would not begin to speculate on that, and neither should you."

Madison held up her hands. "I'm sorry I've upset you. I was only repeating what Zain told me." Darn if she hadn't done it again—called him by his given name.

Elena sighed. "It is not your fault, *cara*. And I beg of you to please not repeat what I have said."

She found it odd that Elena would want to conceal the information from the boys she had practically raised. "Don't you think the princes have a right to know the truth?"

"Some secrets are best left in the past." Elena picked up a towel and began to twist it, a sure sign of distress. "Did you require anything else from me? If not, I have some work to attend to."

Madison knew not to press the matter any further. She needed Elena as an ally, not an enemy. "Actually, I was wondering if you had a final guest list for the reception. I want to go over it with His Highness." Provided he didn't toss her out on her posterior, injuring her pride.

"Yes, I do." Elena walked into the office, emerged a few moments later and handed her two pages full of names. "You'll see that I have made a separate column for the prospective queen candidates and their fathers. I thought you would find that helpful."

She found it appalling. "I suppose Prince Zain will appreciate that information. He can come prepared for when they converge upon him."

Elena surprisingly patted Madison's cheek. "Do not worry, *cara*. He will find none of them to his liking as long as you are here." With that, the woman smiled, returned to the office and closed the door.

Obviously no one could pull the wool over Elena's eyes, and that could present some complications if Madison didn't remain strong in Zain's presence.

Not a problem. The way things were going, she'd be lucky if he ever seriously spoke to her again, let alone touched her.

Eight

He wanted nothing more than to touch her. Only a slight touch. Or perhaps not so slight at that.

Since Madison's arrival in the study, Zain had engaged in several fantasies that involved taking her down on the sofa where she sat reciting names that mattered not to him.

"Who is Layali Querishi?" she asked. "That sounds familiar."

He fixated on Madison's blue blouse, which could easily be unbuttoned, allowing access to her breasts. "She is a sultan's daughter and a popular singer."

"And gorgeous." She crossed her legs, causing the skirt's hem to ride higher on her thighs. "I remember seeing an article about her Australian tour."

"I do not recall her looks." Nor did he care about them. He only cared about running his hands up Madison's skirt as a reminder of what they had given up for the sake of professionalism.

"Do you think that's a good idea?"

Madison's question startled Zain into believing he might have voiced his thoughts. "What are you referring to?"

"Pay attention, Your Highness."

He had been paying attention—to her. "My apologies. I have a lot weighing on my mind." And a heavy weight behind his fly.

"I said do you think it's a good idea to seat all these women together at the same table? That's grounds for a queen candidate catfight."

He could not hold back his smile. "Some might find that thoroughly entertaining."

"Or thoroughly in bad taste. I suggest we separate them to avoid bloodshed."

He started to suggest they discard the list and move on to something much more pleasurable, when a series of raps sounded at the door. Familiar raps that readily identified the offending party.

Madison consulted her watch. "It's late. I can't imagine who would be stopping in this time of night, unless it's Mr. Deeb."

"It's not Deeb."

"Then who is it?"

"My brother."

Thankful his coat sufficiently hid his current state, Zain rounded the desk and opened the door to Adan wearing his standard military-issue flight suit and a cynical smile. He made a circular sweeping gesture with his arm and bowed dramatically. "Greetings, His Majesty, king of the surfing sheikhs."

He had not mentioned that pastime to Madison, but she definitely knew now. He wanted to send Adan on his way but instead gave him the required manly embrace. "When did you arrive?"

"I flew in a while ago." Adan leaned around him. "And who is this lovely lady?"

"I'm Madison Foster." Zain turned to see her standing in front of the sofa. "And you must be Prince Adan."

"The one and the only." Adan crossed the room, took Madison's hand and kissed it. "Are you one of my brother's California conquests?"

"She is a political consultant," Zain added in an irritable tone. "Which means she is off-limits to you."

Adan released her hand but offered up a devil-may-care grin. "I have only honorable intentions."

She returned his smile as she reclaimed her seat. "You also have a very British accent."

"He has an aversion to authority," Zain said. "He spent most of his formative years in a military boarding school in the U.K."

Adan attempted to look contrite. "I have since learned to respect authority and take orders, as long as they are not delivered by my brothers."

Zain wanted to order him out of the room. "Considering the lateness of the hour, I am certain you are ready to retire."

"Actually, I am wide-awake." He had the audacity to drop down beside Madison and drape his arm over the back of the sofa. "How long will you be here?"

"Ms. Foster will be with *me* until after the coronation," Zain answered before she could respond. "And we still have much to accomplish tonight."

"We can take up where we left off tomorrow," Madison said as she came to her feet. "I'm sure you two have a lot of catching up to do after all these years."

Adan clasped her wrist and pulled her back down

beside him, sparking Zain's barely contained fury. "I visited Zain in Los Angeles less than six months ago. In fact, I was his guest at least once a year during his time there."

Many times an unwelcome guest, as he was now. "For that reason, he should return to his quarters so that we might resume our tasks."

Adan ignored him and took the pages from Madison. "What is this?"

"We're going over the guest list for the upcoming wedding reception," she said.

He leaned closer to her. "Am I on it?"

She seemed unaffected by his nearness, and that only served to anger Zain more. "Since you're in the wedding party, there's no need to add your name."

Adan perused the pages for a few moments. "Ah, I see we have a bevy of prospective brides in attendance. Najya Toma's much too young. Taalah Wasem is too stuffy. And I had hoped to claim the third one as my own. No one would turn down a chance to bed Layali Querishi." He winked. "Of course, she is not quite as beautiful as you."

Zain had had quite enough. "If you are finished with your attempts to seduce my employee, I suggest you retire to your quarters now so that we may resume our duties."

Adan reluctantly came to his feet. "You are beginning to sound like Rafiq. Did you leave your sense of humor in the States?"

"Did you leave your sense of decorum in your jet?"

"Women are quite taken with my jet."

Zain pointed at the door. "Out. Now."

Adan had the audacity to laugh. "I can take a hint, brother. And I certainly understand why you would want

Ms. Foster all to yourself." He regarded Madison again. "It has been a pleasure, madam. Should you need protection from this rogue, feel free to notify me immediately."

She needed protection from his rogue brother. "I assure you, Adan, Ms. Foster is in good hands and does not require your assistance."

Adan sent Madison another smile. "Then I will bid you both good-night."

After Adan thankfully left, Zain closed the door and tripped the lock. He turned back to Madison and launched into a tirade on the heels of his anger. "Although you obviously enjoyed my brother's attention, you should know that he is a master of seduction. Stay clear of him."

"That's rich, coming from you." She tossed the papers aside and sighed. "Not to mention he's practically a baby, and he seems perfectly harmless."

He took a few steps toward her. "He is five years my junior. That makes him twenty-eight, and a man."

"And he's three years younger than me, so in my eyes, that makes him cougar bait."

He had not realized she was over thirty, but then he had never asked her age. "Adan would not care if you were twice his age. He recognizes a beautiful woman, he is anything but harmless and he has designs on you."

She rolled her eyes. "Stop playing the jealous monarch, Zain."

He was not playing. "I am only concerned about your well-being."

She tossed the pages aside. "Really? For the past few days, you haven't seemed at all concerned about my well-being, or anything else, for that matter. You've barely given me the time of day."

And it had nearly destroyed him. "I am giving you space as you've requested."

"You're giving me the cold shoulder, and I don't deserve that."

"And you believe I deserve this torture?"

"What torture?"

He slid his hands in his pockets and took two more slow steps. "Each time you are near me, I can only think about touching you. Ignoring you is my only means of self-defense."

"You could at least be civil."

When he reached her, he took off his jacket and draped it over the back of the sofa. "Civility is the last thing on my mind when you're dressed as you are now."

She looked down before returning her gaze to his. "It's a plain blouse and knee-length skirt, Zain, and I've been dressing this way since we met. It's more than decent."

Decent yes, but his thoughts were not. "And I have suffered because of your choices."

She rested her elbow on the back of the sofa and rubbed her forehead. "Fine. I'll wear a full-body burlap sack from now on."

"It would not matter what you are wearing. I would still imagine you naked."

"And that makes you just like every other man who comes in contact with a female."

He leaned forward and braced his palms on the cushions on either side of her hips. "Is that what I am to you, Madison? Only one more man who wants you? Was our lovemaking nothing more than a diversion?"

Unmistakable desire flashed in her eyes. "It was… It was…"

"Remarkable?"

"Unwise."

He brushed a kiss across her cheek before nuzzling her neck. "Tell me you do not want to experience it again, and I will leave you alone."

"You're asking me to lie."

He touched his lips to hers. "I am asking you to admit that you still want me. I want to hear you say that you are as consumed by thoughts of us as I am."

"Stop making it so hard to resist you, Zain."

Using the sofa's back for support, he lifted her hand and pressed it against his fly. "You are making it hard on me, Madison."

She rubbed her thumb along the ridge. "That sounds like a very personal problem to me."

He kissed her then, a kiss hot enough to ignite the room. But when she tried to pull him down beside her, he resisted and straightened.

She glared up at him. "I get it now. You're teasing me and then you're going to walk out of here just to punish me."

"I promise I have no intention of punishing you." He lowered to the floor on his knees to fulfill his greatest fantasy. "Unless you consider absolute pleasure a form of punishment."

When he reached beneath her skirt and slid her panties down, she released a slight gasp. And when he parted her legs, she trembled. He kept his gaze leveled on hers as he kissed the inside of one thigh, then the other, and prepared for a protest. Instead, she remained silent as her chest rapidly rose and fell in anticipation.

"Unbutton your blouse and lower your bra," he said, though he realized she might not answer his demand if she believed he had gone too far.

Yet she surprised him by releasing the buttons with

shaking fingers before reaching beneath the back of the blouse to unclasp the bra.

Seeing her eyes alight with excitement and her breasts exposed was almost his undoing. As badly as he wanted to dispense with formality and seat himself deep inside her, he had something else in mind. Yet before he sought his ultimate destination, he had one final question. "Tell me you want me to keep going."

She exhaled slowly. "You know I do, dammit."

The first curse she'd ever uttered in his presence served to excite him even more. "Then say it."

"I want you to do it."

That was all he needed to hear. He pushed her skirt up to her waist for better access, slipped his hands beneath her hips and lowered his mouth between her trembling legs. He watched her face to gauge her reaction as he teased her with the tip of his tongue, varying the pressure to prolong the pleasure.

When her eyes momentarily drifted shut, he stopped and lifted his head. "Look at me, Madison. I want you to see what I am doing to you."

She blinked twice as if in a trance. "I don't think I can."

"Yes, you can, and you will."

When their gazes locked, he went back to his exploration, more thoroughly this time. She gripped the cushions and lifted her hips to meet his mouth, indicating she was close to reaching a climax. And as she tipped her head back and released a low moan, Zain refused to let up until her frame and expression went slack.

After her breathing slowed and her eyes closed again, he rose to his feet. Leaving her now would be difficult, but he felt he had no choice. He turned and started toward the door, only to halt midstride when she asked, "Where are you going?"

He faced her to find she was clutching her blouse closed, a mixture of ire and confusion in her expression. "I am going to bed, and you should, as well. You should be relaxed enough to enjoy a restful sleep." He regrettably would not. He would lie awake for hours, aching for her and wondering when he would have her again. If he would ever have her again.

"Oh, no, you don't," she said. "You're not going to just leave me here alone after you've somehow managed to turn me into some sort of wild animal in heat."

"I know you, Madison, and this wildness is the part of you that you've kept concealed from the world, and from yourself. You have simply never met a man who encourages that side of you before now. I am that man."

She released the blouse, allowing it to gape open. "A real man would come over and finish what he started."

It took all his resolve not to answer her challenge. "From this point forward, you will have to come to me. But mark my words, we will finish this."

Mark my words, we will finish this...
To this point, Madison hadn't given Zain that satisfaction, although he'd given her plenty during their little office interlude. She'd managed to afford the same courtesy he had shown her by turning the tables on him. She'd made a point to avoid him the past three days, but unfortunately, she couldn't avoid him tonight.

While she claimed a corner of the banquet hall, nursing a mineral water and a solid case of jealousy, the imminent king stood at the front of the room, basking in female attention. Who could blame them? He was a tall, dark presence dressed in a black silk suit, light gray shirt and a perfect-match tie. Both his looks and his status had earned him more than his share of attention. She'd basically been relegated to wallflower status, after she'd made the required rounds among the dignitaries and diplomats she'd personally invited. Normally she didn't like being invisible, yet tonight she didn't care if she blended into the background. It didn't matter one whit if no one noticed her.

"You are looking exceedingly lovely tonight, Ms. Foster."

Madison glanced to her left and met the dimpled baby Mehdi's charming smile. She still couldn't get over his lack of resemblance to his older brothers, who could almost pass as twins. Where their eyes were almost black, Adan's were golden and his hair was much lighter. That didn't make him any less gorgeous in a boyish sort of way. "Thank you, Your Highness."

"Tonight you should refer to me as Adan." He took a step back and studied the crimson cocktail dress she'd chosen instead of the black one Zain had requested she wear all those weeks ago. "Red certainly becomes you."

She smoothed a hand over the skirt. "I worried it might be overkill."

"Your beauty has almost killed some of our elder statesmen. You'll know who they are as they are holding their ribs where their wives have landed elbows throughout the evening."

She couldn't hold back a laugh over that image. "Don't be ridiculous."

"I am only being observant." He nodded toward Zain. "My brother the king has certainly noticed. He has watched your every move all night, and he's presently staring at us, the fires of hell in his eyes."

Madison turned her attention to Zain and confirmed

he had one heck of a glare leveled on them. "He's too involved with his admirers to care about me."

"He cannot give them his proper attention when you are all that he sees."

"That's ridiculous."

"That is the truth." He leaned close to her ear. "Right now he believes I am propositioning you, and if he knew that for certain, he would come over here and wrap his hands around my throat."

She couldn't believe he would even think that about Zain, let alone voice it. "He wouldn't do that. He's your brother."

Adan straightened and smiled. "He is a man obsessed with a woman. I have no idea what you have done to bewitch him, but your spell has effectively created a monster. I have never known Zain to be so possessive. Perhaps he is caught in a web of love and he has no idea how to free himself."

A web of lust, maybe, but Madison didn't buy the love theory. Anxious to end the troubling conversation, she opted for a topic change. "The wedding was nice, although I didn't understand one word of the vows." She also didn't understand how a bride could have looked so sad on her wedding day.

"You did not miss much," Adan said. "It was a merger. The culmination of a business arrangement born out of obligation. An obligation I will eventually face. But since I have no direct claim to the throne, I intend to enjoy my freedom until I am at least forty. Regrettably, Zain is not as fortunate. He will be expected to marry a suitable bride as soon as possible."

Madison didn't need to be reminded of that, nor did she need to encourage more discussion about Zain by commenting on the antiquated tradition. "Speaking of the bride and groom, I haven't seen them in a while."

"They have retired to the marriage bed," Adan said as he snatched a glass of fruity punch from the roving waiter's tray. "And by now Rafiq has confirmed that his bride is not a virgin. Of course, he will not care as long as she spreads her legs in an effort to produce the mandatory heir."

She frowned. "That's rather crass, and how do you know for sure she isn't a virgin?"

"Because another Mehdi brother had her first."

Surely not… "Zain?"

Adan downed the rest of his drink and set the glass on the nearby side table. "Yours truly."

Madison did well to hide her shock. "You slept with your brother's wife?"

"Future wife," he said. "And I did not instigate it. I had recently arrived home from the academy to celebrate my seventeenth birthday at a friend's house. Rima came by after having argued with her true love. She was looking for consolation wherever she could find it. I happened to be searching for a willing woman to give me my first experience. I tried to refuse but, alas, I succumbed to her charms. It was, as they say, the perfect storm."

A perfect mess, in Madison's opinion. "And Rafiq never wondered where she'd gone after they argued?"

He sent her a practiced smirk. "I said she argued with her true love. I did not say she argued with Rafiq."

She had somehow become embroiled in a real-live Arabian soap opera. "Then who is it?" Reconsidering the question, she raised her hands, palms forward. "Never mind. I don't want to know."

When Madison noticed one young woman standing on tiptoe and whispering in Zain's ear, she'd seen enough.

Her feet hurt and her heart ached. She only wanted to crawl into bed and throw the covers over her head. That probably wouldn't stop the images of the king taking another willing woman into his bed.

She set her glass next to Adan's and smiled. "Since the crowd seems to be dwindling, I'm going to head to my quarters now. It's been nice talking to you." And very, very interesting.

He lifted her hand for a kiss. "Should you require a man's undivided attention, I am on the second floor in the room at the end of the hall."

She tugged her hand away and patted his cheek. "You, Adan, are too charming for your own good, and I'm really much too old for you."

"As was Rima."

She wasn't going to jump into that sorry situation again. "Good night."

Without waiting for Adan's reply, she hurried through the expansive ballroom and bore down on the double doors that led into one of the many courtyards. Since the building was separate from the palace proper, she found the surroundings seriously confusing, particularly when only dimly lit by random lights alongside the various pathways. Deeb had accompanied her to the reception, but he had long since left, and now she was on her own. That shouldn't present a major problem. She had a master's in political science, a good sense of direction and she'd always excelled at geography. Give her a map and she could find her way anywhere. Too bad she didn't have a map of the jumbled of walkways.

Madison chose the most direct path and immediately arrived at an intersection. She couldn't remember whether to go right or left and wished she'd paid more attention on her way there. She could see the looming palace, but had no clue how to get there. Maybe she should flip a coin—heads, right; tails, left. Maybe she would end up in Yemen if she took a wrong turn.

Luckily she heard approaching footsteps behind her and pivoted around, expecting to see a security guard who could show her the way. She wasn't prepared to see Zain walking toward her instead.

She refused to do this, her prime motivation for taking off down the hedge-lined brick path to her immediate right. At the moment, she didn't care if she wound up seeking shelter in a caretaker's cottage, as long as she could escape before she did something totally foolish, like taking the pretty prince down into the hedges and having her wicked way with him.

"Madison, wait."

She didn't dare look back. "No."

"You cannot continue."

"Yes, I can. Watch me."

"You are about to hit a dead end."

No sooner than he'd said it, Madison did it—almost ran smack dab into a brick tower with a nice little water feature set off to the side of a small bench.

She had no choice but to face the music, or in this case, the monarch. "Go back to your guests, Zain," she said when she turned around.

He loosened his tie and collar. "The guests have all departed."

She folded her arms beneath her breasts. "You couldn't entice even one of those nubile young creatures into your bedroom?"

He slipped the single button on his coat. "They did not hold my interest."

If he made one more move to undress, she would have to resort to hedge-diving. "I'm sorry to hear that. Now if you would kindly point me in the right direction, I'll be on my way."

When he stalked forward, she retreated, once again finding herself backed against a wall. "I am not letting you leave until you understand that being without you is killing me," he said.

"You seemed quite alive to me tonight."

"Those women meant nothing to me." He braced one hand above her head and used the other to slip the wide strap down her shoulder. "Seeing you in this dress made matters worse, as did watching you with Adan. Had he touched you again, I would have crossed the room and wrapped my hands around his neck."

She almost laughed when she recalled Adan had said those exact words. "You can't go around beating up any boy who pays attention to me while I'm here. And I won't be here much longer."

"Precisely," he said before he leaned down and kissed her bare shoulder. "Our time together is limited and I do not wish to waste more than we already have."

"What happened to me coming to you?" Better still, what was happening to her determination to resist him?

"My patience is in tatters. We have been playing the avoidance game long enough. It's time to release our pride and admit that we need to be together. I *need* to be with you."

And heaven help her, she needed to be with him as much as she needed air, which seemed to leave her when he streamed his hand over the curve of her hip.

If he wanted to finish this once and for all, then they would finish it, even if it meant going out in a blaze of glory. "If you need me that much, stop talking and kiss me."

He did, with enough power to light up the country.

Before Madison knew it, Zain had her bodice pulled down, his mouth on her breast and his hand between her legs. Somewhere in the back of her mind, she realized she should tell him to stop and take it to the bedroom before they went any further. But she was too weak with wanting and too far gone to halt the madness.

And madness it was when he pushed her panties down and did the same with his slacks before he wrapped her legs around his hips and drove into her. His intense thrusts blew her mind and propelled her to the edge of orgasmic bliss. That one-time foreign sound began to form in her throat, only to be halted when Zain planted his palm over her mouth.

At that point, she heard the nearby voices, saw movement between the break of the trees. Knowing that could get caught only heightened the dangerous pleasure, and brought about a climax that shook her to the core. She could tell Zain had been affected, too, by the way he tensed and released a guttural groan in her ear, followed by that same single harsh Arabic word.

The sound of their ragged breathing seemed to echo throughout the area, and Madison hoped the passing party had moved out of earshot. Zain loosened his hold, allowing her legs to slide down where she fortunately found her footing. She still felt as if she were on shaky emotional ground.

For that reason, she had to get away from him. "We need to return to our respective rooms before Deeb sends out a posse and they catch you with your pants down."

He planted both palms on the wall and rested his forehead against hers, his eyes tightly closed. "When I think about you leaving me, even only for a moment, it sickens me."

She could relate to that. "We knew my leaving was

inevitable, Zain. The more time we spend together, the harder it will be to say goodbye." At least for her.

He raised his head, some unidentifiable emotion in his eyes. "Stay with me tonight, Madison. All night. I want to wake in the morning to find you beside me."

And that seemed like a recipe for disaster when it came to her heart. "But—"

His soft kiss quelled her protest. "I am begging you to stay."

Madison had stayed with Zain that night, and every night for the past week. They had grown so close, and she had become so lost in him, she'd begun to believe she didn't know where he ended and she began. And that frightened her, but not enough to stop sleeping in his bed, and waking up every morning to his wonderful face. This morning was no exception.

When a ribbon of light streamed through a break in the heavy curtains covering the window, Madison rolled to her side, bent her elbow and supported her cheek with her palm. She took a few moments to capture a good, long look at the beautiful sleeping prince. The prince who would become king in two days.

His dark lashes fanned out beneath his closed eyes and his gorgeous mouth twitched slightly, as if he might smile. The navy satin sheet rode low on his hips, exposing the crease of his pelvic bone and the stream of hair below his navel. Her face heated when she remembered following that path last night with her lips, causing Zain to squirm when she kept right on going.

She realized she was only a shell of her former self— the woman who had repressed her sexual nature for fear of losing control. Lately, losing control had been preferable when it came to making love with Zain, in many ways, and in many different places—in the study at noon, in the shower several times, in the tunnel leading to the lower-level grounds and on the veranda after midnight, even knowing extra guards had been posted at the corners of the building on all levels. Yet some of the most memorable times came when they took walks in the garden, holding hands and stealing innocent kisses. And the long talks had meant the world to her, conversations about politics and policy and sometimes their pasts. Zain had even reluctantly admitted he harbored some guilt over not having the opportunity to say goodbye to his father, and that made her ache for him.

But the one defining moment in their relationship happened two mornings ago, when she'd awakened alone in his bed, with an orchid on her pillow and a note that read, "You make my days, and my nights, worthwhile."

She'd realized she loved him then. Loved him more than she ever thought possible. Yet none of that mattered. In forty-eight brief hours, he would enter a new era as the king, signaling the end of theirs.

But she still had today—an important day for Zain— so she shook off the downhearted thoughts and kissed his bare shoulder. When he didn't respond, she pressed another kiss on his unshaven jaw, then propped her chin on his chest. "Time to get up, Your Sexiness."

His eyes drifted open and his lips curled into a smile. She would store that smile in the memory bank to get her through the lonely days to come. "I am up," he said in his sexy morning voice.

Madison caught his drift and lifted the sheet. Yes, he had definitely arisen to the occasion, as usual. "I'll rephrase that," she said as she dropped the covers back into place. "You need to get out of bed, get dressed and get ready to address your subjects. On that note, I don't know why you won't give my speech suggestions even a little bit of considera—"

He rudely interrupted her light lecture when he flipped her onto her back and rubbed against her. As far as bedside manners went, she couldn't complain. "My royal staff yearns for your attention," he said as he buried his face in her neck.

She had to laugh over that one. "Aren't we just the king of bad euphemisms this morning?"

He lifted his head and grinned. "I have more descriptive ones, if you'd like to hear them."

Before she could object, he had his lips to her ear and her body reeling with possibilities when he recited a litany of crude, albeit sexy, suggestions. When he looked at her again, she faked shock. "Oh, my. Did you minor in dirty words in college, or have you been watching too much cable TV?"

His cupped her breast in his palm. "You bring out the savage in me."

She could say the same for him. He made her want to growl, especially at the moment when he set his hands in motion all over her bare body.

Right when he had her where he wanted her—hot, and bothered and almost begging—the bedside phone began to ring. He eased inside her at the same moment he picked up the receiver. Madison marveled over his ability to multitask, then became mortified when she recognized Rafiq's voice on the other end of the line.

"I am currently occupied," Zain said. "However, when I am able to pull myself away from this most pressing matter, I will be downstairs in the study."

After he hung up, Madison laughed. "You are so bad."

He frowned. "Last night you told me I was very good."

"No. That's what you told me."

The teasing quickly ended as they concentrated on their lovemaking, on each other with a familiarity normally reserved for longtime lovers. But they were so attuned to one another now, it seemed as if they had been lovers forever. And in the aftermath, when Zain's gentle, whispered words of praise floated into Madison's ears, she started to cry. For some reason, she'd done a lot of that lately, but never in front of him.

As he folded her into his arms and stroked her hair, he didn't question her about the tears. He only held her close to his heart until they finally subsided.

"I'm sorry," she said after she recovered from the meltdown. "I guess my leaving is starting to sink in."

"I am trying not to think about it," he said. "Otherwise, I might not get through my duties today."

She wanted so badly to tell him she loved him, but what would be the point? Nothing had changed. Nothing would. She was still the unsuitable American, and he was still the Arabian king steeped in tradition, destined to choose one of his kind.

So she raised her head and gave him her sunniest smile, even though she wanted to sob. "Speaking of your duties, the time has come for you to impress the masses, the way you've continually impressed me."

His dark eyes were so intense, it stole her breath. "Madison, I…" His gaze drifted away with his words.

"You what?"

When he finally looked at her again, he seemed almost detached. "I want to thank you for all that you've done. I would not have gotten through this process had it not been for your support."

That comment was as dry as the desert, and not at all what she wanted to hear. "And to think you almost sent me packing that first night."

"I am glad you fought me on that, and I will never forget our time together."

Funny, that sounded a lot like an early goodbye. Maybe he was just doing some advance preparation, and she should take his cue. "You're welcome, Your Highness. Now that the party's over, it's time to take care of business."

Nine

He had arrived at this first of two monumental moments with a certain confidence, and he had not managed that alone. Unbeknownst to Madison, he had every intention of taking her advice and speaking from the heart. If only he had been able to do that this morning. The one word he had not been able to say—had never said to any woman—had stalled on his lips. Committing to that emotion would only complicate matters more. She was bound to leave, and he was bound to duty as the leader of his country.

"They're ready for you, Emir," Deeb said as he opened the doors to the veranda.

"Good luck, Your Highness," Madison said from behind him.

Since their last conversation that morning, a certain formality had formed between them. Yet he could not consider that now, nor did he dare look at her and meet the sadness in her eyes. "Thank you," he said as he left her to deliver the most important speech of his life.

He moved onto the balcony containing enough guards to populate a military installation. After taking a few moments to gather his thoughts, he stepped behind the podium, and the cameras began to flash. Zain surveyed the masses spread out on the grounds as far as the eye could see. Among those in the immediate vicinity, he spotted a few familiar faces—Maysa, Malik and his family, as well as several childhood friends—and that served to further bolster his self-assurance. Many of the others looked both eager and somewhat suspicious, most likely because they were waiting for him to fail. He refused to fail.

He pulled the pages containing the prepared speech, then on afterthought, set them aside. He also ignored the teleprompter that Madison insisted he have so he wouldn't falter. If his words did not come out perfectly, so be it. His country would then know he was not perfect, and that suited him fine. He had his flaws, but he had the best of intentions. Now he had to convince the country of that.

After adjusting the microphone, Zain began to speak, immediately silencing the restless crowd. He began with outlining his water conservation plan, which garnered minor applause. He continued by insisting that education was the key to prosperity, and he vowed to fund school improvements. He went on to talk about the importance of family, his love for their country and his commitment to its people. He spoke about his father in respectful terms, highlighting all that the former king had accomplished during his forty-year reign, and that he would proudly serve by his example. That earned him a roar from the crowd and shouts of approval. Perhaps he had finally arrived.

Yet as he remained to acknowledge their support, he could not help but wish Madison was at his side. Wish that he had the means to change tradition and choose his bride by virtue of her attributes, not her dowry. But that would present the possibility of rejection not only by the council, but also the traditionalists who expected him to marry one of their own. And even if he could successfully lobby for that change, would he subject Madison to this life? Would he risk destroying her sense of independence in exchange for assuming the role of his queen? A role that had left some women emotionally broken, including his own mother. He then recalled when Madison had said she would never give up her life for any man, and he could not in good conscience ask that of her, even if the thought of letting her go sickened him.

When he felt the tap on his shoulder, he turned to find Deeb, not Madison, as he had hoped. "The press is waiting in the conference room, Emir."

One hurdle jumped, yet another awaited him—answering intrusive questions. "I will be along shortly." First, he planned to seek Madison's approval, a move he would have never made before her, and not because he lacked respect for women. Because he had been that inflexible. She had changed him more than he realized. More than any woman had, even Genevieve. Madison had served as his touchstone for the past month and, in many ways, had given him the strength to survive the chaos. Her opinion mattered to him. She mattered to him, much more than she should.

With a final wave, Zain returned to the study to find Madison seated across the room in front of the corner television, watching the international analysis of his address. He approached the chair and laid a hand on her shoulder to garner her attention. "Did Deeb interpret for you?"

When her frame went rigid, he removed his hand. "Yes, Deeb translated, and you did a remarkable job. For the most part."

When he moved between her and the TV to ask what she hadn't liked, he noticed she did not look well. Her skin was pale and a light sheen of perspiration covered her forehead. "Are you feeling all right?"

"I'm fine," she said as she abruptly stood. "It's a little warm in here."

When she swayed, he clasped her arm to steady her. "You should sit down again."

She tugged out of his grasp. "I said I am perfectly fine, Your Highness. I'm just going to…"

Her eyes suddenly closed, her lips parted slightly, and as she began to fall, Zain caught her in his arms and carried her to the sofa. He had never felt such concern, such fear and such anger over his staff's failure to immediately act.

He turned his ire on Deeb. "Do not stand there like an imbecile. Summon Dr. Barad. Now!"

Madison came awake slowly, feeling somewhat confused and disoriented. She had no idea how she'd ended up on Zain's office couch, although she did recall being dizzy and starting to free-fall. After that, nothing but a big, black void.

When she raised her head from the sofa's arm, an unfamiliar female voice said, "Stay still for a few more moments, Ms. Foster."

The owner of that voice finally came into focus—an exotic woman with dark almond-shaped eyes and long brown hair pulled back into a braid. "Who are you?" Madison asked in a sandpaper voice.

"Maysa Barad." She lifted a stethoscope from a black bag set on the coffee table. "I'm a local physician and friend of the family."

She was also the woman Zain had visited a few weeks ago, and darn if she wasn't gorgeous. "Where's Zain?" she asked, not caring if she hadn't used the proper address.

"He left and took the goons with him after I told him I couldn't do a proper examination with an audience."

Why not? She'd done a swan dive in front of one. "Any idea what happened to me, Dr. Barad?"

"You fainted. And please, call me Maysa." She pressed the metal cylinder against Madison's chest, listened for a few minutes and then pulled the stems from her ears. "It's definitely not your heart."

She wouldn't be surprised if it was, considering it was close to shattering. "That's good to know."

"Your blood pressure's stable, as well. I took it when you were passed out."

"Just wish I knew why I passed out."

"Are you eating well and getting enough rest?"

She'd been eating like a pig at a trough. "Yes on the eating, not so much on the rest. It's been fairly stressful around here." She didn't dare mention that Zain had been the primary cause of her lack of sleep.

Maysa dropped the stethoscope back in the bag and sent her a serious look. "When was your last menstrual cycle?"

An odd question since she'd never passed out from a period. "Honestly, I'm not sure, because they're not regular. I was born with only one ovary, and my doctor isn't convinced it functions all that well."

"Then you've been diagnosed as infertile?"

This was the complicated part. "Not exactly. I have been told that my chances of getting pregnant without medical assistance are remote and, even then, not guaranteed."

"How long ago was this?"

Madison had to think hard on that one, when all she wanted to do was go back to sleep. "I had an ultrasound ten years ago, but I always go for my annual checkups."

"Then you have no way of knowing for certain if perhaps your ovary is in fact functioning."

"I suppose that's accurate."

"Have your breasts been tender?"

Come to think of it, they had. Then again, they were Zain's favorite toys of late. "Maybe a little, but they get that way right before my period."

"That leads to my next question. Have you had sexual relations in the past month?"

She'd had sexual relations in the past few hours. "Why is that important?"

"Because your symptoms indicate you could be pregnant, provided you have been exposed."

Had she ever, and often. But pregnant? No way. "I'm really not sure how to answer that."

Maysa laid a gentle hand on her arm. "I promise you that anything you tell me will be held in the strictest of confidence. We also adhere to doctor-patient privilege in this country."

As long as Madison didn't have to reveal who she'd been having relations with, she might as well admit it. "Yes, I have been exposed, but I truly can't imagine that I could be pregnant."

"There is one way to find out," she said. "I'll have a pregnancy test sent over in the morning."

Madison felt another faint coming on. "Can you make sure to be discreet?"

"I will." Maysa rose from the sofa and smiled down on her. "In the meantime, I want you to rest here awhile longer, and then retire to your room for the remainder of the evening. If you have any more spells, don't hesitate to have Zain call me."

She mentally nixed that suggestion. "Thank you. I appreciate that."

"Also, even if the test is negative, you should stop by my office and I'll draw some blood to be more certain. It could be you've eaten some tainted food."

Lovely. She hated needles about as much as she hated being viewed as fragile. "I'll let you know as soon as I know."

Maysa reached the door, paused with her hand on the knob and then faced Madison again. "You might want to forewarn the father."

She couldn't even consider telling Zain now. "Believe me, he wouldn't want to be bothered."

Maysa sent her a knowing smile. "He might surprise you."

With that, the doctor left, and Madison tipped her head back on the sofa and stared at the ornate chandelier on the ceiling. She never dreamed she would prefer food poisoning over pregnancy, but considering the poor timing, and the circumstance, a baby was the last thing she needed. Definitely the last thing Zain needed.

Of course, she was leaping to large conclusions without good cause. She'd had unprotected sex with Jay for five years, and that had never resulted in a bun in her oven. Of course, Jay hadn't owned a magic fertility mountain, either.

Ridiculous. All of it. She didn't know why she'd fainted, but she highly doubted pregnancy had anything to do with it.

The day had started off like any other day. Madison had awakened that morning after sleeping almost sixteen hours straight, taken a shower, picked out her clothes—and peed on a stick. Now it had suddenly become a day like no other.

She stared at the positive results for a good ten minutes before it finally began to sink in. She was going to have a baby. Zain's baby. A baby she'd always secretly wanted but convinced herself she would never have.

Myriad thoughts swarmed in her head, followed by one important question. How was she going to tell Zain? More important, should she even tell Zain?

He did have a right to know, but he also had the upcoming coronation hanging over his head. He had an entire country counting on him, too. A country that had finally begun to accept him. A scandal—any scandal—could ruin everything.

Right then she wanted to crawl back under the covers and cry the day away, as well as weigh her options. But when someone knocked on the door, and if it happened to be Zain, she might be forced to make a snap decision.

She tightened the sash on her robe, secured her damp hair at her nape, convened her courage and opened the door.

"Good morning, *cara*," Elena said as she breezed into the room, a tray in her hands and something white tucked beneath her arm.

After taking one whiff of the food, Madison began to feel queasy. "Thanks, but my appetite isn't up to par."

Elena faced her with concern. "Are you still not feeling well?"

She dropped down on the edge of the bed. "I'm still a little weak."

"Then I will give strict orders you are not to be disturbed. But you need to eat something to regain your strength. Perhaps I should bring you some tea."

"No," she belted out. "I mean, schnapps probably wouldn't be good for an upset stomach." Definitely not good for a developing baby.

"I would bring you ginger tea to help with the nausea." She removed the cloth from beneath her arm and held it up. "I have also brought you fresh towels should you decided to take a long bath later."

"I appreciate that," she said, before it suddenly dawned on her Elena was heading into the bathroom, and the blasted test was still on the counter.

She could try to distract her. She could tackle her. Or she could accept that it was already too late, because the minute Elena came back into the room, she could tell the secret was out by the look on the woman's face.

"I see you have confirmed you are with child," Elena said in a remarkable matter-of-fact tone.

"Looks to be that way, but it's possible to have a false positive reading." Her last hope, and a remote one at that.

Elena looked altogether skeptical. "It is possible, but not probable when a Mehdi and a mountain are involved."

She'd drink to that, if she could drink. "You're making a huge assumption. How do you know I didn't have a torrid night with the chef?" *Dumb, Madison, really dumb.*

"The chef is nearing seventy years of age, and he can barely stand. I also knew from the beginning you would not be able to resist Prince Zain, and he would not be able to resist you."

Madison couldn't prevent the waterworks from turning on again. "I swear I never meant for this to happen," she said as she furiously swiped at the tears. "I have never crossed professional lines and I have never been so weak. I also never believed I'd be able to conceive a child."

Elena perched on the edge of the bed and took her hand. "You have never met a man like Prince Zain."

That wasn't even up for debate. "He is one in a million. An enigma and complex and very persuasive."

"He is his father in that respect."

Madison had the strongest feeling there could be a personal story behind that comment. She didn't have the strength to delve into more high drama. "And tomorrow, he's going to replace his father. He doesn't need this complication."

"He does need to see that you are all right. He has been so consumed with that need, he has taken to ordering everyone around like a petulant child."

That was news to her. She figured he'd gotten so caught up in the precoronation activities, she'd been the last thing on his mind. "Then why hasn't he stopped by?"

"Because Dr. Barad ordered him to stay away from you for at least twenty-four hours."

She experienced a measure of satisfaction that he was concerned, but she also feared his reaction when she lowered the baby boom. If she decided to make the revelation.

"Have you given any thought to when you are going to tell him?" Elena asked, as if she'd channeled her concerns.

That's all she'd been thinking about. "I have no idea.

I'm not even sure I should tell him." She held her breath and waited for a lecture on the virtues of honesty.

"Some would say it would be wrong to withhold such important information from Prince Zain," Elena began. "But I know the seriousness of the people's expectations when it comes to their ruler. You could be viewed as an outsider and unworthy of the king. You could be shunned, and so could your child. And Prince Zain's standing could forever be tarnished beyond repair."

She knew all those things, but that didn't make it easier to hear them. "And that's my dilemma, Elena. I wish I were better emotionally equipped to handle it, but I'm not. I'm worried that if I do tell him, he'll be angry and he'll send me immediately packing." That would solve her problem, but it would hurt to the core.

Elena squeezed her hand. "When the rumors surfaced about the paternity issues involving the Prince Zain and the model, I knew they were not true. He would never abandon his child, nor would he abandon the woman he loves with all his heart."

"He's never said he loves me, Elena." But then she had never told him, either.

"He is like any other man, afraid to say the word for fear he will swallow his tongue and never speak again, among other things."

They shared in a brief laugh before the seriousness of the situation settled over Madison again. "If what you say is true, then I would be asking him to choose between me and his child, and his country. And if he does choose us, he might regret that decision the rest of his life, and in turn resent me."

"That is possible."

Madison fought back another onslaught of tears. "Please tell me what to do, Elena."

"Only you can decide, *cara*. And you must ask your-self two important questions. Are you strong enough to stay, if that is what he wants from you, and do you love him enough to let him go if you decide not to ask that of him?"

She did love him enough to choose the latter. She couldn't ask him to choose and risk he'd hate her for it. She'd rather part as friends, and live on a lifetime of memories. As far as what she would tell their child, she'd have to figure that out later when she had a clearer head and a less heavy heart.

Elena brushed a kiss across Madison's cheek before she stood. "Whatever you decide, please know I believe you are more than worthy of Prince Zain's love. If the situation were different, I would welcome you as the daughter I was never fortunate enough to have."

Madison came to her feet and gave her a long hug. "And I would be proud to be your daughter-in-law, Elena." If things were different, which they weren't. "I can't thank you enough for you advice and support."

"You are welcome, *cara*," she said with a kind smile. "And should you be in need of a governess after the baby's birth, please keep me in mind. I would be happy to raise another Mehdi son or daughter."

She appreciated the offer, though she couldn't imagine Elena ever leaving this place. "I will definitely keep it in mind."

"And I will be praying for a bright and happy future for you both."

After Madison saw Elena out, it became all too clear what she had to do. She crossed the room, picked up the phone and pounded out Deeb's extension. When he answered with his usual dry greeting, she dispensed with all pleasantries. "This is Madison Foster. Could you please reschedule my flight for first thing in the morning?"

A span of silence passed before he responded. "You do not wish to attend the coronation?"

She couldn't very well tell the truth, so she handed him a partial lie. "I'm really disappointed I can't attend, but I have a job offer and they want me to start immediately."

"Should I inform the emir you've had a change in plans?"

"No. I'll tell him." Or not.

"As you wish."

After she hung up, Madison curled up on the bed to take another nap. She needed more rest to regain her strength before she took the last step. A step that she didn't want to take—the final goodbye to the man she loved.

When Zain opened the door and saw the sadness in Madison's eyes, he knew why she had arrived unexpectedly in his quarters. She was not there only to wish him well, though she probably would. She was not there to spend one final night in his arms, though he wished she would. She was there to say her goodbyes.

"May I come in?" she asked, sounding unsure and unhappy.

He opened the door wide. "Please do."

Once inside, they fell into an uncomfortable silence before she spoke again. "I went by your office first but Mr. Deeb said you'd retired early, so that's why I'm here. I hope it's okay."

"Of course. You have been here before."

"I know, but never through the front door."

That brought about both their smiles, yet hers faded

fast. "Come and sit with me awhile." *Stay with me forever.* The thought arrived with the force of a grenade. A wish he could not fulfill.

After he cleared several documents from the sofa, Madison took a seat on the end, while he claimed the chair across from her. "You look much better than you did the last time I saw you. Are you feeling better?"

"Much better. I've had plenty of sleep."

He could not say the same for himself. "Did Maysa determine why you fainted?"

"It could be a number of things, but all that matters now is I'm fine."

She sounded less than confident, and that concerned him. "I am happy to hear that. I've been very worried about you since I had to catch you during your fall."

"You caught me?" She both sounded and looked taken aback.

"I would never let you fall, Madison." And he would never forget those moments of intense fear. "Do you not remember?"

She shook her head. "No. I just remember being dizzy, and then I woke up on the couch."

"I was furious when Maysa demanded I leave you alone." He still was.

"Elena told me you were not in the best of moods. I'm sure my little mishap, coupled with the upcoming ceremony, didn't help. So are you nervous about tomorrow?"

No, but she was. He could tell by the way she folded the hem of her causal blue top back and forth. "I am ready for it to be over." Though that meant they would be over, as well.

"I'm sure you are. But it's the realization of your dreams, and that has to make you happy."

Holding her would make him happy. Having her as a

part of that dream would be the ultimate happiness. He felt he could do neither. "You should be happy to witness the fruits of your labor when I am officially crowned."

Her gaze faltered. "I didn't do that much, Zain."

He would strongly disagree. "You managed to mold me into the king I was meant to be, and that was no small accomplishment." She'd managed to steal his heart in the process.

She presented a sincere smile. "Yeah, you were a challenge at times. But I wouldn't take a moment of it back."

Nor would he, and he could not let another minute pass without being closer to her. He pushed off the chair and joined her on the sofa, much to her apparent dismay when she slid over as far as she could go.

"You need not be concerned," he said. "I am not going to touch you unless you want me to do so."

She sighed. "I would love for you to touch me, but that would only make it harder to leave you tonight."

He took a chance and clasped her hand. "Then stay with me tonight. Better still, stay with me after the coronation."

She pulled her hand from his grasp. "And what would my duties be, Zain? Your staff consultant, or your staff mistress?"

He experienced the resurgence of the anger he had harbored all day. "I am not my father. I have never viewed you as my mistress."

"But that's exactly what I would be when you choose your proper royal wife. Of course, you could send me on my way when that happens. And that would probably be best since I couldn't stand the thought of some other woman in your bed."

He could not stand the thought of any other woman in his bed aside from her. "I wish I could promise we could have an open relationship, but that is not possible. We would both suffer for it."

"Then I guess we will just have to suffer through a permanent goodbye."

When she came to her feet, Zain stood, as well. "I am asking you not to go, Madison. I am begging you to stay."

She lowered her eyes. "What would be the point?"

He framed her face in his palms, forcing her to look at him. "Because I care for you, and I want your smile to be my last memory before you leave."

When she laid her hands on his, he expected her to wrench them away. Fortunately, she did not. "If you really cared about me, you wouldn't do this. You'd realize this is tearing me up inside."

"And you would realize it is killing me to say goodbye tonight. I promise I only want to hold you, and to know you are beside me in the morning on the most important day of my life."

"You are asking so much from me, Zain. Too much from us."

Desperation drove him to continue to plead his case. "I am asking you to give us this final night together."

"But I'm not strong around you."

When he saw the first sign of tears in her eyes, he tipped his forehead against hers. "You are strong, Madison, and you have given me strength when I have needed it most." He pulled back and thumbed away the moisture from her cheek. "You said you trusted me before. Trust me now."

"I'd keep you awake with my crying."

"I will gladly provide my shoulder."

He seemed to wait an eternity for her to speak again. "Do you promise not to steal the covers?"

His spirits rose at the sight of her smile. "I promise I will do my best."

"Then I'll stay." She pointed at him. "You have to wear clothes, and you can't try to seduce me."

He held the power to do that, but her faith in him was paramount. "I will remain dressed, and I will be on my best behavior." While battling the clothing constraints and his ever-present desire for her.

"Okay." She hid a yawn behind her hand. "Then let's get on with it before I pass out again."

His worry returned. "Do you feel that you might faint?"

"No, but I might fall asleep on my feet."

As she entered the bathroom, Zain retrieved a pair of unused pajama bottoms from the bureau and ignored the top. He had promised he would remain dressed, but he hadn't said how dressed he would be.

In an effort to hide his bare chest, he climbed into bed, pushed the wall switch that controlled the overhead light and covered up to his chin. She soon emerged from the bath and snapped on the nightstand lamp to reveal she was wearing one of his shirts. Clearly she meant to torture him.

She stood by the bed, a hand on her hip and a frown on her face. "Are you wearing anything, or have you already gone back on your word?"

He reluctantly lifted the sheet. "I am covered from the waist down and I feel that is a good compromise. You know I tend to get warm at night."

"Fine. Scoot over."

After he complied, Madison slid onto the mattress and snapped off the light. When she remained on her side, away from him, normally he would fit himself to her back. Tonight, he felt compelled to ask her permission. "May I hold you?"

"Yes, you may," she answered without looking at him.

He settled against her, slipped one arm beneath her and draped the other over her hip. The scent of her hair, the warmth of her body, sent him into immediate turmoil. After a while, when he heard the sound of her steady breathing, he began to relax. Knowing she was there with him, if only for tonight, provided the comfort he needed. His eyes grew heavy and he soon drifted off.

He had no idea how long he had been asleep when he was awakened by the feel of Madison's soft lips on his neck.

Not knowing if her affection stemmed from a dream, Zain remained frozen from fear of making the wrong move. But when she whispered, "One more memory," he knew she was fully awake.

She was already undressed, and she made sure he joined her in short order. With nothing between them but bare skin, they kissed for long moments, touched with abandon. And when those kisses and touches led to the natural conclusion, Madison took the lead, and he let her. She straddled his hips, rose above him and guided him inside her.

Zain acknowledged this was her means to maintain some control, by leading him into the depths of pleasure, and he gladly followed. He watched her face as she found her climax, and realized he had never seen her look so beautiful. Yet his own body demanded release, and it came, hard and fast.

When Madison stretched out on top of him, their bodies still joined, he rubbed her back gently. He had never felt so deeply for anyone, and he had never cherished her enough until that moment, knowing that she had given him this final, lasting gift of lovemaking. He wished they could suspend time and remain this way indefinitely, but that was impossible.

He refused to consider that now. Refused to take away from this time with her. And when he felt her tears dampen his shoulder, he held her closer and wished he could do more. If wishes were coins, he'd have enough to fill the entire palace. Yet he would never be able to fill the empty place in his soul when she left him. At least he would have some time with her tomorrow, and that thought helped him sleep.

Zain was sound asleep when Madison left his bed right before dawn. She hated to depart without his knowledge, but she didn't want to wake him. She was afraid to wake him. Afraid because he could easily persuade her back into bed and back into his arms. Maybe even persuade her to stay for the coronation, and even longer.

As it stood now, she had a plane to catch at the airstrip in an hour, a car coming in twenty minutes before that, and she still had to take a shower and finish packing. She hurriedly re-dressed in the bathroom, and when she returned to the bedroom, she thankfully found Zain sleeping like a baby.

A baby...

She couldn't think about that now or she'd start crying again, even though she felt all cried out. But she wasn't stupid enough to believe there wouldn't be more tears in her future. A lot of tears, along with a bucketful of regrets. Regret that he couldn't be a part of their child's life. Her life.

Madison took a chance and quietly approached the bed even though she risked waking Zain, but she couldn't leave just yet. The first signs of daylight allowed her to take a mental snapshot of him to help her remember these last moments. He looked almost innocent with that dark lock of hair falling over his forehead. And because he was stretched out on his belly, with his head toward her on the pillow, she could see his eyes move behind closed lids. He was probably dreaming about becoming king, but to her he would always be a desert knight with a winning smile and a hero's heart. Maybe he hadn't rescued her, but he had given her the most precious of gifts.

On that thought, she lifted his arm that was draped over the side of the mattress, and pressed his hand lightly against the place where their baby grew inside her. Someday, when their child's questions about his or her father inevitably began to come, she would simply say *Daddy loves you,* because she inherently knew he would.

As the tears began to threaten, and Zain slightly stirred, she released his hand and placed it on the empty space she had occupied so many nights. Then she leaned down and kissed his cheek. "Good night, sweet prince. I love you."

She walked away, praying she didn't hear him calling her name. But she heard only silence as she left his room for the last time. She experienced relief knowing she could leave before he even realized she was gone.

Ten

"What do you mean she is gone?"

Zain could swear Deeb physically flinched, the first sign of a crack in his unyielding demeanor. "She called yesterday evening and asked me to arrange for her flight to be moved to this morning."

He'd mistakenly believed that when he awoke to the empty space in his bed, she had left to dress for the coronation. "Did she say why she needed to depart early?"

"She mentioned something about a job offer that required her immediate return to the States."

Madison had never mentioned that to him. In fact, she had led him to believe she would be in attendance at his crowning. He wondered what other lies she had told him.

Driven by fury, he grabbed the ceremonial robe from the hanger behind his desk, slipped it on and began buttoning it with a vengeance. "If that is all, you may go."

"Prince Rafiq requests a meeting with you before the ceremony."

His brother should be on his honeymoon, not hovering like a vulture. "Tell him to meet me here in ten minutes, and I will allow him five."

Deeb bowed. "Yes, Your Majesty."

"Will you allow your former governess some of your precious time?"

At the sound of the endearing voice, Zain looked across the room to see Elena standing in the doorway, dressed in her finest clothes, her silver hair styled into a neat twist. "You may come in and stay as long as you wish."

She swept into the room and gave Deeb a smirk as she passed by him. After Zain took a seat behind his desk, Elena claimed the opposing chair. She folded her hands in her lap and favored him with a motherly smile. "I do not have to tell you how proud I am of your accomplishments."

The anger returned with ten times the force. "At least I have your support. Unfortunately, I cannot say the same for Madison, who took it upon herself to leave without telling me."

Elena practically sneered at him. "Remove your *testa* from your *culo.* You have no one to blame but yourself for her actions."

He did not appreciate being blamed for something beyond his control, especially by the one woman he could always count on. "I did not tell her to leave early."

"But did you ask her stay, *caro?*"

He forked both hands through his hair before folding them atop the desk. "I did, yet she refused me."

"How did you ask her?"

"I requested she stay on after the coronation, and then she accused me of asking her to be her mistress."

"If your request was not accompanied by a marriage proposal, then she was justified in her accusation."

He had no patience left for her lecture. "She knows that marriage between us is not possible. There would be severe repercussions."

"Then you are saying you would marry her if the situation were different?"

He did not know what he was saying at this point in time. He only knew he had already begun to miss her, and she was barely gone. "I see no need to speculate on impossibilities."

She leaned forward, reached across the desk and took his hands. "You must ask yourself now if sacrificing love for the sake of duty will be worth it."

"I have never claimed to love her."

"Then tell me now you do not."

If he did, he would be lying. He chose to cite a truth. "I am committed to ruling this country, as it has been ordained by the king."

She let go of his hands, leaned back and laughed. "*Caro,* you never cared about your father's wishes before. You must assume this responsibility because it is right for you, not because he challenged you or because he issued a royal command in an attempt to keep you reined in."

"Do you truly believe that was the intent?"

"Yes, I do. He saw so much of your mother in you. She was also a free spirit and fiercely independent. Since he could not control her, he was determined to keep you under his thumb by making unreasonable demands."

He had never heard her mention his mother in those terms. "I assumed he believed I was the most suitable son to answer the challenge. I should not be surprised he had other motivations, or that he never believed in me."

"He was somewhat calculating, Zain, but he was not a stupid man. He would never have designated you as his successor if he did not think you up to the challenge. And I personally believe you would make a magnificent king, but the demands could suffocate you in the process. I do not want you to live your life regretting what might have been had you chosen a different path."

He felt as though he were suffocating now. "Then I shall prove you both wrong."

Rafiq entered the room, a folder beneath his arm and a solemn expression on his face. He leaned down and kissed Elena's cheek. "The ceremony is set to begin. I have reserved a seat in the front row for you."

She smiled up at him. "Thank you, *caro mio.* And I want you to know that I believe you would make a good king, as well."

Elena quickly rose from the chair and leveled her gaze on Zain. *"Il vero amore e senza rimpianti."*

Real love is without regret....

The words echoed in Zain's mind as Rafiq pulled up the chair where Elena had been seated. "What was that all about?" he asked.

"Nothing." He had no reason to offer a valid explanation for something Rafiq would not understand. He did have a pressing question to pose. "Were you aware of Ms. Foster's early departure?"

Rafiq opened the notebook and studied the page. "No, but her absence is favorable today. You do not need any distractions."

Zain could argue she meant much more to him than a distraction, but he would only be met with cynicism. "How is Rima?"

"She is well," he said without looking up.

"Is she not disappointed that you are here and not on a wedding trip?"

Again, Rafiq failed to tear his attention away from the documents. "My wife understands the importance of my duties, and today my duty is to see that the transition goes smoothly." He finally looked up. "You have a full schedule. The press conference begins immediately following the ceremony, then you will be expected to attend a luncheon with several of the region's emissaries. This evening, you have the official gala."

He would rather eat lye than spend an evening suffering through another barrage of sultans attempting to foist their daughters off on him. "How many people will be in attendance?"

He closed the notebook. "Several hundred. I have to commend Ms. Foster on her assistance with the attendees. She somehow arranged for the U.S. vice president to be there, along with the British prime minister."

"She did not mention that to me."

"She wanted to surprise you."

Zain was surprised to learn the news, but not surprised she pulled it off. He checked his watch to see that he had little time before the ceremony, and found his thoughts turning to Madison. He wondered where she was at this moment, if she happened to be remembering their night together, or attempting to forget him. Perhaps he would call her later, or perhaps not. After today, he could offer her nothing more than a conversation that could cause them only longing, and pain.

He rose from the chair, removed the royal blue sash from the box on the corner of his desk—the sash that his father and his father's father had worn during their reign—and placed it around his neck. "I am ready now." Was he ready? He had no choice but to be ready.

"Before you go," Rafiq began, "I want you to know that although we do not always see eye to eye, I am proud of your accomplishments thus far, particularly your water conservation plans. I have lobbied the council members and I am happy to report all but one are now on board."

"Who is the holdout?"

"Shamil, and that is because I have not been able to reach him since my wedding that he did not bother to attend."

Zain found that odd since Shamil had been Rafiq's closest friend, the reason why Shamil had been appointed to the council. "Perhaps he is traveling."

"Perhaps, but that is not a concern at the moment. Let us away before we are late."

As Zain walked the corridor leading to the ceremonial chamber, with Deeb and Rafiq falling behind him, each step he took filled him with dread. Not dread over assuming the responsibility, but dread over making a mistake he could not take back. When they passed the area lined with attendees held back by braided gold ropes, he could only see visions of Madison. The remembrance of Elena's parting words overrode the burst of applause.

Il vero amore e senza rimpianti...real love is without regret.

And when the doors opened wide, revealing those who had received a special invitation to witness the ceremony, he stopped in his tracks.

"What are you waiting for, brother?"

Zain had been waiting all his life not for this moment, but for a woman like Madison Foster. Nothing else mattered—not his birthright, not duty, only his love for her. He would live with constant regret if he did not at least try to win her back, and that was much worse than the fallout from his next decision.

He turned to Rafiq, slipped the sash from his neck, and placed it around his brother's. "The crown is yours, Rafiq, as it should have been from the beginning. Wear it well."

Confusion crossed Rafiq's expression. "Are you saying—"

"I am abdicating."

"Why?"

"If I told you, you would not understand. Suffice it to say that I have learned commitment must come from the heart. Though I will remain committed to my country and intend to see my conservation plans implemented, my true commitment lies elsewhere."

Rafiq scowled. "You would give up your duty for a woman?"

"I am giving up my duty for love."

"Love is inconstant, Zain. It drives men to weakness."

"You are wrong, brother. It drives men to honor." Zain laid a hand on Rafiq's shoulder. "I am sorry you are so trapped in your love of duty that you will never know real love."

With that, he turned on his heels and left, ignoring the silent, esteemed guests who apparently had been rendered mute from shock.

When he reached the study, he stripped out of the robe, tossed it aside and began to mentally formulate a plan.

"Is there anything I can assist you with, Emir?"

He should have expected Deeb to come to his aid, as the faithful assistant had for years. "Call the airstrip and tell them to ready the second plane for immediate departure. After that, ask one of the staff to pack my bags."

Deeb moved into the room and stood at attention. "Where will you be going and for what length of time?"

He unlocked the drawer containing his passport. "I will be going to Washington, D.C., for an indeterminable about of time." He would only be there a matter of hours if Madison tossed him out on his *culo*.

"If you are going after Ms. Foster, she has not yet departed."

Zain's gaze snapped from the folder to Deeb. "Why is it that you are only now telling me this?"

"I assumed the plane would have taken off by now. It seems the pilot has delayed the flight due to inclement weather."

Zain peered out the window and as predicted, the sun was shining. "The rain stopped hours ago."

"Yes, Emir, it did," Deeb said.

The pilot must be an imbecile, or overly cautious, but either way, Zain was pleased. "Call the airfield and make certain the plane remains as it is."

"As you wish, Emir. Shall I accompany you?"

Zain pocketed the passport, rounded the desk and placed his hands on Deeb's shoulders. "No. You shall go home to your wife and children and spend a lengthy sabbatical in their company. I will make certain you are paid your wages until you resume your duties as my brother's assistant."

Deeb smiled, taking Zain by surprise. "I truly appreciate your consideration, Emir, and I hope that we meet again soon."

Perhaps sooner than he would like if he did not hurry. "Now that we have finalized my arrangements, I am off to see a woman about my future."

Delays, delays and more delays.

Madison leaned back in the leather seat and muttered a few mild oaths aimed at the idiot responsible for the three-hour wait on the tarmac. Unfortunately, she had no idea who that idiot might be, since she couldn't understand a word of the offered explanations.

But she couldn't complain about the service she'd received in the interim. She been plied with food and drink and even shown the onboard bed by the flight attendant. She preferred to nap in the seat, belted in, until they were safely in the air, hopefully by next week.

She checked her watch for the hundredth time and confirmed the ceremony should be over by now. Zain was probably being presented to the press as the newly crowned king of Bajul. She was happy that he had finally realized his dream, and sad that she couldn't play a part in it. Even sadder that he wouldn't be a part of his child's life.

When someone knocked on the exterior door at the front of the plane, Madison hoped someone had arrived either to inform them of takeoff, or to explain why they couldn't seem to get airborne. She watched as the attendant pulled down the latch, and then the woman bowed. Madison wondered if some dignitary had delayed the flight in order to hitch a ride. If so, she hoped he or she didn't expect a friendly reception from her.

But when she saw the tall, gorgeous guy step into the aisle, she realized she'd been wrong—very wrong.

As if he didn't have a care in the world, Zain flipped his sunglasses up on his head and dropped down in the seat beside her.

"What are you doing here?" she asked around her astonishment.

He presented a world-class grin. "I've decided you could use some company on your journey."

He had lost his ever-lovin' royal mind. "You can't do that. You just became king. They're not going to tolerate you running out on your obligations on a whim."

He lifted her hand and laced their fingers together. "This is not a whim. This is a plea for your forgiveness."

"I forgive you," she said. "Now leave before they oust you from the palace on your royal behind and strip you of your crown."

"They cannot do that."

"Maybe not, but since you've worked so hard to re-store your reputation as a non–flight risk, don't you think it would be beneficial to actually prove that is the case?"

"My reputation is no longer a concern."

Had she taught him nothing? "It should be, Zain, if you're going to be an effective king."

"I am not the king."

Her mouth momentarily opened before she snapped it shut. "If you're not the king, then who is?"

"I abdicated to Rafiq."

She took a moment to sort through the questions running through her brain at breakneck speed. "Why would you do that when this has been your dream forever?"

He brushed a kiss across her cheek. "It was my father's dream, or perhaps I should say his ploy to keep me under his control, according to Elena, who told me that this morning. Being with you is my real dream, although I did not know that until I was faced with what I stood to lose if I lost you."

Alarm bells rang out in Madison's head. "What else did Elena tell you?"

"She told me that if I chose the crown over you, I would only live with regret, and she was correct. I want to be with you as long as you will have me."

She was still stuck on his conversation with Elena. "And that's all she said?"

He frowned. "Should there be more?"

"I guess not." She felt relieved that he appeared to be

in the dark about the pregnancy, and thrilled that he had returned to her without that knowledge. But still… "I'm worried you're going to regret this decision to give up everything you've worked for and what you still have left to achieve. Not when you've made it so clear how much you love your country."

"I love you more."

She couldn't quite believe her ears. "What did you say?"

"I said I love you more than my country. More than my wealth and more than my freedom."

After his declaration began to sink in, Madison said the only thing she could think to say. "I love you, too."

He gave her the softest, most genuine smile. "Enough to marry me?"

Not once had she let herself imagine that question. "Zain, we haven't known each other that long. In fact, we've never really dated. Maybe we should just start there."

He lifted her hand for a kiss. "A wise woman recently told me that an immediate connection to a person leaves a lasting impact."

"Elena's words?"

"No. Maysa's. She told me that when I talked nonstop about you the night I went to see her. And she is right. I have felt connected to you since the day we met, and I want to make that connection legal and legitimate in everyone's eyes."

If he was willing to take that leap of faith, why wouldn't she jump, too? After all, they had a child to consider—information she needed to reveal, and soon. But before she could force the words out of her mouth, the door to the cockpit opened, and in walked none other than Adan, wearing his military flight suit and his trade-mark dimpled grin.

Zain shot out of his seat and moved into the aisle. "What are you doing here?"

Adan responded with a grin. "I am flying the plane, of course, and you should thank me. I'm the reason why we have yet to take off."

"I do not understand, Adan."

Neither did Madison, but she couldn't wait to hear the youngest Mehdi's explanation.

"I delayed our departure because I suspected you would come to your senses and realize you could not let a woman like Madison leave."

"You came upon that conclusion on your own?" Zain asked in a suspicious tone.

Adan looked a little sheepish. "All right, I admit that Elena formulated the plan, and I agreed to it. And if it had not worked, I planned to whisk Madison to Paris, which by the way is where we will be stopping for the night to refuel."

"You have a woman waiting for you there," Zain said.

Adan grinned again. "That is a distinct possibility."

Zain pointed to the cockpit. "Fly the plane."

"That is my plan, brother. And feel free to utilize the onboard bed during our flight."

"The plane," Zain repeated.

After Adan retreated, Zain returned to Madison and clasped her hand once more. "Let's marry in Paris."

Oh, how she wanted to say yes. But first, she had a serious revelation to make. "Before I agree to marriage, there's something I need to tell you."

"You are not already married, are you?"

She smiled. "No, but I am pregnant."

He stared at her for a moment before comprehension dawned in his stunned expression. "You are serious?"

"Yes, I am serious. I wouldn't joke about a thing like that." But she wasn't beyond using humor to defuse his possible anger over the secret. "And that's the reason why I fainted. It wasn't bad food or your overwhelming charisma, although that does make me want to swoon now and then."

When he failed to immediately comment, Madison worried that her attempts at levity hadn't worked. That brought about her explanation as to why she had withheld the information. "I wanted to tell you, Zain, but I didn't want you to have to choose between the baby and your obligation to your country. And I also need you to understand that it's not that I didn't want a child, I just thought I could never have one. I never wanted to deceive you, but—"

He stopped her words with a kiss. "It's all right, Madison. I could not feel more blessed at this moment."

Neither could she. "Then you're okay with it?"

"I will be okay when you say that you will marry me."

Madison held her breath, and finally took that all-important leap. "Yes, I will marry you."

Any reservations or hesitation melted away with Zain's kiss. In a few months, she would finally have the baby she'd always wanted and thought she would never have, with the man she would always love.

Epilogue

"Here are your babies, Mrs. Mehdi."

After the nurse placed the bundles in the crooks of Madison's arms, she could only stare at her son and daughter in absolute awe. Not only had her lone ovary functioned well, it had worked double time. She only wished their father had been there to see them come into the world.

As if she'd willed his presence, Zain rushed into the room sporting a huge bouquet of red roses and an apologetic look. "The damn plane was delayed because of the rain," he said as he set the flowers down and stripped off his coat.

No surprise to Madison. Wherever there was rain, there was Zain. "It's okay, Daddy. Just get over here and see what you've done."

He slowed his steps on the way to the hospital bed, as if he were afraid to look. But when he took that first glance at his babies, his eyes reflected unmistakable joy, and so did his smile. "I cannot believe they are finally here."

Neither could Madison. "After fourteen hours of labor, I was beginning to wonder."

He leaned over to softly kiss her. "I regret I was not here with you to see you through this."

"That's okay. Elena stayed the entire time and held my hand, worrying like a mother hen."

"Where is she now?"

"I sent her back to the condo. She mentioned something about napping beneath the California sun so she could work on her tan."

He smiled as he brushed a fingertip across their daughter's cheek. "She is beautiful, like her mother."

Madison pushed the blanket away from their son's face to give his father a better look. "And our baby boy is so handsome, just like his uncle Adan."

That earned her a serious scowl. "You are determined to punish me for my late arrival."

"No, I'm just trying to cheer you up, but I guess under the circumstance, that's not going to be easy to do."

"No, it is not." He scooped their daughter into his arms with practiced ease, as if he'd been a father forever, not five minutes. "Holding new life in your arms helps ease the sadness."

It had definitely been a time of sadness back in Bajul, as well as a week full of unanswered questions. "How is Rafiq doing?"

"It is hard to tell," he said. "He seemed all right at the funeral, but he is not one to show any emotion."

Madison had learned that firsthand. During the the two times she and Zain had returned to Bajul, she couldn't recall seeing Rafiq smile all that much. Then, neither had his bride. "I wish I had known Rima better. Do they have any idea what happened with the car, or why she was even in it alone that time of night?"

When the baby began to fuss, Zain lifted their daughter to his shoulder. "No true explanations have emerged thus far. As it was with my mother's death, we may never know."

For months Madison had considered telling her husband about the conversation with Elena involving his mother, but she'd decided to put that on hold for the time being. Today should be about the joy of new beginnings, not sorrow and regrets.

The nurse returned to the room and when she caught sight of Zain, Madison thought the woman might collapse. It didn't matter if they were seventeen or seventy—and this woman was closer to the latter—females always responded the same way to Zain. "Is this the babies' daddy?" she asked.

No, he's the chauffeur, Madison wanted to say but bit back the sarcasm. "Ruth, this is my husband, Zain."

When Zain stood to shake her hand, Ruth grinned from ear to ear. "It's a pleasure to meet you. Is it true you're a sheikh?"

"Yes," Zain said. "But today I am only a new father."

Madison couldn't be more proud of that fact, or the way he pressed a soft kiss on his daughter's forehead. She was definitely going to be a daddy's girl.

The nurse lumbered over to the bed and took Madison's baby boy out of her arms, much to her dismay. "Where are you going with him?"

Ruth patted Madison's arm. "Don't worry, Mommy. He'll just be gone for a little while. Now that he and his sister have warmed up a bit, it's time for their first bath."

She was a little disappointed to give up her children

so soon after their birth, but it would allow her and Zain some time to reach one important decision.

After Ruth carted off the twins, Madison scooted over, gritted her teeth against the lingering pain of childbirth and patted the space beside her. "Come over here, you sexy sheikh."

He turned his smile on her. "Is it not too soon to consider that?"

She rolled her eyes. "I just gave birth to the equivalent of two five-pound bowling balls, so what do you think?"

"You have a point." He kicked off his Italian loafers, climbed onto the narrow bed and folded her into his arms.

"We need to decide on their names," she said as she rested her cheek against his chest. "We can't just refer to them as 'He' and 'She' Mehdi indefinitely, although it is kind of catchy."

"How do you feel about Cala for our daughter?" he asked.

Zain had never suggested that name before now, but Madison supposed his trip home to mourn after the end of a young woman and her unborn child's life had somehow influenced his choice. "It's perfect. I'm sure your mother would have loved having a granddaughter named after her."

"Then we shall call her that. And our son?"

She lifted her head and smiled. "Why not settle for what we've been calling him the past five months?" The nickname they'd given him the day they'd learned the babies' genders during the ultrasound.

He grinned. "Joe?"

"Short for Joseph, which just happens to be my great-great-grandfather's name."

"Joseph it is."

Now that they had covered that all-important decision, she needed to address one more. "Do you have any regrets about giving up the crown and leaving Bajul?"

"Only one. We never made love on the rooftop."

She elbowed his ribs. "I'm serious."

"I have a beautiful wife and two perfect children. How could I possibly regret that?" His expression turned somber. "Do you regret that you have put your career on hold for me?"

Something Madison had sworn she would never do, but then she's never imagined loving a man this much. And during the last conversation with her mother, she'd actually admitted it. "I haven't put my career completely on hold. I'll be doing some preliminary consulting for the senator's campaign the first of the year."

"And you do not mind traveling to Bajul in a few months and staying for a time?"

"As long as we wait until my parents come for their visit, I'm more than game. Besides, I've told you that I feel it's important that our children know their culture, and you still have important work to do on your conservation plans."

He planted a quick kiss on her lips. "Good. While we're there, we will return to the lake and relive our first experience."

The experience that had brought them to this day. This new life. This incredible love. "That sounds like a plan. You bring Malik's truck, and I'll bring my overactive ovary. We might even get lucky a second time."

"I cannot imagine feeling any luckier than I do now."

"Neither can I."

When the nurse returned their children to their waiting arms, completing the family they had made, Madison and Zain settled into comfortable silence, as they'd done so many times since they had taken that giant leap of faith, and landed in the middle of that sometimes treacherous territory known as love.

Madison felt truly blessed, and it was all because of one magical mountain, and one equally magical man. A man who might not be the king of his country, but he was—and always would be—the king of her heart.

* * * * *

REUNITED WITH HER SECRET PRINCE

SUSANNE HAMPTON

To my amazing family and friends who have supported and encouraged my writing journey…and unknowingly given me the most wonderful inspiration for my characters.

PROLOGUE

IT WAS THE twelfth of June, a perfect summer's day in the northern hemisphere, and one that nurse Libby Mc-Donald would never forget.

It was the day her life changed for ever. Perched precariously on the edge of her bed, she struggled to fill her lungs with air as her emotions threatened to overwhelm her. Her life was suddenly spinning out of control and Libby was powerless to change anything, which was completely at odds with her character. She was, without exception, calm even in the most stressful times but this was not Cardiology or the ER and she was not triaging patients; she was suddenly trying to triage her escalating fears. And failing miserably.

Her emerald green eyes darted from the test results to the floor and back again as her fingers nervously tapped on the side of her bed, making a sound barely audible above the beating of her heart. It was as though if she didn't stare too long in the direction of the test strip, it wouldn't be real. But it was real. There were no faint lines. There was no ambiguity about it. Libby was going to have the baby of the man who had exited her life as mysteriously as he had entered it.

The boldness of the two lines on the pregnancy test were almost screaming the result at her.

And reminding her of her poor judgement when she fell in love so quickly and realised in hindsight that while she had thought he was everything she was looking for and more, she had fallen in love with a man she really didn't know at all.

Her life would most definitely be nothing close to the 'white picket fence' perfect one that she had imagined. The one where she was happily married to the man of her dreams, living in a rustic cottage by the ocean with a baby on the way. In reality, while Libby had a baby on the way, she was renting a condo in Oakland, about 20 minutes from San Francisco and not not too far from her retired parents. And she was still paying off her student loan while trying to save for a car to replace the ageing one in the driveway.

There was nothing perfect about her life in her mind, at least not any more. Less than two months earlier she had thought it was as perfect as any woman could dream possible when she'd unexpectedly found herself falling in love. He was a six-foot-two dark-haired, handsome and charismatic doctor and they had been working together at the hospital for almost a month when she had taken a leap of faith and changed their relationship status from colleagues to lovers by inviting him home late one night. While it had been out of character for Libby since they hadn't been actually dating, it had felt right.

They had spent many hours working together in ER and they had been sharing lunch whenever possible and having lengthy discussions about their mutual love of medicine over late-night coffee when ER was quiet and they could steal away to the twenty-four-hour cafeteria.

He had encouraged Libby to consider specialising in Cardiology when she'd told him how much she enjoyed rotations in that department and he had gone so far as to find out the next study intake for her.

She had tried to hide her growing feelings for him but at times that had been almost impossible. Observing him with patients, many seen under extreme duress, Libby's admiration had grown by the day. He had been equally as kind and caring as he was thorough and responsive, and she had watched as his knowledge and experience had changed the outcomes for many critically ill patients. Her professional respect had blossomed into something so much more.

Libby could not help but notice that his demeanour had seemed a little sombre and distant at times, but his mood had always seemed to lift when he'd seen her and she'd felt like she was floating whenever he was around.

She had only dated two men before him, one just out of college for a year before they'd both realised they were better off as friends and then there had been another six-month relationship with a medical student that had been set up by their mothers. When it had ended it had broken their respective mothers' hearts but not their own. And neither relationship had been overly passionate, closer to lukewarm, so she had decided to concentrate on her studies and her career.

But that fateful night when she had acted on her growing feelings, he had made her believe she was the only woman in the world. The way he'd held her and made love to her had made her naively trust that he was the man who would love her for ever. As she'd lain in the warmth of his tender embrace, with the dappled moonlight shining through the open drapes, listening to him gently sleeping, she'd hoped that since they had crossed over from colleagues to lovers, she would learn more about his life outside the hospital and over time something of his family, his past and his dreams for the future.

Libby had thought in her heart she had found *the one*.

But the opportunity to learn anything about him outside medicine had never come as the next morning she had awoken to find him gone. His side of her bed had been cold and empty and she'd soon learned the devastating truth that he had left town. He had given notice at the hospital that morning via email and disappeared. Very quickly she'd discovered he was not *the one*.

Almost eight weeks later she was facing the biggest challenge of her twenty-nine years and the fact that the one night they had shared had changed her life from nurse to single mother despite them taking precautions. There would be no better half to help her. No partner to share the joy and the pain.

Libby no longer cared to know anything about the man, his life or his past. What she did know was that she would have to face this alone and she also knew that she could never again allow her emotions to cloud her judgement. And never let her heart rule her head.

Collapsing back across the bed and staring at the ceiling fan as it slowly made circles in the warm air, Libby couldn't pretend, even to herself, to be surprised by the confirmation of her pregnancy. Her hands instinctively covered her stomach. There was no physical sign but in her heart she was already protective of her baby. Even in the pharmacy as she'd purchased the test that afternoon, she'd thought her action was redundant.

She had been feeling nauseous for almost six weeks and she had eaten more olives, fish and bread than she cared to remember in the preceding days. Which for anyone else might not be odd, except Libby detested olives. But, like a woman possessed, she had driven to the late-night supermarket close to midnight in search of black olives. They had to be Kalamata olives. And artisan bread. And that week she had started visiting the fish market and she ordinarily hated the smell of fresh fish.

Her cravings were Mediterranean, just like the father of her unborn child. The man who had shattered her heart and her trust.

Suddenly, there was a knock on the front door, breaking through the jumbled thoughts that were threatening to send her mad.

'Hello…anyone gorgeous at home? Other than me, I mean?' the voice chirped loudly.

She recognised the voice of her best friend, Bradley. The rock in her life since nursing school. She had been expecting him but was clueless as to how he would react as he hadn't known she had even been interested in someone and Libby had never kept secrets from Bradley. Slowly she sat up and then climbed to her feet. Her legs were still shaking and her mind racing.

'The door's unlocked and I'm in my room, Bradley… There's something I need to tell you.'

Thirty minutes later, they both sat staring in silence at their empty iced tea glasses. Bradley had moved Libby into the kitchen and insisted that she have a cool drink and something to eat. He had brought home two cupcakes from the local bakery and there were now only crumbs on their plates. She suspected that he needed something to calm his nerves as much as her. Learning about her pregnancy had come out of left field for him.

'He's a lying, deceitful bastard on every level.'

'I feel so stupid. I mean, I didn't really know him, not outside work, but we just clicked. We talked for hours literally and it seemed right. But it was so wrong. And I don't have that much dating experience, not in last few years anyway. I guess I read too much into it.'

'He clearly wanted you to read into it. He's a dreadful excuse for a man.'

'I'm an idiot.'

Bradley patted her hand with his. 'You're not an idiot. Love just makes us do crazy things. Heaven knows, I've fallen for the wrong man more times than I care to recall.'

Libby nodded. She was done with talking about the man who had broken her heart. And there would be no more tears either. She had shed enough in the weeks since he'd left to last her a lifetime and now she needed to focus on herself. And her baby.

'I know it's a lot but *we've* got this,' he said with his chin definitely jutted and his hands on his hips. 'I'm in this with you, all the way.'

'That's so sweet, Bradley, but I made a mess of everything. Not you. You've got a whole wide world out there. You don't have to tie yourself down to me and...' Libby paused as her gaze dropped to her stomach. 'And my baby.'

'What sort of gay best friend walks away from his best friend for ever and her baby? Not me, that's for sure,' he retorted, standing and reaching for both cups. He walked to the dishwasher, put them both inside then spun on his heel to face her with a look of determination. 'You will be the most amazing mommy ever and I will be the most awesome, stylish uncle that any little poppet ever had. Ooh, I wonder if the baby will have your stunning red hair? Here's hoping as I can see the tiny wardrobe already, hues of green and copper and, of course, yellow. Goodness, there're so many choices ahead of us...'

'What would I do without you?' Libby cut in.

'You'll never know 'cos I'm not going anywhere. This baby will be loved and cherished. And my adorable niece or nephew will have anything in life that he or she wants.'

Everything except a father, Libby thought, but said nothing as she swallowed the lump in her throat and blinked away the last of the tears stinging the corners of her eyes.

'And we will throw the best birthday parties ever!' Bradley continued, his face animated with excitement and his hands moving around wildly. 'I can see them now. Like tiny carnivals with rides and cotton candy and a petting zoo.'

Libby's lips began to curl upwards as her spirits lifted just a little. 'You're spoiling the baby and we still have seven months to meet him or her.'

'Of course it's my responsibility as Uncle Bradley. I'm in your baby's life for ever.'

Libby felt a stab in her heart, wishing the father of her baby would be in their lives for ever too, but that would never be. She had no clue where he had gone. The hospital could not give Libby a forwarding address and he had not mentioned leaving to anyone other than his short, and apparently sudden, resignation email.

Clearly, she meant nothing to him. Neither had their time together been as special as she had imagined. It had all been in her head. She had romanticised the entire affair. She feared he might feel the same about the child they had created but she would never know because there was no way for her to tell him.

As he sat staring out across the brilliant blue water Dr Daniel Dimosa's thoughts unexpectedly returned to the gorgeous redheaded nurse who, only months earlier, had unknowingly made him forget about the uncertainty of his future, if only for a few short weeks. She was sweet and kind and the woman he'd wanted but knew he couldn't have. Not for ever, at least.

Daniel had fought the attraction over the time they had spent together while he had been Acting Head of ER. He had valiantly attempted to keep their relationship professional. But he had failed. Her nursing skills, genuine empathy with patients and wonderfully warm, kind manner was nothing he had witnessed before. She would work past her shift to allay the fears of patients and their families, go the extra mile to transfer her knowledge to inexperienced medical students, and make all the medical team around her feel included and important. And against everything he had promised himself, he had begun to fear he was close to falling in love.

No matter how much he'd tried, Daniel couldn't ignore his feelings for her. He would look for excuses to spend time with her even over a coffee in the early hours of the morning at the twenty-four-hour cafeteria, but he'd still kept the conversation about their mutual love of medicine. Nothing about the past and nothing about the future.

He couldn't allow himself to make promises he couldn't keep. Daniel had known it was only a matter of time until he would need to leave. He had long known he could not in any good conscience promise a future to any woman and for that reason he had kept his love life to flings with women who wanted nothing more.

And for that reason Daniel had left that night without saying goodbye or offering an explanation. It wasn't his to offer. Instead, he had climbed from the warmth of the bed they had shared and disappeared into the night. He had left without waking the woman who was beginning to steal his heart. He thought back to the moment he had gently moved the strand of red hair resting on her forehead and tenderly kissed her one last time as she'd lain sleeping like an angel. His heart had ached with every step he'd taken away from her. Knowing he would never see her again. Never make love to her again. Never hold her again.

He knew it had been a mistake to take their relationship from that of colleagues to lovers but the passion had overtaken them and he had given in to his desire to have her in his arms, if only for one night.

Before he'd closed the door he'd silently mouthed, *I will never forget you, Libby.*

Then he had walked away, knowing there was no choice.

He had done it to protect her…and now he had to do everything he could to forget her. And he hoped she would do the same.

CHAPTER ONE

'I LOVE YOU, BILLY.'

'I luff you, Mommy.'

'You need to be a very good boy for Grandma while I'm gone,' Libby said, blinking back tears as she squatted down to the little boy's eye level and ran her fingers through his thick black hair. 'I'll only be away for a few days, and I'll miss you very much.'

'I'll be good. I promith,' he said, and threw his little arms around her neck.

'Grandpa's waiting in the car to take me to the airport. I need to go now but I'll be back soon.'

'Grandma told me seven sleeps.'

'That's right,' Libby replied, then kissed his chubby cheek. 'I love you to the moon and back.'

'I luff you this much,' he said, stretching his arms as far as he could.

Libby stood up, ruffled his hair gently and redirected her attention to her mother. 'Please call me if you need me, anytime, day or night. My cell phone will always be on. I'll call every night but if Billy gets a sniffle or a tummy ache or just needs to talk to me during the day or night, please call me.'

'I will, I promise. Billy will be fine with us. Now go

or you'll miss your plane,' her mother told her as they all walked to the car, which was idling in the driveway with her father at the wheel and her luggage already in the trunk. Libby climbed into the front passenger seat and as the car drove away she watched her son holding his grandmother's hand and waving goodbye. She felt empty already and the car hadn't left the street.

'Now, don't you go worrying while you're away, poppet,' her father said as they merged into the freeway traffic. 'We'll take good care of our grandson.'

'I know you will, Dad,' she said, trying to blink away the tears threatening to spill onto her cheeks. 'It's just I've never been away from Billy and it's…it's…'

'I know it's hard, Libby, but, believe me, it's probably going to be a lot tougher on you than him. Worrying and missing your child is all part of being a parent,' he said with a wink and a brief nod in Libby's direction. 'But we'll keep him busy and your mother has an itinerary to rival a royal visit. I swear you get your organisational skills from her. We're off to the zoo tomorrow and the playground the next day, and on Thursday Bradley's heading over to take him out for ice cream and a walk on the beach, and he's got a play date with the neighbours' grandchildren on Saturday… Oh, I almost missed out a day. Your mother booked tickets for that new animated car movie at the cinema on Friday. I tell you we will all sleep well this week from sheer exhaustion.'

Libby McDonald listened to all her father was saying. She appreciated everything her parents had planned for Billy so much but it didn't help as her heart was being torn a little with each mile they travelled. She was thirty-three years of age, mother of the world's most adorable little three-year-old boy, single by choice, and she loved her son more than life itself and didn't want to be away from him.

'You might have fun in the Caribbean. It's not every day you get asked to fly to the other side of the country to tend to a wealthy patient for a week on a luxury yacht. What was his name again?'

'Sir Walter Lansbury,' Libby replied as she looked out of the car window, feeling no excitement at the prospect.

'That's right.' Her father nodded as he flicked the indicator to change lanes. 'He's quite a philanthropist and a generous benefactor to the Northern Bay General Hospital. Even had a wing named after him, your mother told me.'

'Yes, he's very generous and that's why the hospital board agreed to his request to have me as his post-operative nurse while he cruises through the Caribbean for seven days and nights. It's quite ridiculous really. He should be at home, recovering, at seventy-nine years of age, not gallivanting on the open seas five weeks after a triple coronary artery bypass graft.'

'Sounds like he's a bit of an adventurer.'

'Or a risk-taker and a little silly.'

'A risk taker without doubt,' her father remarked. 'But he wouldn't have amassed a fortune if he was silly.'

Libby didn't answer because she was completely averse to risk-taking and Sir Walter taking one with his health made him silly in her opinion. She had taken a risk falling in love and that had all but ensured she would never take another unnecessary risk. She planned everything about her life and she liked it that way. Libby McDonald hated surprises and risks in equal amounts. Her life was settled and organised and was almost perfect, except for the occasional night when she couldn't fall asleep and her thoughts turned to Billy's father. But they were becoming fewer and fewer and she hoped in time she would all but forget him.

'We never know what the universe has in store for us. This trip might be a life-changing experience for you,' her father continued as he checked his rear-view mirror and took the next exit from the freeway. 'All I do know is that Sir Walter has secured himself the finest cardiac nurse in the whole country.'

Libby smiled at her father's compliment but she was far from convinced he was right. She felt certain there had to be other nurses who would jump at the opportunity but the hospital board had insisted she go. And there was no get-out-of-jail-free card attached to an order from the board. It was signed and sealed and in less than a week she had been packed and on her way to nurse the generous benefactor she had cared for after his heart surgery. How she wished at that moment that she had been in ER and not in his recovery team.

Later that day, Libby's flight finally landed in Miami and she caught a cab to the Four Seasons Hotel where a room had been booked for her by Sir Walter's assistant. Being a few hours ahead of the west coast it was getting late in Miami and the sun had set so she ordered room service, called home and said goodnight to Billy and, after eating dinner, she ran a hot bath. Surprisingly she had managed to doze just a little on the five-hour flight. Business class, courtesy of her temporary employer, was as luxurious as she had heard. But with no sleep the night before as she'd tossed about in her bed at home, she was close to exhaustion when she finally climbed into her king-size hotel bed and drifted off to sleep.

The next morning Libby woke, went for a brisk walk before she ate breakfast in her room, checked out of the hotel, and caught a cab to the marina. She was due there at eleven. Her stomach began to churn as the cab drew closer. The previous day's uneasy feeling was returning and while it was in its infancy, she feared it could gain momentum quickly.

She lowered her oversized sunglasses and looked through the cab window at the busy road leading to the wharf and prayed that the week would pass quickly and there would be no surprises. None at all. Pushing her glasses back up the bridge of her nose, Libby collapsed back into the seat, second-guessing herself.

Suddenly her thoughts began to overwhelm her. The sensible, well-organised life she had created felt a little upside down and it weighed heavily on her. Her throat suddenly became a little dry and her palms a little clammy. The air-conditioner in the car suddenly didn't seem enough and she wished she hadn't agreed to the week-long assignment on the open seas.

She knew she would miss Billy terribly. He was her world and her reason for getting up each day, the reason she kept going, determined to create a life for the two of them.

Suddenly her cab driver made a U-turn and her hand luggage fell onto her lap and she heard a thud as her suitcase toppled over in the trunk. She rolled her eyes, quite certain that Bradley had packed more than she would need. But she hadn't argued as she'd had no idea what she would need. She had no clue since she had never done anything like it before.

Libby McDonald had been playing it safe, very safe, and now she felt at risk of becoming a little…lost at sea.

'We're about two minutes away, miss,' the driver said. 'I'm taking a shortcut through the back streets as the traffic jam ahead would make it fifteen.'

'Thank you,' she said, smiling back at him in the rear-view mirror. His voice had brought her back to the present. It was not the time or the place for doubting herself. She had to quash her rising doubts because there was no turning back.

The cab was weaving around a few narrow streets until finally Libby could see the ocean and rows of yachts of all shapes and sizes.

'I think this is your stop,' he announced, finally coming to a halt.

Once again, she dropped her glasses to rest on the bridge of her nose and, in an almost teenage manner, peered out of the cab window again. She spied the yacht—gleaming, magnificent and standing tall and pristine in the perfectly still blue water. It was the most magnificent ship she had ever seen. Not that she'd seen any up close and personal. Her experience was from travel shows on cable television but she had not expected it to be so grand and beautiful in reality. Regal was the word that came to mind as her gaze roamed the structure and her eyes fell on the name emblazoned across the bow, *Coral Contessa*. That was definitely the one. She had been told that Sir Walter Lansbury had named it after his beloved late wife, Lady Contessa.

Libby's stomach knotted with trepidation. The yacht was going to be both her workplace and temporary home for the next seven days. Suddenly motion sickness, or something like it, came over her even though she was still on dry land.

While she had worked in both Emergency and Cardiology at the hospital for over seven years, she knew nothing of nursing on a ship. And that bothered her. Libby had consulted with the cardiologist a few days before she'd left for her trip and had been reminded that their patient had had a post-operative elevated blood pressure and a BMI that indicated he needed to lose at least twenty pounds. To the frustration of his specialist, Sir Walter loved bad food, cigars and strong liquor and he didn't take his health as seriously as he did the stock market.

Initially, Libby had also been concerned about the number of passengers and crew and whether she would be responsible for everyone, and how many that would be in total. She had been reassured by the hospital that there would be no more than twelve to fourteen other passengers and eleven crew members, including the two-person medical team. They felt confident most of the passengers would come on board in good health and remain that way for the duration of the cruise.

She would be focused on her client and occasionally managing passengers' nausea, the effects of too much sun or too much alcohol, the odd strained muscle or twisted ankle. There was always the risk of more serious conditions but Libby hoped her cruise on the *Coral Contessa* would be uneventful, busy enough to keep her mind occupied but not overwhelming. Nothing would go wrong, she reminded herself, if the number one patient followed their advice.

Everyone agreed Sir Walter would be better off not

going to sea five weeks after heart surgery and instead resting at home but, being headstrong, he clearly wasn't accepting that. She hoped the ship's doctor was equally headstrong and together they could manage their patient.

Libby wasn't entirely sure if the impetus for her decision to accept the job offer had been Bradley's contagious excitement or another one of her parents' well-meaning heart-to-heart talks about her taking chances and moving on with her life.

She was still young, they constantly reminded her, and she had so much to experience and a whole world to see. And Billy needed to grow up knowing she was not only the best mother he could wish for but also a strong independent woman who had a career and a life. Just thinking about him, her fingers reached for the antique locket hanging on a fine silver chain around her neck and she held it in the warmth of her palm. Inside was a photograph of the beautiful dark-haired, blue-eyed boy. He was the image of the father he would never know.

Libby stilled her nerves and blinked away the unexpected threat of tears she was feeling at the thought of being away from her little boy. It was only a week at sea, she reminded herself firmly, and her parents wanted so much to spend quality time with their beloved grandson. But she and Billy had never been apart for more than a day in three years. He was the light in her life and she wasn't sure how she would cope.

True to his word, Bradley had thrown a birthday party for Billy every year and had hosted his third birthday two days before Libby had left. Their family and friends had come and showered Billy with presents as they always did, and those with small children had brought them along to enjoy the celebrations, including a face painter. Bradley had enthusiastically dressed as a giant sailor bear. He thought he'd looked like a furry member of the Village People—Libby wasn't sure but the image still made her smile.

There had been way too much cake, far too many sweets and more balloons than Libby had ever seen, courtesy of her mother. Everyone had had a wonderful day but Libby had been preoccupied at times throughout the afternoon with doubts about her impending trip, although it had been pointless to fight the inevitable. The trip was going to happen. And everyone except Libby seemed very happy about that fact.

That night Bradley had insisted on helping her pack. He'd included a swimsuit and a light denim playsuit and a stunning silk dress that skimmed her ankles. It was deep emerald-green silk with a plunging neckline and nothing close to the practical clothes she generally wore, a going-away present from Bradley.

'Take a risk for once!' Bradley had told her when she'd unwrapped his parting gift. 'You have the body for it, so flaunt it!'

Libby had frowned at him.

'It's perfect for you and what's the point in having a stylish BFF if you don't listen to me? Besides, it matches your gorgeous eyes so you have to take it.'

Libby had laughed and given Bradley a big hug. At six feet four he was almost a foot taller than her and she always felt secure in his hug, if not always secure in his choice of clothes for her. The outfit was very far removed from her usual conservative style. She wasn't sure she would wear it, because even if she was brave enough, she felt quite sure she wouldn't have the occasion to do so, but Bradley had insisted. He had released his arms from around her tiny waist, ignored her concerns, packed all of his choices in her luggage and had returned to her closet to find some sandals to complete the look.

'Let's face it, *all* of your cute outfits and shoes have been Christmas and birthday gifts from me,' he had said, with a pair of unworn gold high heels he had given her for Christmas the year before balanced in one hand while he pulled another dress from a hanger, along with a sarong and a wide-brimmed straw hat. He placed all of it neatly into her open suitcase. 'Anything conservative is staying home. I refuse to let my absolute best friend in the world morph into a soccer mom. You're too young for that. At least wait until Billy's actually old enough to play soccer.'

Libby smiled as she remembered his remark and silently admitted that what he'd said wasn't too far from the truth. She knew she would never wear most of the outfits Bradley had packed but she didn't argue. There would apparently be two ports of call, which meant that if Sir Walter wanted to go ashore she would visit the islands with him, and if not she would remain on board.

Bradley had done his research and had told her that golden sandy beaches, translucent underwater caves and exclusive private isles were awaiting her. He told her to go ashore whenever she had the chance and not to be a party pooper by staying in her cabin. As he'd held up the travel brochures, he'd insisted she should do everything she could. Clearly, he was going to live the next week vicariously through her.

Libby wasn't fussed about any of it and, to be honest, wanted to get the trip over and done with so she could get back to her real life, but she didn't tell him that. He was excited for her so she let him tell her all about the sightseeing. At least one of them was excited.

Together they'd continued to pack and had selected shorts, T-shirts, jeans, lightweight jackets and a summer dress that Libby thought were far more her style. It became a compromise, with Bradley less than enthusiastic about some of Libby's clothing choices but agreeing if it didn't mean his choices were sacrificed to make room for them. At the end of the packing, she'd looked at her bursting luggage, convinced it would be way too much since she was working on the ship not socialising, but again Bradley had insisted.

Through social media, he had found out that the luxury, multi-million-dollar yacht had a pool, an intimate movie theatre and even a rock-climbing wall, and he reminded her that while Billy would be well taken care of by his doting grandparents and his fabulous fashionista Uncle Bradley, she needed to have some fun.

'She's a beauty,' the cab driver told her, breaking into Libby's reverie as he climbed from the cab and popped the trunk.

'Yes, she is,' Libby agreed, as she collected her belongings from the back seat and met him at the rear of the car.

'I'm sorry I'm a bit awkward with bags,' he began as he reached into the trunk. 'My fingers are a bit twisted. I think it might be arthritis.'

Libby looked down at the hands of the driver as he took hold of her bag. 'May I take a look?' she asked softly.

'Sure, why not? Are you a doctor?'

'No, I'm a nurse,' she replied as she reached for his hands.

He held both hands quite still for Libby to examine. Immediately she could see quite clearly there was a thickening and tightening of tissue under the skin of both hands. It was affecting the ring and little fingers. Both fingers on the right hand were almost completely closed into his palm. She recognised the problem immediately.

'How long have you had this condition?'

'A few years now but it's been getting worse lately,' he told her with a voice that signalled acceptance of his fate. 'I'm worried if both hands close I might not be able to drive and that would make life tough for the family. I'm fifty-two years old and I'd like to drive for another ten years if I can. My daughter's getting married next year and she wants the big wedding with all the bells and whistles so I can't be out of work.'

Libby said nothing as she continued to examine his hands. 'I'm not an expert but you may have a condition called Dupuytren's contracture.'

'Is there a treatment for it?'

'If it is what I think, it can be managed,' she told him. 'And it's definitely worth your while seeing someone. You would need to be referred to a specialist. My father had the condition and that's why I'm aware of it.'

'My ma told me it was arthritis and there was no hope. It's in my genes, she told me. My pa had it, but he died nearly twenty years ago 'cos of his diabetes.'

'Again, I am not an expert but if you make an appointment with your regular doctor…'

"I haven't seen a doctor in over ten years,' he cut in. 'I've been healthy as an ox and haven't needed one.'

Libby was well aware that there was a genetic predisposition to the condition but Dupuytren's contracture could be aggravated by cirrhosis of the liver and the presence of certain other diseases, including diabetes, which she was now aware was in his family along with thyroid problems so a visit to the doctor was well overdue. It could uncover a hidden condition that needed to be managed. The man's hands might be a sign that something even more serious was happening out of sight.

'I would make a time and get a general check-up and blood work while you're there. We should all do that every year. I'm sure you want to be heathy and happy and dance with your daughter at her wedding.'

'I do,' he said. 'I'll make a time next week to see a doctor. Honest, I will.'

Libby smiled and paid the fare, including a generous gratuity, and then reached down for her belongings.

'Thank you for taking the time to talk to me. Not many people do that nowadays. Everyone's in a rush. It was real nice of you,' the driver continued as he slipped the cash into his shirt pocket. 'You're a princess and I think you're a real good nurse.'

Libby smiled again and then reached for the suitcase that he had managed to pull from the trunk and place on the kerb. 'You take care of yourself.'

'And you have a great trip. Hope you meet a prince on that yacht,' the man said before he climbed into the cab.

Libby suddenly felt a little flustered with the thought as she struggled to manage her belongings. She didn't want to meet a prince—or any man for that matter. She just wanted to get the next week over and done with and return to the only man who mattered to her: her son. With a bag across her chest and a laptop case slipping from her shoulder, she reached for her large suitcase sitting on the pavement where the driver had placed it and tried to calm her nerves. It's only a week, she reminded herself. *Only a week.*

Accepting her fate, she drew in a deep breath, put a smile on her face and hoisted the slowly slipping laptop bag back up onto her shoulder and made her way to the walkway onto the yacht. The sun was shining down and she could feel the warmth through her thin T-shirt. As she climbed aboard, she could see the shining deck, perfectly arranged with black wicker outdoor seating, scattered with oversized striped cushions in striking colours. Everything about it was stunning, even the sky and sea matched perfectly.

Under different conditions she might have enjoyed herself. But Libby had a job to do and then get home. She had no intention of socialising. She had no intention of doing anything other than tending to the medical needs of Sir Walter.

Brushing away wisps of red hair that had escaped her ponytail, Libby hoped that the days ahead would pass quickly.

Dr Daniel Dimosa stood at the bow of the *Coral Contessa*, looking out across the perfectly still blue water. His mood was reflective, borderline sombre. It was the first day of his final ocean placement, then it was time to return to his family. The time had come. He looked down at his phone and reread the last message from his mother.

My darling son,

Thank you so much for agreeing to return to your home and your rightful place.

Your father's condition has deteriorated further since

the last time we spoke. He has not made any public appearances in the last week and he must abdicate very soon. There are days that he struggles to remember his advisors' names. Thankfully, he is still very aware of who I am, and my prayer is that our love for each other is strong enough to help us through the most difficult times ahead.

I know the people of Chezlovinka will be elated to see you take up your role as Crown Prince, just as your father and his father before him. Without you, my darling, I know there would be unrest and instability and I fear what may become of our land and the future of the people who so rely upon us.

Your loving mother xxxx

Daniel knew he had no choice but to stop running from his past and stop wondering what might have been. There were still question marks over the future, but he would deal with those in time. His own time. In his heart, he knew that he was destined to follow in his father's footsteps, perhaps in more ways than one. Early onset dementia was a genetic disease and he was not certain that it had eluded him.

He knew he would miss the spray of salt water on his face, the sounds of the gulls whenever they drew closer to shore, and the serenity of the endless blue horizon. And most of all the freedom to practise medicine. He drew a deep bitter-sweet breath of warm, humid air. Sadly, his love affairs with both the sea and medicine were drawing to an end at the same time.

Daniel knew he had to face the fact that his current way of life was over and no matter how much he wished it could be different, it couldn't. He was a realist. His path and his fate had been chosen the day he was born and now he had no choice but to return to his homeland. He had seven more days as Dr Daniel Dimosa before he turned his back on his life as a doctor and returned to his life as Crown Prince Daniel Edwardo Dimosa.

The breeze picked up and Daniel felt a familiar emptiness in his heart. He had grown accustomed to a life with no ties but it didn't stop him wishing for more and wanting to feel again how he had felt in San Francisco all those years ago. But he would never put a woman he cared so deeply for through what his mother had faced since his father's diagnosis five years earlier. The worry of not knowing when her husband and the man she had loved her entire life would look at her as if she was a stranger.

His expression fell further as he admitted to himself that this would be the last time he was on US soil for a very long time. It would make this trip even more poignant.

While the day was warm and calm at that moment, weather at sea was more unpredictable and prone to drastic change. Not unlike some of the women Daniel had bedded over the last four years while he'd been trying to forget the sweet, loving redhead who had so unexpectedly captured his heart. Wherever the ship docked there were women who were happy to share one night of pleasure with no strings attached. It was enjoyable, and both parties were happy to walk away knowing it would never be more than that. He forgot them as quickly as he met them and he felt sure they did the same.

A tic in Daniel's jaw began on cue, the way it always did when he thought back to the woman he had loved so briefly. With all of his being, he wished he had handled it differently or, better yet, never become involved. He wished he had been in a place where he could have explained everything and told her the truth but he hadn't been. He had been sworn to secrecy and he couldn't break that promise.

Daniel was a man of his word—both as a doctor and as Crown Prince Daniel Edwardo Dimosa.

Travelling had been all he had known for so long and he was reluctant to leave that way of life, but he was needed at home so his choices were limited. Daniel's father had carried the burden of royal responsibilities for a long time. Now, at only sixty years of age, his condition had worsened and Daniel would not turn his back on the man he both loved and admired and who was slowly being trapped inside his own deteriorating mind.

By taking over the throne, it would allow his father to retain his dignity and see out his final days away from the scrutiny of the public eye. And keeping that secret was paramount to the economic security of the principality. There was really no debate. Daniel needed to be there for his father and for the small European principality of Chezlovinka.

Over the years there were times late at night when his thoughts sometimes wandered back to the woman he had left behind. He hoped she had forgotten him, married and had a family. She deserved that and more…even if it wasn't with him.

'Dr Dimosa,' the young concierge began, 'I thought I'd let you know the ship's nurse has just boarded and has headed to her cabin. You asked me to notify you.'

'Thank you,' Daniel replied, turning momentarily to

acknowledge the young man then just as quickly turning back to the view.

His life was to be one of duty to the principality he was destined to rule. It would be a life without freedom.

And one without love.

CHAPTER TWO

LIBBY STOPPED OUTSIDE her allocated cabin and reached into her bag for the door swipe card she had been given by one of the three stewards. They had offered to take her bags to the cabin but she'd wanted a few moments alone to take in her surroundings, to be alone with her thoughts and steady her unsettled nerves.

She was huffing and puffing, as well as flustered and anxious again by the time she reached her cabin and felt quite silly having a bag large enough for a month-long vacation. What was she doing? Why hadn't she fought the board's decision? And why had she allowed Bradley to pack so many outfits into such a large suitcase?

Everything was suddenly a little overwhelming again.

She should be home with her son instead of on the other side of the country, and sailing even further away. It was like the other side of the world to Libby, and her world was her boy. She didn't want to be anywhere without him.

'Hello, there.'

Libby turned quickly to find a young woman with a mop of blonde curls and a wide smile approaching her.

'Oh, my goodness, it can't be,' the woman began, then

took a step backwards and faltered momentarily. 'Libby McDonald? Is that you?'

Libby realised instantly that she knew the woman. Standing before her was one of her closest friends from junior high.

'Georgie? Georgie Longbottom? I can't believe it's you.'

Without hesitation, the two embraced with wide grins and genuine elation.

'How long has it been?' Libby began as she released her hold and stepped back a little. Her previous apprehension and nerves were temporarily replaced with a much-needed feeling of comfort and familiarity as their eyes scanned each other with their smiles still broad and their shared joy palpable. 'It must be…almost twelve years?'

'Thirteen actually. I remember because I returned to London at the end of my sophomore year. Our crazy fun year at Seaview High was the best year of my school life,' Georgie confessed, then paused for a moment as a wistful smile washed over her pretty face. 'To be brutally honest, it was probably one of the best years my life, full stop. We were fancy free and had no idea just how tough the real world can be.'

Libby nodded, silently admitting the carefree days of the final years of senior school had been some of the best for her too. The reality of Georgie's words brought her back to reality. They were not seventeen, wide eyed and looking for an adventure any more. The Caribbean adventure that Libby was facing now was not one about which she was feeling any real level of excitement.

Life had certainly not turned out as Libby had expected…in so many ways. And it sounded as if life had not been perfect for Georgie either but Libby didn't want to dwell or complain or ask too many questions, at least not immediately, of the friend she had not seen in for ever. She wanted to live at least for a little while in the unexpected joy that seeing Georgie had brought to her.

'That was a wonderfully happy year, wasn't it?'

'Absolutely,' Georgie replied as she reached for Libby's laptop bag that was slipping from her shoulder. 'What's your role on board?'

'Sir Walter's nurse. What about you, what brings you on board?'

'I'm Walter's chef again for this trip,' she replied. 'He's a lovely man and easy to work for. I've done the Caribbean trip a few times for him. I've also catered some of his large, exclusive parties in his UK residence. He has a place in Miami, another in San Fran and one in London, and I own a restaurant not far from his London home. He tells me often enough to boost my ego that my restaurant is his favourite in the world. Anyway, he invited me to have a working holiday in the Caribbean, overseeing the galley crew and making some fabulous desserts, and I couldn't say no.'

'That's so exciting and what a compliment. I never knew you wanted to be a chef,' Libby confessed. 'I never even knew you cooked.'

'It's a long story, but I found my passion in life after I left school. But enough about me. I want to hear all about your life and since your cabin is right next to mine, I'm sure we'll have lots of time to catch up. I saw your name on the room register half an hour ago. I knew you always wanted to be a nurse so I wondered if it could possibly be you, but I didn't want to get my hopes up because there's more than one Elizabeth McDonald in the world.'

'Yes, it's not an exotic or exciting name…'

'And you think Georgina Longbottom sounds like a rock star?'

Both girls laughed.

'Hey,' Georgie continued as she took Libby's laptop bag and put it on her own shoulder. 'Let's get you unpacked before the staff meeting.'

'I think I've over-packed.'

Georgie smiled again. 'I would have to agree with you on that…and from memory that's not like you. I was always the one with too many bags when we'd take off down the coast for a few days to one of those music festivals. You were always the sensible one with everything packed neatly into a backpack. Quite the minimalist. Clearly things have changed in regard to that.'

'My friend Bradley made me pack…'

'Bradley,' Georgia cut in, looking her friend in the eyes with a cheeky smile and her head tilted. 'Is he your other half?'

'No, Bradley's other half is Tom and he's super nice. I'll tell you all about him when we get inside, if I can fit all of this in the cabin.'

'We'll manage. The cabin's quite tiny but we can put the suitcase under the bunk.'

'Bunk?'

'Yes, bunk, but you have the cabin to yourself as there aren't too many staff on board so you have the choice of top or bottom bunk. It's not a stateroom like the guests have but it's quite nice in there.'

Libby smiled as she tried to recall the last time she had slept in a bunk. Then it came to her. 'Like at Big Bear camp?'

'Maybe a little, but this cabin has a porthole. It moves

with the motion of the waves but you'll get used to it,'
Georgie remarked with a half-grin.

Libby nodded as she retrieved her swipe card from
the unlocked cabin door and they stepped inside. She
was definitely older and she prayed wiser but the fact
that she was on a luxury yacht so far from home had her
doubting her wisdom. Seeing Georgie made her feel a
lot better about the situation but it also brought back a
time that had been uncomplicated and for the longest
moment she wished she was that innocent again. A time
when everything was exactly what it seemed. A time
when she could trust people's intentions.

Libby drew a deep breath. 'I think the next seven days
are going to be a lot better with you on board,' Libby
said, feeling a little more relaxed than she had thirty
minutes earlier.

'Have you been on many ships other than this one?'
Libby asked, pushing unwanted thoughts of romance
from her mind as she quickly checked out the cabin and
found a small bathroom with a toilet, wash basin and
shower. It was clean and compact like the rest of the ac-
commodation and with Georgie's help she was quickly
becoming more comfortable in her surroundings. She
was gaining control in small ways and it was making
her relax just a little.

'No, just Walter's. I'm busy running the restaurant so
I can't afford the time to do it for anyone else.'

'You're back so I guess you must have enjoyed it.'

Georgie nodded. 'Yes, I did. It's stressful at times
but so much fun and you end up becoming good friends
with the other team members. Or even more sometimes.'

'Romance at sea. That sounds like a dreadful idea,'

Libby said with a look of disdain. She couldn't think of anything worse at that moment.

'It's happened before and the doctor on this trip is ridiculously handsome—tall, dark and single—but he's too aloof for me. The crew all say he's a nice guy but he's way too mysterious. I'm over that type but maybe you...'

'Absolutely not. I'm definitely not looking for romance,' Libby cut in, shaking her head and feeling shivers run over her body. Tall, dark and mysterious was everything in a man she never wanted again.

'Never say never.'

'No, I can say never. Believe me, I'm not interested in anything other than looking after my patient, seeing some sights and then heading home to my...' Libby stopped, pulling herself up again from mentioning Billy. She decided to leave that conversation for later. She was already too emotional and she didn't want to talk about Billy and risk crying.

'Your...?'

'My...um...family. It's the first time I've been away in for ever.'

'Sometimes being thrown into new situations out of your comfort zone is the best way.'

'I'm not sure about that but I guess I'm going to find out.'

Daniel was waiting to meet the nurse who he had been told had boarded and was settling into her cabin. While there were still thirty minutes until the scheduled briefing with the captain, the rest of the ship's staff had already made their way to the deck. He wasn't sure why he was feeling anxious, but he couldn't ignore the stirring in the pit of his stomach. It was almost a feeling of déjà vu and it made him feel less than his usual relaxed self. There was more than enough time to prepare for the dozen or so passengers and their host and the *Coral Countess* would not be setting sail for another two hours, so there was nothing he could put his finger on at that moment, yet he was still uneasy.

The cabin that had been converted into a makeshift hospital room was next to Sir Walter's suite. With only five weeks since the long heart surgery, Daniel had requested it be set up to resemble as closely as possible a hospital room with everything he and the cardiac nurse would require should Sir Walter have any post-operative complications. It was uncommon but not impossible to suffer issues a few weeks post-op and he wished that Sir Walter had delayed the trip a little longer.

Daniel's sense of unease wasn't abating and he put it down to the fact that this would be his last voyage. He ran his fingers through his dark hair, took another deep breath and began pacing the pristine deck overlooking the helipad again, his mind slowly filling with remorse, regret and more than a little melancholy as he thought back over his life at sea and how it was coming to an end. At forty-one years of age, he had spent ten years of his medical career consulting in different hospitals all over the world and almost four tending to the needs of passengers on both private yachts and larger cruise liners. And twice he had tended to the needs of their families when one of the passengers had died at sea.

Daniel sighed as he thought back over the good, the bad and then the sad moments in both his personal and professional life. It had certainly been a mixed bag but he did not regret his decision to leave Chezlovinka and taste freedom for the last decade. He was also very grateful to his mother for encouraging and supporting his desire to pursue a medical career and now he would repay her by returning to rule so his father could abdicate.

Daniel lifted his chin defiantly at the thought of the life that lay ahead for him. There was so much he didn't know about his future. All that was certain and all that he could control was the next seven days on the *Coral Contessa*.

Georgie looked down at her watch. 'We'd best be off, then. We don't want to be late.'

'Late for what?' Libby asked, her blue eyes widening suddenly.

'Our briefing with the rest of the ship's crew, including our hunky mysterious medic. I mentioned it a moment ago.'

Libby shook her head and climbed to her feet. 'Of course, I'm sorry, you did mention it. I'm just a bit distracted.' Meeting the ship's doctor was not her focus. She was still worried about Billy and how he would cope without her. And how she would cope without him.

The last thing she wanted was to appear unprofessional in front of the rest of the crew so she was grateful that it was only Georgie in the cabin. She nervously brushed her jeans with her hands. There was no dust but it helped her to regain her composure.

'Hey, you'll be fine. Once we set sail you'll realise this is a piece of cake.'

'I hope so,' Libby replied, and quickly pulled a comb from her purse and hastily redid her ponytail, catching all the unkempt red wisps.

'If Dr Dimosa is easygoing underneath his moody Mediterranean demeanour, the trip will be a joy for you.'

Libby froze on the spot. Her stomach fell. 'Dr Dimosa is the ship's doctor?' she said, forcing the words past the lump that was forming in her throat. It was made of tears and anger and complete disbelief.

'Yes, Daniel Dimosa. He's the one I was talking about. Do you know him?'

Libby's pulse began to race and her stomach sank further. Dr Daniel Dimosa? *Her* Daniel? The man who had broken her heart and left without a word.

Billy's father.

Libby felt the colour drain from her face. Suddenly the cabin began to spin and she grabbed the edge of the desk to steady herself. An onslaught of emotions rushed at her as the blood drained from her head to feed her pounding heart. Libby felt herself falling and she was powerless to stop herself from crashing to the floor.

CHAPTER THREE

'WHAT EXACTLY HAPPENED before she fainted?' Daniel called down the corridor as he walked quickly with his medical bag in his hand. Concern was colouring his voice as he neared the cabin where Georgie was waiting outside. 'Was there a critical incident, or any sign she wasn't well?'

'No, nothing. I just told her that we needed to head to the deck for the captain's briefing with you.'

'How is she now?'

'She's conscious but on the floor still.' She motioned with her hand as she opened the cabin door but paused outside. 'I placed a pillow under her head and called for you. I asked her to remain where she was until you arrived. The fall was very sudden and it doesn't make sense…unless she has an underlying health issue that she never mentioned during our conversation.'

Daniel moved past Georgie, stepped inside and looked over to the young woman lying on the floor. He was forced to steady himself on the frame of the doorway. His whole world changed in an instant. Nurse Elizabeth McDonald was Libby McDonald. The woman he had loved and left. The same woman who had never completely left his thoughts.

And the woman he had never thought he would see again.

* * *

Daniel stared in silence, so many conflicting thoughts running through his mind. Over the years since they had parted he would sometimes be reminded of her by the sight of a woman with long red hair in the crowd or hearing a laugh like hers. And he would wonder what would have happened between them if only his life had been different.

But it wasn't different and now more than ever he knew that.

He stilled his nerves, crossed the small cabin like a man possessed, and knelt down beside her. While her breathing was laboured, she was conscious and staring at the ceiling. He fought an unexpected but strangely natural desire to pull her into his arms.

'Will she be okay?' Georgie asked, breaking into his thoughts.

He had to remind himself that he was the ship's doctor, nothing more, although being this close to Libby again was suddenly making him wonder how easy that would be.

Placing his fingers on her neck, he took her pulse. It was racing but strong. Her eyes were open and looking towards the ceiling. And they were the most brilliant green, just as he had remembered. She was alert but saying nothing. Her pupils, he could see, were equal in size and not dilated.

'Libby, it's me. Daniel.'

Libby closed her eyes and turned her face away from his as he spoke. She said nothing to even acknowledge his presence in the cabin.

He knew he deserved her reaction. 'I had no idea you

were the nurse on this trip. I guess I never thought of you as Elizabeth.'

Still nothing.

'I've always thought of you as Libby.'

She slowly turned back to face him. He saw her eyes were as cold as ice, her lips a hard line on her beautiful face. 'I don't care how you thought of me,' she said coldly, before she rolled her face away from his again, and he watched as she wiped at a tear with the back of her hand. 'Just leave, Daniel. I don't need you here.'

'I'm not going anywhere,' Daniel said before he turned to Georgie. 'Please leave us alone. I can take it from here.'

From Georgie's expression he could see she was clearly perplexed but she did as he asked and walked from the cabin, pulling the cabin door closed behind her.

Using her elbows as support, Libby tried to ease herself into an upright position.

'Please don't move,' he told her, and placed his warm hand gently on her wrist.

'Don't…don't touch me,' she said, pulling her arm free. 'I need to leave, now.'

'I'm checking your vitals before you're going anywhere.'

'Take them if you must,' she said curtly. 'Give me a clean bill of health then I'm leaving the ship. There's no way on God's earth I'm spending the next seven days working with you.'

'Let's deal with that in a minute. First you have to remain still while I check your BP.' Swiftly and efficiently, Daniel removed the blood pressure cuff from his medical bag and wrapped it around the arm she had reluctantly given him. The result took only a few moments. 'Ninety-eight over fifty.'

'I have low blood pressure,' she spat back as she quickly unwrapped the pressure cuff and shoved it in Daniel's direction. 'It's nothing out of the normal range for me. I'm fine.'

Daniel looked at the cuff lying in his hands and then back at Libby. There was so much he wanted to say but couldn't. And things he was feeling that scared his cold heart.

He had to stay focused and ignore his reaction to the woman who was so close to him he could smell the perfume resting delicately on her skin. What they had shared was in the past and had to remain there, he reminded himself. He had left her bed in the early hours of that morning for good reason.

Nothing had changed. In seven days he would leave the yacht and begin to transition to ruling the principality; he wasn't about to risk the distance he had purposefully put between Libby and himself when he had walked away.

It was not just about two people any more. He had to think of his father and the people of Chezlovinka.

'I understand why you're reacting the way you are,' he began, his voice low and controlled. 'It's justified and I deserve it but it was a long time ago.'

'You think you understand? Really? I don't think you could possibly understand,' she said in an almost breathless voice as she glared at him again.

'I understand more than you'll ever believe.' He was fighting his mind's desire to remember back to the wonderful weeks they shared and their last night together.

'I doubt it because if you truly did, then you wouldn't

have left San Francisco without the decency of an explanation. It's been four years, Daniel. That's more than enough time to reach out.'

'I couldn't, Libby. It's complicated.' He moved back, creating distance between them. Distance she clearly wanted and he definitely needed.

'Complicated? That's the best you can come up with after all this time?' she responded, shaking her head. 'That's beyond pathetic but I don't care any more.'

'I don't know what else to say,' he began, knowing that she wanted and deserved more but he was not ever going to be in a position to let her know the truth.

'Don't bother trying, Daniel. There's nothing you could say that would make a scrap of difference now. It could have once, but that was a very long time ago.'

Daniel took a deep breath. 'As I said, I had my reasons…'

Libby looked away, staring at nothing. 'We all have choices in life. You're just not telling me the reason why you made yours.'

Daniel chose to say nothing because there was nothing he could say. He couldn't admit that he had never meant to take their relationship as far as making love to her that night because he had not been free to become involved. He could not tell her about his family, his destiny to rule the principality, or the secret they were all forced to hide from the world to maintain the stability of the small principality. His hands were tied.

'Honestly, Daniel, I don't give a damn.' Libby's voice was cold and matter-of-fact. 'But you can do the right thing now by getting out of my way and letting me off this ship. Find yourself a new nurse and give my sincere apologies to Sir Walter.'

Daniel shook his head. 'I wish it was that simple but it's not. Unfortunately, you can't leave the yacht, Libby.'

'Just watch me.'

'No matter how angry you are with me, you can't just leave,' he replied as he ran his fingers through the black waves of his hair. 'I need to have a qualified cardiac nurse to assist with his care.'

'Are you serious? I'm expected to care what you need?'

'No, but you need to consider what Walter needs, and that's an experienced nurse. He's five weeks post-operative. I can't have just anyone on board.'

'Then get an experienced temp from an agency,' she cut in angrily. 'I'm not that special.'

Daniel disagreed silently. Libby was very special in many ways but he would never be able to tell her that. 'It can't happen, Libby. I'm sorry. It's just not possible.'

No matter how many nights he had ached to have her lying in his arms, to feel the warmth of her body next to his and taste the sweetness of her kiss again, Daniel knew now more than ever he had to keep her at arm's length. He had to keep their relationship the way it had begun all those years ago before he'd overstepped the mark.

'I need to have a competent nurse with your experience and qualifications,' he told her, quickly re-establishing the professionalism that was required.

Libby stared at him for a moment, her eyes roaming every inch of his face before turning her gaze back to the ceiling. Daniel felt even more confused. While she had every right to be angry and distant, it was as if there was something more behind her words. He wasn't sure if it was just more anger but there was something. Something she was holding back from saying.

'I'm sure there's a nurse who can fit the bill,' she said in a voice devoid of emotion.

'We need clearances and we're leaving in less than two hours. The process can't happen that quickly.'

'Call someone. Expedite it. I'm sure Sir Walter is well connected.'

Daniel shook his head. 'No one is that well connected, not even Walter. There's a process that can't be fast-tracked when you're sailing in international waters and that's removing the most obvious and pressing fact that we have a patient with specific needs. Walter's condition is precarious. He needs a highly skilled nurse and you agreed to travel with him. You have a duty of care and you signed a contract.'

'The board at the Northern Bay General Hospital signed that agreement…'

'On your behalf and, again, for good reason, they have put their reputations on the line. Walter is one of America's wealthiest men and I imagine he's also a very generous benefactor to the hospital. He's also in need of high-quality, specialised care. For all of these reasons, you have to stay on board. I'm sorry, Libby, there's really no option. The ship can't set sail without you and I don't think you want to have Walter and the board suing you for breach of contract.'

Libby slowly got to her feet as Daniel rose to his with his hand extended to her. She ignored his offer of assistance and used the bunk to steady herself.

'Then write me a sickness certificate and clear me to leave so they can't sue me. Tell them I have an unexpected medical condition.'

'But you don't have any condition, Libby. I can't lie.'

He watched as she took a deep breath and considered his words. Again, her demeanour was so different from that of the woman he had met all those years before; the hurt clearly still ran deep but there was something else. There was something less carefree about her. Something behind those beautiful eyes that he couldn't quite work out.

'You lied to me…'

'I didn't lie, Libby. I left without an explanation. I never lied.'

'Well, if you find that acceptable, how about I do the same now? I'll just leave without an explanation, if you believe that's acceptable behaviour,' she said in a controlled but clearly hostile voice. 'I deserve the right to walk away just like you did. The only difference is that you'll know why…and it's your choice whether to tell them or not.'

Daniel nodded, accepting the truth in her words. 'I deserve that.'

'Yes, you do and I deserve your help to get me off this yacht now.' She closed her eyes and shook her head.

Daniel wished he could help her but he couldn't. 'If I could I would but—'

'Write the certificate and I'll be gone. It won't matter if Walter delays setting sail for one day. They can all stay aboard here in the port and party into the early hours.'

'Unfortunately, even a delay of two hours let alone a day to secure a new nurse would cause Walter to miss his niece Sophia's engagement party.'

'Engagement party? What engagement party?' she demanded as she slumped back down on the lower bunk shaking her head. 'I thought this was just a week's cruise.'

'It is, with a small engagement party in San Lucia. He's brought his favourite chef from London to oversee the catering. Guests are coming in from all over the world to meet him there.'

'So, that's it, then. It's a fait accompli. I'm forced to stay.'

'I'm sorry, Libby.' Daniel's long fingers rested on his clenched jaw as he looked at the woman over whom he had lost countless nights of sleep—from both guilt and the realisation that he would never find a woman like her again.

Her face held a mix of anger and hopelessness. 'Trapped on this ship and expected to work with you? It's so unfair and you know it.'

'It is unfair, but I will find a compromise. I will make our working time together minimal. We can visit Walter at separate times and any incidents with the other passengers we will handle the same way unless there's an emergency...' he began, just as he received a pager alert. He looked down momentarily at his device, then moved towards the door. 'If you agree to those terms we can work this out for the next week.'

Libby chewed the inside of her cheek anxiously. For her there was more to think about than just not wanting to spend any time with Daniel. There was Billy to consider. Daniel had no idea he was father to her son. How would he react to knowing that? Would he even believe Billy was his child? And if he did believe her, would he actually care? It was a dilemma she'd never thought she would have to face. She tried to calm her breathing as

Daniel left, closing the door behind him. She was stuck between a rock and a hard place and there was no choice but to agree to Daniel's terms. Being sued was not an option. She had lost her heart once to the man—and almost her mind—when he'd left, and she wasn't about to lose her home and her future because of him.

There was so much at risk by staying but even more by leaving. For nearly four years she had resigned herself to never seeing Daniel again, never having to think about telling him that he had a son. And now she was going to be at sea for seven days and seven nights with the father of her child. The father of the little boy who was so much like him. The deep blue eyes that looked up at her every night when she tucked him into bed were his father's eyes. The black hair that she smoothed with her hands in the morning when Billy ran to her, arms outstretched, for a cuddle was his father's hair. The skin that turned a beautiful golden hue in the summer sun, that too was his father's Mediterranean skin.

But when Daniel had disappeared, Libby had had neither the money nor the desire to hire someone to find him. To tell him that he had a son he might not even have wanted.

But now it was an option. Now there was the opportunity to tell him and she was confused, *terribly* confused about how he would react to the news. The man she had fallen in love with and who she had invited into her bed would care, but the man who had walked away might not care at all and that would break her heart all over again.

Libby watched as the door slowly opened again. Her heart picked up speed and she felt it pumping erratically. She dropped her gaze as Daniel stepped back inside the cabin. She didn't want to look at him. She was worried she would see her precious son in his eyes and consequently soften towards Daniel. She needed time to think. Time to work out in her mind what was best for her son. Not for her and not for Daniel. Her thoughts were only on what was best for Billy. He was the innocent one and needed to be considered above anyone else. Did she have the right to hide Daniel's son from him? Did his behaviour, leaving without an explanation or a forwarding address, take away his right to know he was a father? But if she told him, and he became a part of his son's life in some capacity, could he leave again without warning and the next time break Billy's heart?

She needed time and a clear head to sort it out. She wasn't going to rush into making a life-changing decision for Billy.

Libby wondered if time on the yacht would allow her to learn more about Daniel, get to know the real man and try her very best not to let their failed relationship influence her decision. Libby knew she had to make a truly informed choice, not just react emotionally. Perhaps that was what fate had planned—time for her to learn as much as she could about Daniel and allow her to make the very best choice for Billy.

'Your decision?'

Libby continued looking down at the cabin floor as she shifted her feet nervously. Little did he know that she had two decisions to make…

'Let's be honest, Daniel, I don't really have much of a choice. It's been made for me. I have to stay.'

'Thank you, Libby. It's best for everyone.'

'We'll see,' she told him. Her heart was still beating out of her chest. She had so much at risk. There was much to protect and consider for the next week.

'There's one more thing,' he said as he turned to leave. 'I'm sorry, Libby, but you'll still have to attend the briefing with the senior members of the crew on the stern deck in thirty minutes. It's a regulation procedure. After that I will do my best to ensure there's minimal contact between us.'

Libby nodded. She was still struggling to process it all.

'Fine, but I want minimal contact, Daniel. I don't care how you arrange that but you need to make it happen,' she said, her words short and her tone curt. 'And don't even try to change the terms of this arrangement. If you do, I swear I'm getting off this ship at the first port and you'll be the one explaining why.'

CHAPTER FOUR

'ARE YOU OKAY, LIBBY?' Georgie asked as she stepped back inside the cabin, her big brown eyes even larger than before. 'I was so shocked when you fainted.'

'I'm okay. I think I was just overwhelmed. Maybe I didn't drink enough water and my blood pressure fell.'

Georgie's expression changed and Libby watched as her old friend closed the cabin door slowly, and purposefully moved closer as if she was about to learn a secret that could bring down a nation. 'Libby, from the day we met all those years ago at school we connected and we could never hide anything from each other. Nothing's changed; it's like we were sisters in a previous life.'

'I know but...' Libby began, then stopped, knowing she couldn't lie to her friend.

'Is there something you want to share with me? The way he looked at you, and the way he spoke, it was more than a little bit obvious you two have chemistry and if it's old chemistry, then it just re-ignited in this cabin.'

'It's nothing.' Libby stiffened at the question and felt her pulse pick up again. But nothing had re-ignited, she reminded herself. It was just the shock of seeing him and the decisions that came with having him so close to her.

'Oh, really, nothing? One, he called you Libby

and, two, he said, "It's me, Daniel." And if that wasn't enough, he asked me to leave the cabin. Why would he do that unless he wanted to have a private conversation with you? You two definitely have history. You can tell me to butt out but I know there's something there.'

Libby couldn't talk her way out of it. She respected Georgie too much. She had no choice but to tell her part of the story. Just not everything.

'We dated briefly, *very* briefly a few years back. It feels like a lifetime ago.'

'I knew it,' Georgie said crossing the room and sitting on the bed beside her friend. 'However brief, and however it ended, it's clear to me that it was rather an intense relationship. It's so obvious that it wasn't just a casual fling for either of you.'

Libby closed her eyes and drew a deep breath. Once again, she was feeling overwhelmed with the reality of it all. Georgie's questions, while well intentioned, were confrontational and almost too much to handle. 'It's complicated.'

'I'm sorry, Libby, I didn't mean to pry. You don't have to go into it. I overstepped good manners and I do apologise, truly. I mean, by the look of you now and the expression on his face, what you shared might be better left alone, at least for now.'

'I'm sorry, Georgie. I'm not up to talking about it. Maybe later.'

'Absolutely. Whenever you're ready,' she replied as she reached out and embraced Libby. 'Like they say in the Hollywood movies, "I have your back, girl."'

With the kindness of Georgie's embrace, Libby found a ray of hope amongst the rubble that had suddenly become her life. Trapped at sea with Billy's father, the man whom she had loved deeply but briefly, was a disaster she had not seen coming. 'Thank you.'

Georgie finally released her hold. 'Men...can't live with them and apparently you can't sail without them.'

Libby nodded. She was still on very shaky ground with her emotions but somehow she had to dig down and find the strength to get through the cruise and make what could be the single most important decision in her life. And in her son's life. Her stomach was churning as she battled with doubts about making the right decision for everyone. And her own feelings about Daniel. Were they truly dead and buried?

'I guess if I have to go to the briefing, I might as well get it over and done with,' she announced, getting to her feet and lifting her chin and making her way to the cabin door, her heart pounding with every step.

Moments later, Libby and Georgie arrived on the deck where they found the rest of the crew waiting. Libby looked around her but didn't take in too much. It was by far the biggest yacht at the dock—and the most luxurious—but Libby was oblivious to all of it. Nothing was registering with her. Her mind was racing in many directions, all of them leading back to Daniel.

'Hello, there, I'm Captain Mortimer but you can call me Eric.' The captain acknowledged Libby and Georgie's arrival with a smile. He was a man in his late fifties, not particularly tall, with a kind face and short hair just beginning to grey at the temples. He was dressed in a white uniform, complete with epaulettes and a captain's cap, all with the *Coral Contessa* insignia.

Sir Walter really did like a very professional-looking crew; the younger, blond and slightly taller man next to Captain Mortimer wore the same uniform. There was nothing casual about this yacht. 'I have the pleasure of navigating this magnificent vessel for the next eight days and with any luck this weather will hold up and it will be quite lovely. We'll be setting sail this afternoon and cruising out across the Caribbean Sea for the next three days.

'On day four we'll be docking at Martinique. You can work out between yourselves who'd like to go ashore that day. We'll anchor there for about six hours to allow the guests to tour the island. At seventeen hundred hours we'll once again set sail with the intention of docking the next day around eleven-hundred hours in San Lucia.

'On this second and final stop we will remain in port for the day and the night so those who missed leave on Martinique can take some time in San Lucia. On the sixth day we hoist anchor at zero six hundred hours for the trip back across the Caribbean Sea to Miami. Any questions?'

Libby heard every word from the captain but didn't retain too much as she was distracted by Daniel's presence so close to her after so many years. It was like a nightmare and one she wished she could wake from to find herself in her bed, in her home, hearing the giggles of her son playing in his room.

She blinked, hoping to make this reality disappear, but it didn't. She tried not to look in Daniel's direction but was powerless to prevent herself. She was drawn to him like a moth to a flame that would undoubtedly burn her if she got too close. He cut a powerful silhouette dressed in the starched white uniform too, a stark contrast to the darkness of his tanned skin. She watched as he stood alone, resting his lean fingers on the railing and staring out to sea. His look was far away but he didn't appear cold or arrogant. She couldn't help but notice he looked like a man in pain.

She didn't want to stare at him; she wanted to be able to look away; she wanted to hate him—and part of her did, but there was something in his expression that confused her. The pain in his eyes looked real. It was coming from somewhere deep inside and for some inexplicable reason Libby suddenly cared. Her reaction didn't make sense.

She should have been happy to see him looking sad but she wasn't. She was seeing a man who looked like he was at war with himself. The cleft in his jaw was just as she remembered it. The blackness of his hair falling in soft waves, like the ocean, had not changed. In fact, everything about him was just the way she remembered, except for the almost overwhelming sadness. That was new. And somewhat perplexing for her.

For the first time in a long while Daniel was unsure how to behave, how to manage the situation and his own feelings. So he chose to remain silent and look out to sea. Look towards where they would be travelling for the next week and wish it to be over. He couldn't change the outcome so every moment would be difficult for him as he now knew it would be for Libby too. She had every right to be angry with him. His behaviour, without explanation, had been appalling. And he couldn't provide any explanation.

While he had imagined his last assignment at sea would be challenging, he could never had dreamt just how much.

He did not want to make it obvious to anyone else that he and Libby had once been as close as two people could ever be so he would make all communication minimal. Theirs had been a love affair that should never have happened. But he still wished with all his heart that it had never had to end.

'Let's go around the group and introduce ourselves and since we'll be working and living closely together for the next week perhaps tell us something interesting about you,' Captain Mortimer began, bringing Daniel back to the task at hand. Meeting everyone. 'Well, you know me so let's begin with our First Mate, Steve.'

'Thanks Eric, I'll keep it brief since I don't want to bore you all with stories of my perfect childhood, college sporting prowess or my new golden retrievers. I'm Steve Waterford. I've been First Mate for about five years now, and it's my second stint on the *Coral Contessa*. I was raised in Boston and still live there with said dogs when I'm not at sea. Boris is six months old and Molly's three months old and into everything, including my boxers drawer.' Steve smiled and then looked towards the casually attired man at his left, who was rolling his eyes but smiling. His head was clean shaven and he had a beard and wore heavy black glasses.

'Probably too much information, Steve. I'm Laurence Mitchell and I'm the Chief Engineer and I've been working on various yachts and cruise ships for just over six years. I've worked three stints with Eric and Steve. I'm a native New Yorker and also still live there when I'm not on the high seas.'

'I'm Stacey Langridge, the *Contessa's* purser,' the tall blonde woman began. She too was in uniform. 'This is my second cruise with Eric and I think I've worked with Steve more times than I can remember but I'm new to this ship. I grew up in SoCal near Venice Beach but now I live in Miami. I made the move over here about a year ago with my husband. No dogs in my life…although I've dated a few over the years.' She laughed then followed suit and looked to her left.

'I'm Daniel Dimosa, I'm half of the medical team.' Daniel kept his words brief. He had no desire to socialise or to mention anything about his personal life so he looked over in Georgie's direction, willing her to step up next.

'Georgie Longbottom. I'm from the UK, although I'm quite certain my accent gave that away. I'm the owner of a restaurant in London and, at Walter's request, the ship's chef for the second time on this yacht and, as fate would have it, my best friend from sophomore year in San Francisco when I was on an exchange is standing next to me. We haven't seen each other in for ever, so there's a lot of catching up to do.'

The group all then looked at Libby. Daniel could not avoid doing the same. He could not help but notice she nervously but purposely made eye contact with them all but not with him. He could also not help but notice that she was as beautiful as he remembered, perhaps even more so. Her stunning red hair was tied away from her face in a ponytail. He recalled it flowing across the white pillowcase as she lay naked beside him in the warmth of her bed.

He dug his fingers into his palms, trying to keep his mind from wandering back to that time. He couldn't let the memories overtake him. He had to stay on task. Thinking even for the briefest moment of the way it had been would be pointless. He could not change what had happened or make amends. She was angry and hurt even after all the time that had passed and she had every right to feel that way, although he thought she would have moved on by now and not reacted the way she had when she'd seen him. Perhaps—and understandably—she would have been cold and distant but her reaction was more than that. He had never made contact, never written or called so he had given her no reason to think of him.

'Elizabeth McDonald, but I prefer to be called Libby, and I'm from Oakland, which is about twenty minutes outside of San Francisco. I have nursing experience in both A&E and Cardiology and recently I was one of Sir Walter's nurses pre- and post-operatively. And, this is my first time on a ship.'

The group all smiled back. All except Daniel. His look was sombre and he didn't take his eyes off Libby. He couldn't. He was momentarily caught up in thoughts of the past. Daniel knew he had to get a grip on his feelings. Something tugged at his heart as he stood watching her from across the room and it scared him to the core.

Daniel Dimosa had a battle with his feelings on his hands.

'Okay, I guess now we know a little about each other and too much about Boris and… I've forgotten the other one's name already,' Eric said in a light-hearted manner.

'Molly,' Steve interjected. 'And to think I was going to give you one of their pups.'

'No, please, that's not necessary. In fact, my wife would be mortified by the thought,' Eric said, shaking his head. 'So, let's get down to the briefing. You know most of it but it's regulation to go over it so I will, particularly as a few of you are new to this particular ship.

The previous voyages of the *Coral Contessa* have been without incident and I hope this trip will be the same.

'We're on a US-owned ship sailing in international waters. In keeping with guidelines, all staff are on call twenty-four hours a day. You will be assigned eight-hour shifts but you will have a pager in case you're needed twenty-four hours a day. It is not to be switched off at any time and I expect that you report here immediately if called. Neither Steve nor I will call unless it's an emergency. There's always the chance we could find ourselves in a situation where we need additional support or we may need your assistance to help seriously sick or injured patients to disembark so I need to know I can always reach you.

'Georgie is fluent in French and Italian, Stacey in Spanish, and I also speak a little Greek so we should be able to assist Sir Walter's international guests according to the information I was provided. Oh, and Steve is fluent in golden retriever but we won't be needing that on this trip.'

The team laughed, except for Libby. She stood staring into space, not capable of reacting, and Daniel understood why. She was feeling trapped and, while it wasn't his fault, Daniel felt guilty. Her distaste at being in the same space as him was understandable.

He watched as Georgie leaned over and gave her a hug. There was a very real bond between Libby and Georgie and one that, it appeared, had not diminished despite their years apart. He was not surprised because Libby was hard to forget. She was genuine and compassionate and so much more he didn't want to remember, but all of it was coming back to him at lightning speed.

CHAPTER FIVE

'SIR WALTER AND his remaining guests are due to arrive shortly. His grandson and guest arrived early and have already boarded and are in their stateroom. We are scheduled to set sail at fifteen hundred hours,' the Captain announced. 'So please take this time to get to know your way around your home away from home and meet the rest of the crew who have been on board for quite a few hours, some since yesterday, in preparation for the voyage.'

Daniel was still coming to terms with the situation. It was surreal seeing Libby and he had to keep reminding himself that after this week he would never see her again. Their paths would never cross. There was nothing to bind them together and everything to keep them apart. He had to make sure he did not let old feelings creep into the present. He could not truly make amends and he did not want to lie or hurt her further. She had made it clear she wanted their time together to pass quickly and she was only here because she had no other option. How he wanted it to be different but that wasn't in the stars for them.

The senior crew were dispersing but Daniel needed to speak with Libby about Walter's condition and in general about her role on the yacht, and after that he would keep his word and restrict all interactions to a professional minimum.

'Libby, can you please stay back?' Daniel asked. 'I would like to clarify a few things as this is your first time as a ship's nurse.'

Libby paused in mid-step and turned back. Daniel could see by her expression her distaste of the idea.

'Do you want me to stay too?' Georgie asked in a lowered voice.

'I'm good, Georgie, thank you,' she said softly. 'I'm sure this won't take long and then I'll head back to my cabin.'

'Five minutes, tops,' Daniel responded, making it clear he had heard both of them.

Georgie walked away, leaving Daniel and Libby alone for the second time that day. Libby crossed her arms and glared in silence at him. Her hostile body language told him everything he already knew.

'Libby,' he began. 'I will keep this very brief, but I do need to explain what we do and don't have access to on the yacht in regard to providing treatment to Walter and any other passengers.'

'I'm quite happy to go and find that out for myself,' she retorted as she paced the deck.

'I'm sure you could do that but it might be more efficient if I was to give you a brief overview because we don't know what the next few days might hold in terms of Walter's health. What we do know is that we have an almost eighty-year-old man who has undergone a triple coronary artery bypass graft and insists on behaving as if he has never seen the inside of an operating theatre. You and I are both aware that he is not fully recovered and he is as stubborn as the next billionaire and believes he knows best in every aspect of his life…' Daniel's words were cut short by the arrival of a uniformed young man.

'I'm Stan, one of the stewards, and I need you to come quickly. There's a young woman on the top deck. She gashed her head and one of the stewardesses is sitting with her. There's a load of blood.'

'Let's go,' Daniel said, immediately following the young man.

'I'm coming too,' Libby answered.

Within moments, the three of them climbed the circular staircase leading to the top deck to find a young woman dressed in shorts and a bikini top sitting in a deck chair. A stewardess stood beside her, holding a blood-soaked white hand-towel against the young woman's forehead. She had visible injuries, including grazes and cuts to the exposed skin on her shoulders, upper arms and face. There was a first-aid kit lying nearby.

'Do you know what happened… Rose?' Daniel asked as scanned the stewardess's name tag.

'Natalie had a tumble on the top deck,' Rose replied matter-of-factly. 'One of the engineers found her. It looks like she fell from the climbing wall, which had been cordoned off as it was unattended, and she had been on it without a harness. I asked her not to move; I thought she might have neck injuries. I've done first aid and knew she should remain still and wait for you as she might need a neck brace but she ignored my instructions.

'She climbed to her feet and then collapsed back down in the chair. I brought the first-aid kit up with me when I was called.'

'Do you know if she was conscious when she was found?'

'No, they said she was unresponsive. The engineer initially thought she had hit her head and been killed in the fall,' Rose told him. 'Poor man, he was quite shaken up by it.'

Daniel took a pair of disposable gloves from the open first-aid kit and Libby followed suit, slipping on a pair and moving closer to the young woman.

'I can take over and give your hand a rest,' she told Rose as her gloved hand replaced the stewardess's and held the bloodied towel in place.

'Natalie,' Daniel began, looking directly at the young patient. 'I'm a doctor, my name is Daniel and this is Libby, the ship's nurse. We need to take a closer look at your injuries.'

'It's not that bad,' the young woman mumbled. 'I just need to wash up and have some painkillers for my head…and I'll be fine. Honest I will.'

'I think you'll need a bit more than that, Natalie,' Daniel said firmly before turning to the stewardess. 'Thank you, Rose. Libby and I have got this. We can take it from here.'

Her reaction to hearing the words from Daniel took Libby by surprise. They reminded her of how Daniel would say that in ER. 'Libby and I have got this,' he'd said more times than she could remember…or cared to remember at this time. They had been such a great team. Everyone had recognised how well they'd meshed on the job. They thought the same way, Libby pre-empting what Daniel would need. There had been an unspoken trust. They had worked like a hand and glove… Libby just wished it had been the same in their personal lives.

'We haven't even set sail yet, so it's not a good omen for the rest of the trip,' Rose commented before leaving the area. The young woman was still sitting upright but swaying a little. On closer inspection, Libby could see there were deep grazes to her elbows and knees with trickles of blood on her left leg. Her right slip-on-style shoe was missing but as Libby's eyes darted around, there was no sign of it close by.

'I'm going to carefully take the towel away from your head so we can look at the wound,' Libby told her softly to allay any fear. Libby had stepped into medical mode and made a conscious decision to leave their personal issues behind.

The young woman remained very still as Libby released the towel. She knew immediately it was a deep wound and would require stitches or else there would be an unattractive scar running across the victim's forehead above her left eye. Some of Natalie's blonde hair was matted into the bloodied area. The length of time between the fall and being found might have been more than first thought.

'It appears the bleeding has ceased for the time being at least,' Daniel told Libby as he leaned in and examined the wound very closely. The scent of his musky cologne filled her senses and her immediate reaction was to pull away but she couldn't. She was still supporting the young woman so she had to stay closer to Daniel than she'd ever thought she would again. She swallowed and tried to calm her racing heart. It wasn't anger surging through her veins. It was something she had forgotten how to feel.

'She will need stitches,' Libby remarked in a tone that gave away nothing of how she was feeling.

'I agree,' Daniel responded. 'However, I would suggest that since it's in a prominent place on your face, a plastic surgeon would be your best option.'

The young woman nodded but appeared unperturbed with the news about her face.

'I'm just going to check your pulse,' Libby cut in.

'I need to ask you some questions while Nurse McDonald takes your observations.

'What is your name and date of birth?' Daniel went on.

'Natalie.' The young woman paused and looked up, her eyes darting about as if searching for the words. 'Natalie, Natalie... Martin.'

'And how old are you?' Daniel asked, not taking his eyes away from his young patient as he observed her reactions.

'I'm eighteen...no, no, I'm nineteen,' she told him as she reached up to the wound area with her blood-stained fingers.

Gently but firmly Daniel directed her hand away from the wound. 'Your hands are contaminated. You need to refrain from touching the wound until it's dressed.'

'Can you please tell me today's date and the day of the week?' Libby asked.

'Monday, June tenth.'

Libby looked at Daniel. It was Sunday, June eleventh. The woman was lucid but still a little disoriented.

'Natalie, are you in significant pain anywhere other than your forehead and the scratches on your legs?' Daniel asked as he reached for a stethoscope.

'It kind of hurts all over but if you can clean me up and give me some strong painkillers I'll be okay.'

'Pulse is seventy,' Libby announced.

'Is that good or bad?'

'Your observations are good, Natalie, but it's not as simple as a strong pulse and a few painkillers. I need to better understand how you're feeling as there can be underlying issues from a significant fall. Is there any significant targeted pain or generally a battered and bruised feeling?' Daniel continued the line of questioning. Libby was aware he was not convinced that the injuries from the fall were as clear cut as they could see.

Natalie's loss of consciousness for a still undetermined period of time and a fall from a height were concerning him. He was a thorough doctor and not one to compromise a patient's health care so he was taking his time and remaining calm. He always had.

'The back of my head is the worst,' she said very slowly, purposely rolling her head in a circular motion. 'But a shot or two tonight and I'll be fine.'

'Best not to move your head that way, and I might remind you that at nineteen you're underage and would not be served alcohol on this ship. Please stay as still as possible and let me look at the back of your head,' Daniel said as he walked to the other side of the examination table and carefully checked the posterior skull region.

'As I suspected, there is an area of your skull that is somewhat depressed. For a conclusive prognosis we will need to do X-rays and you're going to need to be in hospital under observation.'

'For how long?'

'Overnight at least. I'm not sure how far you fell and for how long you were unconscious. Both are concerning me.'

Libby began to clean the wound. Careful not to dislodge the blood clot, she freed some of the matted hair and applied an antiseptic solution and sterile gauze dressing. Daniel reached over and his hand brushed hers lightly as he held the dressing in place while she reached for a soft wrap bandage.

'I'll wrap the wound,' she began, trying to steady her breathing. Even through the gloves she had felt the warmth of his hand on hers and she was surprised at her reaction. 'I don't want to use anything adhesive on her skin.'

'Good call,' Daniel replied.

The young woman was agitated but staying still enough to allow Libby to dress the wound.

'Can the plastic surgeon come on board to see me?'

'No, Natalie, the only course of action now is to clean up the wound, give you a temporary dressing and then arrange for you to disembark and transfer immediately to the local hospital. I would prefer that you are transported in an ambulance so I will make a call now and arrange for that. They may have a plastic surgeon on staff at the hospital or refer you to one. I'm not conversant with the local hospital's scope.'

'I'm not leaving,' she announced loudly. 'I'm going to the engagement party with my boyfriend, Ernest. You know, Walter's his great-uncle and he owns this yacht. You can't force me to leave.'

'I'm sorry, Natalie, but that's exactly what I'm doing and I can guarantee you that Sir Walter will not argue the point,' Daniel responded. His voice was firm but not at the volume of hers. 'It's not in your best interest to remain on board with your injuries. You need to get to the nearest hospital as soon as possible for a complete assessment…and I mean as soon as possible.

'Head injuries are not to be taken lightly—the extent

of your injuries from the fall may not become obvious immediately and the damage to your skull is concerning me. There's a risk of internal bleeding. You need a CAT scan and may be admitted to the intensive care unit dependent upon the results. While you feel fine now, don't be cavalier about the seriousness of the fall.'

'Cava what?'

'Cavalier. It means don't dismiss how serious the injury could be,' Libby explained.

'But Ernest can watch me and tell you if there's anything wrong.'

Daniel reached for the ship's phone. 'We might well be out at sea when either of you notice a problem. And that would be too late.'

'There's a helipad. I can get taken back to shore anytime.'

'While there is a helipad, there's not a helicopter on board. You could lapse into a coma without warning and it would be too late to call for the coastguard and I'm not prepared to take that chance with your life.'

'Are you serious? A coma?'

'Yes, there's always a risk, however slight, with a severe blow to the head of what we call extradural blueing from the middle meningeal artery or one of its branches and as a result a haemorrhage inside your skull. I understand it's all medical jargon to you, but I'm letting you know that it has the potential to be serious. Your well-being is my priority, Natalie, not your social life. Take another trip with Ernest, but next time don't climb an unattended rock wall.'

Ten minutes later Libby watched as paramedics arrived and secured Natalie on the barouche in preparation for the ambulance trip to the Western Miami General Hospital. Daniel provided them with the background and a copy of the medical notes that Libby had taken during the examination.

Ernest had come to say goodbye but he had chosen to remain on board. He told her not to worry and that she would be fine. He'd have shots in her honour at the party and send selfies to her. Libby could see the young woman's disappointment and anxiety about being transported to hospital was heightened by the sadness of doing it alone. Her boyfriend had chosen partying with his family over her and that had to hurt. Particularly at nineteen.

'Thank you for your assistance, Libby.'

Libby nodded to Daniel and turned to leave. Her work was done. Now she knew she needed distance more than ever.

'I will be suggesting tighter controls over the management of the climbing wall. I might suggest it's closed altogether unless there's someone experienced managing it twenty-four seven. Perhaps I'll speak to the chief stewardess and ascertain the number of young people on board who may be tempted to do something similar. I don't think there're any others but I'd rather be safe than sorry.'

'That's a sensible idea,' she said, not wanting to remain near him even a moment longer. She admired him immensely as a doctor and she worried that might somehow influence how she felt about him as a man. It had once before. From the first day Daniel had stepped into the Northern Bay General Hospital A&E where Libby had been nursing, she had been drawn to him, and history was at risk of repeating itself.

He was a skilled and knowledgeable doctor and she had adored working with him as she'd felt that every moment she did so she learned more and became a better nurse. He had taken the time to explain procedures and the reason for his diagnoses, prognoses and treatment plans, however unconventional or, at times, unpopular they might have seemed. He was thorough and methodical, leaving nothing to chance. He was also very handsome and charismatic and none of that had changed.

An empathetic bedside manner was not at the forefront on this occasion but it was understandable. Daniel wanted what was best for the young woman, and wasn't about to be swayed by her pleas. He didn't mind being the bad guy in her opinion if it meant saving her life—or at the very least keeping her pretty face from being disfigured by ugly scarring.

But Libby had to save herself from being drawn back in. She had to get away as quickly as she could because she could not afford to be swept away by her feelings.

Forgetting the past was not an option and she could not let his professional abilities overshadow the ruin he had left in his wake and the decision that still weighed heavily on her mind. She walked away from Daniel without another word.

Libby arrived back at the cabin and found Georgie waiting outside her door. She gave her the abbreviated version of the events with the climbing incident as they stepped inside.

'I wondered what took you so long. I thought it might have been a heart-to-heart with Daniel,' Georgie said as she leaned against the bathroom door.

Libby was in the tiny space, washing her hands, and

shook her head. 'Not interested. That time has passed. He's had years to reach out and explain what happened and he didn't. I'm done wanting to know.'

'Good for you. There's plenty of fish in the sea and the Caribbean is the perfect place to go fishing. Speaking of that, how about we step out and have a quick look around the yacht? I've done all the prep in the galley for tonight's dinner, which is a seafood buffet, and I've left it with the other two crew members who can manage for the next hour or so. I'll head back and put the finishing touches to it and make the dessert later. We can find somewhere to sit and enjoy a little sun. Walter wouldn't mind at all. Believe me, if he's fed well—and he will be—then all will be well in the world.'

'I'm not really in the mood, but you go,' Libby replied, deep in thought as she made her way to her still unpacked suitcase for a clean top. She had noticed a few tiny spots of blood on the one she was wearing. 'I don't want to ruin your fun.'

Socialising was the last thing on her mind. She felt like a prisoner in a glamorous floating penitentiary and wondered how she would stay sane for the next few days. No matter what she'd said to Georgie, in her heart it wasn't over and she found her mind wandering to thoughts of him and their time together…and to the son they shared.

The brief time tending to Natalie together had made it all so real again. Everything that she had struggled to forget was returning as vividly as the day it had happened. The good, the wonderful, the exciting, all of it, along with the heartache and the confusion. It was overwhelming her.

Without thinking, she reached for her pendant. Her

every reason for living was her son and she was not yet ready to share that secret with Daniel. He was a man who could sweep her off her feet, make her feel like she was so special and then disappear overnight without an explanation. Daniel was a brilliant doctor but Billy deserved more than that. He deserved stability and a loving father who would not disappear on an unexplained whim.

There was also the niggling question of whether, upon learning he was a father, Daniel might demand shared custody and Libby had no idea where Daniel lived. That was something that Libby had neither the funds nor the emotional strength to fight. She just needed time to decide whether Billy would be better off with Daniel in his life and, if so, when she would tell him.

There was much that Daniel would have to explain and prove for her to make such a huge decision and she worried that seven days and nights might not be a long enough time. Libby felt certain that if it wasn't for them being on the ship together, he would not have given her another thought.

She just wished she felt the same.

'You can't turn into a hermit because of Daniel,' Georgie said firmly. 'We've known each other since we were sixteen and you haven't changed. You're so sweet and lovely and I don't want to see you lock yourself away because of him.'

'That's not the reason…'

'Libby.' Georgie looked at her friend. 'That's a porky pie and we both know it.'

Libby frowned in Georgie's direction with no clue what her friend was talking about.

'A porky pie is a lie,' she continued, without Libby

responding. It was a lie. Daniel was the reason for her simmering anxiety and her lack of enthusiasm about everything, except getting off the ship. Disembarking the *Coral Contessa* was the one thing she was looking forward to very much but she knew something had to be resolved one way or the other before she did.

'Libby, I didn't mean to be rude or forward in any way. I just meant that you're making up an excuse not to get out and about because of whatever happened between you and Daniel. But locking yourself in the cabin won't change anything. All it will do is waste the experience of your first time on a yacht.'

'Maybe I'm making an excuse but it's complicated, Georgie, and…to be honest, I guess I'm still in shock. I never thought I'd see him again in my life.'

'Your fainting made it very clear that even hearing his name was a huge surprise and not a pleasant one. It's always complicated when men are involved. They generally manage to make a complete mess of things most of the time.'

'More than you know.'

'I guessed it didn't end well and, again, I'm not prying. You can share as much or as little as you want with me, but I'm going to share some things I know about the man.'

'Things you know about him? What things?'

'Daniel is handsome and could have pretty much any woman he wanted within ten miles of the ship but from what I've heard from the other crew members he's single and has never become involved with anyone he works with and that's not because there haven't been offers. Passengers and crew alike literally throw themselves at him, but he keeps his distance.'

'How do you know this?'

'Ships' doctors don't exist in huge numbers, and Stacey and one of my galley crew have worked with him before on larger cruise ships. It's a tight-knit community and someone as handsome and eligible as Daniel is fodder for gossip. Only there isn't any about him. He's the ultimate elusive bachelor and a gentleman. His liaisons, and there will be some, no doubt, must be fleeting and kept ashore and discreet with no drama. He's never married and he's quite private about his personal life and his family, if he has any, but he's an amazing doctor and a good and fair colleague. That's it.'

'That's a lot of background,' Libby said, still uneasy about how quickly the crew of the *Coral Contessa* had updated Georgie about Daniel. All the more reason to keep her secret safe. That would no doubt spread like wildfire and she didn't need that. Her anxiety was suddenly on the rise again.

'He's squeaky clean and that makes him even more desirable…and almost a celebrity. There are a lot of Latin lovers at sea, but he's not one of them.'

'No offence, Georgie, but I don't think I want to hear any more. I'm not ready to hear wonderful character references about my ex,' Libby said as she sat down on the bunk and slumped back against her pillows.

'I don't know how to make you feel better about the situation, Libby. I told you what I know so you can feel better about yourself. By your reaction you were clearly in love with the man and I wanted you to know, whatever happened, he's a decent man so your instincts when you fell for him were right.'

Libby closed her eyes and wished she could open them and find herself in her own bed in her own house and not staring at the lower deck of a yacht about to sail through the Caribbean. She should have paid more attention to her initial doubts about the trip and fought harder not to be sent on an adventure at sea. The reality was closer to a disaster.

'I know your intentions are good and I appreciate what you're trying to do but I don't trust my instincts about much right now.'

'Then trust mine,' Georgie said as she stepped closer again. 'You can't change anything except yourself into a swimsuit. Let's get some sun while we can. There's another few hours before Sir Walter's guests claim the sundecks for their own.'

'Like I said, you go. I'd rather stay here and call home.'

'Call home while I slip into my swimsuit and then we'll go for a walk at least. Wallowing inside your cabin won't change anything. The sun at least has a chance to change your mood and lift your spirits, so let's give it a chance. We need to relax with a fruit cocktail, non-alcoholic of course since we're working, but maybe later tonight we can switch it up for a champagne. It's not often you find yourself at sea with your absolute best friend who you haven't seen in over a decade.'

CHAPTER SIX

'ISN'T THE SUN GLORIOUS?' Georgie asked her reluctant companion. 'The view's stunning and we haven't even set sail yet. I think we're going to have a lovely time.'

'Mmm,' Libby responded, staring straight ahead as the two strolled around the deck. She had called home and spoken to Billy and her mother and everything was fine. Billy was about to have lunch and then help his grandfather build a big red racing-car bed. Her parents were spoiling their grandson and he was clearly so excited about sleeping in a racing car that night that he didn't have too much time to talk to her. Knowing that Billy was happy and not missing her was a relief.

She had changed into white shorts and a navy striped T-shirt. Georgie was in a pink and green floral bathing suit but Libby had no intention of baring that much skin. Knowing that Daniel was on board was making her self-conscious, not to mention that Bradley had packed the skimpiest of bikinis in her suitcase.

The crew were busily preparing for the final passengers yet to arrive and tending to the needs of those already on board. Sir Walter was the most important passenger and he was yet to arrive. Libby had not seen him since he had been discharged from hospital a week after his surgery and she was genuinely looking forward to seeing him again. If only it were under different circumstances.

'I'll take "mmm" for the moment but by tomorrow I'll be looking for a smidgen more enthusiasm.'

'That might be my limit, I'm sorry,' Libby said as she drew breath, unable to forget for even an instant that Daniel was at any time only a deck away from her. The thought of him was making her heart and her body react in ways that made her very uneasy. It was the most confused she had been in four years.

Georgie returned a half-smile and Libby suddenly felt pangs of guilt. Her behaviour was less than gracious after Georgie's earlier excitement to see her and the support she had shown when she'd needed it most. Libby knew she needed to lighten up. She had agreed, albeit reluctantly and under duress, to be on board for the next seven days…or six and a half, she told herself as the first day was almost half-gone.

'I'm sorry, let's walk around and find a seat in the sun. You're right, it will be lovely.'

After just over an hour of Miami sunshine, incessant chatter and a delicious pineapple smoothie each, Georgie excused herself to return to galley duties. Libby was returning to her cabin to change into her uniform when a steward caught up with her.

'Sir Walter has just boarded and wants to see you.'

'He's early. I didn't think we would see him for another hour and I haven't changed into my uniform.'

'He won't mind, I'm sure,' he told her as he led the way to their host, who was making himself comfortable on a sun lounger on the deck at the bow of the yacht.

He had an entourage of people with him but, as Libby quickly and thankfully noticed, no Daniel.

'Hello, Nurse Elizabeth. It's lovely to see you again, my dear. I hope you're not upset that I kidnapped you for a few days?'

'Hello, Sir Walter. I'm happy to be here,' she lied. While lying was not a habit of hers, it was not Sir Walter's fault that his yacht was the last place on earth she wanted to be. She wanted to appear gracious and not dampen his excitement about the cruise and his daughter's engagement party. 'I just want to keep you on your path to a full recovery on this cruise.' That was not a lie. That was Libby's sole focus. Daniel was not a focus of hers. Although avoiding him was.

'We'll see about that.' He laughed. 'You see, I'm going to enjoy what time I have left on earth and not fuss too much with healthy hoo-ha. If I want a beef Wellington with gravy then I shall have one, and I do not like exercise. At all.'

Libby knew she would have her hands full with Sir Walter. It appeared that both men of significance on the *Coral Contessa* were going to challenge her reserves.

She just needed to dig deep and rise to the occasion.

'So now we've caught up, why don't you take a look around my little yacht, make sure you know where everything is and I can sit here and catch up with my friends. I'm feeling as fit as a bull and I don't need you…'

'Are you sure?'

'Couldn't be more sure,' he told her. 'And I know you have one of those pager things, so someone will find you, or the doc, if I my ticker starts acting up.'

* * *

Libby left Walter and his group, and took an unaccompanied tour of the yacht. It was magnificent on every one of the four decks, all of which were serviced by a glass elevator. The decor was like that of an Italian hotel from a magazine, with white marble floors, ornate gilded furnishings and a ceiling in the formal dining area that was reminiscent of the Sistine Chapel.

As she passed one of the two oversized columns near the bar, a steward pushed on a small panel and to Libby's surprise the entire column opened and she saw it was filled with shelves of polished crystal glasses and decanters. Opulence was the word that came to mind everywhere she looked. She'd had no idea what a yacht of that much splendour would be worth but she knew she couldn't earn enough in a million lifetimes to buy one. Libby looked around, knowing she had something far more valuable in her life. Something money could never buy. She had her son.

After roaming for a little while longer and stumbling across the room towards the bow of the yacht, which housed a speedboat and two jet-skis, Libby thought she had seen enough. A boat on a yacht was too much for her so she made her way to her cabin to shower and change into one of the uniforms that had been hanging in the wardrobe. She pulled her slightly damp hair into a low bun at the nape of her neck and checked her appearance in the mirror on the back of her cabin door. Libby was very conscious that she wanted to appear professional and there to do her job.

It was a message she wanted to send to everyone. Including Daniel.

* * *

Libby returned to find Walter with a lit cigar in one hand and a short crystal glass of what she felt certain was whiskey over ice in the other hand. She could not mask being upset to see him smoking and drinking. She was disappointed and angry in equal amounts and suspected that was why he had sent her on a sightseeing trip around the yacht. He was completely disregarding everything he had been told in hospital before and after his bypass surgery.

He had been warned that smoking could increase his chance of blood clots and he risked a serious chest infection along with a slower healing process. It was behaviour far more dangerous than consuming a beef Wellington and she intended to tell him exactly what she thought.

'Sir Walter—' she began as she drew near, her voice not masking her distress at the situation.

'Walter, remember, I want you to call me Walter,' he returned with a laugh under the wide-brimmed hat he was now wearing.

'Fine, I will call you Walter and in return I want you to put that cigar and that drink down now. You cannot be smoking or drinking after your heart surgery.'

Walter stared back at her in silence. Libby didn't care if he fired her. In fact, that would be a blessing but it wasn't her motivation in telling him off. Keeping Walter alive and assisting him back to good health was all she cared about.

'I'm going to be blunt,' she said, staring into his eyes. 'What you're doing is reckless behaviour and you know it. You're barely five weeks out from major surgery that saved your life and you're sailing around the Caribbean, smoking and drinking and acting like a teenager. You've contracted me to be on board as your nurse and what I'm seeing is, well…silly behaviour on your part. I'm not going to stand around and pretend it's all right. I just won't. The walls of your arteries were lined with fatty plaque caused by a diet high in animal fats, refined sugar, smoking, inactivity and excessive alcohol. And you're indulging in all of that again!'

Libby lifted her chin defiantly as Walter looked back at her, taking his time to reply. It was as if each was staring the other down, not unlike the prelude to a gunfight.

'I am neither silly nor reckless in spending what time I have left sailing, young lady. This yacht and the Caribbean are the closest I get to being with my beloved late wife, Contessa. She was the love of my life and if I go, it will be while I feel close to her. I told her as much when I held her hand as she died and I know she will hold mine in the bow of this yacht if I die on it.'

Libby was taken aback at the emotion in his voice, the sentiment in his words and the tears forming in the corners of his weary eyes. She softened her tone but kept resolute in her message. 'I do understand what you're saying and how you're feeling, Walter, but you don't have to die anytime soon. You can sail as much as you like and feel close to your beloved wife for many years to come but you must stop smoking and drinking heavy liquor.'

'Well, maybe I don't want to live a great many years,' he retorted, turning away from her. 'Maybe I'm lonely and tired and I want to enjoy what little time I have left, and if I hasten the end, then so be it.'

'Please forgive me for saying this, but I think that's being quite disrespectful.'

'Disrespectful? And to whom am I being disrespectful?' His head turned back to Libby, his eyes wide and his lips cutting a thin line in his clearly irritated face.

'To the doctors and theatre nurses who saved your life.'

'They're paid to do that. It's their job, just like it's your job to take care of me for the next week so I make it to my niece's engagement. Not that I completely approve of her fiancé but nonetheless you and the doc will keep me alive to see that day.'

'And what about the day after?' Libby said, taking the empty seat beside him. One of the family entourage had quickly moved away when the polite but somewhat heated discussion had erupted. 'What about living to see her children, your great-nieces and-nephews? To bounce them on your knee and look into their gorgeous cherub faces. Don't you want to live to do that?'

'Using unborn children to get your point across,' he said butting his cigar on the ashtray nearby. 'Now, that's hitting below the belt.'

'I'll do whatever it takes, Walter, to make you see reason. You've survived a massive operation and now it's up to you to take care of yourself and since you're from the UK, if you do as your medical team say you may even make a hundred and receive a letter from the Queen. Wouldn't that make your day? You could frame the letter and hang it in your suite or perhaps behind the bar for everyone to see.'

'Using Her Majesty now. To what ends will you go? Have you no shame, Libby?'

'No shame at all when it comes to your health. I will do and say whatever I must to keep you healthy.'

'Well, the whole hundredth birthday and the Queen

won't work,' he argued with a raised eyebrow. 'My hundredth birthday is twenty-one years away so I'm sure if I make it that far it won't be the Queen who'll be writing to me. She'll be in a better place by then.'

'The reigning monarch, then,' Libby cut in. 'Does it matter who signs the letter from Buckingham Palace? Let's just get you to the age to qualify first.'

'Lovely thought, but I'm painfully aware that while the survival rate for bypass patients who make it to five weeks after the operation is pretty darn good, everything changes after about seven or eight years. The chance of me falling off my perch jumps considerably so I'll be lucky to see my ninetieth birthday let alone my hundredth. Anyway, I've decided I'm going to damn well enjoy the next few years and leave the rest to fate. I'm most certainly not going to spend what years I have left sitting in an armchair, looking out of a bay window with a mohair rug on my knees…and a cup of Earl Grey tea in my hand.'

'With all due respect, Walter, there's quite a lot of space between a nursing home and smoking cigars and drinking whiskey in this very ornate floating bar.'

Walter eyed Libby in silence again. His lips once again formed a hard line in his wrinkled face but he didn't look annoyed. She couldn't read his expression at all. Libby knew she should never play poker with him as he was giving nothing away. Her stomach suddenly dropped.

Had she gone too far? She really liked Walter but she couldn't sit by and watch him risk his health unnecessarily, but neither did she want to appear unprofessional and cross the line. Under his gruff exterior, he was a kind and generous man and, quite apart from her duty of care as a nurse, she had grown fond of him while he had been in her care in hospital. She wanted to see him live as many years as he could and not throw them away on cigars and alcohol.

His lips turned to a smirk as he grudgingly placed his glass on the table.

'I like you, young lady. You have what I think you Americans called *spunk* and what we British call unbridled determination. Some might even call it stubbornness, but a word of warning: I too have stubbornness in bucketloads. It's how I built my empire and I'm not going to roll over and play dead anytime soon. You'll have your hands full if you think I'm going to change my ways easily.'

Libby climbed to her feet. She'd been worried that she had overstepped the mark but by his tone and the fact he'd said he liked her, clearly she hadn't said too much.

'I'm up for the challenge, Walter.'

'And what challenge would that be?'

Libby turned to see Daniel standing far too close for her liking and quickly she turned her face back to her patient. Her heart had instantly picked up speed and she hated herself for the way she was reacting. She should be angry whenever she saw him. Furious, in fact. But she wasn't.

Her body had no shame, she realised. Immediately upon hearing the timbre of his voice or seeing his tall, dark silhouette or when the scent of his cologne overtook her senses, she lost all reason and self-respect. And Daniel's effect on her wasn't lessening in impact. She had already witnessed how handsome he looked in his crisp white uniform with its stark contrast to his tanned Mediterranean skin. She didn't need to look at him again and be reminded of that. Everything about him and the way he made her feel frightened her.

She was just grateful that all of what she was thinking and feeling was not obvious to anyone else.

'It appears, Daniel, that Libby thinks she can change my *reckless* ways and make me see a ripe old age so I can get a letter from Buckingham Palace,' Walter told him with a wink. 'But I'm trying to tell her that it's pointless to try to change a man. Once we're out of nappies, or diapers as the Americans call them, no woman can change us. It's really quite pointless to try, don't you agree?'

Libby closed her eyes. The words resonated in her heart. Daniel, she suspected, was a man who didn't want to change. He was a man who was happy with the way he lived his life. Loving and leaving women with no thought for the hurt he caused or the hearts he broke.

'I believe, Walter, that under the right circumstances and with the right incentive, a man can change.'

Libby was taken aback by Daniel's answer to Walter's question. *The right incentive?* Did that mean she hadn't been incentive enough for him to change his philandering ways all those years ago? And what did he mean by the right circumstances? She was terribly confused and she felt anger starting to brew deep inside. Strangely, she liked the feeling of anger. It gave her perspective and control over the situation.

'Codswallop!' Walter bellowed. 'That's all New Age, politically correct codswallop. I have no intention of changing my ways, no matter how sweet or how pretty the messenger may be.'

Libby shook her head at the backhanded compliment as she refused to look in Daniel's direction. She didn't want to see the reaction on his face.

'Let's not debate whether men can change,' Libby suddenly interjected to put the conversation, and her thoughts, back on a professional level. 'Let's get back to the issue at hand. Your health and the responsibility of your ship's medical team.'

'Let me see if I have this correctly. I'm paying you both very well—not to mention handsomely donating to a hospital in San Francisco—to have you accompany me on this trip with the sole purpose of preventing me from having fun and reprimanding me at every available opportunity?'

'No.' Daniel stepped closer as he spoke. 'Walter, Libby and I are here to ensure you have the best chance of a full recovery. You must understand that the surgery you underwent is not a cure for coronary heart disease. It's a second chance if you change your ways, but if you don't you will be right back to square one in a very short period of time and we don't want that.'

'Oh, dear, I have no chance here. You're both singing from the same hymn sheet,' he said with an expression of defeat crossing his face. 'Fine, I will refrain from my wicked ways for the next week but after that, when you two are out of my sight, all bets are off. I will do as you ask for the next week purely because I can't handle seven days of incessant nagging...in stereo.'

With that he stood up and stretched his back from side to side. 'I think I will have a nice shower and change for dinner. Georgie is preparing some of my favourite food and I intend to enjoy it...without a cigar or whiskey, as ordered by my keepers, but I'll damn well have dessert if I fancy it. And if either of you try to stop me, I'll have you thrown overboard and you'll be swimming with the fish tonight.'

Daniel smirked and Libby's lips formed a half-smile as Walter left. Suddenly his entourage followed suit and dispersed, leaving Libby and Daniel standing together.

Libby looked out to sea for a moment before she began to walk away. Being alone with Daniel as the sun began to set was a recipe for disaster. The setting was far too romantic and she knew, despite all the unanswered questions and her simmering anger, there was the smallest chance that she might still be vulnerable to him.

And she could not afford to go down that path again. There was so much more at stake this time.

'Please don't go, Libby,' he began. 'I know I said I'd find a way to ensure we're not working together but perhaps we could sit and talk sometime. I do think fondly of the time we spent together.'

'Not fondly enough to get in touch any time over the last four years,' she spat back at him coldly.

CHAPTER SEVEN

'MR HUDSON.' LIBBY addressed the man she had directed to follow her inside the makeshift infirmary. She paused as she closed the door. 'Please come in.'

'It would be my pleasure,' he told her, then continued, 'But you can call me Maxwell.'

Libby drew a short breath. His response had been followed by a peculiar stare in her direction. Her intuition was telling her that Maxwell's gaze was not purely patient-nurse. His eyes seemed to hover on her lips, not meeting her eyes at all. It was odd but she shrugged it off. Maybe his hearing was compromised and he was lip reading. Some of the older patients she had cared for over the years did that, although Maxwell appeared to be in his late forties but she couldn't be sure. He was not particularly tall and quite stocky in build, with a receding hairline so his age was difficult to pinpoint.

'Please sit down,' she said, motioning towards the chair adjacent to the cabin desk as she stepped inside the en suite bathroom and washed her hands. 'The doctor is not available, but I can take some notes and see what the issue is and call for him if there's anything urgent. He isn't too far away.' Just far enough to allow her to feel more comfortable.

'He can't go too far—we're on a ship. Unless he jumps overboard and then it would just be you and me.'

His response was odd and made her feel uncomfortable. And the way he was looking at her when she reappeared with freshly scrubbed hands even more so.

'It was a joke,' he said with a snigger and a raised eyebrow. Still standing a little too close for Libby's liking, he continued, 'I'm sure he wouldn't jump off the ship—at least not while you're on here.'

Libby was not impressed but was determined to remain professional and move past the blatant flirting.

'What appears to be your problem today?' Libby asked in a monotone.

Maxwell stared at her in silence, his eyebrow still arched.

'Is everything all right, Mr Hudson?' Libby continued in the same professional but unemotional tone, only a little louder.

'Call me Maxwell. It's less formal,' he said with a smirk.

'Maxwell, as I said, please take a seat…' she motioned again to the chair '…and tell me what the problem appears to be.'

He sat down without taking his eyes off her. 'It's my back. I fell asleep in the sun and now I'm burnt.'

'I see. Please remove your shirt and I can take a look.'

Maxwell began unbuttoning his brightly coloured shirt, patterned with flamingos and palm trees. His eyes remained fixed on hers and he mimicked a male entertainer as he slowly undid each button, making Libby's discomfort grow by the second.

'I don't see a ring, pretty lady.'

* * *

Libby had a fairly good idea where the conversation was heading and she had no intention of helping it along. Quite the opposite, she was going to stop it dead in the water by ignoring it.

'It's such a lovely day and I'm sure you want to get back to the group so let's look at your sunburn.' Her tone was courteous and professional as she slipped on latex gloves. She trusted she was making it clear she was not interested in his line of questioning.

'I'd rather stay in the cabin with you.'

Libby drew a deep breath. The man had the faint smell of whiskey and a strong smell of suntan lotion and bad cologne. The combined scents were as unpleasant as his personality. 'Well, I have a lot to do, so let's get you seen to and back out there.'

'It must be a bit dreary not being able to join the party,' he continued, still not following Libby's clear line of conversation.

'I'm on board to work. That's the only reason I'm here and I'm happy about that. Looking after Sir Walter will keep me busy enough.'

'When you finish your shift, you should come up on deck and get some sunshine with me.'

'I don't have a shift, I'm on call all the time. Now please turn around so I can look at the sunburn.'

'It's not that bad actually.' The man's mouth curled into a grin that immediately turned Libby's stomach. She had feared the worst and very quickly her fears were being realised.

'I came here to see you.'

'Then we're finished here.'

'Not so fast,' the man said. Standing up and moving

closer, he grabbed her wrist with his stubby fingers. 'I watched you sitting by the pool yesterday with your girl-friend, in your skimpy shorts, and I did some digging around to find out about you. It seems you're single... and available.'

Libby tried to pull free but the man moved even closer. His breath was warm on her neck as he stared into her eyes. Suddenly, being in such close proximity to him, she noticed the stench of alcohol was not so faint.

'Let go of me now.' Her voice was raised and her tone cold as she pulled her arm free and moved to the other side of the room. A sense of panic was stirring in-side. She was alone in the cabin with a drunken, lech-erous man.

'Come on, don't play coy. The doctor's not here. It's just you and me. The rest of the group are up on deck, a long way from us, so let's make friendly.'

'Get away from me,' Libby yelled, trying to quell her anxiety. The situation had escalated from uncomfort-able to dangerous very quickly. Her heart was picking up speed and she felt the heat rising from her core. Her fight-or-flight response was kicking in as she backed up to a wall-mounted telephone.

'Come on, you and I both know you signed up to have some fun. If you weren't the type to *party* you would've stayed on dry land,' he said as he reached for the zip on his shorts. 'And I'm the man who can give you a good time, right here, right now. I've got plenty of time to seal the deal.'

The door opened abruptly as the man reached for Libby. Seemingly unperturbed, he ignored the sound and continued to fumble with his shorts.

Daniel was standing in the doorway. With powerful

strides he crossed the room, grabbed the man by the collar and spun him around. Libby could see the rage in Daniel's eyes. She had never seen him like that before. With her emotions on a roller-coaster, it both frightened and calmed her at the same time.

'Don't ever speak to a woman like that again,' Daniel roared. The volume and tone of voice commanded attention.

The man straightened up and looked Daniel up and down. Ignoring the uniform, he continued to display a level of arrogance that Libby found appalling.

'Chill out, buddy. Go back on duty and do your steward thing. It's all good…the little lady's happy to chat with me.'

'Nurse McDonald is most definitely not happy to speak with you. She's made that clear. Now leave.' Daniel stood his ground and Libby felt very safe and protected by the man she had wanted to hate.

'Like I said, chill out. It's all good.'

'I said leave. Now.'

'Make me,' the now irate passenger said with a cocky expression on his alcohol-flushed face. He suddenly began shifting unsteadily from side to side on his feet as if he were in a boxing ring.

As Daniel stretched out his long arm to escort him outside, the man took a swing at him, his right hand clenched into a fist, trying to connect with Daniel's ribs.

'Daniel, be careful,' Libby called out with concern etching her voice. Concern for the man she had never wanted to see again in her life but was so relieved to see at that moment.

Daniel dodged the man's punch as it cut through the

air. 'Don't be stupid,' Daniel told him. 'Just leave before you get hurt.'

'By who? You?' the passenger laughed scornfully as he tried yet again to punch Daniel but this time taking aim at his stomach.

Libby could see that Daniel had no choice but to act in self-defence. He deflected the man's punch with his forearm, then, grabbing the man's arm, twisted it behind his back and forced him to the floor in a secure hold, his knee resting firmly on the man's back.

'Please dial nine, Libby. It will put you through to the bridge. Ask the captain to send down the first mate and a steward to take care of this creep. I'm going to insist this excuse for a man is escorted off the ship when we arrive in port tomorrow morning.'

Without hesitation, Libby did as Daniel asked and explained the situation before turning back to see Maxwell restrained, red faced and unable to move as Daniel still had him pinned to the floor. Maxwell's eyes were darting about, his cheek pressed against the floor, and he was muttering inaudible comments to no one in particular. Perhaps his sober self was having regrets, she thought. She didn't care. He was a predator and she was relieved that Daniel was going to have him removed from the ship. Under the influence of alcohol or not, he was a risk that needed to be mitigated.

'You can't throw me off.'

'I can and I will,' Daniel said in a voice that continued to bring reassurance and calm to Libby. 'I'll speak with Walter immediately.'

'But I'm family,' Maxwell muttered. 'He won't throw me off. He'll throw you two off for treating me this way.'

'I don't think so, buddy. You're a risk to every woman

on the ship and I'm not going to allow that risk to remain on board.'

The first mate and two stewards arrived within minutes to find Daniel still restraining Maxwell.

'There's always one who overdoes the alcohol and oversteps the mark,' the slightly taller of the well-built trio said. 'We can take it from here. I assume you'll be speaking with the captain or Sir Walter. This guy's probably family so it might be difficult to drop him off at the next port. If they keep him on board we'll just have him followed when he's out of his cabin.'

'I don't care who he is, he's getting off this vessel, no ifs, no buts about that. He's gone.'

Thwarted in his attempt to seduce Libby, and no doubt feeling humiliated by the ease with which Daniel had grappled him to the floor, the man had ceased struggling. He lay in a crumpled heap with Daniel clearly in control. But it was not lost on Libby that without Daniel it could have ended very differently.

It could have ended very badly.

As the door closed, leaving them alone, Daniel turned to Libby and looked at her for the longest moment before he spoke. His blue eyes were piercing her soul with the intensity of his gaze. It was as unnerving as it was comforting.

'Are you all right, Libby?' he finally asked in a voice that was strong and masculine but coloured with layers of warmth and tenderness.

His concern seemed genuine and his expression was serious but Libby could not answer for a moment. She was once again seeing Daniel and the man she had been so very close to, not the man she had wanted to forget.

His eyes were drawing her in just as they had in the past. They were like two brilliant blue crystals but they were far from cold. And, against her will, their warmth was thawing her heart.

'I'm…fine,' she managed to say, with so many mixed emotions colouring every thought. His eyes looked so much like her precious son's that it caught her breath.

'I'm not so sure,' he replied and crossed the room, gently pulling her into his arms.

Libby wanted to fight him, she wanted to pull away but she couldn't. She fell into his embrace. Into the warmth of his chest and the strength of his arms around her. It was everything she needed at that moment. The past was gone and the future didn't matter. Libby just wanted to remain in the comfort of Daniel's arms for as long as she could.

There was a knock on the open door and they both turned to see Walter standing there with the chief stewardess beside him. Daniel dropped his arms and Libby stepped back, immediately creating space between them.

'I heard what happened, Libby,' Walter began. 'I'm so sorry, my dear. Are you all right?'

'I'm… I'm fine, thank you.' Her voice quavered from the reality of what had almost happened with Maxwell… and the embrace she had shared with Daniel.

'It appears you're fine because of our doctor.'

'Yes.' Libby nodded and looked fleetingly at Daniel. He was staring back at her, his concern for her evident in his expression. Her heart was torn with so many emotions. He had come to her rescue despite the way she had spoken to him the day before. Despite the way she had pushed him away.

'You're a strong woman, Libby,' Walter continued. 'I know that first hand but what you just faced is not something to brush off lightly. Maxwell is leaving the yacht tomorrow morning. The captain has called the coastguard and they're picking him up first thing and what they do with him, frankly, I don't care. For what he just did, I'd drop him in the middle of the ocean, to be honest, if I could get away with it. I've never liked him but he married his way into the family years ago and we've never been able to shake him. Well, we have now. And for good.'

'Thank you, Walter.'

'Don't thank me, Libby, thank Daniel. He was your knight in shining armour, rushing to your rescue, and it's a good thing he did,' Walter interjected. 'Now, you need to have a good rest in your cabin or on deck. You do not have to fuss over me for the rest of the day. I've told the steward to lock Maxwell in his cabin and if he tries to leave they can find a broom closet. I don't care where they damn well put him. They could strap him to a jet-ski for all I care.

'We'll let him sleep off the booze in preparation for his exit from the yacht, and the family, tomorrow. I'll be glad to see the back of him. He's been a leach for years but now he's crossed the line. I'm just so very sorry he stayed long enough to do this to you.'

'It wasn't your fault; no one could have known.'

'While that may be true, my dear, I'm going to try to make it up to you by having your belongings brought up to one of the empty suites on this deck.'

'There's no need, really.'

'Yes, there absolutely is a need,' Walter argued. 'That excuse for a man tried to assault you and would have succeeded if it wasn't for Daniel. The suite is adjacent to Daniel's and I think it might be reassuring for you to have him close by.'

With that, Walter and the chief stewardess left the cabin.

The suite next to Daniel's cabin? Libby wasn't sure that was such a good idea. For anyone.

'I'm truly sorry that happened...' Daniel began.

'You have nothing to apologise for,' Libby cut in, never having expected to say those words to him. 'I... I don't know what I would have done if you hadn't arrived.'

'Don't think about it, Libby. It's over and he's gone. For good, so you can relax for the rest of the journey knowing you don't have to look over your shoulder.'

Libby drew in a deep breath in an effort to still her nerves—about the attack and about being in the arms of her saviour. Both were playing on her mind.

'But how did you get here so quickly?' she asked with a curious expression on her face.

'I was just outside the cabin.'

'From when he arrived?'

'A minute or two afterwards,' Daniel told her, nodding his head and running his fingers through his hair. 'I know how you feel about me, Libby, and your determination not to spend time with me, and I don't blame you. I do understand. But I'd previously seen the jerk being incredibly disrespectful to the female crew members. He looked like potential trouble.

'I know the type too well. Too much sun and too much alcohol. I was going to raise the matter with Walter and the captain tonight but when I heard he was heading to see you with a medical condition I followed him and waited nearby. It's not that I don't trust in your ability to manage a situation as a nurse, Libby. Believe me, I've witnessed how you handle the most volatile situations in the ER but this was different. You were alone in a cabin and I feared it could go very wrong.'

Libby said nothing. Her anxiety was abating by the moment and, against her better judgement, her desire to once again be in Daniel's strong arms was growing by the second.

'When you raised your voice, I knew that, despite your rules, I had no choice but to step in.'

Libby looked at him sheepishly and in a way she had not expected to ever again. He was not the man who had broken her heart, he was her handsome protector.

'I'm glad you did,' she said softly.

Daniel looked at her in silence for the longest time and she felt her heart melting. All the feelings she had buried were starting to resurface and she wasn't sure how to fight them. Or if she even wanted to try. The urge to feel his strong arms around her again was over-whelming. And unexpected. Libby suddenly saw Daniel for the man she had fallen in love with all those years ago. She was looking at the man who had captured her heart. And the way he was looking at her at that moment made her wonder if perhaps he had not forgotten what they had shared either. There were questions that needed answering…but did she want to know the answers now? They had a week to unpack the past. It was a silly way to think but her heart was leading her thoughts.

She was so confused at that moment. Adrenalin was still surging through her body, along with something else. A warm feeling. A feeling of safety. A feeling of something she couldn't define.

But she liked it and realised she'd missed that feeling. And she'd missed him.

CHAPTER EIGHT

DANIEL STOOD LOOKING at Libby. He wanted her with every fibre of his being. He wanted to pull her back into his arms and carry her to his bed. He wanted to make love to her more than anything he had ever wanted. But he couldn't. It wasn't right for so many reasons. She was vulnerable. And he knew whatever they would share would only be for a few days. It couldn't be for ever. And Libby deserved better than that.

Libby deserved a forever man. And he could never be that. He had to step back. He had to walk away again but this time in the light of day and before he lost the ability to do it a second time.

'As long as you're okay, I should go,' Daniel said abruptly, pulling them both back to reality.

As he stepped away he fought the need to taste the sweetness of her mouth. It was a battle he had to win against his own desire for the woman so close to him he could smell the soft scent of her skin. He would recognise that scent anywhere. It was Libby's scent. It had been in his memory for the longest time.

But they could never be that close again.

No matter how much he wanted to be with Libby, Daniel knew he couldn't. That would be taking advantage of the situation. Taking advantage of her need to feel comforted after what she had just faced. Daniel knew that walking away all those years ago had been cruel but he believed his reasons had made it justified. Doing it again would be unforgivable.

He had to accept that being together wasn't in the stars for them. Fate had very different ideas for his future and he knew he cared for Libby too much to put her through what lay ahead for him. He wished with all his heart that the life ahead for him was a simple one that could include the most beautiful, kind, wonderful redhead he had ever met, but it couldn't.

His life would play out very differently from the one she deserved.

As he made his way to the door, he turned back to her. 'I'm sorry for what happened today, Libby. And, trust me, he will be gone in the morning. You'll never see his face again.'

Libby was taken aback. Daniel had just pushed her away. It was just as she had asked but that had been before she had fallen into his arms again. Before she had realised that she loved that feeling.

And wanted more.

Her heart sank a little. Her knight in shining armour was just passing through. Yet again. She felt so stupid for getting her hopes up and letting her heart be tempted, if only for a moment, toward the path that had broken it so completely all those years ago.

Biting the inside of her cheek, Libby watched Daniel leave the cabin and close the door behind him. And close the door on any chance for them, she told herself.

She would never be that stupid again. Clearly, she

meant nothing to him or he would not have behaved so dismissively. He would not have walked away, leaving her standing there like a stranger he had rescued. Like any other colleague, not a woman who had fallen in love with him. Who had slept with him, no matter how long ago it might have been.

Libby couldn't help but wonder why the universe had brought Daniel back into her life for only a few days. Perhaps it was to let her know he was not the right man for her. To remind her of what he had done and could do again.

To remind her that she was a strong woman, a mother and a nurse, and that was all she needed to be. She didn't need Daniel Dimosa and now she had five days to prove that to herself.

And to work out exactly what sort of man he really was. And if there would be a place in her son's life for him.

Daniel had no choice but to put distance between them. He was close to losing the ability to see reason and surrendering to his desire to pull Libby to him and tell her everything. Tell her that he hadn't wanted to leave her all those years ago. Tell her why he'd had to go but how much he wished he'd never left. But he couldn't do any of that so keeping her at bay was his only defence.

Sombrely he walked back to his cabin and shut the door. He needed to shut his heart on Libby. He went into the bathroom and washed his face with cold water. Staring into the mirror as he patted his skin dry with a hand towel, he knew he was in trouble. Libby McDonald was still in his heart and now she was within reach. And tonight she would be even closer. Her cabin would be right next to his. She would be lying in her bed with only a thin wall between them. A wall he would gladly break down, if only he could.

Stepping away from the mirror, he crossed to the open doors of his balcony. Looking out across the still blue water, all he could see was Libby's beautiful face.

He was struggling to understand why the world had brought them together, only to tear them apart.

That night, as he lay awake in his bed, Daniel thought back to the day he had first laid eyes on Libby at the Northern Bay General Hospital in San Francisco. With a short-term contract as head of ER, Daniel had instantly been taken by the beauty of the redheaded nurse who had efficiently organised everyone and everything in sight. As she'd rushed from one bay to the next, directing paramedics and nurses alike, he'd also seen the sweetness of her face and, as he'd drawn closer, the kindness in her eyes. The way she had engaged with the anxious patients and their loved ones was nothing quite like he had witnessed before.

The days had become weeks and as he'd spent more time working closely with Libby in ER, the more and more he'd come to appreciate her extraordinary ability as a nurse. She'd managed the younger nurses as if she had been doing it for decades yet he'd felt sure she was only in her late twenties. And the desire to impart knowledge and give guidance along the way to the young nurses and the medical students had had her staying back some days long after her shift had ended. She'd swept them up on a journey with her in the love she had for nursing.

Libby was born to have a career in medicine, he'd soon realised. She was a natural and, against his better judgement, and everything he had told himself and the rules he had lived by, he'd soon felt himself falling for her. When they'd worked the same shift in ER she had pre-empted his needs and together they'd managed the most difficult cases, some with wonderful outcomes, others ending in tragedy, but they had done it in a way he had never experienced before. And she'd brought comfort to every situation.

Daniel rolled over in bed and stared at the ceiling as his mind travelled back to the night they had crossed the line. The night he had reached out for her not as a colleague but as a lover.

It had been the most wonderful evening, a hospital fundraiser with an Easter theme. There had been oversized glitter-covered eggs in floral arrangements on every one of the one hundred and fifty tables, and six-foot stuffed rabbits placed at the entrance dressed in waistcoats and top hats. Daniel had worn a tuxedo as it had been a black-tie affair. The women had worn glamorous floor-length gowns, adorned with jewels, some real and some costume, and the men were a sea of black suits.

But Daniel had seen none of it once Libby had arrived. His breath had been taken away as she'd walked into the room wearing the most stunning white sequined gown. As she'd turned to greet another guest, his eyes had roamed the bare curve of her back. Her red hair had been swept to one side and as she'd caught him staring at her, she'd smiled the most beautiful smile back at him. Immediately, he'd realised she was not only the most gorgeous woman in the world, and without doubt the most amazing nurse, she was dangerously close to being the love of his life.

He'd noticed they were seated on opposite sides of the same table so he had politely, and with the other guests' approval, rearranged the seating to be next to her. They'd chatted all night about everything and anything. And then Daniel had asked her to dance.

It had been a dance like no other. As he'd taken Libby in his arms, her body had moulded to his, the softness of her perfume filling his senses. Her hair had brushed against his face and when she'd laughed and rested her head ever so lightly on his shoulder, he'd never wanted the night to end.

It had been after midnight when the band finished and their last dance had come to an end. Daniel had offered to drive Libby home and she'd accepted, with a smile that had lit up the room and his heart. When he'd walked her to the door, he leaned in to kiss her goodnight on the cheek but his lips had moved to find hers in the porchlight. Passion had overtaken them both and she'd invited him inside.

It had been the most wonderful night. He would never forget it but he would always regret it too. He should not have crossed the line.

With only a sheet covering his body, Daniel turned and stared out to sea. The curtains were open as they always were and the moonlight was dancing on the gently rolling black waves, painting them silver. Daniel had seen it many times before but tonight was different. Tonight he knew that Libby could be looking at the same darkened horizon from the window in the suite next to his.

The next morning, he woke with a resolve to keep his promise to himself and his family, no matter how difficult it might be. He was returning to Chezlovinka in four days. He could not complicate it further, neither would he ever hurt Libby again. There was a divide between them that he could never again cross. This time he could not afford to get swept up in his feelings.

Libby had finished breakfast when he arrived on deck, looking for her. He had taken a call from the chief stewardess when he'd stepped from the shower about a crew member who was unwell.

'Good morning, Libby.'

She turned and smiled a half-smile in his direction. 'Good morning, Daniel.'

He wanted to ask if she had slept well but decided to stay away from any personal conversation and keep it about work only. 'I hope you can put yesterday behind you. The coastguard picked up Maxwell early this morning.'

Libby nodded. 'Good to hear.' Her reply was without emotion and it made Daniel wonder what she might be thinking, but he knew he had no right to ask.

'If it's okay with you, we need to make a crew cabin call.'

'Why do you need me?' she asked curtly as she placed her plate back on the end of the buffet with others that had been used by guests.

'It's a young woman. She sounds a little distressed and is complaining of gastro symptoms. I hope to hell it's not, because we know that can spread through the ship very quickly. Her symptoms do sound vague but I'm also hoping it's not appendicitis. I would ordinarily go alone, as it's nothing I can't manage, but she asked for a female doctor. When we explained that wasn't possible, she asked for you to attend with me.'

'That's fine. Whatever she wants,' Libby replied matter-of-factly.

He suspected it was not her ideal situation, but she was showing him professional courtesy and he appreciated that.

'Thank you, Libby. I've got my bag with extra gloves, masks and a couple of disposable gowns just in case it is gastroenteritis,' he told her as he began walking in the direction of the glass elevator.

'If it is, how do you plan on controlling that on board?' Libby asked as she followed him.

'If I consider it a risk, I'll take away her swipe card and secure the cabin. If she has a cabin buddy we will keep an eye on them too and quarantine her in another cabin if possible. I don't like to do it but sometimes it's necessary even on a yacht this size. There's still four days' cruising to go and it would be unfair to the other passengers and particularly nasty for Walter.'

'Let me take that,' she said, reaching for the small bag. Her soft skin brushed against his as her fingers took the handle. His heart unexpectedly began racing as he had not been expecting her touch.

Libby suddenly released hold of the bag and stepped away from the elevator door. Neither made eye contact but each automatically created a distance between them. Daniel's reaction reaffirmed to him that it was going to be the most challenging four days of his life. He was still unsure how Libby felt but he realised it was best he didn't know.

They reached the cabin within a few minutes and Daniel checked his pager.

'The young woman's name is Alexandra and she just confirmed that she's been vomiting for two days now.'

Libby pulled from her bag the two disposable gowns, masks and a pair of gloves for each of them, which they immediately donned before knocking. Daniel had a swipe card that opened every one of the ship's cabins in case of an emergency.

'Come in,' a very drained and weary female voice called out.

Daniel and Libby stepped inside the tiny cabin with no windows. It was on the lowest deck and not too far from Libby's original cabin. Alexandra, still dressed in pink pyjamas, was sitting on a chair with her head resting in her hands. Her complexion was drained of any hint of colour.

'Hello, I'm Dr Dimosa and this is Nurse McDonald but please call us Daniel and Libby,' Daniel said, then looked at Libby for approval.

It was after the fact, but Libby nodded her agreement; she was happy to use her less formal first name and with what they were facing she wasn't overly fussed whatever they called her.

'I'm Alex,' the woman said in a strained voice and little energy behind her words. 'I've seen you both around but I didn't know what you did. I'm a cleaner. I do some galley work now and then but mainly clean the suites.'

'Please tell us what's happening and how you're feeling now,' Daniel said.

'I've been throwing up for two days and I'm not sure if it's something I ate or sea sickness but whatever it is I feel dreadful.'

'When did this start? And what were your initial symptoms?' Daniel continued, as he reached back to find Libby was already holding the digital thermometer he wanted. He couldn't help but smile to himself. Naturally she had known what he would be needing next; she always had.

'It was about two days ago, when I woke up. I thought it was something I ate because I felt a bit queasy,' the woman began.

Daniel rested the thermometer gently inside the woman's ear and it quickly beeped the reading. 'Thirty-six point five,' he reported to Libby, who was already taking notes. 'You don't have a temperature. Not even a low-grade fever.'

'Is that good? What does it mean?'

'It means your body's not fighting a bacterium or virus so there must be another reason for the nausea,' he said as he turned to find Libby reaching for the thermometer, discarding the disposable cap, wiping the handle clean with antibacterial wipes and returning it to the medical bag. She was her ever efficient self.

'But what can you give me to make it stop? I've been vomiting for hours and my stomach hurts,' the woman asked. 'And I want to get back to work.'

'Before I give you anything, I would like to know what we are dealing with.'

'I feel like death warmed up again, but...' she paused as she made her way to the bunk and lay down, pulling the covers up to her chin protectively '...it did improve both days after lunch.'

'So the nausea stopped completely after lunchtime?'

'Yes, I had some dry toast and then by dinnertime I was fine and then it started again the next morning. Last night I was fine again and I ate a good dinner and could work but now today it's back,' she said with her eyes starting to close. 'I'm exhausted with all of this throwing up. Is it seasickness? I've never worked on a boat before.'

'No, Alexandra, I don't think so.'

'Then what is it?' she mumbled wearily, her blue eyes as pale and drawn as her skin.

'Your lack of fever and the transient nausea are leading me to believe it might be a case of morning sickness…'

'Morning sickness?' The young woman almost yelled her response as she sat bolt upright. 'Are you telling me I'm pregnant?'

Libby silently agreed with Daniel's diagnosis. While it wasn't how she had felt when she'd been pregnant, it was a common symptom during the first trimester of pregnancy. For her entire pregnancy she had been overtaken by cravings for food she couldn't ordinarily stomach and, once she had given birth, never ate again.

'I'm putting it forward as a possibility,' he said calmly. 'We would need to confirm with a pregnancy test and then bloodwork.'

'I can't be pregnant. It's not possible,' she said, shaking her head as she slumped back against the pillows.

'You haven't had sex in the last month?'

Alexandra looked down at her hands, they were trembling slightly in her lap.

'Or months,' Daniel added. 'If you are pregnant, you may have conceived a few months ago and be further along in the pregnancy.'

'This is a mess,' she said, turning back to face Daniel and Libby with tears welling in her eyes. 'I haven't had a period in over eight weeks but I thought it was the stress of the separation. I left my husband six weeks ago.'

'I'm sorry,' Daniel and Libby said simultaneously.

Libby leaned in and instinctively put her arm around the young woman to comfort her.

'We were told we couldn't have children naturally—' Alexandra continued.

'Again,' Daniel cut in as he looked at the woman with compassion, 'I'm not saying that you are pregnant but it's something we need to consider as the symptoms do align.'

'I can't believe it,' she returned, as she began shaking her head again. 'If it's true, the timing couldn't be worse. I just secured the job with Sir Walter and I really need to keep it. I'm employed to clean the yacht when he cruises and look after his house in Miami the rest of the time. He's a good boss and I need the money to pay rent now that I'm not living with my husband.'

Daniel nodded. 'Walter is a good man, Alex, and I can have a word with him once we know if you're pregnant and see what sort of arrangement can be made for maternity leave. Do you have any other support at home?'

Libby pulled her arm away slowly and turned her attention to the medical bag nearby. She wondered if there was a pregnancy test inside. It was a long shot but if there was one on board it would either confirm or negate the pregnancy diagnosis and ensure any decisions made by Alexandra were based on fact.

'No, my mother and father passed away in an accident in Mexico three years ago. It was just my husband and me and now…now it's just me.'

Libby was surprised to find a two-window pregnancy test. While it was what she wanted, it wasn't what was normally in a medical bag—but, then, she surmised that a medical bag on a cruise ship was not a regular medical bag. She checked the date then held it up for Daniel, her eyes signalling her intention to suggest Alex take the test. He nodded his response.

'There's a pregnancy test here,' Libby announced in a low and equally calm voice. 'Would you like to go to the bathroom and find out one way or another? As Daniel said, you'll need bloods when you return to shore but these over-the-counter pregnancy tests become more accurate all the time.'

'How does it work?'

'It will detect the hormone chorionic gonadotropin. When an egg's fertilised and attaches to your uterine wall, the placenta begins to form and produces this hormone, and it appears in your bloodstream and your urine. As you get further along in pregnancy, the hormone levels rise more rapidly, doubling every couple of days. That's why if the test is positive, you'll need to see your obstetrician in the next week or so to gauge how far along you are in your pregnancy.'

The young woman reached in silence to take the test kit from Libby and then swung her feet around and slowly moved to stand up. She was still visibly weak so Libby held her arm as she made her way to the bathroom.

'Do you know what to do?' Libby asked. 'It's a two-window test so two lines indicate positive and a single line is negative. But, remember, while the positive result is generally accurate, the negative may not be definite and if the symptoms continue you may want to visit your GP for bloodwork.'

'I've done this too many times before and each time it's been negative and that never changed with a blood test,' she said as she stepped inside the tiny bathroom.

'We're nearby, if you need us,' Libby said without

making any further comment as she closed the bathroom door.

Libby was distracted thinking about the anxiety surging through Alex behind the small bathroom door. She knew and understood it first-hand. For Libby it was a lived experience, and one she would never forget. She reached for her locket and held it in her gloved hand, wondering if in the not-too-distant future Alex would be holding a much-loved child in her arms.

She looked over at Daniel and felt a pang of guilt. He had no idea what she'd been through on her own. Part of her was still angry and part of her felt sad for him that he had not been able to share the joy of the little boy who was his son.

If he had known, perhaps he still would have stayed away. Perhaps he would have returned, not for her but for his son.

'If she's pregnant,' Daniel suddenly said, breaking her thoughts and completely unaware of the enormous decision weighing heavily on her mind, 'Alexandra's nausea might be temporary with any luck, and she might be a mother-to-be who has cravings more than sickness. My mother was apparently like that when she was pregnant with me. Lived on olives, grilled fish and homemade bread for months.'

Libby's eyes grew wide. She couldn't believe what Daniel was telling her. He was describing exactly her pregnancy diet with Billy.

The door opened tentatively and Alex stood there crying, her body visibly shaking, with the test in her hand.

'There are two lines. I'm pregnant. I'm actually going to be a mother,' she said through tears. 'I'm so happy and so sad and so confused. It's all I ever wanted and now I'm not sure I can do it. Not alone.'

Libby, still reeling a little from Daniel's story, crossed to Alexandra and took her arm to lead her back to the chair. 'Sit down and catch your breath. It's a lot to take in. Particularly when it's unexpected.'

'I'm… I'm happy. I'm actually so happy but I'm not sure what to do. It's all so surreal to me and part of me still can't believe it. We went through three rounds of IVF and three negative pregnancy tests and my husband said he couldn't go through it again.

'It wasn't just the cost. The devastation of the last negative test made me go a little crazy. I wanted a baby so much and my husband shut the door on the idea. He said the hormones I had to take made me so sick and he didn't want me to go through that again. He said he loved me too much to do that but his decision ripped us apart. I wanted to try just one more time. I knew he would be the best father and we would be so happy. With no parents, a family of our own meant the world to me. But he wouldn't. He said it wasn't meant to be.'

'I understand, and I might be out of line here,' Libby began, 'but your husband sounds like a very caring man who made that decision from concern for you.'

'I know. I still love him, I always will, but…we did nothing but argue and then I went into my shell and shut him out because I wanted a baby so badly.'

'And now that's become a reality,' Daniel said, rubbing his chin. 'While it's unexpected, I'd say it's a great outcome.'

'But what if I lose the baby? What would happen? I would go completely crazy and I can't put him through that,' she said as she moved to the bed and curled up into a foetal position, pulling the covers over her. 'I can't do that to him, I can't.'

'It looks like we're both at risk of being out of line,' Daniel started, 'but I think you might be selling your husband short on this one. There's no indication that you'll miscarry, so if you don't tell your husband he will have missed the joy of these months. The joy of finding out he's going to be a father. That would be a very special time for him. Don't take that away from him. My advice, both professionally and as a man, would be to let him know.'

'But what if something goes wrong with the pregnancy?'

'You're jumping to the worst-case scenario,' Daniel said as he drew closer and looked intently at Alexandra. 'As I said, unless the obstetrician has identified an issue and told you there would be a risk, you should not be overly concerned. You're young and appear otherwise healthy so make sure you see your GP and obstetrician and start an antenatal plan, and seriously take this time to consider bringing your husband up to speed with the fact he's going to be a father. Give him the chance to step up. I'm not a counsellor, but you said you still love him so at least give him the chance to tell you and your baby the same thing.'

Libby felt a lump rising in her throat with every word that slipped from Daniel's lips. The previous pang of guilt threatened to become a tsunami of regret.

Her mind was spinning and her stomach churning in a way they never had before.

She and Alex each had a huge decision to make.

But Libby had only five more days before the opportunity might be gone for ever.

CHAPTER NINE

LIBBY SPENT THE following days concentrating on Walter.
He didn't like any fuss, so she caught up with him after
he had enjoyed his breakfast on the deck, after lunch
and then just before he retired to his luxurious cabin for
the night, checking his blood pressure and his wound.
Despite the less than healthy diet, her patient was pro-
gressing very well. The wound was healing nicely and
his blood pressure was back within normal limits. The
sea air certainly agreed with him.

When she wasn't with Walter, she returned to the
quiet of her suite to call home and check in with Billy
and her parents—and more importantly avoid seeing
Daniel. She had done some soul searching after hearing Daniel speak openly and honestly to Alex about her
need to tell her husband about her pregnancy. It wasn't a
decision she was making in haste, the way she had done
the night Daniel had driven her home. She was going to
tell Daniel that he had a son.

Her decision was born from thinking hard about the
words Daniel had imparted to Alex, both as a doctor
and as a man, and knowing in her heart they were true.
Libby didn't want to keep Daniel from his son to punish him. With hand on heart, she knew her immediate

reaction had been to protect Billy but she had to trust that in letting Daniel know, whatever the outcome she had not prevented Billy from having the opportunity to know his father.

Now it would be up to Daniel whether he wanted to take on that role. And what that role in Billy's life might look like in the coming years.

The time alone in her cabin was giving Libby the space she needed to think about everything.

She could not be sure that Daniel would not leave Billy the way he had left her four years ago, without an explanation and with no way to contact him, but it was a chance she had to take. She just had to get the timing right. If he reacted badly and they still had a few days at sea, it would not be fair on Walter and the rest of the passengers. Libby decided she would tell him the night before they docked. It would give her sufficient time to tell him everything, answer his questions, and then he could process his feelings about it alone, not trapped on the yacht surrounded by a group of strangers.

Libby had no reason to socialise too much. Georgie was busy with preparations for the upcoming engagement party and the day-to-day running of the galley. It was busier than she had thought so they both caught up every evening for half an hour to chat and then head to bed early. That was the time when Libby called home because there was a time difference.

She missed Billy, Bradley and her parents. She had no intention of raising the fact that Daniel was on the yacht to either Bradley or her parents as she didn't want to be swayed by their bias. They would naturally want to protect both her and Billy and none of them had known Daniel. Not the man she'd fallen in love with, at least.

They had only known him as the cad who had broken her heart. So their opinion no doubt would not favour Daniel.

Libby headed down to see Walter on the morning they docked at Martinique. She needed to know if Walter intended to go ashore with his guests. If so, she would accompany him; if not, she would remain on the yacht and head to her cabin until his next medical check was due.

'Are you heading to the island today, Walter?'

'I've done it more times than I care to count,' he told Libby as she packed away the blood pressure monitor and stethoscope and sat down beside him. 'And between you and me, I could do with some peace and quiet with that lot gone for a few hours.'

Libby smiled, happy that she could just relax.

'How's my ticker doing anyway?' he asked. 'Is sacrificing my whisky and cigars paying dividends?'

'Absolutely. Your blood pressure is perfect and your scar is healing so well you'll hardly notice it when you're sunbathing on your next cruise.'

'My next cruise will be without those monkeys,' Walter scoffed as he looked in the direction of the guests disembarking the yacht. 'The extended family on Contessa's side are the worst. They're noisy, obnoxious and for the most part quite ungrateful...not to mention the clothing. I loved my wife; she was a beautiful, stylish woman, not unlike Grace Kelly, but her family are quite a different matter altogether. They have the most terrible dress sense. Abominable is more to the point. I know she wasn't adopted but I've always wondered where she fitted in. It's fortunate that I met Contessa first; if I'd met them I might have run in another direction.'

Libby bit the inside of her cheek so she didn't laugh as she watched the dozen or so family members heading ashore. She had to agree that their clothing was very loud and there were myriad patterns with a Hawaiian feel to them. She could only imagine what Bradley would have said.

'I do love my side of the family, of course,' he continued. 'My brother and his wife passed away a few years back now but they had the most gorgeous daughter, Sophia. She is the image of her mother and since Contessa and I were not blessed with children of our own, we unofficially adopted her when she was seventeen and she came to live with us for a little while until she went to college.

'As I said, she is the most perfect creature ever created and I love to spoil her whenever I can, which is why I'm throwing her this party. She's all grown up now—twenty-nine and an investment banker. She looks more like a model but she has a heart of gold and a mind like a steel trap. I think that's why we get on so well.'

'You modelled too?' Libby asked with a cheeky smile.

'I like you. You're funny. My side of the family will like you too; they're all flying in to San Lucia tomorrow. Should be a splendid night and I'm so excited to be seeing Sophia again. She did visit me in hospital but it was a whirlwind trip on her way to France to meet her fiancé's parents.'

'I'm sure she'll be excited to see you too.'

'You're very kind, Libby,' he said with a smile as he reached for his freshly squeezed juice. 'Tell me about your family. Do you have any shockers like the ones who just headed off to scare the locals?'

Libby laughed. 'My family is a little quieter. I adore them and I'm their only child,' she said, and without thinking she reached for her locket and held it in her hand as she spoke. 'My mother and father live quite close to my home in a suburb in San Francisco.'

'I think being close to your parents is lovely. It doesn't happen much nowadays. Everyone is on the go and travelling all over the world for work, never in one place for too long.'

'My parents are both retired and rarely travel, and being a single mother it's wonderful having them there to help out...' Libby stopped in mid-sentence. She hadn't meant the words to slip out and wished she could take them back. She'd been so careful not to mention Billy for five days and now she had just told him everything. Well, almost everything.

'Oh, you're a mother?'

She shifted in her seat uncomfortably but knew it was too late. Trying to hide the fact would only make it worse. 'Yes, I have a son.'

'Tell me more. How old is he and what's his name?'

'Billy...he's just turned three,' she managed to tell him, all the while wishing she had never opened up about her personal life.

'Just turned three... Hey, when was his birthday?'

'Last week, on the tenth of January.'

'That's three days after my birthday. He must be a lovely little chap.' He chuckled, then leaning in he whispered, 'You know, I was told by my mother that I was an Easter Bunny surprise. Of course, I worked out as I grew up that meant I was the result of a night of lovemaking in April after perhaps too many chocolates and champagne for my mother and more than likely a Guinness or two for my father.'

Libby froze. She couldn't laugh along with Walter. She swallowed as she remembered the Easter fundraiser the night Daniel had driven her home. There had been no chocolates or Guinness but there had definitely been a night of lovemaking that April. She felt heat rushing to her cheeks. She had tried to push the night from her memory but now it was coming back to her at lightning speed.

'It's lovely to know a little more about you, Libby,' he said, putting the glass down again, to her relief completely unaware of her reaction to the conversation. He reached for a scone. 'But I'm going to cut our chat short because you are too young to stay on board with an old man who you just confirmed is as fit as a Mallee bull...'

'A Mallee bull?' Libby asked with a quizzical look. Her mind was spinning with what she had confessed and now they were talking about bulls.

'It's Australian slang for healthy. Comes from the Mallee region in Victoria, where there are a lot of cattle and where I invested in a sheep station. They can be an odd bunch in the land Down Under, and they use funny terms like that. I've picked up one or two on my travels there.'

'I never heard it before. I've learned something today.'

'And you'll learn more by heading ashore and exploring the island. Georgie told me you haven't travelled much so don't waste this time sitting with me when you can enjoy life in the Caribbean.'

Libby was still trying to calm her nerves. She had never expected their conversation to be so revealing. It was unexpected and she hoped it would not complicate her plans to tell Daniel about Billy in a few days. 'Thank you, Walter, but I'm very happy to stay on board today.'

'Hogwash,' he retorted. 'I've arranged company for you for the day, so there's no point arguing.'

'You've asked Georgie to go with me?'

'No, my dear,' Walter replied. 'She's up to her neck making an engagement cake for tomorrow night's party, so I asked Daniel. He was quick off the mark to accept the invitation and he should be here any minute.'

Libby suddenly felt her heart pick up speed. She had hoped to avoid Daniel for the next few days until she was ready to confess everything.

'Goodness, you suddenly look flushed, my dear. Let me pour you a glass of water,' Walter said as he reached for the pitcher of chilled water and filled a glass. 'Take this.'

Libby accepted the glass and drank the water quickly. 'Thank you. I'm sorry about that. I don't think I had enough fluids today,' she lied. She had no choice. She could not tell Walter that the thought of spending the day with Daniel was not what she wanted or needed.

'Make sure you take a bottle of water with you today, young lady. Can't have my nurse unwell on the island. Daniel might have to carry you back on board,' he said with a laugh.

Libby heard footsteps and turned her head slowly to see Daniel approaching from the other end of the deck. He was wearing a white T-shirt and beige shorts. His tanned feet were slipped inside dark-coloured espadrilles and he had a baseball cap covering his hair. He was dressed for a day on the island. And he looked so very handsome. Just as she knew Billy would one day.

Libby quickly climbed to her feet. She needed a few moments to calm her nerves. Her thoughts were racing and she felt emotionally dishevelled. Time alone together was definitely not in her plans.

'I'll go and change into something more suitable,'

she told Walter, unsure of exactly what she intended to do but she knew if she could find an excuse not to go, she would. 'Please let Daniel know I'll be back as soon as I can.'

With that, Libby made her way to the glass elevator without passing Daniel. Ordinarily she would take the spiral staircase to the next deck but that would mean crossing paths with him.

As she stood waiting for the glass doors to open, she heard Walter call out cheerily, 'Good morning, Daniel. I can see you're all ready for your island date with Libby.'

Libby's hand began shaking as she pressed the call button again. *A date?* Was that just Walter's perception or was there any possibility that Daniel saw it that way too? She wished more than ever that she had never accepted the assignment to care for Walter. She would never have seen Daniel again and her life would not once again have been turned upside down by him. Her emotions were firmly strapped in on the roller-coaster and she couldn't escape.

The doors opened and she stepped inside and turned to see Daniel looking in her direction. Her heart began racing again. While she intended to go through with her decision to tell him about Billy, she was growing more concerned by the minute that her feelings for him were unfortunately still very real. The way her heart skipped a beat when his hand accidentally brushed against hers, how she'd felt so safe in his arms after the horrible situation with Maxwell, and finally seeing him appear on the deck ready for their *date*.

All of it was telling her that she was at risk of losing her heart to the man again if she didn't take control of her feelings and the reality of the situation. Her focus had to be on letting Daniel know about Billy in the right way and at the right time, and establishing a relationship with him that would allow him to be in Billy's life if he chose to do so. Full stop. Nothing more. Nothing romantic. No risk to her heart. None at all.

Trying her best to keep everything in perspective and on the task at hand, Libby changed into something more suitable for sightseeing. She chose a floral summer dress that skimmed her knees and flat white sandals. With a straw hat in her hand and a cross-body purse holding the few things she would need, she made her way to the door, knowing the day ahead would be challenging but an important part of telling him about Billy.

As she descended the highly polished oak staircase to the deck again, she decided the time she would be spending on the island with Daniel was purely an opportunity to find out more about him. Perhaps he had changed. Her stomach churned a little; she couldn't deny she was worried that he would raise the topic of their past and that it would hurt her to hear the truth. Or perhaps he would keep everything close to his chest and still stand behind the only explanation she had heard so far: *it was complicated.*

Had it just been a one-night stand that she had mistaken for more? Had Daniel been planning on leaving the hospital anyway and had assumed she knew? There were so many questions but she wasn't going there. The day was all about Billy. Libby needed to know enough about Daniel to know she was right in her decision to open up her life and that of her son to the man who had broken her heart. She had to make sure, as best she could, that he wouldn't break Billy's heart too.

* * *

'Ahh, there you are,' Walter said with a smile as Libby drew closer. 'You were quicker changing than my wife ever was. Must be the nurse in you. Always efficient and, I must say, looking very pretty.'

'Thank you, Walter,' Libby replied, not looking in Daniel's direction.

'I agree,' Daniel said, thinking that she looked far more than just pretty. He thought she looked stunningly beautiful. Just as she always had. Just as he had remembered her over the years.

'Then off you two go. Make the most of this beautiful weather and don't worry about me. You have your pager and I have the captain, the chief stewardess and a whole crew, so I'm well covered. And as a bonus I have a day of peace without those blessed, noisy folk who drive me to drink!'

Daniel nodded and Libby smiled a half-smile before they turned and made their way to the gangway. Libby held on tightly to the railing and Daniel suspected the rocking of the yacht in the shallower water made her a little nervous of falling into the marina. She didn't have to worry, he thought. He would be there to catch her for the next few days. In fact, if the world had been a different place, and he'd had any control of the future, he would always be there to catch her...in his arms.

'What would you like to do, Libby, shopping, sightseeing or an early lunch?'

Libby looked at her watch. 'Lunch sounds lovely.'

Daniel looked around. It wasn't his first time on the island and he had a favourite street market he wanted to show Libby that wasn't too far away so they could be back if there was any emergency on the yacht.

'This way,' he said, and began walking past the street vendors selling fresh fish and produce. He watched as Libby looked around, her eyes wide as she took in the sights and smells of the colourful French Caribbean island. 'It's not too far.'

It took all of Daniel's self-control not to reach for her and pull her close as they walked. He wished he could hold her hand and as lovers visit the island together for the first time. But he could not behave the way his heart was wanting. He had to allow his head to control every part of his behaviour. He just wanted to spend time with Libby and hopefully heal the hurt he had inflicted, although he wasn't sure how he could do that.

It didn't take long for them to reach the bustling street market.

'Martinique is a French Caribbean island so the food is French with a Caribbean twist,' Daniel told her as they made their way to a stall where he could see the food he loved and hoped that Libby would also enjoy.

'What exactly does that mean? I've not eaten much French food and I have no idea what Caribbean cuisine would be like.'

'The two most popular dishes are Boudin Creole and Boudin Blanc. I think you'd like the Boudin Blanc. The Creole is made from pork, pig's blood, onion and other ingredients…' Daniel paused as he noticed Libby's nose wrinkling up as he spoke. 'Just as I thought. Blanc it is.'

'What's in the second one?' she asked, her face not masking her concern.

'It's a white sausage made from pork, without the blood, and includes prawns, crabs, sea snail or fish.'

'That sounds much nicer.'

Daniel ordered two portions of the Boudin Blanc in his best French and then stepped back to Libby.

'I didn't know you spoke French.'

'I suppose there was no need to use it when…' He paused, feeling awkward about how to frame that time. He'd wanted to say *when I fell for you*, but he knew he couldn't tread that path.

'When we worked together,' Libby cut in, to his relief, and then continued, 'I guess not. San Francisco probably doesn't have a large French population.'

The brightly dressed woman behind the counter called Daniel's name and he stepped up and collected two plates of food and they made their way to a table for two nearby. The chairs didn't match and the table was faded by the sun but he noticed that Libby didn't seem taken aback by it. Daniel sat the plates down and then pulled out her chair for her. She immediately leaned down towards the plate in front of her.

'It smells delicious.'

'It is, believe me,' he said. 'I'll just get us some drinks. What would you like?'

'Water would be lovely, if it's okay to drink the water on the island.'

'I'll get bottled water for you.'

Daniel bought two bottles of water and returned to find Libby looking around her. The sun was dancing on the red waves of her hair and kissing her bare shoulders the way he remembered. While he loved being with Libby, there was an ache in his heart for what he could not have.

After their lunch Daniel suggested a walk by the shore.

'That sounds lovely,' Libby told him as they left their table and began walking down towards the beach.

Their conversation was light and mostly about the island.

'You seem to know a lot about Martinique. It's very beautiful and serene,' Libby said as she looked out across the creamy white sand to the still, blue water.

'For the most part it's a very pretty island…'

'For the most part?' She repeated his words with a questioning inflection as she slipped her sandals off and walked barefoot on the soft sand.

'Like most places in the world today, there is a risk at times. It wouldn't be advisable to wander around the largely empty back streets of Fort-de-France after dark. It's an area best left alone after the sun sets.'

Libby nodded and continued looking around. 'The names of the places and the food just roll off your tongue. How many times exactly have you visited?' she asked as they walked a little further.

'I can't be sure. I've lost count over the years, to be honest, but I do love it. I've worked on the cruise ships that call in at Martinique with tourists for the last few years.'

Libby looked at him then looked away back out to sea. 'I'm sure you've seen many exotic places.'

'Yes, I've travelled all over the world. I've been the ship's doctor on trips through the Caribbean, the Bahamas, Alaska and even all the way over to Australia and New Zealand.'

Daniel noticed Libby's mood suddenly shift and she fell silent, appearing to be deep in thought. She looked up towards the cloudless sky then walked away towards the shade of a huge palm tree.

'That must have been a culture shock from ER in a major hospital?' Libby said as she sat down, smoothing her dress out on the sand and crossing her ankles. 'I mean, one day you're in an inner-city emergency room and the next you're travelling the world on a yacht or cruise liner.'

One day in your bed and the next on a plane to the other side of the country, Daniel thought. He suspected the question was not just about the culture shock but more about the shock of his hasty departure.

'Libby,' he began as he sat down beside her, 'everything about the time with you in San Francisco was unexpected. You have to believe me, I didn't plan for any of it to happen and I wanted to explain everything to you but as I told you before, my life is complicated.'

'Perhaps we should leave that alone, Daniel,' she cut in without turning to face him. 'But I do want you to know that I would never have slept with you if I thought it was going to be a casual one-night stand and that you'd be gone before the sun came up. That's not who I am.'

'It wasn't just a casual one-night stand.'

Libby looked out across the water, saying nothing.

'It meant so much more to me than that,' he told her.

'Let's not go there, Daniel. I really don't want to spend the day talking about the past,' she said, turning to face him. 'That was not my intention. We need to make peace with whatever it was that happened between us.'

'Libby, believe me when I say that I'm truly sorry I caused you pain. I swear that if I could take it back I would.'

'Which part, sleeping with me or leaving in the middle of the night?'

'Leaving,' he told her honestly, not sure if she had heard him. 'Until my dying day I will never regret making love to you.'

CHAPTER TEN

LIBBY WOKE UP THE next day remembering Daniel's words but not knowing whether to believe them.

'Until my dying day I will never regret making love to you, Libby.'

Goddamn it, why did he have to say that?

None of it made sense to her and now he was making her life even more complicated. Whatever he said, it didn't change anything. His life was apparently *complicated.*

Well, life *was* complicated, for so many people, including her. Daniel didn't have the monopoly on a complicated life.

And he had no clue just how complicated hers had become because of him.

They had returned to the yacht without saying anything else to each other. She had to find the right time to tell Daniel about Billy and at the same time ensure she set ground rules. Billy deserved that. She wished her son had a daddy who would kiss him goodnight every evening and hug him every morning. While Daniel clearly couldn't be that man, she hoped he would find a way to be a part of Billy's life. Not be someone who might show up every few years or who Billy might bump into occasionally on an exotic island in the Caribbean.

There was a hurried knock on the door and Libby jumped out of bed, threw on her robe and rushed to open it.

Georgie was standing there with a look of panic on her face. 'I'm so sorry to bother you this early but Alexandra's throwing up again and I can't have her near the food, particularly not the engagement cake.'

'Come in,' Libby said, opening the door wider. 'Of course, it's the engagement party tonight. I'll help you in any way I can. I just need to check on Walter…'

'Daniel's already doing that,' Georgie cut in as she closed the door. 'He said he'll look after Walter, get him dressed and to the party on time. The other guests can make their own way there and the lovebirds flew in last night. They're staying at the resort already with the rest of the UK guests who also flew in late yesterday. The party is on the beach near the resort and the event planner arrived two days ago and has a local team already setting up before we dock.'

Libby curled her unruly bed hair into a makeshift bun and reached for a hair tie on the nearby table to keep it in place. 'It sounds like it's all organised, a bit like a military exercise. Let me know what you need and I'm there.'

Georgie gave her the biggest hug. 'I knew I could count on you.'

'Always.'

'Okay, we dock in San Lucia in a few hours so perhaps have your shower, get ready and pack a dress for the party…'

'I'm not going to the party,' Libby corrected her

friend. 'I'm going to help you so I can wear shorts and a T-shirt because I'll be out of sight.'

'That's just it. I only need you to help me with some dessert preparation in the galley as I'm such an annoying perfectionist and I have to have someone I trust to manage quality control. Alexandra is as fussy as me but, as I said, unfortunately she's out of the picture, so you're my go-to. I'll also need you to help me put the cake together when we get to the party. It's baked and decorated but I have to assemble it on the beach.'

'We can't do that on the yacht?'

Georgie laughed. 'Can you imagine what could go wrong carrying a five-tier cake across the sand?'

'Five tiers? How many guests are coming?'

'I think close to a hundred and fifty. Some are sailing in and others have flown in. It's quite the social event. There are whispers that a couple of Hollywood A-listers will be there too.'

'Goodness, it sounds like all the more reason for me to stay in the background and look after the last-minute bits and pieces for you.'

Georgie appeared to ignore Libby's remark and, making her way to the closet, she opened the doors where there were only uniforms. 'Where are all your clothes?'

'In my suitcase,' Libby replied matter-of-factly.

'But you have a huge space in this stateroom. Why on earth are you not using it?'

'Because I wear my uniform most days and the rest of my clothes I can pull out of my suitcase and throw on.'

'Do you have *anything* glamorous in said suitcase?'

'Glamorous? But it's an island party. Wouldn't shorts or a cotton dress be okay?'

Georgie shook her head. 'No, they wouldn't. There

will be the most fabulously dressed people at the party and you are absolutely not going to look like Orphan Annie. You, my friend, have to look equally fabulous.'

Libby suddenly thought Georgie sounded decidedly like Bradley.

'Where's your suitcase?' Georgie asked as she looked around the room.

Libby pointed to the second closet on the other side of the dressing table. 'It's in that one.'

Without wasting a second, Georgie sprang into action, crossed the room and found the suitcase lying inside the closet. She dragged it out onto the carpeted floor, opened it and began looking through the clothes like a woman on a mission. Within seconds she came upon the emerald-green silk dress. 'This,' she announced, climbing to her feet with the dress in her hands like a triumphant explorer with a golden chalice, 'is perfect. Just perfect. Do you have any shoes?'

'There are some gold strappy sandals in there somewhere but honestly, Georgie, please just let me help out in the kitchen and leave the party to the guests. I won't know anyone anyway.'

Georgie ignored Libby's pleas and continued to rummage around until she found the gold shoes in a plastic bag at the bottom of the suitcase. She unzipped the bag and held them up. 'Gorgeous. Not too high for navigating the walkways that are being erected on the sand leading to the floating pontoon.'

'A floating pontoon?'

'Yes, a floating pontoon with a Caribbean band. I'm not sure if you're aware that Walter is one of the wealthiest men in the UK, if not the world and he doesn't do things by halves—neither does his niece Sophia, I've heard. That's why I have to get this cake to be just per-fect and you will be responsible for ensuring no one, and I mean no one, including those strange family members sharing the yacht with us, goes near the cake before the lovebirds cut it. I don't want anyone hovering too close and being tempted to touch it. That's why you must be dressed up and looking your gorgeous self so you can blend in and still be on cake duty.

'There was a strict direction from the event plan-ner that they did not want anyone snapped in photos not looking the part. Alexandra even brought a lovely dress with her but I can't risk her throwing up at the party. Can you imagine Walter's reaction to that? Not to mention the guests having a fit and jumping into the water to get away. Now, that would make the front page of the tabloids!'

Libby could see Georgie's point and agreed to help her friend out. 'Okay, I'll pack my things into…actually, I don't know what to pack them in but I'll find some-thing and then I'll jump in the shower, get dressed and head down to the galley to help you.'

'You're the best friend ever,' Georgie said, hugging Libby again and then making her way to the door. 'Don't rush. We don't dock for a few hours so there's plenty of time to do the prep work on the desserts. And you will be my pseudo apprentice sous chef.'

Libby thought that sounded outside her skill set but she could definitely manage some simple prep work in the galley and guard the cake, but that was her limit. She had only been cooking for Billy and herself for the last few years so her repertoire consisted of simple healthy food with lots of vitamins but no fancy plating. She hoped Georgie wasn't going to expect too much.

About thirty minutes later there was another knock on the door and Libby, still dressed in a towel and drying the mop of her hair, rushed to open it. 'I won't be long, Georgie—' she began, and then, lifting her head, realised it wasn't Georgie. It was Daniel standing there with a suit bag in his hand.

'Georgie asked me to drop this off to you for your dress. The stewards are all busy.'

Libby wanted to slam the door shut, partly from embarrassment and lingering anger but mainly from feelings she wished she didn't have for the man. But she knew that would be bad manners considering he had brought her the suit bag to transport her dress to the party. Words had temporarily escaped her but suddenly she realised that if she reached for the bag, there was a very real possibility she might lose her towel. Libby had no choice but to invite Daniel into her stateroom.

'Um…er…please come in. You can leave the bag over there,' she said, motioning towards the chair beside the desk. 'I'll just finish getting ready so please let yourself out.' With that, Libby crossed the room, her heart racing and her head spinning again, and stepped inside the bathroom. She slipped on the large guest bathrobe behind the door to make her feel less exposed as she stepped back out, determined to send him on his way. She had to be firm and set boundaries—for her own good because she was scared by her reaction to him.

'I appreciate you bringing the suit bag, but I don't want to hold you up,' she told him, trying to hide how self-conscious she felt. 'Georgie told me you're tending to Walter today while I'm helping her so it looks like we'll both be busy.'

'Yes, we will,' he began. 'But it wasn't just the bag that brought me here. We need to talk.'

'I think we did that yesterday and nothing really changed. Lunch was lovely and I enjoyed your company, but you have a complicated life. And that makes two of us,' she said, closing her robe even tighter around her otherwise naked body. She felt vulnerable to her own feelings with Daniel so close. 'Let's leave it at that, Daniel, for the moment. There's something I want to talk to you about but now is not the time.'

'I agree. Yesterday proved to me that we need to talk about what happened so we can have closure.'

'Fine, whatever you think, Daniel. Please just go. We can talk about it another day. I have to help Georgie prepare for the party and I'm running late.'

Libby shut the bathroom door on Daniel as her fingers reached for the locket around her neck. Her heart was racing as she accepted that all hope for them was gone in an instant. He wanted closure. Not that it should have come as a surprise since he had not reached out since leaving but it did sound very final. She held the locket tightly in her clasped hands, praying that she was doing the right thing for Billy's sake by telling Daniel he was a father. Perhaps that closure would include walking away from the son he had never met but if so it would be best to know now.

Disappointed he had not been able to speak with Libby, Daniel headed back to the bridge to check the arrival time with the captain. He needed to have Walter ready for the party and had offered to assist him to dress. Daniel had lain awake until the early hours of the morning, thinking about Libby. She was so close and yet so far from his reach. He wanted to step back in time and do everything differently but that wasn't possible. He had allowed himself to fall for her when he'd had no right to do so. And no right to let Libby believe he was free.

Each moment in such close proximity to her had been torture to him. Knowing she was in the suite next to his, breathing softly as she'd slept, had made his body ache to hold her. He'd ached to tell her how much she meant to him and that his feelings would never change, no matter how far apart they were, but that was unfair. She needed to be free to move on.

He'd tossed and turned in the huge lonely bed as he'd thought back to how natural it would have felt to reach for her hand as they'd strolled around Martinique. How easily he could have kissed her while waiting to order their food and how much he'd wanted to pull her into his arms as they'd walked barefoot across the warm sand. She was everything he wanted and couldn't have.

It had been three a.m., the yacht being tossed about in unruly waves, and Daniel had been no closer to sleep than when he'd climbed into bed four hours before. The Caribbean seas could be temperamental but that had never bothered him before. He had become accustomed to rough water and strong winds. Sleep had never evaded him in bad weather the way it had for the last five days in the calmest of waters. Thoughts of Libby had been keeping him awake. Thoughts of what he had done and how much he continued to hurt her by keeping the truth from her.

Daniel had decided, before finally succumbing to sleep, that he could not live with himself knowing he had caused the sadness and confusion so evident in Libby's beautiful eyes. It would be unfair to let that continue when he had the power to change it. Or at least temper it a little. He would let Libby know enough about his life so that she understood his feelings were real and that the reason he had left was just as real. He would explain his role in Chezlovinka and the need for him to return to take over from his father.

Just spending a few days with Libby had made Daniel realise he could trust her to keep the secret of his father's illness and that it was imperative he return to his homeland—a principality so obscure she would know nothing about it. But at least she would know he did care for her and that what they had shared had been real. It just couldn't be for ever. Her life was in San Francisco, his was a life of serving his people on another continent but the time they had spent together would always be in his heart. She deserved to know that much.

He just had to find the perfect time to tell her before that time ran out.

CHAPTER ELEVEN

LIBBY DRESSED QUICKLY in shorts and a T-shirt and hung her party dress in the suit bag behind the door with her gold sandals, a small gold evening clutch and some long emerald costume jewellery earrings that Bradley had packed. All the while, Libby was thinking about Daniel and wishing that anyone but him had been the ship's doctor.

Her life could have remained simple but at least there were a few days until she told Daniel everything…and he told her whatever it was he had kept from her.

Then they would both, according to him, have closure. Libby wasn't so sure.

As she zipped up the suit bag, she thought that Georgie and Bradley should have their own make-over show called 'How to save the poor nurse with zero styling ability and a million things on her mind'.

Georgie was already under way with the desserts when Libby arrived in the galley.

'How many tarts have you baked?' Libby asked, astonished at the sight of a galley stacked to the ceiling with handmade individual pastry cases.

'Two hundred.'

'For one hundred and fifty guests?'

'You never know, they may like a second and Walter doesn't want anyone missing out on his favourite dessert—Persian custard tartlet with mango, papaya and guava.'

'That sounds exotic and delicious. What can I do to help?'

'It would be wonderful if you could cut up the fruit the way I have done as an example,' Georgie said as she began to make the custard filling with more cream and eggs being taken from the cool room than Libby had seen in her entire local supermarket.

Libby spied the cut fruit resting on a chopping board. It looked perfectly presented. Libby knew her work was cut out for her to ensure her fruit looked as lovely. She reached for an apron and began to peel the first of dozens of mangoes. 'What about the savoury food? Please tell me you're—or *we're*—not preparing that as well?'

'Good God no.' Georgie laughed. 'The chefs in the resort are preparing that part of the menu.'

'That's a relief,' Libby said as she put the first peeled mango in the huge bowl in front of her and tried to push away thoughts of Daniel and the conversation they would have before the end of the cruise.

The two women and a galley hand spent the next few hours preparing the different elements of the fruit tarts and packing them away in the cool room for transportation to the resort when they docked. Libby had seen the engagement cake resting in the cool room and it was magnificent. Once upon a time she had dreamed of an engagement party and a wedding, both with stunning cakes and all the trimmings, but now she didn't believe in happily ever after.

The chief stewardess arrived to alert them that the

yacht would be docking in fifteen minutes. This gave the team time to pack everything ready to be transported to the cool rooms at the resort. It would be like another military operation with everything cut and carefully placed in containers along with three enormous pots of custard that had been chilling.

'When will you do all of the work putting two hundred desserts together?'

'Once we dock, I'll follow the crew to the resort and once mains are served I will begin final preparation. I don't like to chill the pastry so I keep the other ingredients cold and construct and plate the dessert at the last minute. It's so much nicer to bite through room-temperature pastry into a chilled filling. It just adds that bespoke touch at the end of the meal, and Walter loves it done that way.'

'You're such a fussy pants, aren't you?' Libby joked with her friend as they busily gathered everything and stacked it all safely on a trolley for collection by crew members. 'But so is Walter. He loves the whole regalia of uniformed crew and it does look lovely, I must admit.'

'It's the little touches that make the difference,' Georgie replied with an expression that showed she was ready for battle. The engagement cake had to be transported too and Libby could see that was weighing on Georgie's mind. This was a huge event and a lot of the focus would be on the work undertaken by Georgie.

'It will be the best engagement party that San Lucia has ever seen,' Libby said.

'I have a feeling that tonight will absolutely be a night to remember for everyone!' Georgie responded with a wink.

* * *

Daniel assisted Walter to dress for the party. The proud uncle was wearing a tuxedo and bow-tie and requested Daniel do the same.

'The invitation says black tie, so I will truss up like a turkey for the next few hours only because I'll never hear the end of it from Sophia if I don't…and because that is what Contessa would expect of me.'

Daniel noticed Walter turn away abruptly as he spoke and he suspected it was to hide a tear or two.

'It will be a wonderful night, Walter. Everyone will have the best time and you're looking very suave,' Daniel told him. 'Sophia will be proud and Contessa will without doubt be watching all of the celebrations with you.'

'Hmm, do you think so?'

'Absolutely.'

'All right, enough of the mushy stuff,' Walter said gruffly, and he brushed non-existent lint from his jacket sleeves and crossed to the door of the largest suite on the yacht. 'Let's get this show on the road. I think it will be a night to remember.'

The party had begun and Libby stood in the perfect, balmy night air, looking around in amazement at the most beautiful setting she had ever seen. Fairy lights were strung across four giant pontoons only a few metres from shore. Two of the pontoons had tables and chairs, one had a dance floor and there was one for the band, and all four were joined by arched bridges that were also lit by fairy lights and covered in an array of brightly coloured Caribbean flowers, including hundreds of enormous coral-coloured hibiscus flowers. It was a sudden splash of colour and a stark contrast to the predominantly white decor.

The pontoons were secured by large pylons driven through the water and deep into the sand so they didn't shift with the movement of the tide that gently lapped beneath. It was postcard perfect and Libby was standing guard in front of the most stunning engagement cake that she thought had ever been made by anyone anywhere in the world. It was divine in every aspect and Libby was still amazed that it had made it onto the floating pontoon without dislodging one piece of the delicate filigree flowers that cascaded down the five layers like a waterfall of pastel shades of coral tipped with gold leaf over a naked Belgian chocolate torte. It was a piece of art and Libby had watched Walter look over more than once or twice with a smile born of pride in Georgie's work.

Georgie had also been correct in saying that stray hands might be tempted to touch the cake and the potential perpetrators were just as she had expected—the extended family that had sailed in with Walter. Libby had to be firm in reminding them to keep their fingers away from it.

Sophia and her fiancé, Etienne, arrived and the party was soon in full swing. Sophia wore a striking coral-coloured dress that skimmed her shoulders and fell to the floor and her blonde hair was styled in a high ponytail secured with a silk hibiscus flower encrusted with diamonds. Her fiancé was wearing a tuxedo, as were all of the men at the event. Libby thought Walter's niece looked absolutely beautiful and she told him as much when he passed by.

'Thank you. I told you she's the spitting image of her

mother.' Then, stepping back and running his gaze over Libby, he added, 'And you look very beautiful yourself.'

'Why, thank you, Walter.'

'But I'm still not completely sold on her fiancé,' Walter leaned in and whispered in her ear. 'He's an actor apparently but I've been told I don't get a choice in the matter.'

'He seems lovely and the way he looks at her shows he is a man in love, and that thought should bring you comfort.'

Walter nodded. 'I guess when you pare everything back, finding true love is all that really matters in life.'

'Yes, it is.'

Walter reached for Libby's hands in a fatherly way. 'Tell me, my dear, are you married? I know you have a little boy but you never mentioned a husband neither do you wear a ring.'

'No, I'm single.'

'Not met the right man yet?' he asked with an impish wink as he sipped on his lime and soda.

'I thought I'd met him but he had other ideas. It's complicated.'

'All matters of the heart are complicated but, just between you and me, if you're looking for a potential boyfriend, I think Dr Daniel is more than a bit keen on you. I've seen the way he looks at you when no one's watching. It's all happened quite quickly since you only met on my yacht, but that level of emotion can't be feigned. It was love at first sight for Contessa and myself so I never judge the speed at which Cupid's arrow hits,' he said with a wink.

'Anyway, I'm not sure how you feel about him, but his face lights up when anyone mentions your name. I've not raised it with him because it's not my place, and he's a bit of a closed book. I thought I'd test my theory yesterday so I asked him to accompany you to Martinique and, just as I thought, he jumped at the chance. I'm quite intuitive when it comes to people. You know, Libby, he's not a bad looking rooster and you'd have medicine as a common interest. You could do worse…if you're in the market for a husband, I mean.'

'I'm not in the market,' she snapped quickly.

'Well, maybe not now, but keep our Dr Daniel in mind for the future. Who knows, he might grow on you. It took me a while to win my gorgeous wife but eventually she fell in love with me. Anyway, enough of my matchmaking, I'd best be off and mingle with all the other guests… And by the way, you're doing a wonderful job keeping Contessa's relatives away from the cake. Georgie told me you were on duty. Excellent job, keep it up.'

Libby felt her back stiffen, her heart begin to race and her thoughts become airborne swirling above her, unable to be reined in. She was having a fight-or-flight response to what Walter had told her before he'd rushed off to mingle with the guests. It was fortunate he had left her alone because she was both stunned and speechless.

Just when Libby thought their conversation about Daniel was finished, Walter came back. 'By the way, he's looking your way from over at the bar. You've certainly got him mesmerised…and a man mesmerised is a man in love.'

Libby instantly turned to see Daniel standing at the bar with a drink in his hand. His smile widened and as much as she didn't want to smile back, her lips seemed to take on a mind of their own and curled upwards. He looked so handsome in his tuxedo. But Libby had to admit that Daniel looked handsome in anything he wore…and even more handsome when he wore nothing.

Suddenly, she was so angry at herself for having romantic thoughts about Daniel. In fact, any thoughts about him. He was a closed book—even Walter agreed about that part and the rest of what he'd said was disturbing. She turned her attention back to the cake and away from him. Guarding the cake was her job for the night until Sophia and her fiancé cut it, and then she could return to the yacht and close the door on the world.

It wasn't long before the happy couple made their way to the cake. Mains had finished and the Persian tartlets arrived and were quickly devoured by all the guests, with a number asking for seconds, including Walter. Libby took a few small steps backwards as the couple posed for the photographs by the professional photographer and guests alike. She hadn't realised how close she was to the edge of the pontoon but that soon became evident. Her stomach sank with the realisation that her left heel was off the pontoon and hovering over the water. Suddenly, she lost her balance and with her arms flapping ungraciously she fell backwards into the water. There were gasps from the guests and Walter signalled the band to stop playing. Daniel sprinted from the bar where he had been standing most of the night and dived into the water in his tuxedo. While it wasn't overly deep or cold, it was eerily dark and the moment Libby felt Daniel's strong arms around her, she felt safe. Humiliated but safe.

'Are you all right?' he asked as he gently swept away the damp curls clinging to her face.

'I'm fine thank you…' she began, trying to catch her breath. 'But I can't believe you did that. Your tuxedo is drenched now and we both look silly. You should've let me look silly on my own.'

Daniel smiled. 'You don't look silly, you look beautiful. I've wanted to tell you just how beautiful you looked all night. Now you look wet and beautiful.'

Libby looked back at him in silence and realised just why she had fallen in love with him. And why it had been impossible to forget him.

'Is everything okay?' Walter called out from the edge of the pontoon, where he stood surrounded by an army of concerned guests, including Sophia and Etienne.

'We're fine, just felt like a late-night swim,' Daniel said as he took Libby's hand and led her from the water to shore. 'We might head back to the yacht…for some dry clothes.'

Libby didn't remember much about the walk back to the marina and the yacht. With Daniel's hand still holding hers, she felt like she was home even though she was four thousand miles from San Francisco. She couldn't pull her hand free despite how much she knew she should. She was tired of doing everything alone and she loved feeling protected. Perhaps she was making another mistake, she wasn't sure, but at that moment it felt right. Her heart felt light and she couldn't remember ever feeling this happy.

Finally, they reached the *Coral Contessa* and one of the stewards, who must have seen them making their way towards the yacht, greeted them with two large white towels.

'Late-night dip?'

'Something like that,' Daniel said as he wrapped one of the towels around Libby and pulled her close.

The steward departed as quietly as he had arrived, leaving them alone on the deck. Daniel looked at Libby and knew it was time to tell her everything. He cared deeply for her and he knew in his heart he could trust her. She had given him no reason not to trust her. He wanted her to know everything. He knew it wouldn't change the outcome but she deserved to know it all.

His family was going to have him for the rest of his life so he deserved to give Libby what she needed to move on with hers. Daniel looked into the blackness of the star-filled sky. The dark canvas above them was dotted with tiny sparkling beacons of hope and, while there were none in Daniel's mind, he knew he was doing the right thing.

'You have to stop saving me,' Libby said softly. 'You're starting to make a habit of it. First rescuing me from Maxwell and now Caribbean sharks.'

Daniel smiled. He would willingly rescue Libby for the rest of his life if he could. But he couldn't.

'I want to tell you something, Libby.' He turned to her and began, 'It's something I've wanted to tell you for a very long time and I tried to tell you this morning.'

'That you actually still care for me and that's why you jumped into the water to save me?'

'That…and something else…'

'If it's true that you still care for me then the something else can wait until tomorrow,' she told him as she stood up and looked into his eyes. 'Let's not talk any more…let's just have tonight and talk about the rest to-morrow.'

Daniel was surprised but he didn't want to argue. He

felt the same way. He hadn't made any promises and he never would. Libby knew that, and yet she wanted to spend the night with him and he wanted her more than words could say. What he needed to tell her could wait until the morning.

His arms reached for her like a man possessed, his mouth hovering inches from hers. 'Are you sure?' he asked, his voice low and husky.

Libby nodded and with her head tilted upwards she stood on tiptoe to meet his lips. Unable to wait a moment longer, his mouth met hers with a tenderness and urgency that she returned. His hands gently roamed the curves of her still-damp body as their kisses become more passionate. Her back arched against the hardness of his body and his lips began to trail kisses down her neck. Within moments, Daniel scooped her into his arms and she buried her head against his chest as he carried her to his suite and to the bed that would be theirs for the night.

CHAPTER TWELVE

DANIEL WOKE IN the morning with Libby lying naked in his arms and he wished with all of his heart he could wake that way for ever. Gently she stirred and, turning to face him, she smiled the most angelic smile he had ever seen.

'Good morning,' he whispered, and kissed her tenderly.

'Good morning, yourself,' she said, and kissed him back.

Daniel rolled onto his back and looked towards the ceiling while Libby rested her head on his chest. 'Would you like some breakfast?'

'No,' she murmured. 'I'm fine right here. I don't want to leave bed, it means we have to face reality and I'm not ready yet.'

Daniel turned his face away and looked into the distance. He had to agree, but he also had to tell Libby the truth.

'Nor me,' he told her with a melancholy tone to his voice. 'It couldn't be more perfect but there's something I do need to tell you. I tried to last night...'

'I know,' she said. 'I'm sorry I stopped you.'

'I'm very glad you did,' he said, kissing her softly.

'But now we really do need to talk. It's important that you know everything.'

'I have something I need to tell you too, Daniel,' Libby began.

Daniel smiled a bitter-sweet smile, knowing he would love to spend his life learning everything there was about Libby, but instead he had to tell her the harsh realities of his so they truly could have closure.

'To understand why I did what I did four years ago, you need to know about my background, where I came from—'

'I'm not going to judge you by where you grew up,' Libby interrupted him, and stroked his arm. 'I don't believe in that whole "born on the wrong side of the tracks" idea. I think you are what you make of yourself; it's not where you came from.'

Daniel couldn't help but smile again at what Libby had said. She obviously thought he came from a disadvantaged background and was trying to make him feel better. Her heart was huge and accepting and she didn't have a judgmental bone in her gorgeous body. He couldn't have loved her more and that made it all so very sad. Libby deserved better than a life with him.

'No, Libby, I didn't struggle growing up. In fact, it was quite the opposite. I grew up with great privilege.'

'I see,' she said with a curious look on her face. 'What sort of privilege? An elite school and a nanny?'

'Yes…and some.'

'And some?'

'My family is the royal family of a small principality in Europe.'

'You're a member of a royal family?' she asked in an incredulous tone. 'An actual royal family?'

'Yes, but it's not a huge country. I doubt you've heard of it. My Father is the Crown Prince of Chezlovinka.'

'Chezlovinka? The principality that borders Greece.'

'You've heard of it?'

'Yes, I've heard of it,' she replied with curiosity on her face as she propped herself up on the pillow and looked into his eyes. 'I studied it in my final year of college.'

'You studied Chezlovinka?'

'Yes, it's a beautiful Mediterranean country...' Libby paused, her eyes wide with shock and a little disbelief. 'But I never saw any images of you.'

'My mother was very protective and she kept me from the scrutiny of the media so I could have a relatively normal childhood and early adult life. She was the one who encouraged me to pursue medicine. I studied in London.'

Libby was silent for a moment. 'Oh, my God, that means you're a prince.'

'Yes,' he nodded. 'Prince Daniel Dimosa.'

'So that's what this is all about. Now it makes sense,' she said, pulling the covers up around her and moving away. Her forehead wrinkled with a frown as she stared at Daniel. 'You're a prince and I'm a commoner. I get it. You need a princess and I'm a long way from that.'

'No, Libby, you're not a long way from that. You're kind and intelligent and empathetic and everything a princess needs to be, but there's a dark side to the story, as there always is in fairy tales. My life isn't about palaces and joy. It will be filled with sacrifice and duty and I don't want you to have to sacrifice anything in life. I want you to have everything you want and I can't give you that.'

'I understand, Daniel. You're letting me down gently,' she said softly as she closed her eyes.

'No,' Daniel said, reaching for her and pulling her close again. 'That's not it at all, Libby. You're far too good for the life I could give you.'

'That's sweet, Daniel, but it's not true. You will have a wonderful life there.'

'It is true, Libby.'

'You don't have to say anything else, Daniel. I wouldn't fit in to your royal lifestyle and you can't fit back into mine. My life is simple. I'm just a nurse from San Francisco.'

'Don't say that,' he cut in firmly. 'You're the most amazing woman I've ever met and I would fly to the end of the earth for you, but a life with me is not one I would wish on anyone. Least of all you.'

'You're a wonderful man, Daniel. I understand that you wanted to protect me from the scrutiny of a life that you are very accustomed to but one that's a very long way from mine,' she said as she moved away a little and looked at the ceiling fan gently circling above them. 'You need a woman who comes from the same place in society, not a woman who may be a liability. You don't need a woman clumsy enough to fall off a pontoon and embarrass you.'

'Libby, you could never embarrass me. And I would dive off a million pontoons for you but it's not about you. It's about my family.'

Libby reached for the towel on the floor and slipped from the bed and into the bathroom and returned in a bathrobe.

'Your family? What do you mean?' she asked as she began to collect her clothes from the floor.

'It's my father. He's not well and I need to return to take over the country. I knew it would happen one day and that's why I didn't want to become involved with you. I'm sorry I lost the ability to see reason and walk away. I was selfish to want one night with you. It was unfair and I had no right, but a part of me was in denial.'

'I guess I understand. It's sort of how I behaved last night… I just wanted one night with you and to hell with the consequences.'

'And, believe me, I'm glad you did, but one night is all it can be. I'm sorry.'

'I know it was just one night. You said upfront you wanted closure between us and I'm a big girl. I went into last night knowing that. You have nothing to be sorry about.' Her voice was still barely more than a whisper and filled with sadness.

'I told you yesterday when we were on Martinique that my life was not my own to live. It's not mine to make my own choices—many have been made for me by virtue of being a member of the royal family and some by virtue of being my father's son.'

'Isn't that one and the same?'

'Not quite, but I must return home. My father's condition will never improve. There's no medication or treatment that can change the prognosis.'

'Is your father's illness terminal?' she asked as she sat on the edge of the bed just out of his reach.

'Yes, but we have no idea how long he has left. My father's is a cruel fate because he has early onset familial Alzheimer's disease. He's wasting away inside his own body.'

Daniel suddenly felt relieved saying it aloud to Libby. He hadn't told anyone before and now he had it was as if half the weight of the world had been lifted from his shoulders. Nothing had changed, and nor would it, but he felt more at peace than ever before. He had never expected to feel that way. He'd thought he would feel tortured and racked with guilt for betraying the family, but it was as if he had been betraying Libby for the longest time by not letting her know.

Libby's expression fell into one of all-consuming sadness. 'Oh, Daniel, that is so very sad. I'm so sorry. I can only imagine how hard it must be on you and your mother and everyone around them.'

'It's been difficult but my father has been able to manage until now. It's been an early onset but also a slow onset. But the symptoms have worsened over the last month so my mother sent for me. I will be heading there next week. I can't delay my return any longer.'

'The people of Chezlovinka must also be saddened by the news of your father's illness.'

'That's just it,' Daniel said with a resoluteness to his voice. 'They can't know. I have to step up and take control so my father can quietly abdicate and keep his dignity. It would cause doubt in their minds about him and about me and about the future of the country. There's been too much unrest in the world lately to bring more uncertainty to them now.'

'I understand you don't want to upset them with news of your father but why do you say the same about yourself? It's a disease afflicting your father, not you.'

'That's just it, Libby. It could affect me. My father's condition is caused by a mutation in a single gene and a single copy of the mutant gene inherited from either parent will cause the disease in the child. There is every chance I have inherited the mutated gene and my life in a few years may be just like his.'

'But you don't know that for sure.'

'No, but I also have no guarantee it won't and the people of Chezlovinka are not naive. If they learn the nature of my father's illness, they will quickly work out that it's genetic and one day in the future I too may be affected. They need stability and that's why I will head back to my country and begin grooming my successor so that in the event I do succumb to the disease, he can ascend to the throne.

'I have looked into altering the constitution to allow my adopted paternal cousin, Edward, who is studying law at Cambridge, to reign over the principality. Because he was adopted at birth by my father's brother and his wife, there would be no risk of the disease continuing in the family but he would carry on the Dimosa name.'

'And you have to keep this secret to yourself.'

'Not entirely. I can't. My father has deteriorated to a point now that he has a loyal team of nurses who have all agreed to assist and say nothing outside the palace walls.'

'But what about you? You must know how I feel about you. I can be there for you, if you'll let me.'

'You're the most wonderful woman, Libby, and you know how I feel about you too, but I can't ask you to do that. I can't ask you to give up the life you have and risk spending your life caring for me. I don't want that life for you. I don't want you to have to look after me the way my mother has looked after my father and will continue to nurse a man who soon may not even recognise her.'

'But you may not have the condition, Daniel. And if you did it wouldn't change the way I feel about you.'

'It would change everything to me,' he said. 'I can't allow you to risk being trapped with a man who is trapped inside himself.'

Daniel wanted to add *And one who didn't want chil-*

dren. Libby would be the most wonderful mother and he wasn't prepared to risk having a child who might also carry the gene. Daniel was adamant he wouldn't be tested until he showed symptoms. No good would come of learning his fate early. He felt certain that he would not have been spared the same destiny as his father and he didn't want his mother to have the worry of her only child being trapped like her husband. If he didn't have the test, he didn't have to lie to his mother about the prognosis.

Libby wiped the tears that were spilling down her cheeks. 'If you truly care for me, why don't you let me make that decision?'

'I'm giving you the chance to find a man who comes without the risk of a disease that will rob you of a long and happy life. I don't want you to be a care-giver. You should be a man's wife and lover for ever without the risks that being with me would carry.'

'It wouldn't change my feelings for you whatever the result but if it's forcing you to make this decision to shut me out, why won't you get tested? You would know what the future held and then be able to make rational decisions based on fact.'

Daniel drew a deep breath. 'I will be tested one day but not now. I need to be strong for my family and my country. I need to focus on them and not me. If it was confirmed now that I had the gene for early onset familial Alzheimer's disease, then every day I would live with that knowledge and I would not be able to hide that from my mother. It would not be fair to add further to her worries. She shouldn't lie awake concerned about both of the men in her life.'

'I do understand, but perhaps not knowing is also a worry for your mother…'

'Maybe I'm being selfish, Libby, but if I learn the truth, and it's as I suspect it will be, then I may not have a single moment of peace. I will live my life in fear of how it will play out.'

'But, Daniel,' she told him, 'that's how you're living your life now.'

Daniel looked at Libby in silence, considering her words…and wondering if she was right.

Libby reached for her locket as Daniel climbed from the warmth of the bed in silence and, slipping on a bathrobe, stood by the window, looking out to sea.

'There's something I need to share with you,' she said as she followed suit and climbed from the bed. Pulling the sheet around her, she crossed to him. 'Something that may change the way you feel about everything. About your future…and even about being tested.'

Daniel turned back to her and held her tightly to him. 'There's nothing in the world that can change my future, no matter how much I wish it to be true. And I will not consider testing until it's absolutely necessary. I need to think of my mother and my country, not myself, at this time. I'm sorry, Libby, but there's nothing you could say that would change how I feel or what lies ahead for me.'

'I disagree. I know there is.' She began stepping back and started to open the locket that hung around her neck, the one that held the picture of Daniel's son, *their* son, who looked so very much like his father.

Suddenly the yacht was tossed by a wave with such force it sent Libby back into his arms. 'Are you all right?'

'I… I think so,' she stammered. 'I've never felt anything like that. Are we going to be all right? That was a huge wave. The water hit the window and we're on the top deck.'

'We're back out in the Atlantic Ocean, and I'm guessing there must be bad weather ahead. Please sit down. Don't leave the cabin,' he began as he grabbed some casual trousers and a shirt from the closet and dressed quickly, looking outside to see ominous dark clouds had overtaken the sky. 'I'll head to the bridge and check with the captain to see what's happening. I'll also call in to see Walter on the way. I shouldn't be long.'

'Please don't forget I need to speak with you,' Libby said as she sat down, still draped in a sheet. 'It's important.'

'We'll talk, I promise, as soon as I get back.'

CHAPTER THIRTEEN

DANIEL CHECKED HIS watch as he closed the door to his cabin where he had left Libby. It was seven o'clock and the scheduled time to give Walter his daily early morning medical check. He made his way to the master suite at the end of the corridor, all the while being tossed from side to side with the motion of the yacht in the waves. His arms were outstretched and he kept his balance with his hands firmly against the corridor walls.

Suddenly, he realised it had been the first day he hadn't checked the time upon waking. It was his habit to check and plan the day but that morning, with Libby so close, knowing the time had been the last thing on his mind. But everything he had told her weighed heavily on him—not that she would betray his trust but that she wouldn't accept his resolute position on setting her free.

He had a swipe card to open the door in an emergency and when there was no answer to his knocking, he did just that, but quietly. Walter, he found, was still sleeping and it appeared that the waves tossing the *Coral Contessa* about hadn't broken his slumber. Daniel let him be. He had heard the guests rowdily return in the early hours and had assumed Walter would have been one of them, so he was not surprised that his patient was still happily asleep under his covers.

Daniel guessed that most of the other guests would be doing the same, as they had both eaten and drunk themselves merry in San Lucia.

The captain had made mention the night before that they would be heading off at six in the morning for two days at sea on their way back to Miami, so they would be able to sleep off the effects of the party for forty-eight hours if necessary, but Daniel was concerned that with the rough weather he might need to check on the nausea medication supplies after he visited the bridge. Then he would return to Libby so they could continue their talk. While it wouldn't change anything, he wanted to spend every last minute of this time with her before they parted for ever. It felt good that there were no secrets any more. It was how it should be.

Daniel arrived at the bridge and received an update on the weather from the captain. They were in the tail end of a storm that was heading south and further out to sea, but they were still feeling the effects of the waves.

'We're on the clean side of the storm,' Eric told him, dividing his concentration between the navigation panel and the undulating horizon ahead. 'Unless there's a sudden change, we'll have the shallower waves and lower winds this side. We're surrounded by thirteen thousand tons of yacht so there's not much risk to us.'

'So we shouldn't be concerned about the waves hitting the top deck a little while ago,' Daniel said, remembering the force that had thrown Libby off balance.

'Before the storm shifted southerly, we were slammed by towering walls of water but they've subsided now and the skies should clear up soon. The seas will still be a little rough for another two hours but nothing as severe as we've just encountered. After that, it should be smooth sailing back to Miami. However, I've asked the stewards to inform guests not to go out onto their balconies for the next few hours until I give the all clear.'

'Do you think they would actually consider doing that in this weather?'

'You'd be surprised,' Eric said, rolling his eyes but still looking ahead.

A steward appeared at that moment to inform Daniel that a guest had been thrown from his bed in the last big wave, lacerating his head. He was bleeding profusely and another thought she had a sprained ankle after falling on the way to the bathroom. Concerned there might be more injuries over the next two hours in the rough seas, exacerbated by the effects of the too much alcohol at the party, Daniel needed Libby to assist him. He knew she had her pager, so he sent her a message and asked her if she could change and head to the infirmary as soon as she could while he left the bridge and headed to get his medical bag and then go to the head injury patient first.

Within minutes, Daniel was at the first patient call and knocked on the cabin door. A clearly distraught woman opened it and invited Daniel inside. 'There's so much blood. I think he'll need stitches,' she told him as she took a sip from her wine glass.

Daniel could see the injured man sitting on the bed slightly slouched over. He appeared to be in his late sixties and was holding a white hand towel on the area over his left eye. There didn't appear to be too much blood on the makeshift bandage.

Daniel opened his medical bag, donned gloves and with some sterile swabs crossed to the man.

'I'm Daniel and I'm the ship's doctor. You've no doubt seen me around the ship. What's your name?'

The man looked him up and down. 'I'm Stan and I've not seen you on the yacht but I saw you dive into the water last night. That was an odd thing to do at a party.'

'It was very peculiar, I agree,' the woman chimed in.

Daniel chose to ignore their comments. 'Let's look at your injury, Stan. If you could drop your hand, I'd like to take a look at the cut.'

Slowly the man released the pressure he was applying to the towel and Daniel leaned in, prepared to see a deep wound, but instead found there was a slight abrasion. A graze of sorts. There was little sign of bleeding.

Daniel wiped the area with the swab. 'Would you like me to cover the skin with a dressing?'

'You're not stitching the wound?' the woman asked with the glass still in her hand. 'I think he needs stitches or he might start bleeding again. He could bleed all over the cabin.'

'Yeah, you should just stitch it and be done with it,' Stan agreed.

'There's nothing that requires stitches…'

'Are you sure?' the woman asked as she swayed with the movement of the yacht, though that wasn't the only reason for her inability to stand upright and perhaps for Stan falling out of bed. Daniel could see a small pile of minibar-size bottles of liquor on the dresser. It appeared that the party had continued in their room. He applied an adhesive dressing to the clean area and reassured them that the injury was not as serious as they had first thought. He left their cabin and called instructions through to the stewards to keep an eye on the pair and perhaps not refill the minibar that day.

Daniel arrived at the infirmary to find Libby inside with another guest.

'When did the nausea begin?' he heard Libby ask the man as she drew closer.

'When the big wave hit, we both started throwing up.'

Daniel looked around but there was no one else there. 'You said *we*. Is there someone else suffering from nausea?'

'Yes, my wife, but she didn't want to come down. She decided to go out on the balcony and get some fresh air. She thought it might help.'

'In this weather? She's out on her balcony? Which room?'

'The first deck, cabin nine.'

Daniel raced to the phone and called for a steward to head to the room immediately and he did the same, leaving Libby to attend to the man's nausea. Daniel needed to check on the man's wife. There was still another two hours of bad weather and rough seas ahead and Daniel didn't want anyone on their balcony, particularly if they'd spent the night drinking. The steward was already at cabin door nine, already knocking when Daniel arrived.

There was no answer so Daniel used his swipe card to open the door and, just as he had feared, the woman was leaning over the railing and vomiting. He crossed the room with long purposeful steps and pulled her inside just as a large wave slammed the yacht. It was low on the side but still powerful and Daniel and the steward shook their heads in unison, both aware that it could have ended very differently if they hadn't arrived in time.

'Can you knock on every cabin door and remind guests again that they are not to step outside under any circumstances? And don't refill any minibars until we dock in Miami.'

Daniel then headed to see his next patient with the suspected sprained ankle. He arrived to find Stella lying on the bed with her foot elevated. He looked around the room and was relieved to see no sign of empty bottles. Stella was in her early forties and travelling with her mother, who had headed off to bring her back some breakfast. Daniel remembered seeing them both dancing at the party. On close examination of her ankle, foot and lower leg, he could see it had been damaged in the fall. There were a number of points of tenderness and pain when she attempted even the slightest movement.

'It appears to be just a sprain, Stella, so I'd advise you to rest and avoid movement that causes discomfort. I'll order up some more ice and I'd like you to pack that around your ankle for about twenty minutes and repeat that every two or three hours during the day.'

'Better today than yesterday. I would have missed the party and the dancing…and seeing you dive into the water in your tuxedo to save your wife.'

Daniel said nothing. Libby was not his wife and never would be. Spending the night with her in his arms had made the thought of saying goodbye and never seeing her beautiful face again overwhelming but he had the next two days with her and he intended to make the most of that time.

'Should I see my doctor when I get back to New York?' Stella asked.

'If the pain's not subsiding after a day or so I would

definitely make an appointment with your GP. He may need to arrange an X-ray or MRI. However, I'll return later to check on you and I may compress your ankle with an elastic bandage to manage any swelling and we will have a better idea if you have sustained a fracture, but at this time I believe it's just sprained.'

After ordering an ice pack for Stella, Daniel headed back to check on Walter. He was his most important patient and had been left alone in the rough weather. He apologised when he arrived at Walter's suite.

'I'm fine,' Walter told him. 'I'm an old sea dog. I quite like it when the sea gets angry and tosses us about. It's invigorating. Lets you know you're alive.'

Daniel wasn't convinced but didn't argue the point. He just checked Walter's blood pressure and was happy it was still within normal range and the wound was continuing to heal. Perhaps the trip to the Caribbean was just what the doctor should have ordered.

'So how did the pair of you dry out after your midnight swim?' Walter asked as Daniel closed his medical bag and slipped off the latex gloves. 'Quite heroic of you to dive in like that.'

'It was only a few feet of water...'

'That's not the point. Women love to be saved and I'm sure Libby appreciated your chivalry,' he said, smiling. 'I did notice you two didn't come back to the party. I assume you took the time to become better acquainted.'

'We decided to stay on the yacht and talk,' Daniel said, running his lean fingers along his chin.

'I hope you stepped up and finally kissed her,' Walter said with one eyebrow slightly raised.

'I'm not telling you—'

'You don't come across a young lady as lovely as

Libby more than once in your life,' Walter cut in. 'And I'll take your lack of a denial as a yes. It's about time because I could see you had feelings for her from the moment you met and she'd be perfect for you. I suspected it was a case of love at first sight...'

'Actually, Walter, we knew each other before this cruise.'

'You knew each other? Libby never said a thing to me and I thought I knew everything about her.'

'You know everything about her? You must have spoken to her for longer than I did.'

'Well, I know she lives close to her parents.'

'In San Francisco. It's where we met.'

'She's never travelled much before this trip.'

'I think she's a bit of a homebody,' Daniel said with a smile as he crossed to the door to return to the woman about whom they were speaking.

'And she's the single mother of a three-year-old little boy.'

Daniel stopped in mid-step and his expression was suddenly no longer light-hearted as he turned back to face Walter. 'Libby has a son?'

'Yes. Billy's his name and his birthday's only a few days after mine.'

'Which is when, exactly?'

'January tenth. He had his birthday a few days before we sailed. I told Libby he was an Easter bunny conception like me.'

Daniel felt the blood drain from his face. An Easter conception?

'How old did you say her son was?' Daniel asked.

'Three, she told me.'

Surely not. It couldn't be. His mind was racing. They

had slept together on the night of the Easter gala almost four years ago.

'But don't worry, there's no husband. Libby told me she's single. When I asked about the father of her child, she told me it didn't work out. She mentioned something about it being *complicated*.'

Complicated? Daniel rushed from the room without saying another word. He had to find Libby. He had to know if she had been keeping something from him. He'd told her everything about his life and she hadn't told him about her son. Why would she hide that unless it was deliberate? Unless there was a chance the little boy was his son.

Daniel knew she would not be in his suite so he headed to hers. He needed to know why she had been hiding her son from him. He suspected he knew the answer already. He knocked on her door like a man needing the oxygen inside the room to breathe.

After a few moments Libby opened the door and he stepped inside and slammed it closed behind him.

'I know you have a son. I need to know, is he my child?'

Libby was stunned by Daniel's question and the look of fury in his eyes. She had wanted to tell Daniel herself and not have him learn about their son from someone else.

Her heart began to pound inside her chest. Her chin was quivering, tears building by the moment as she nodded her reply.

'Walter told you, didn't he?'

'How I know doesn't matter. I just want to know, is he mine?'

'Yes, Daniel, he's yours. You have a son.'

Suddenly, her reasons for keeping her secret from him for all these days escaped her. She was searching for something that made sense. Something she could tell Daniel that would justify her actions. It all seemed wrong now. Very wrong. She'd had every opportunity to tell him for the last week and she had chosen silence. She told herself that she had been looking for the right time but was there ever going to be a right time? Or had she been looking for a reason not to tell him?

'Was it as simple as just wanting to punish me?' he asked with both anger and sadness colouring his voice.

'No, it wasn't that. I wasn't punishing you—'

'I disagree, Libby. I think you very much wanted to punish me for leaving you the way I did after we slept together.'

'I was eight weeks pregnant when I found out.'

'Why didn't you contact me then?'

Libby looked at him with her guilt quickly morphing into something closer to resentment. 'By that time you had long gone. As we both know, you'd slipped away before the sun came up the morning after we made love.'

'You could have found me if you wanted to,' he told her without taking his gaze from her.

'How dare you! I tried to find your contact details through the hospital HR records but they were closed. And it was well above my pay grade to request that they be opened. I guess a *prince* can have anything he wants but a commoner like me has to play by the rules.'

Libby was furious at the accusations Daniel was throwing at her. He had no right to put all of the responsibility back on her when he was the one who'd left without saying a word. Or leaving a forwarding address.

'After I left without an explanation, you had every right to be angry,' he replied, softening his tone slightly but still sounding cold and distant. Then just as quickly it grew in harshness as he spoke. 'But keeping me from knowing about a child, Libby, for all these years, that's more than just punishing me. You've been punishing *our* son too.'

Libby felt an ache in her heart as those words slipped from his lips. It was true what had happened, although it had not been deliberate. But the way he had called Billy *our son* brought a sting of tears to her eyes. Now that she knew why he had left, she knew Daniel was not the cold, callous man she had created in her own mind over the years but she couldn't change the past. Nor could he. They had both kept secrets that could tear them apart for ever.

She knew she should have told him after they'd left the engagement party. She should have told him before they'd made love. Or that morning. There were so many times when she should have told him.

'Billy did not deserve to be denied knowing I was his father or I denied knowing I had a son,' he said, pacing the room with long purposeful steps that led nowhere.

'I tried to tell you this morning...'

'So you were only going to tell me because we spent the night together? If that hadn't happened were you going to leave the yacht and not look back? Why didn't you tell me the first day you saw me? Or on Martinique, or any of the other times we were alone? Did you want to cement us, rekindle what we had before telling me?'

'No. I didn't want to rekindle anything with you.'

'I think you did. That's what all of this was about. You wanted to know if we would reunite before you told me about my son. I remember you saying, "Let's have the night and to hell with tomorrow." And clearly to hell with me knowing I had a son if it didn't work out between us.'

Libby was furious again with the way he was speaking to her, accusing her of only telling him when she'd got what she wanted. It wasn't true.

'I never said to hell with tomorrow…'

'Maybe not the words but it was what you meant when you said, "Let's have the night."'

'How can you twist my words like that?' she asked, holding back the tears that were building as the accusations poured from his mouth.

'I'm not twisting anything, Libby. I'm telling you how I see it.'

'I wasn't sure you would even care…'

'You had no right to make such a sweeping assumption about me, Libby. You don't know me.'

'That's right, Daniel. I don't really know you because you kept your real life a secret from me. And perhaps there's more you've kept from me.'

Daniel stopped in his tracks and stared across the room at Libby. 'I laid my life bare for you this morning, Libby. Everything was out for you to know. Nothing was hidden because I trusted you and in return you couldn't even tell me that I have a three-year-old son. Now I know my trust was misguided.'

'I was trying to tell you about Billy this morning…'

Daniel shook his head. 'I guess you didn't try hard enough, did you?'

CHAPTER FOURTEEN

DANIEL STAYED IN his cabin with his thoughts for as long as possible. The rough seas had abated and the captain had given the all clear for the passengers to venture onto their balconies again. Daniel spoke to him about the minibars being left unstocked, at least overnight, and they agreed it would be in the best interests of the few somewhat intoxicated passengers in order to ensure they were safe and not likely to do anything silly. They could have a drink with dinner in the dining area but not in their cabins.

Daniel's mind kept wandering back to Libby and her son. Their son. He wanted to know more about the little boy. What he liked to do. What he looked like. His favourite colour and favourite food. Daniel wanted to know everything. But most of all he wanted to know he was safe. Safe from the genetic disease that ran through the Dimosa family. But that was Daniel's responsibility. Not Libby's or anyone else's.

That lay squarely with him. He knew what he had to do.

Daniel ate his lunch and dinner in his cabin. He didn't want to see anyone. He had so much to think about now.

More than he could have ever imagined when he'd set sail on the *Coral Contessa*.

Libby remained in her cabin too. Georgie had called by but Libby had told her friend she was tired and would rather stay inside and they would catch up the next day.

Libby couldn't stop thinking about the angst written all over Daniel's face when he had confronted her. She knew that while she'd had her reasons for keeping Billy a secret initially, she should have told Daniel before he'd discovered it from someone else. She had been the judge and jury and found him guilty three years before and she hadn't lifted that life sentence.

She lay on her bed thinking and rethinking everything from the day they had met until that morning. The tears flowed for what might have been but what was most apparent to Libby was Daniel not asking for proof of his son's paternity. He trusted Libby's word that he was the father. While he was angry and hurt, he had never doubted her the way she had doubted him.

She knew in her heart that Daniel had done the wrong thing for the right reason. He had wanted to protect her from a life in a country far from home, potentially nursing him, and she had repaid that chivalrous behaviour by denying him knowledge of his son, even when she'd had the chance.

Libby didn't expect that Daniel would want to see her again and she wasn't sure how they could move forward but she knew somehow that they would work out visitation for Daniel with Billy. Of that she was certain. Libby knew her first instincts about Daniel had been right all those years ago. He was a good man and she would make sure his son got to know that too.

But there was something else she wanted to do. Daniel deserved to share in Billy's life up to that day. She opened her computer and began the task of piecing together her son's life from the first ultrasound to his third birthday. Every precious moment—Billy's first steps, his first words and everything else that she thought would bring Daniel closer to knowing his son.

It took all night but finally, at seven the next morning, it was complete and saved to a USB that she slipped into an envelope with her number in San Francisco if Daniel wanted to make a time to meet his son. She quietly left it by his door.

It was night time before they docked in Miami and there was a knock on Libby's cabin door. She was almost packed, just leaving out shorts and a top to wear the next day.

She was expecting Georgie as they had arranged for drinks on the deck. While it wasn't something she was keen to do, Libby knew she owed it to her friend.

'One minute,' she called out.

'I will wait as long as it takes,' the deep voice replied.

Libby froze. It was Daniel's voice, not Georgie's. Taking a deep breath to steady her nerves, she tentatively crossed to the door. It took a moment longer for her to open it.

'I didn't expect to see you,' she said honestly.

'I guessed as much as you left your telephone number in the envelope,' he told her without taking his eyes away from hers.

'I thought if you were ever in the area you might like to call and make a time to meet Billy.'

'I want much more than that,' he said. 'We need to talk. May I come inside?'

Libby nodded and stepped back from the door. Her worst nightmare was about to be realised. Daniel, she surmised, wanted to talk to her about more than visiting his son. There was the very real risk that he might want joint custody. And she knew he had the right to ask for that.

'Every child has the right to know they are loved unconditionally by their parents, no matter how their parents feel about each other,' he began, confirming her suspicions as he crossed to the balcony doors. They were open and the cool evening breeze was softly moving the sheer curtains. Slowly, he turned to face Libby. 'I want our son to know that I will love him until I take my last breath.'

'I know you will, and I'm so sorry, Daniel,' Libby began. 'I know I should have told you but I stupidly thought I was protecting Billy from being hurt. He's my world. He's my everything.'

'Protect him from me? How could you think I would hurt him?'

Libby collapsed back onto the bed, her tears beginning to flow. 'Because you hurt me and I didn't want him to love you the way I did and have you walk away. I couldn't let him know you and love you, only to have you disappear. I thought it would be better for Billy to never have you than to lose you because that is an unbearable pain.'

Daniel looked at Libby in silence and she felt her heart breaking all over again.

'I'm sorry, Daniel, I'm so sorry.'

'You said you loved me. Do you still feel that way?

Do you still love me, Libby?' he asked, staring deeply into her eyes as if he was searching her very soul for the answer.

She nodded as she wiped the tears away with her hands.

Without saying another word or asking another question, Daniel crossed to her and gently pulled her up and into his arms.

'Then I should be the one apologising, Libby. I'm sorry I left you that night. I'm sorry I stayed away and I'm sorry I let you down.'

'I know now you had your reasons—'

'None that were good enough to put you through what I did. I've made some calls and I'm taking the genetic test. Not for myself, I'm taking it for Billy and for you. And I swear, if you give me a second chance, I will never disappear again.'

Libby raised her face to him. 'You want a second chance with me?'

'More than anything I have ever wanted.' Daniel's lips hovered very close to hers as he whispered, 'I love you, Libby. I have since the day I met you and I will never stop loving you, if you let me.'

EPILOGUE

LIBBY GAZED THROUGH the lead-light window at the picturesque palace grounds. The pastel-hued roses were in full bloom, the immaculately trimmed deep green hedges were framing the flower beds, white pebbles along the meandering pathways glistening in the early morning sun. And the sky above was azure and cloudless. It truly was fairy-tale-perfect, and so much more than Libby could have dreamed possible for her Easter wedding day.

The test results had arrived the day before and they were negative for Daniel. He had not inherited the mutated gene from his father, which meant that Billy was not at risk either, but Libby had agreed to marry Daniel without knowing. When he had proposed, on the condition they wait for the test results, she had insisted the wedding was going ahead no matter what the report said. She would love him for better or worse and she meant it. Daniel and Billy had bonded almost immediately upon meeting. They were like two peas in a pod. Billy was his father's son in more ways than just good looks and Libby knew they would never spend another day apart.

'Only a few more buttons and I'll be finished,' her mother said softly as she poked her head around her daughter's waist and smiled at her reflection in the antique oval mirror. 'You truly look like a princess. Just beautiful. You do know it's almost guaranteed your father will cry when he sees you.'

'I don't think so. Dad's not like that. I've never seen him cry,' Libby replied, with a hint of disbelief creasing her forehead.

'He cries on the inside. You can't see it but he cries and today there will be tears of happiness that might just overflow,' her mother said, returning to her original position as she looped closed the last few pearl buttons that secured the back of the stunning silk wedding dress. It had been made by a team of local seamstresses and had taken three weeks to complete. It was a tradition for all the royal brides of Chezlovinka.

The ornate ivory gown skimmed her shoulders, with a band of antique lace from Daniel's mother's wedding dress. The sleeves were of the same lace and they had been cut to a point that framed her manicured hands. The bodice was cinched at the waist with a low back and a long train.

The door suddenly burst open.

'Oh, my Lord, you look like a princess!' Bradley pronounced as he came rushing to the bride. He was dressed in an emerald-green-and-black-striped silk suit with lapel embellishments. Libby thought momentarily it was a little more Broadway than Chezlovinka but that was Bradley. She smiled as he grew closer, his arms outstretched. He was never understated. He was loud and fun and she wouldn't change a thing about him. He was her best friend and that would never change.

'That's just what I told her,' Libby's mother said, and she spun around with her hand outstretched not unlike a traffic controller. 'But absolutely no hugging, you two. You'll crush the dress.'

Bradley stopped in mid-step. 'Of course. I wouldn't dream of crushing that divine creation.'

Libby laughed. 'A little hug would be fine.'

The two embraced cautiously before Bradley stepped back. 'Honestly, Libby, you look like a china doll, a red-haired china-doll bride. You couldn't look more beautiful. Or more perfect.'

'That's so sweet of you.'

'Honey, it's the truth and I hope Daniel knows just how lucky he is—'

'He does,' a little voice interrupted.

All three turned to see Billy standing in the doorway. 'Daddy did my bow-tie this morning and he told me that he is the luckiest man in the world because he's got Mommy and me for ever and ever.'

Libby felt her eyes begin to fill with tears.

'Oh, no, you don't,' Bradley cut in. 'You can't cry, you'll ruin your make-up. No smudgy bride on my watch.'

Libby laughed and Bradley pulled his crisp handkerchief from his top pocket and gently mopped the tears at risk of staining her cheeks.

'What would I do without you?'

'I have no clue and Tom and I will be visiting this quaint part of the world often so you won't have to find out,' he said with a smile. 'Plus, you have to come back to visit us at least twice a year. We can't have Billy losing his accent. I just won't allow him to grow up with some posh European way of talking that I can't understand.'

The door opened and an immaculately dressed woman with an earpiece entered. She smiled but it was a somewhat strained smile and her general demeanour, behind her chestnut chignon, midnight-blue suit and nude stilettos, was that of a woman on a mission.

'Bradley, this is our wedding planner, Simone,' Libby said.

'Lovely to meet you,' Bradley replied, after giving her the once-over and approving of her outfit. 'I'm guessing it's time to get this show on the road.'

'The groom and the wedding party are in place, along with the rest of the royal family and international guests,' Simone announced with a heavy Western European accent. 'You are only a five-minute carriage ride to the church but you need to leave now.'

'This is it, and the last time I can call you Libby McDonald,' Bradley said, as he carefully lowered the antique lace veil. 'Next time we meet, you will be Your Royal Highness.'

Libby leaned in as the veil dropped over her face. 'You will always call me Libby, that won't change. Not ever.'

Moments later, after the short trip in the open carriage to the two-hundred-year-old church, Libby stepped down onto the red carpet and smiled at the crowd as the bridesmaids hurriedly smoothed her dress and straightened her veil and ten-foot train.

'You look stunning, Libby. You're a true princess,' Georgie whispered, then took her position as Maid of Honour.

There were gasps of joy and waves from the people who had gathered there, many of whom had been waiting since dawn to see their beautiful new princess. She waved and smiled back at them with genuine joy filling her heart. She should have been overwhelmed but knowing that Daniel would soon be her husband and finally they would be the family she had always wanted lessened her nerves.

Despite Simone's exemplary planning, protocol had been thrown to the wind when it came to Billy. He had travelled in the carriage with Libby and his grandfather but once they'd come to a stop he had jumped down, patted the large grey horse nearest to him then raced inside the church on his own. It had been planned that one of the groomsmen would walk Billy to Daniel, who was waiting at the altar, but Billy was far too excited to see his father.

Georgie and the other bridesmaids and flower girls did follow protocol and walked on cue to the church doors and as the organ music began they walked in step inside and out of Libby's view.

'Well, it looks like there's a whole lot of pretty important people who've travelled a long way to see you,' Libby's father said as he patted her hand. 'We'd better not keep them waiting. Not sure if they can still behead for such a thing in this part of the world, but let's not find out.'

Libby giggled from behind the veil and, taking her father's arm, walked inside the church. Organ music filled the church, the beautifully dressed guests were seated in pews decorated with white roses and lily of the valley, but Libby saw none of it. All she could see was the most handsome man in the world turn to see her. Her soul mate, the love of her life, and the father of Billy and their future children was waiting at the altar, dressed in his red military attire and a smile that spoke to her heart. It told her everything she needed to know.

Prince Daniel Dimosa was the man of her dreams and she was about to become his wife.

As she took her first step down the aisle, she read his lips as he said, 'I love you, Libby.'

Libby's heart was bursting with happiness. She had found her prince and her happily ever after.

* * * * *

COMING SOON!

We really hope you enjoyed reading this book.
If you're looking for more romance
be sure to head to the shops when
new books are available on

Thursday 27th February

To see which titles are coming soon, please visit
millsandboon.co.uk/nextmonth

MILLS & BOON

FOUR BRAND NEW BOOKS FROM
MILLS & BOON MODERN

The same great stories you love, a stylish new look!

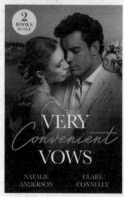

OUT NOW

Eight Modern stories published every month, find them all at:

millsandboon.co.uk

OUT NOW!

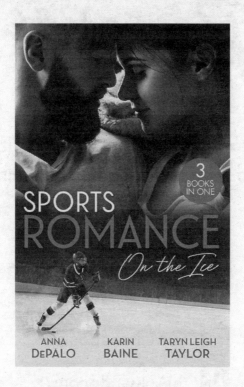

LET'S TALK

Romance

For exclusive extracts, competitions
and special offers, find us online:

(f) MillsandBoon

X @MillsandBoon

(O) @MillsandBoonUK

(♪) @MillsandBoonUK

Get in touch on 01413 063 232

afterglow BOOKS

Afterglow Books is a trend-led, trope-filled list of books with diverse, authentic and relatable characters, a wide array of voices and representations, plus real world trials and tribulations. Featuring all the tropes you could possibly want (think small-town settings, fake relationships, grumpy vs sunshine, enemies to lovers) and all with a generous dose of spice in every story.

♪ @millsandboonuk
◎ @millsandboonuk
afterglowbooks.co.uk
#AfterglowBooks

For all the latest book news, exclusive content and giveaways scan the QR code below to sign up to the Afterglow newsletter:

SCAN ME

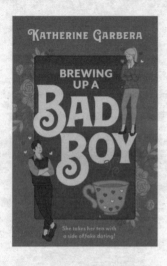
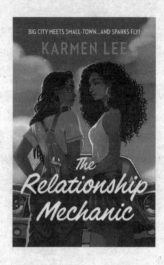